Praise for Robin W. Pearson

" *'Til I Want No More* feels like an extended afternoon at a family reunion barbecue, complete with mouthwatering food, spilled family secrets, and voices of faith that never lose hope. This brilliantly written story reminds us that God is bigger than the struggles that all families face, yet as a woman of color, I love that Robin's courageous characters look and sound like me."

BARB ROOSE, speaker and author of *Surrendered: Letting Go and Living like Jesus* and *Joshua: Winning the Worry Battle*

"Robin W. Pearson has done it again—she truly knows how to captivate her readers and have them eagerly turning each page, anticipating what is going to happen next. *'Til I Want No More* is no exception. Maxine's journey of love, longing, and finding her identity and worth is relatable to so many women, all of whom will be able to resonate with the many emotions of this bride-to-be as she seeks to find the joy and sense of belonging she's been missing."

ANGELIA WHITE STONE, CEO and editor of *Hope for Women* magazine

"Robin W. Pearson writes strong characters who wrap their arms around you and pull you into the family circle, a hubbub of loyalty, secrets, faith, and yes, forgiveness. Nobody's perfect—but maybe that's the best theme woven through this book."

BETH K. VOGT, award-winning author of the Thatcher Sisters series

"Pour yourself a glass of sweet tea and sit back to enjoy this delightful new story from Robin W. Pearson. Once again her soulful Southern voice brings heart-tugging family relationships into the spotlight with realism and meaningful emotions."

CARRIE TURANSKY, award-winning author of *No Ocean Too Wide* and *No Journey Too Far*

"Robin W. Pearson has given us another story that sinks deep into the heart of a family. Her Southern touch adds to the charm and authenticity of her characters, while causing the reader to root for their full restoration."

CHRISTINA SUZANN NELSON, award-winning author of *More Than We Remember*

"Pearson's excellent debut explores forgiveness and the burden of secrets. . . . Pearson's saga is enjoyable and uncomfortable, but also funny and persistent in the way that only family can be."

PUBLISHERS WEEKLY, starred review

"Pearson delivers a poignant debut that explores the faith of one African American family. . . . The writing is strong, and the story is engaging, and readers will be pleased to discover a new voice in Southern inspirational fiction."

BOOKLIST

"Robin W. Pearson's debut novel is a contemporary fiction masterpiece. . . . Set in North Carolina, readers will feel the heat, smell the food, and hear the bees buzzing in the background. . . . Pearson has created a story that makes you feel like you're in the same room as the characters. Do not miss this one."

CHRISTIAN FICTION ADVISOR

"Readers will cry, laugh, sigh wistfully, and even rage a little at this moving story. *A Long Time Comin'* is a wonderful tale of love, family, secrets, relationships, and forgiveness that will teach us all how to live well in the midst of real life."

THE BANNER MAGAZINE

"Robin W. Pearson delivers a fresh new voice for Southern fiction, treating readers to an inspiring journey through the complex matters of the heart."

JULIE CANTRELL, *New York Times* and *USA Today* bestselling author

"My mouth watered at the mustard greens and ham hocks. Feels like home. You'll fall in love with Evelyn and Granny B and a cast of memorable characters so rich you won't want the story to end. We can only hope we'll be reading more from Robin W. Pearson!"

CHRIS FABRY, bestselling author of *Under a Cloudless Sky* and *The Promise of Jesse Woods*

"With a deft hand and an unflinching eye, Pearson tackles the cobwebby corners of her characters' lives and in doing so reveals truths that ultimately help us all to heal . . . even when we've convinced ourselves we don't need to."

SARAH LOUDIN THOMAS, author of *Miracle in a Dry Season*

"Robin W. Pearson's authentic faith and abundant talent shine through in this wholehearted novel. Bee and Evelyn will stir your heart and stay with you long after the last page of *A Long Time Comin'* is turned."

MARYBETH MAYHEW WHALEN, author of *Only Ever Her*

"In *A Long Time Comin'* Robin W. Pearson takes readers behind closed doors and into the heart of a family."

ANN H. GABHART, bestselling author of *Angel Sister* and *The Refuge*

"Robin W. Pearson's singular style and fully realized cast of characters ring proudly throughout this novel. Her masterful voice is a welcome addition to the genre of family sagas rooted in hope and faith."

LIZ JOHNSON, bestselling author of *The Red Door Inn*

"The lyrical weaving of family narratives, past and present, is masterful—certainly to be compared with writers such as Sue Monk Kidd and Barbara Kingsolver. . . . Buy this book. It gripped me . . . from page one."

JANET HOLM McHENRY, bestselling author of *PrayerWalk*

"*A Long Time Comin'* is a tender and sweet story of a cantankerous grandmother and her dear family members. . . . Her characters are charming, endearing, and flawed. I hope we have many years to come of reading Pearson's work."

KATARA PATTON, author

'Til I Want No More

A Novel

'Til I Want No More

Robin W. Pearson

Tyndale House Publishers
Carol Stream, Illinois

"But now, thus says the Lord, who created you, O Jacob,

And He who formed you, O Israel:

'Fear not, for I have redeemed you;

I have called you by your name;

You are Mine.'"

ISAIAH 43:1

To my daughters, whose worth is far above rubies,

and my sons, who are mighty men of valor.

January

"If you don't allow God to confront your past, your past one day is going to confront you. . . . Esau is comin.'"

REVEREND LEE CLAYPOOLE

Chapter One

"YOU KNOW TROUBLE AIN'T CATCHIN'." Ruby Tagle's dark eyes flicked in her granddaughter's direction. "Nobody's gon' sneeze and give it to you or your Theodore."

"Did you hear your grandmother, Maxine?" Vivienne Owens stood on her toes and stretched to retrieve a small jar from the kitchen cabinet. It skittered away to the far end of the shelf.

"Yes, ma'am, I heard Mama Ruby, but I never said I thought trouble was contagious." Maxine smiled a little as she hopped down from the stool. She reached up and set the glass container on the counter. At five-six, Maxine had her mother by three inches, by her estimation, the only way she outmatched her.

"Yes, Vivienne, the girl never said she thought trouble was contagious." Roy Tagle opened the pimientos with a *pop!* and handed them to his sister.

1

Mother arched an eyebrow at her younger brother. "I don't need none of y'all to tell me what she said. My ears are workin' just fine. You see, I listen like a mama, not an uncle." She spooned sweet peppers into the bowl in front of her. "Now, Maxine, you've been havin' these crazy dreams for weeks now, ever since you set that appointment with Theodore's pastor. You just need to sit down somewhere."

In other words, calm down.

But Maxine couldn't calm down. She'd met Theodore in September, right after he'd relocated from New Orleans to Mount Laurel. Only God's hand could've directed him to that North Carolina crossroads of Eastern and Lexington-style barbecue. He proposed on a chilly December night at the end of a cooking class led by Manna, the Tagles' catering company. As Ruby pulled out the mini chocolate soufflé with a joyful "Voilà!" that sounded more like deep South than South of France, Teddy had dropped to one knee, to no one's shock but Maxine's. He'd toasted her with a crystal flute filled with semisweet chocolate topped off with a one-carat diamond. Now, six weeks later, sporting her emerald-cut ring, she was in her mother's kitchen, dizzy from her whirlwind romance and its effect on her life, a life it had taken her thirteen years to rebuild and only a *yes* to blast to smithereens. Again.

"It's not that simple, Mother. I can't just tell my heart to obey and expect it to fall into line."

"But you can control that mind of yours. Think on the truth, and stop runnin' around here like Chicken Little. The sky isn't fallin' on you just because your friends separated. What happened to them isn't gonna happen to you and Theodore. Isn't that right?" Vivienne looked to Mama Ruby as she stirred the potato salad, using one pink-gloved hand to hold on to the bowl.

Ruby nodded.

"I didn't say it was, Mother." To mask the shiver snaking through her, Maxine moved her shoulders to the gospel beat of the Jackson Southernaires, crooning from the Bluetooth speaker. She wished she could blame her chill on the clouds cloaking the pale-blue sky, but she knew it had nothing to do with the twenty-degree temperatures, unusual for North Carolina. The three women had been going back and forth for over an hour, since Maxine had shown up on her mother's doorstep holding her box of silk chrysanthemums.

"The thought breaks my heart, that Evelyn didn't talk to me about what she was going through. I thought she was spending the summer helping her grandmother, not running away from her husband."

Mother's spoon clanked against the side of the bowl. "Then I take it you've told her all about what *you're* going through."

Maxine swallowed a lump in her throat that felt the size of Pilot Mountain and stepped a little closer to the flames flickering brightly in the fireplace behind her. She fiddled with the ribs of her gray corduroy skirt. "I'm only saying I can imagine what Evelyn went through. Pregnant, her heart in broken pieces. Trying to avoid the whispers, pointing fingers, the dissection of her problems, the gossip from church folk. Did you know she's having a little girl?"

Though they weren't blood kin, Maxine and Evelyn Lester had considered each other family since middle school, after Evelyn had shown up at the Tagles' farm looking to buy butter beans more than half their lifetimes ago. Thing was, Evelyn's grandmother had dispatched her there with an empty bushel basket but without two nickels to rub together. Ruby simply pointed Evelyn to a spot on the porch beside her own granddaughter, and Maxine and Evelyn bonded as they shelled butter beans for the next few hours. Maxine already called herself "Auntie" to the baby Evelyn carried.

Her mother frowned and shook her head, dislodging a strand from her silver-streaked bun. "Is that what this is about? *Her* baby girl?" She aimed a gloved finger at her daughter. "If so, you need to keep in mind that it didn't have anything to do with you. Baby or no baby. Besides, her marriage is fine now. Just fine. What I'm asking myself is how you two can know so little about each other, considerin' you're best friends and all."

Vivienne returned her attention to the bowl, but Maxine figured her mother's murmuring had little to do with the potato salad.

The chair creaked as Mama Ruby propped an ample hip on the stool Maxine had abandoned. "Goodness gracious, Maxine Amelia, you don't know your end from your beginnin'. You ain't even married yet. You might not think trouble is catchin', but you're already signin' yourself up for divorce care and your weddin' is months away." Her grandma pointed to the wireless speaker. "And, Roy, turn down that music. Cain't even hear my own thoughts let alone help this child here with hers."

Uncle Roy obeyed.

Mother scooped out a teaspoonful of the creamy mixture and turned to Maxine. "Here, taste this for me. What does it need?"

"Mmm. Nothing."

Her mother nodded in response and sprinkled kosher salt

over the bowl and swirled it around with her mixing s[
She used a fresh spoon to offer Uncle Roy a sample. W[
he nodded, Mother finished off the potato salad with papri[
and covered the sixteen-inch melamine bowl with plastic wrap.

Maxine pursed her lips and stifled a sigh, wondering why
her mother made such a show of asking her opinion. "Like
I said, it's just sad. For them, not me. I'm too nervous about
starting a marriage to fret over ending one."

"That's because you have some sense. Getting married is
nothing to sniff at." Uncle Roy squeezed Maxine's shoulder.
"Viv, I'll take that to the pantry fridge and start moving the
rest to the truck." He hefted the pumpkin-colored dish to
shoulder level and left the room.

Mama Ruby wrapped an arm around Maxine. "First
things first, don't listen to your uncle. He hasn't met the
right woman yet who makes him want to set another place
at the table. And next, don't let your mind play tricks on you,
awake or asleep. Their problems are not your problems. Stop
thinkin' of this pastor as a one-man judge and jury. From
what I hear, Atwater is good people."

Her grandma was squishy in all the right places. Accepting
the comfort of her embrace and her words, Maxine planted
a quick kiss between the wrinkles on her velvety cheek.
Then she opened the long, rectangular box on the quartz
countertop and lifted out one flower after another, setting the
counter ablaze with purple, cranberry, and orange blooms.

But she didn't miss Mother rolling her eyes heavenward.

Mama Ruby must not have missed it either, for she
chuckled and pointed at her daughter. "Amen, Vivienne! This
child here needs to look to the hills and trust God's authority

and care, not just her husband's—" she spared Maxine a side eye—"that is, her *future* husband. Trusting Him has kept me and Lerenzo married. And it keeps Manna in business."

That's easy to say when y'all run your catering business while holding hands. I'm just trying to keep a fiancé. Maxine snipped the stems and leaves and arranged the artificial flowers in the olive cut-glass vase. "All I know is, these seven sessions with the pastor are going to feel like a long, drawn-out game of *Truth or Consequences.*"

Mother huffed as she scrubbed her work space. "Maxine, you can't be nobody but yourself. Everybody else is taken. Focus on your Theodore and the life you're planning with him. Guilt is the rust on the sword, let me tell you. It's been thirteen years, and you need to be done with all this."

Done with all this. Really Maxine didn't think she'd ever be done with "this," the burden she'd been toting around half her life. It had grown heavier since adding the weight of her engagement ring. Sunlight danced through the picture window overlooking the backyard, and she tilted her face toward it, hoping the warmth would seep through her skin and fill the cracks only she knew existed. But still, her finger shook as she twirled a cinnamon ringlet and looped it around an earlobe. Thirteen years had passed, but it felt like yesterday.

"I don't know what you're tuckin' in your heart's back pocket, but I should tell you John and I talked about it." Mother squinted at Maxine before she shrugged as if giving up. She strode from the sun-splashed kitchen, throwing over her shoulder, "I know you're thirty years old, and you don't need his permission, but you have your daddy's blessing, whatever you decide, whenever you decide."

Daddy. Maxine and her stepfather got along like mayonnaise and mustard, but more often than not, Maxine respectfully—and teasingly—called him First John and his namesake, her little brother, Second. Daddy, he wasn't.

"I know who you thinkin' 'bout." Her grandma's low, soft voice smelled like Brach's cinnamon discs. "But if the Lord hadn't taken Henry in that car accident, he would've agreed with Vivienne."

Maxine whispered back, "Well, if my real daddy would've been here, we wouldn't even be having this conversation. I wouldn't be in this pickle. You know I love my stepfather, but First John only adopted me to hush Mother's clamoring, not to fulfill some burning need of his—or mine, for that matter. Having his blessing is all well and good, but I've got bigger fish to fry."

Mama Ruby held up her hands in the universal sign of silent surrender. She walked to the double wall ovens and fiddled with the dials.

Mother clip-clopped back from the storage room in her daisy-covered clogs and set her handful on the counter. She peeled off plastic wrap and aluminum foil, revealing a frozen pound cake. She usually baked three or four at a time and pulled them out to order for Manna's customers. Then she'd add a freshly made glaze.

Maxine scooped up the discarded plastic and dropped it in the trash. She leaned against the counter, twiddling with her flower trimmings. "Evelyn was always so focused on her work—teaching and writing—not on being a mom."

Mother peeked over her half-moon–shaped glasses as she

set the cake aside and consulted her iPad. "Having a baby doesn't end the world. It didn't end mine."

"Well, it almost ended mine." Maxine held her mother's eyes. Neither blinked for a moment, but then Maxine looked away. "And you're not a seventeen-year-old."

"You're not seventeen years old . . . now." Mother closed her tablet with a decisive click. "Just what *are* you doin' with those flowers?"

"I ordered these so I could try out colors and arrangements for my wedding bouquets." Maxine repositioned a blossom. "I have a feeling Teddy wouldn't take the news that he's a father quite as well as First John did."

"Your Theodore isn't becomin' a daddy no time soon. So no need to send out birth announcements." Her grandma opened a bag of dark-brown sugar and spooned some into a small pot bubbling away on the gas cooktop.

Mother opened the refrigerator and drew out a large, glistening ham covered in pineapple slices. She set it down. "I like the purple and cranberry. Are you sure about the orange?"

"You know orange is my favorite color, and it's perfect for my fall wedding." Maxine shifted a stem. "And as far as birth announcements go, that's exactly what I'm doing by sharing information the world doesn't have the right to know. This is mine. I'm not holding on to this solely for my sake. . . . Excuse me, Mother, what are you doing?"

Her mother plucked two orange mums, leaving only one in the center surrounded by a mixed spray of purple and cranberry, like the setting sun on the horizon. "There. Better. See? Your weddin' is December 5, which feels more like the

Christmas season than the fall. And the fact is, tellin' Teddy is the right thing to do, something we don't have to tell you."

Mama Ruby's voice carried from the stove. "You ever heard of gettin' a *little* married or bein' a *little bit* pregnant? Well, you can't tell that man a little bit of truth. In my day, we called that a lie. And since I'm standin' on my own two feet, I'd say it's still my day."

"Mama Ruby—" Maxine began.

"*But* there's a proper time and place for it, Maxine. A lesson I learned as a young girl." Mama Ruby never looked away from the syrupy mixture she would pour over the ham when it was ready. "You probably heard this story I'm 'bout to tell you, but I'm gon' say it anyhow. Just like Scripture, the same stories have many applications.

"I remember when my brother planned to leave with Mr. Baker to sign up for the Army. At first, my mama didn't say nuthin', but not too long after he left, she sent me to get him off that bus. She didn't want him to go because she knew if he ever left Spring Hope, he wasn't ever comin' back.

"As much as I hated to, I did as I was told. I didn't even ask my daddy what he thought of the matter 'cause nobody got in her way. Billy and I was thick as thieves, and I knew what that trip meant to him. So I took the long way round gettin' to Mr. Baker's, hopin' that bus would be long gone. I even went by Fulton's and bought myself five cents' worth of candy. But sure 'nough, that bus was still sittin' there when I came walkin' up, lickin' my peppermint stick."

"Couldn't you have told your mother how you felt?" Maxine couldn't imagine her grandma ever holding her tongue, even as a child.

"Child, didn't nobody care how I felt. It was my job to obey. Young people these days, thinkin' they got a say in everything . . ." Mama Ruby shook her head.

"Ain't that the truth." Laughing, Vivienne took the spoon from Mama Ruby and stirred the glaze.

"Besides, that's not the point. Follow where I'm leadin', girl. Now, when I got there, Billy was already on the bus. You should've seen his face when he saw me walk up. His eyes just got bigger and bigger, wellin' up. Mr. Baker must have suspected I'd be comin' 'cause he opened up those doors straightaway and asked me, 'You come for Billy?' Well, I looked from him to my brother, sittin' in that window, and I couldn't do it. I just could not break his heart and pull him off that bus in front of all those other boys."

Maxine stopped spinning the vase. "So what did you do?"

"I put a hand on my hip and said, 'Mr. Baker, Mama will have your head if somethin' happens to Billy, so you'd best take care of him.' He looked like he knew I was up to no good, but he closed them doors and drove away. Billy was still wipin' his face when he stuck out his hand through the window and waved good-bye. I can still see him grinnin' as I handed him one of my peppermint sticks."

"What did you say when you got home, Mama Ruby?"

"At first, I reported I was too late to stop Billy from leavin'. Which was mostly true, if you want to pick through the meat to get to the bone—at least accordin' to your way of thinkin'. It *was* too late. His heart was long gone, and he needed to follow it. But that wasn't the whole tale. It wasn't the truth, and my spirit knew it. Tellin' that lie ate me up until I confessed it to my daddy. He made me tell the whole story, and then I got the whuppin' of my *life*. That was okay though. Forgiveness don't always soften the consequences."

"I don't mean any harm, but what does all that have to do with Maxine?" Mother set the spoon in a dish on the counter and lowered the flame.

"Everythang. I could've told Mr. Baker that I was sent there to get my brother, but that wouldn't have been right. It wouldn't have helped nobody to make him get off that bus. My mama had to let go sometime, and Billy did, too." Mama Ruby readjusted the dial on the stove when Mother turned her back and walked back to the island. Her grandma lifted a finger to her lips and shook her head at Maxine.

Maxine waggled her eyebrows and nodded in response as Mama Ruby, the secret sous-chef, continued.

"That truth you've been carryin' around all these years? Of course you're goin' to come clean, just like I did. The same Book that raised me raised you. But *when* to tell it is just as important as what to tell and who to tell. That decision will affect a lot of lives, like the one I had to make. Only God knows the what, when, who, and how, Maxine. Not me. Not your mama. We'll help you deal with the consequences, painful as they may be." Mama Ruby reached into her apron pocket and withdrew a pad of paper and a Sharpie. She marked off an item on her list.

"I just don't know what the right decision is! If I tell Theodore, I have to tell Ce—"

"Hey, y'all! Ooh, pretty . . ."

Mama Ruby's green marker clattered to the floor.

Maxine's whole body froze. She turned incrementally, like the second hand on a clock. It seemed like a full minute passed before she faced the high-pitched voice coming from the mudroom that connected the kitchen to the storeroom. "Celeste . . . ?"

Uncle Roy grinned over the head of the thirteen-year-old girl clad in a denim miniskirt, pink-and-orange long-sleeved tee, and pink leggings. He pushed the glass-paned wooden door closed as she bounded into the kitchen.

"Oh, Maxine, your flowers came!" Celeste's low-topped blue Chuck Taylors squeaked happily on the hardwood floor. She leaned over and kissed Mother on the cheek. "Mmm-mwah. It smells good in here, Mama. What's going on?"

Chapter Two

MOTHER AND FIRST JOHN had tearfully whispered, "I do" in a church in Spring Hope where Reverend Farrow had eulogized Maxine's daddy and Vivienne had collapsed at the end of the two-hour funeral service. The pastor had jumped down from the pulpit to help two pallbearers carry her out. Right past the open casket bidding a grim farewell at the front doors. Years later, Reverend Farrow baptized Maxine's brothers in that redbrick church, dunking Zander and the twins—Robert and Second John—in the pool covered by the floorboards behind the altar.

Reverend Farrow didn't get to baptize, dunk, or even sprinkle Celeste. Maxine took care of that before she returned home the winter after she turned eighteen, swaddling her baby girl in a green- and yellow-flowered blanket, a gift from a benevolence ministry. Maxine had found Jesus while standing in front of a singing Christmas tree in the mall in Valdosta, Georgia. Determined to make sure she and her daughter were washed as white as a rare, Southern snowfall, she pressed a local preacher to baptize them both three days later. It took another sixty days to work up the gumption to pack her few belongings and return to her mother.

When her mother and stepfather opened the door to Maxine that night, they only had eyes for their prodigal daughter on their back stoop holding her torn army-green duffel bag. At first. Then they spied the tiny hand curled around Maxine's finger and the striped baby bag on her left shoulder. At that moment, both the teen and the infant became *their* babies. They made quick work of severing Celeste's parental ties to "that boy." Every morning, noon, and night following, the couple thanked God for the blessings of forgiveness and second chances.

Adopting their grandbaby seemed natural. And doing it right away before they moved back to North Carolina from Alabama made the most sense for all concerned. Maxine could pick up her teenage life she'd dropped by the wayside and go on to college. Their toddler son, Zander, would get a baby sister to tease. Celeste would be raised in a home with a father and a mother. First John and Vivienne felt they'd done right by everybody. Not right as the rain that fell once the summer clouds burst at the seams, but as right as the crooked path that wound through the woods back to their wrought iron gate. It always led their family back home. No more loss, no more brokenness . . . until Maxine started falling to pieces years later, awake and asleep.

"Da—?" Maxine's eyelashes fluttered against her cheeks before she sat up, wrestled with the light cover, and untangling it, threw it aside. Another . . . vision. Not quite a nightmare but too unsettling for such an innocuous word as *dream*. Her eyes searched her bedroom. She found only splashes of hazy yellow and green, filtered through the half-closed shutters, dotting the creamy walls of the garage apartment she rented from her parents.

Maxine had hoped to recover that week's lost sleep with a power nap, but the afternoon light skittering around the edges of the room chased away her drowsiness. She relaxed bit by bit into her pillows as the prickly memories of those moments before she fully awoke evaporated with the warmth of the afternoon sun. She picked up her phone and noted the time: 1:47. Her pillows muffled her groan. If she didn't hurry, she'd miss her date with Teddy.

"Do you have anything you're keeping from me? Tell me now, or forever hold your peace."

"Theodore Franklin Charles, didn't your mama teach you not to talk in church?" Maxine's questionnaire skittered under the pew and landed in the row behind them. She spun and looked over her shoulder. Thankfully it was mid-afternoon on a Thursday. The only other people in Grace Chapel were the twelve disciples having supper with Jesus on the wall over the altar. Still, she lowered her voice a notch and leaned close enough to her fiancé that her breath made the sandy curls above his left ear dance. "What are you talking about?"

Using his trusty Paper Mate pen, he tapped the sheet of paper on his clipboard as he drawled, "They've been asking the same questions for the past fifty years."

At her look, he shrugged and conceded, "Okay, maybe twenty-five. But these days, we need to dig deeper than 'Do you go to church regularly?' to stop the real epidemic killing Christian marriages. So you're a church member. The devil goes to church, Maxine."

"Teddy, this is just a form about premarital counseling." Maxine glanced around the sanctuary, her heart a heavy, slow-moving stone thumping painfully against her rib cage. She tried to keep her fingers from trembling as she set down her empty clipboard and dropped to her knees as if to pray for Theodore's soul or perhaps her own fearful one. Instead, she stretched, her right arm brushing the smooth mahogany beneath the seat. When she still couldn't reach her questionnaire, she mumbled, "Excuse me" and edged past him, tugging down her pale-pink-and-white tweed skirt so it didn't catch on his brown leather Chelsea boots.

Maxine scooted back to her spot on the plush, bloodred pew. "So tell me about this Reverend Atwater. What do I need to say to convince him to like me?" Maxine winked at her fiancé.

Theodore squeezed together the fingers on her right hand and studied her. "You've convinced *me*. That's all that matters."

"We didn't talk about what happens if we miss a class or, heaven forbid, fail a lesson." She nodded toward his questionnaire. "I mean, it's obvious you're going to be that kind of student who tests the teacher."

"Who fails premarital counseling?" He released her hand. With a flourish, he signed his given name on the last page and leaned his clipboard against his chest.

Who indeed? Maxine's heart stopped hurling itself against her ribs and resumed its normal, less painful rhythm as she admired his dancing brown eyes and crooked grin.

"I'm an award-winning educator, the headmaster of a private school." Teddy inched closer to Maxine and kissed her cheek gently. "I don't fail anything, especially anything related to you, my love."

Maxine leaned into him, turning her face to brush his cheek with a kiss of her own. She wrinkled her nose. Scratchy. "Well, this award-winning headmaster needs a shave. Your five-o'clock shadow feels more like seven."

"I didn't have time this morning. My fiancée made me meet her at sunrise to eat quiche."

Her laugh echoed through the empty church as she swatted him with her clipboard. "It was not sunrise! We need to think about our menu, Teddy, and that was the only time Mother could bake a sample. It tastes better straight from the oven."

"Well—"

"Theodore. Maxine. Did you two get a chance to complete the forms?"

For a second, Maxine's eyes flew toward Jesus and His disciples before she ascertained the softly accented baritone wasn't of heavenly origin. She and Theodore turned to their right toward the well-dressed man standing there with his left hand gripping the pew and his right extended in greeting. Fumbling with their clipboards, like guilty kids caught cutting up in school, they stood.

"Pastor Atwater, hello. This is . . . my . . ."

"His fiancée, Maxine Owens. It's good to see you again, Pastor." Maxine tucked her papers under her arm and reached out to shake hands as she considered her flustered fiancé.

Reverend William Atwater smiled. "And you." His long fingers released hers and clapped Theodore once on the back. "Son, you seem a little out of sorts. You all right?"

Theodore cleared his throat. "No, sir. I mean, yes . . . I . . . we were just talking, and I didn't hear you come up. You surprised me."

"Like a thief in the night?" Reverend Atwater's mustache twitched as he chuckled. "Why don't we come to my office—and I'll take those forms, even though they're about as good as unsweetened iced tea. Oh, and you have lipstick on your cheek." Smiling, he turned and led the way from the sanctuary.

Maxine swiped at Theodore's chin line, snickering, "He heard us!"

The wide-eyed, formerly confident headmaster looked more like one of his six hundred students than their fearless leader. "You mean he heard *me*. Looks like you'll be teacher's pet." He intertwined his fingers with hers. "It's time to pay the piper, see what the boss has to say."

Maxine picked up her coat and risked one more look at the painting above the altar before she and Teddy fell into step with the lanky, silver-haired minister.

"So, Maxine, tell me about yourself." Reverend Atwater

ushered them into his office and motioned them toward matching green damask-covered chairs positioned in front of his desk.

Maxine crossed her legs and fiddled with the fringed hem of her skirt. "Well . . ."

Theodore reached over the mahogany arms of their chairs and covered her cold hands with both of his. "*Well*, Pastor, my fiancée is the oldest of four—"

"Five. I'm the oldest of five. Zan is sixteen, Celeste is thirteen, and Robert and Second John just turned ten." Maxine returned one hand to her lap and left the other clasped in his.

Reverend Atwater looked up from the forms on his desk. "That's quite a gap between you and . . ." His eyes followed his finger as it searched the paper.

"Zan—Zander. My biological father, Henry Clark, died in a car accident when I was eight, and my mother married my stepfather when I was eleven. After he adopted me, they went on to raise four more children together."

"Raise? Your brothers and sister are adopted?"

Maxine coughed but shook her head.

Theodore's index finger tickled Maxine's palm. "Nothing could be further from the truth. You'll see for yourself when you meet them what a beautiful blend they all are of Miss Viv and First John. It's like they just spit them out. Are you okay, Max?"

"Miss Viv? First John?" Again, Reverend Atwater consulted the clipboard in front of him.

"Umm . . . ," she croaked. "That's what Theodore—Teddy—calls my mother and stepfather, Vivienne and John Owens.

I'm sorry. Do you mind if I get some water?" She released Teddy's hand.

"Let me, Max." Theodore gently pulled her back to a seated position, but before he could rise, the pastor pushed away from his leather-topped desk and unfolded himself from his chair.

"No, please. Let me." He strode over to a cart parked in the corner. It held a crystal pitcher of ice water and several glasses. "Maxine, is Theodore always this helpful? He's barely letting you get a word in. I thought he'd had more than his say out there in the sanctuary."

"About that, Pastor . . ." Teddy cleared his throat.

"No offense intended, Theodore, and none taken." He laughed and handed over her water. "But let's hear what Maxine has to say."

"It's just she's—"

Reverend Atwater placed an icy glass in front of Teddy and shushed him with one raised, gray-streaked brow. Then he trained his expectant, hazel eyes on Maxine, who was rubbing her engagement ring this way and that with her left thumb.

"Teddy's right, Pastor. I am feeling . . . a bit out of my element." Maxine sipped her water. "But I can surely speak for myself. In fact, I do so all the time in my magazine column, My Daily Grace. And very well, in fact, according to my editor. Jean credits my column with the slight uptick in subscriptions, which we desperately need."

The pastor swiveled from left to right in his high-backed chair. "Aah, she speaks! My wife and I are part of that 'uptick' at your magazine. We subscribed after Teddy shared the news of your engagement. I have to say, Maxine, you seem—how do you say it?—a mite less forthcoming in person."

She uncrossed her legs and sat a bit straighter. "That's the nature of my calling, I think. I tend to 'talk' more with the words I write than the words I speak. Something Teddy will have to get used to." She glanced at the man in question.

Theodore took a deep breath and smiled.

"So you do most of your preaching with your pen while I do mine from the pulpit?" Again Reverend Atwater swiveled in his chair.

"I don't know about you, but I'm usually the choir I'm preaching to." Maxine started to sweat under the spotlight over their conversation. She cocked her head toward the door leading to the sanctuary. "As you may have heard out there, Teddy and I were talking about the purpose of these meetings. I understand you want to get to know us—at least, get to know *me*—but what will we talk about for almost a year? Will you include a membership class as a bonus?"

The pastor chuckled with her. "So you intend to join our church?"

"Of course she does!"

Still laughing, both Maxine and the older gentleman turned at the outburst.

Theodore winced. "I'm sorry, but it's not in me to sit still."

"Believe me, I know. I've prayed over you often enough since you moved here from the Big Easy." Reverend Atwater shook his head at the younger man. "But, Maxine, that is *your* intent?"

She smiled at Teddy. "*Of course.* Leave and cleave."

"Hmm." The pastor ruffled the pages, but he didn't look

down this time. "Yes, leave and cleave. Well, you have some time before you need to wield any sharp objects.

"As far as your questions about why we meet for such a long time, well, I think we'll all discover that as we go along. Seven meetings may sound arbitrary, but I assure you, it isn't. Seven is the biblical number of completion. And it isn't as long as 'until death do you part,' now, is it?"

Maxine pictured her eight-year-old self, standing by the window in her mother's front room, waving good-bye as her daddy climbed into his car that long-ago night. Reverend Atwater's voice drew her back to the land of the living.

"I'm looking forward to this time together, and there's nothing to be nervous about. I'm not trying to uncover any deep, dark secrets or put my stamp of approval—" his fingers made quotation marks—"on you. If God has brought you together, who am I to say anything different? I just want to help you both discover more about each other and your expectations for marriage. And it looks like we've already started to peel the onion."

"What do you mean?" Theodore shifted in his chair.

"We've already learned Maxine's a woman of few words—spoken, at least. You'd better start listening closely, son. Learn to pick up on some context clues." He looked from one to the other. "Okay then. Let's pray and seek the Lord for His will for you as a couple and for you individually." Reverend Atwater stood and reached out a hand to each of them.

Teddy sprang to his feet and stretched out his hand to grip the pastor's.

Maxine rose a little more slowly, to make sure her shaky

legs would hold her. "Does that mean you plan to meet with us separately?"

"If need be. If that's what you'd like. But I try to see you two as God sees you. As one."

Her icy fingers reached for both her fiancé and the pastor. "I wonder what else God sees when He sees me."

Reverend Atwater smiled. He squeezed her hand and bowed his head. "That's for Him to know and for you to find out. Let us pray."

Chapter Three

"WHAT DID YOU THINK about Reverend Atwater?"

Maxine plucked a brown packet of raw sugar from the basket in the middle of the wrought iron table. "He's not as cute as a certain headmaster, but I like him."

"I knew you would." Teddy sprinkled salt and pepper over his BLT.

"Did you now?" She tapped the packet inside her left palm, tore it open, and emptied the sugar into her teacup.

"Yes, because he's a lot like you: he's great one-on-one, and his messages resonate. But generally, he thinks more than he says." Teddy took a bite and swallowed.

Silenced by his assessment, Maxine folded and refolded the napkin in her lap. At first, she'd thought it a hoot to bring her readership along on her yearlong trip down the aisle.

She'd connect weekly wedding updates on her website to her monthly magazine column. Now she wondered what she'd been thinking. Sacrificing her privacy to boost sales made her insides itch.

Apparently Teddy was itching to talk about Reverend Atwater. His feet were firmly planted in the man's pulpit. "Will you feature him in My Daily Grace?"

Maxine smoothed the cloth and let it go. "Probably, since he's an important part of our trip to the altar."

"If your post is due Saturday, you'd better get to it. Especially since we're fresh from our first meeting. Speaking of meetings—" he checked his watch—"I hate to cut short our date, but I'm meeting with the art department at five thirty."

"Art *department*? It's two people, Teddy." Maxine emptied another packet into her tea, then stirred slowly. She took a cautious sip.

"Well, you tell them that." He picked up his sandwich. "You felt comfortable with him?"

"Comfortable with whom?" Though Maxine knew who Teddy meant, she enjoyed making him squirm a bit. She relented when she saw him nearly choke on his last bite of bacon, lettuce, tomato, and ciabatta bread. "Yes, I felt very comfortable with Pastor Atwater. And I think it's cool we're being married by my pastor and counseled by yours. A meeting of the minds." Maxine tucked into her collard green egg rolls, the only reason she ever ate at Sassafras.

"Hmmm . . . a meeting of the minds. That's one way to put it." He took a draft of his sweet tea before wiping away the mustache of droplets over his top lip. "A nice title for your post, too." He used a fork to pilfer some greens from her plate.

"You seem quite invested in my article. You want to write it?" Maxine watched him stop short of popping the food into his mouth, almost relished the sound the stainless steel made when he dropped the fork with a clang onto his plate.

"Excuse me? Did I say something wrong?" Teddy slowly retrieved his napkin from his lap and wiped his hands.

But her fire flickered out as quickly as it flared. Retreating, she graced him with a view of her curly auburn crown as she busied herself with searching for yet another pack of raw sugar, tearing it open, and stirring, stirring, stirring. "No, but it seems I did."

"You haven't said much at all."

Maxine sighed and set her spoon in the saucer. "Didn't the pastor say something about listening closely to this woman of few words?"

"Not this few. Not usually. 'There is no following her in this fierce vein.'"

Maxine squinted at him. "*A Midsummer Night's Dream.* From Sherlock to Shakespeare. You're quite the bulldog today. Am I the bone?"

He shook his head. "Never, babe. Or should I say, always. I love you, and I'm interested in your work. In you. In *us.* I told you, I don't intend to fail anything that relates to you."

Maxine watched him silently eye his plate.

"You *are* still writing about our wedding plans?" Teddy's voice was quiet as his tapered index finger traced the diamond-shaped ironwork in the table.

More than a few uncomfortable seconds passed before

Maxine reached across the table and covered his wandering hand with one of hers, bringing it to rest. With her free hand, she picked up a collards-stuffed bite of egg roll and slid it between his lips. "Just call me Bridezilla. I'm sure I'll get scarier than this in the months to come. You're going to see an entirely different side of me." She kissed his fingers, then moved to refresh her tea.

"Maxine? Hey!"

Maxine dropped the pot with a thump, rattling her cup. Pale-green tea splashed into the saucer. Out of the corner of her eye, she saw Theodore scoot back his chair. "Evelyn!" Maxine could barely speak over the lump in her throat as, in one big gulp, her eyes consumed the pregnant woman grinning at them.

"No, please, don't stand." Evelyn set down her Sassafras take-out bag and moved her right hand in Theodore's direction, as a conductor would indicate a decrescendo to the woodwind section. She wrinkled her nose after he stood. "Gracious, I'm interrupting your—" she glanced at the slim watch on her wrist—"lunch?"

Maxine stopped dabbing the table and joined Teddy. She reached deep down, retrieved a smile to cover her shock, and plastered it on her face. "We're just having a quick meal."

Their visitor's eyes alighted on the nearly six-foot-tall man for a moment before flitting back to Maxine's face. Eyebrows raised, she inclined her head in his direction.

Maxine rounded the table to her side and brushed her cheek with a kiss. "Evelyn Lester, this is the man I told you about—Theodore Charles. Theodore, Evelyn."

"Well, I think I did a better job of introducing you to

Reverend Atwater." Chuckling, he edged around the table and extended his right hand.

"Not according to my recollection." Maxine elbowed him in his side.

"Reverend Atwater?" Again, Evelyn's eyes leapfrogged from one to the other.

"Teddy's pastor." She opened the door a little more so Evelyn could put both her feet on their conversation's welcome mat. "We met with him for premarital counseling."

Her mouth a lowercase *o*, Evelyn's tummy bumped against the table as she stepped closer. "Premarital counseling? A lot happened while I was dealing with my Granny B. You're getting married? I knew your mystery man was special, but you neglected to mention this big news!"

"Not as big as some things, I guess." Maxine nodded toward Evelyn's obtrusive body part that had nearly capsized her cup. "I didn't bring it up the other day because I wanted to hear about you, the baby, and Kevin." She leaned closer to her fiancé to explain, "Evelyn's husband, Kevin Lester."

Evelyn's left hand splayed against the side of her abdomen. "As you can see, I'm about to pop any minute. Kevin's at Mama's house now, with my brother. I've . . . *we've* been spending more time there since everything happened with Granny B. Actually, we have a big family thing planned later." Evelyn sucked in a breath and her eyes widened a bit.

Seeing the emotions do a two-step across Evelyn's face, Maxine's own eyes narrowed. She wondered about the hidden thoughts percolating in her friend's head. She watched Evelyn's shirt stretch tightly across her middle, listened to her struggle for words as she filled the couple in on her husband and his company, her grandmother's illness, and her new baby girl on the way.

Celeste.

"Maxine?"

She dragged herself from her stupor to find both Evelyn and Theodore staring at her. Maxine's smile wavered but never quite righted itself on her face, so she stopped trying and shrugged. "Oops, you caught me. I've got a lot on my mind these days. What did I miss?"

"Your fiancé asked how long we've known each other, and I told him we were raised eating grits and bacon together."

"Then you should be able to tell me why Maxine uses *Mama Ruby* instead of calling her Grandma or Grandmother. Is that a North Carolina thing?" When silence rolled in like a fog after his question, Teddy turned to Maxine.

Maxine imagined herself straining to pick up a set of barbells. She kept sliding off weights until finally, she stripped the truth to its bare bones. "My mother left me with my grandparents for a couple years after my daddy died. During that time I started calling my grandmother Mama Ruby because she became a mother to me. That's when I met Evelyn." This time she mustered a smile to lighten the mood. "Evelyn's Granny B introduced me to tender greens, and my life was forever changed."

Evelyn's eyes twinkled. "Forever changed? Really? So why was I not good enough to meet this guy?"

If anyone's not good enough . . . "Guilty again. It all happened so fast, Ev."

"I see that." Evelyn tapped Maxine's shoulder in what

seemed a gentle rebuke. "Theodore, you do know you've got a passionflower on your hands."

"Maxine? *My* Maxine? No-o-o, she's a peach blossom."

More like a wild Irish rose, Maxine thought. Her eyes met Evelyn's before blinking, her trembling fingers reaching for his steady ones.

"And please, call me Theo or Teddy. I keep looking around for my dad when you say 'Theodore.'"

Evelyn crinkled her nose at him. "Well, if Maxie calls you Teddy, I guess I should too, but if I'm not mistaken, passionflowers and peach blossoms both flourish in hothouses."

Cringing inwardly, Maxine pretended not to notice Teddy's smirk. She took the wheel and turned the conversation around. "*Hot*house, Evelyn? You're starting to sound like Granny B and Mama Ruby." She checked her watch. "Didn't you say you had a family commitment? I hate to hold you."

Evelyn's laughter petered out. Her fingertips tapped her midsection and she shifted the large white paper bag with the tip of her boot. "Thanks for reminding me. I do need to get these back to Mama's and meet . . . Kevin and . . . the family. And I should let y'all get back to your date. Theodore—I mean Teddy—it was good to meet you. Maxie . . ." She leaned in as much as she could and kissed her former classmate's cheek. She pulled a curl and let it spring into place. "I'm glad you're letting your hair down." She retrieved her bag with one hand and waggled the fingers of the other. "Kiss your mama for me."

Maxine and Theodore stood quietly, watching her waddle away. Then he sat down and inched his heavy iron chair closer to the table. "Maxie, huh? A hothouse flower?" The corners of his mouth lifted as he picked up another crouton and crunched it.

As she returned to her seat, Maxine felt his eyes follow her, as if she would suddenly sprout crimson petals and velvety green leaves right there on the spot and he didn't want to miss the transformation. She dug up a chuckle. "She's a funny one, that Evelyn. Not many people call me Maxie."

"She seems nice. And it also seems like something is going on with her husband, or at least it did. Kevin, is it?" Theodore wiped his hands and dropped his crushed napkin on the crumbs on his plate.

"You think so?" *And here I am, broken myself, whispering, pointing, and dissecting somebody else's problems. Didn't I warn Mother?* "Maybe she was distracted. You know how pregnant women can be."

"No-o-o, actually, I don't. Is that something from the bylaws of the women's-only club I don't know about? Oh!" Theodore abruptly looked at his watch. "This has been fun, babe, but if I don't leave now, I'll late for my meeting with the art . . . teachers." He stood and pushed his chair under the table.

Maxine half rose and met his lips for a lingering kiss. She caressed his cheek. "I love you. Talk to you later?"

"Of course." He winked and bent to retrieve his leather briefcase. "Good-bye, my hothouse flower." Without a backward glance, he wove through the tables and chairs toward the front door of the café.

A wilted Maxine reclaimed her seat. Bemused, she picked up her cup and took a slow slurp. *Ugh!* She hated lukewarm tea. She twisted to get her purse from the back of the chair.

"Not to your liking, Maxie?"

Maxine whirled one hundred eighty degrees, and her elbow caught the delicate china she'd just set down. She gasped and stretched for it as it rolled toward the edge of the table, but all ten fingers bobbled the teacup and just missed grasping the handle. In those precious seconds before it shattered on the concrete floor, Maxine noted the torn brown sugar packets around the saucer, the smudges on Theodore's drained glass, the green tea dripping through the wrought iron mesh, and the surprised server who'd chosen that moment to slip the check onto the table.

It only took seconds, but her life as she knew it ended as her heart resumed beating. Maxine's eyes crept up from the leather Timberland boots, to the dark-washed denims and chambray shirt, and finally to the widow's peak of the man before her. *His hair. It's longer and curlier than I remember. And he has a beard!*

"JD?"

Chapter Four

"WELL, SOME PEOPLE STILL CALL ME THAT."

More than Celeste's lifetime ago, that's what everybody had called him. JD. And in the time it took her heart to regain its natural rhythm, that's how far Maxine traveled, to a long-ago, crisp Friday night. She saw herself sitting cross-legged on a blanket on the back of JD's Chevy pickup, throwing Mountain Dew tabs at him, aiming at friends as they streamed through the parking lot after the football game.

"JD, get down! Connor's going to see you."

"Shh, JD. That's Mrs. Shepherd. She'll tell Mother."

"Jay, I love you."

Maxine, the former passionflower, blinked quickly to chase away the vision. She leaned against the table edge and forced herself to focus on the living memory before her. *What do people call you now?*

"Maxie, Maxie." He shook his head. "Wow. It's been a long time." He shifted his weight from one foot to the other and moved his weathered bomber jacket from his left arm to his right. The ice in his coffee clinked. "How are you?"

Maxine stuttered apologies to the server and busboy who were clearing away shards and splashes. She pressed a few bills into the server's hand and then stood and made her way around them, landing a breath away from . . . JD, this person she couldn't simply close her eyes and wish away or discard like broken glass. She swallowed. "I'm, uh, good. I mean, well. I'm doing well. And it's Maxine now. You threw me a bit because no one ever calls me Maxie." *Until today. That makes two people.*

"I admit I haven't heard *JD* in a long time myself. Maxine, huh? That'll take some getting used to." He shifted to his other foot.

For a moment, both their eyes were drawn to the tinkling ice. Maxine watched the condensation on his glass pool and drip once, twice to the floor. She took a step back as the busboy swiped the spot before swishing back to the kitchen with the mop and bucket. Watching him go, she finally took stock of the crowded café, heard other people munch and chat away around them. Sassafras, once her shelter in a storm. Feeling exposed to the elements, Maxine retrieved her mustard-colored peacoat and slipped it on. "What are you doing here?"

He wiggled his coffee cup.

Maxine shook her head. "I meant here, in Mount Laurel. Wait. Is that what Evelyn was talking about? *You're* the 'family gathering'? When I ran into her, we talked about your brother and the new baby. You never came up."

"I was supposed to meet Ev and Kevin later at her mom's house, after my job interview." JD took a breath. "I'm moving back."

"Back where? Back here? To Mount Laurel?" Maxine drew her coat closed as if to protect herself from the news.

Maxine and Evelyn had always walked through life in step before their paths had abruptly diverged. Losing their fathers at a young age. Growing up sweating in their grandmothers' kitchens. Loving Lester men. Sometimes one skipped just ahead of the other; often, one friend had to carry or drag the other along. As Maxine gaped at the man laughing at her, she chalked up another thing they had in common: their propensity for wearing secrets like bulletproof vests. "What's so funny?"

"Don't you live here? Then why is it so preposterous that I would move back?"

Not so much preposterous as disastrous. Maxine draped her small purse across her body and fiddled with the clasp. She forced her hands to work the buttons on her coat.

"Maxie. Maxine, are you okay? You seem . . . different."

Maxine's trembling fingers paused for a moment on her last button. Her words wriggled up from her chest and through the wool neckline of her coat to make it between her lips. "Well, yes, my hair is natural now, I'm about ten pounds heavier even though I've stopped drinking Mountain Dew . . . among other things. I'd expect I'm a lot different than I was at seventeen. Did you expect you'd find me still wearing your letterman's jacket?"

"Actually, I didn't really expect to see you at all. Not today anyway."

His soft words finally lured her eyes to his, and it seemed that once they were hooked, she couldn't extricate them. She flailed about, searching for syllables or phrases she could string together into something coherent. She took in a shallow breath and finally managed to exhale, "You look good."

"Thank you. I was thinking the same."

Maxine raised a brow.

"About you, I mean, of course. You look really good."

"Good, but different?"

"You were always a dog with a bone."

Hearing the same accusation she'd hurled at Teddy, Maxine made a harsh sound, akin to a bark. Several diners glanced their way.

"JD, I—"

"Maxie, you—"

Their words orbited each other for a second before the black hole between them swallowed their voices and they were left staring silently at each other. Then his arm breached the air space and his right hand cupped her elbow. "How about I walk you out? They probably want to use this table anyway." He nodded toward the server hovering near the kitchen's swinging doors and held his cup above his head before he set it down atop a five-dollar bill. Then JD steered her through the labyrinth until they reached the double glass doors. He pushed open one side to propel her through.

The brisk air was ammonia for Maxine, jolting her alert. She freed her arm from his clasp and backed up a step, watching him as he braced open the door for a couple entering the restaurant. Maxine hadn't finished poring over his face when he turned to her.

"Do you feel better?"

Maxine shook her head, stunned that he could still read her. She sought sanctuary from the nearness of JD in the scene around them: the storefronts across the street framed by the steel-gray sky. A cardinal-red Jeep Wrangler traveling faster than the posted twenty-five miles per hour. A worn pink bunny flung from a passing stroller.

"I couldn't tell if you were going to laugh or cry in there."

"I couldn't either." Maxine turned her back on the young woman running to retrieve the stuffed animal and faced the man-who-once-was-JD. She didn't have the emotional energy to hide herself from him. "It's been a long day, and as they say, 'I have promises to keep.'"

"'And miles to go before I sleep . . .' Still reading Frost." The left corner of his mustache rose a millimeter as he looked askance at the large clock above the bank that presided over the intersection. "It's just 4:45. You don't have a minute or two to catch up with your former—?"

"No." Maxine waggled her left hand in front of her face, as if her diamond ring could catch the fading afternoon light and throw it back in his face. "I'm getting married."

"Is that so? To the dude who left you holding the check?"

"He didn't leave me holding the ch—you saw Teddy?"

"Teddy? As in bear?" He stroked the silky hair framing his jawline, a black Magic Marker tracing his face. "So you're marrying a teddy bear. I hope that's working for you."

Maxine reached into her pocket for her keys. "His name is Theodore Charles. And it's 'working' just fine. I do have to go. But it was . . . good to see you, JD. Good luck with that job." She withdrew her keys and quick-stepped toward her car parked a few spaces from the door.

"Maxine!"

She whirled around.

This time both ends of his mustache moved as his bottom lip curved gently. "It was nice running into you. And you'll definitely see me again."

Maxine's toes barely grazed the dewy grass, but it didn't matter. The lacy hem of her white dress caught on the taller blades. Soon, her feet and ankles were sopping wet. Her hand brushed against the cold granite on her right and she read the names etched in ornate script, large enough for God above to read: Devon and Michelle, 43 years. *She scattered chrysanthemums on the mound. A couple more steps and on her right another stone erupted from the ground:* William and Lena, 15 years. *More blooms. She tripped over a small, non-descript marker memorializing Jacob and Faith, 7 months, and when she landed on her knees with a* smack! *on the squishy dirt, she read* The Lesters *on the monument in front of her.*

Before she could strew flowers across the grave, a hand clasped her shoulder. She looked up and behind her, shielding her eyes against the blazing sun. It obscured the face looming above her, but she could see his hand reaching for her. She took it and allowed him to pull her to her feet, leaning hard on the firm yet soft hand that cupped her elbow. "Dead. These marriages, my family. It's over," Maxine whispered, shaking her head. She dropped the rest of her flowers and brushed her hands against her long white skirt. She ignored the brown streaks of earth on the chiffon billowing behind her in the sudden breeze.

"Oh, Maxine . . ."

"How do you know me?" She squinted, trying to see what her heart seemed to hear so clearly.

He laughed. "I've always known you. My covenant with you is forever."

"Always known me?" When Maxine rolled over in bed, her pillows swallowed her murmurs. A few hours later the morning sun burned away the remaining tendrils of her dream, diaphanous as the dress she'd worn during her graveside inspection.

"You saw that boy two days ago?" Vivienne threw the ball. A large white puff of fur shot after it.

"You mean JD." Maxine watched her mother's standard poodle bound through the dead leaves toward them. He dropped the tennis ball at Vivienne's feet.

"I don't care if he calls himself Kunta Kinte. What else did he say?"

"Nothing. Nothing much, anyway."

"Good boy, Milo." Her mother stopped long enough to stroke his head. She lobbed the ball again. "You know, I noticed you the other day. You rolled in right past me when I was settin' up the smoker in the driveway, but I figured you wanted to stew in private. What's he doing here?"

After seeing JD, Maxine had driven home from Sassafras, barely able to focus on the traffic signals, driving too fast through the fog enshrouding Mount Laurel and too slowly to keep up with the speed of her thoughts. "He interviewed for a job. I guess he's moving here?"

"I know you're not askin' me! What in the world?" Mother frowned. She turned away from Milo as he darted among the spindly pine trees that towered around them, hunting for his toy.

Maxine followed her mother's gaze. Both sets of eyes rested a minute on Celeste, who knelt by the stream running along the edge of the property. Maxine looked away from the girl and Vivienne as her thoughts drifted beyond the treetops. She squatted to pick up a miniature pinecone and added it to the considerable collection in her pocket. "Moving back here, and of all times . . ."

Vivienne threw the fuzzy yellow ball and watched Milo sniff at leaves rustled by the breeze and chase squirrels chittering all around them. The dog seemed to give up on the game as he trotted down to Celeste. "Well, it's home. You came back, didn't you? Two times, as a matter of fact."

The first time, Maxine had been a runaway teen, and she'd had nowhere else to turn. The second, she was a young adult, and there was nowhere else she'd wanted to be. Her spiritual amnesia had helped her pretend that her life BCC—before Christ and Celeste—had not only been forgiven; it had never happened. Celeste was her sister. But now, JD's return served as yet another striking reminder of the life she'd left in the bottom of the baptismal pool in Valdosta. Here it was, soaking wet but resurrected. "You're starting to sound like JD," she muttered.

"Like that boy? Do I now?" Mother whistled, and Milo trotted back. "Those are words I never expected to hear."

"What I mean is, that's what he said to me the other day. But it made sense for *me* to move back to Mount Laurel. My . . . family is here."

"But he has *family* in the area too." Vivienne glanced again at the stream's edge. "Maybe he came back for his mama. You know she's suffering from early onset Alzheimer's. Annie has never been my favorite person, but she sure could use all the love and support she can get right now. To surround herself with what and *who* is familiar—even if we consider him unwelcome."

"Mother, you know there has never been an *if* for you when it comes to JD. He was unwelcome, period. Regardless, knowing he was gone gave me breathing room. One minute I'm planning my wedding to Teddy, and the next . . ."

"And the next, you're still planning your weddin' to Theodore." Vivienne clipped the leash to Milo's collar and tugged him in the direction of the house. "Seeing that boy doesn't change any of that. Not even your guest list." She cupped her mouth and called, "Celeste!"

"That's not funny, Mother. Why are we heading back?" Though she hadn't wanted to go on the walk in the first place, crunching through the leaf beds had helped drown out the noise of her thoughts.

"Because I have sweet potato pies in the oven, and Celeste has a science lab to finish. Don't you have a column to write?"

"Aaaaaaah!" Maxine's scream set a flock of blue jays to

flight. The angry flutter of their wings rained down needles on them, and the birds mocked her with their shrieks. "Everybody is so worried about this column!"

Celeste crunched toward them. "Hey, what's up?"

"Your sister's got so grown she forgot herself." Vivienne cut her eyes Maxine's way. "But thirty or not, I don't appreciate you raisin' your voice to me even if you're tellin' me Santa Claus is comin' to town. I'm not *everybody*."

"I'm sorry, Mother, but I'm just tired of hearing about what I'm *supposed* to be doing." Maxine threw a pinecone into the woods.

"Maxine, if you don't stop . . ." Vivienne struggled to restrain Milo, who was determined to retrieve what he must have considered toys tossed for his pleasure. She uttered a low *tsssst* and tugged twice on the leash, settling the dog. Vivienne none too gently clutched Maxine's fingers. "You're lettin' all this get the best of you."

"What do you mean—the best of you?" Celeste tucked the vials she held into a pocket in her backpack and slung it over her shoulder.

"Mother thinks I'm succumbing to the pressures of work and wedding planning. What do you think, Sis?"

"Well, maybe if you . . ." She looked from one woman to the other, then swallowed. "I think you're just as crazy as always. Over-the-top and you don't know how to chill." Celeste laughed and dodged the playful punch Maxine aimed at her shoulder and reached for the leash. "Milo and I are going to take the long way back to the house. That okay, Mama?"

"Just don't make it too long. You have work to do. And

you need to eat—something with lots of fat and protein, preferably. Those jeans are whippin' your behind."

"They are not!" But Celeste twisted around and checked. "Anyway, I hid a slice of pizza from Zan. I was having that for lunch. Come on, Milo. Bye, Max!" She loped off, Milo dancing beside her, itching to charge whatever would run from him.

Freedom. What does that feel like? She took a breath so deep it rattled her whole body. "I thought Teddy was the best of me. I know Celeste is." She stared into the pale-blue sky, though she could've been blind to the clouds and deaf to the jays that still fussed at them from high in the pines. She could only focus on her current predicament. "But I'm afraid that I'm going to lose my best, that JD is going to get the best of me. Again." Tears forged a wet trail to the corners of her mouth.

Vivienne tightened her grip on Maxine's hand. "Maybe that boy—"

"JD."

"Whatever. His showin' up here could be the motivation you need."

"Motivation?" Maxine swiped at her face with her gloved hands and fixed her eyes on her mother. "To do what exactly?"

"To action, Maxine. You thought you could just float along through the rest of this year until your wedding, trading this identity you created for another one—wife of Theodore Franklin Charles, headmaster. Just because you told everybody to stop calling you Maxie doesn't mean that's not who you are."

"So you think I'm still that wild girl in high school?"

Again, Maxine's outcry ruffled the feathers of the wildlife around them.

"Of course not, Maxine. But when you were a girl, you were either looking for a daddy you'd lost or cuttin' and runnin' from the one I'd brought home for you. Since then you've been hiding from your mistakes instead of owning up to the choices you made. Bad ones and good ones. The sassy mouth and rebelliousness might not be you, but all these knee-length skirts, acoustic Christian music, and the 'Miss Vacation Bible School' aren't you either."

Vivienne stroked Maxine's cheek down to her chin—which she cupped as she stared into eyes that mirrored hers. "But it doesn't matter what anybody thinks about your past—"

"It'll matter to Teddy."

"Maybe so. However, the covenant God made with you overrides the one you're plannin' to make with Theodore. That first relationship makes the second possible, something I didn't realize when I was your age. But you know better. Now let's go home . . . *Max-ine*."

"My covenant with you is forever." Maxine thought about her dream as she watched her mother pick her way through the fallen branches, underbrush, and fallen leaves. She considered pitching a tent where she stood, planted next to a fir tree in the woods. But after a moment she followed Vivienne, stooping to pick up miniature pinecones every other step as if they would help her find her way home.

Chapter Five

MAXINE INCHED HER CHAIR CLOSER to her walnut desk. She gazed into the backyard, squinting so she could see the creek. Something about the inexorable nature of the slow-flowing water motivated her in the churning out of her column. She became someone else—"Maxine the Ready Writer," so different from the insecure woman who weighed every word before she opened her mouth, as if saying too much or too little would keep her from wearing her wedding dress. Because it would.

After studying the water's steady shimmer for a moment, she opened her laptop and typed the words *My Daily Grace*.

Da-da-ling!

Maxine jumped. Somehow she must have deactivated her "Do not disturb" feature. *Da-da-ling!* She peered over her orange-covered laptop and retrieved the phone from the top right corner of her desk and read the text. Hey, babe. Why aren't you working? ♥♥♥

She smiled and set the phone back in its customary place. *Buzzz. Buzzz.* "Okay, now, Teddy. You know I have a deadline." *Buzzz. Buzzz.* Maxine focused on the creek as she closed her laptop and answered. She didn't wait to hear her fiancé's greeting before warning him, "Once I say, 'I love you,' I'm hanging up."

"Well, that's a first."

"Excuse me?"

"Maxie?"

"Jay?"

"Looks like we're both having trouble letting go of the past."

Maxine knew JD was referring to the name she used to call him. The name she thought she'd forgotten. She ignored the mirth lacing each syllable of his low voice. "Speaking of letting go, why are you calling me? And how did you get my cell phone number?"

"I asked my sister-in-law—"

"You mean my so-called friend who didn't tell me you were back in town?"

"Yes, one and the same. She ran into you the same day, while she was at that restaurant."

"Sassafras."

"Yes, where we talked."

"We didn't really talk, JD."

"Well, if you want to get specific, it's where you knocked over your teacup and nearly passed out after you laid eyes on me." The humor had evaporated from his voice.

Maxine's exhalation ruffled the silky chrysanthemum petals in the arrangement on her desk. "Seeing you didn't make me break my teacup—"

"Oh, was it hearing my voice?"

Of course, it had been seeing him, hearing him, and remembering him. Not any one of those things, but everything together, all at once. Yet she could not, would not tell him that. That was something Maxie would have done. "But I'm Maxine."

"I know who you are. I called you, remember?"

He'd heard the whispered reminder she thought she'd only felt in her spirit. "Jay . . ." She choked on his name. "JD, you didn't answer me. Why are you calling? I hope you don't think we can possibly pick up where we left off. I told you I'm engaged. My wedding's in December." Maxine listened to the rustling on the other end of the line.

"To Teddy Bear. Yes, you told me."

In the sudden silence, Maxine focused on the pale-greenish-brown sliver of water through the trees. She imagined its twists and turns, its gentle movement toward some distant river that finally emptied into the Atlantic. So intent was she on the ocean's waves in her mind's eye, she nearly missed hearing his next question.

"Tell me, Maxine, why would I want what I had as a boy? I've put away a lot of childish things in the past thirteen years. I don't want what used to be."

"Then why?" Maxine shut her eyes to the creek and the chrysanthemums and leaned back in her chair.

"Because I want what *should* be. I want to know my daughter."

My Daily Grace—Still, Waters

When my siblings were little, we spent our summers building boats out of leaves and twigs, and we raced them on the little creek running through the woods behind my folks' house. Come winter, we skidded around on the frozen parts, only returning to my mother's kitchen once our pants were icy wet and our fingers were almost too stiff to bend. I can still see that family of deer who made their home there one October. Poor things, I think they were hiding out from the hunters.

Even now that creek winds its way through my life. I take comfort knowing it was there before I was born and it will be there after I'm gone. A few years ago, I thought we'd lost it for good. But after a two-day downpour we were asking ourselves, "What drought?" And yes, it continues feeding the area wildlife—from frogs and snakes and rabbits to the deer who still find shelter in our woods. Really, I'm the one who gets the most from that creek. I don't race boats there or wade along its shoreline, but I have a special spot where I can sit and cry and pray about whatever is ailing me and hide from whatever is hunting me down. When the water winks at me from the window as I work, it soothes and calms me. Its silent presence reminds me what once was, points the way to what can be.

Now I know things will change, "Lord willing and the creek don't rise," like my grandmama used to tell me. The waters just may dry up for good. Those deer I love to watch from my deck will find new, safer places to forage for food and raise their young. A tree may fall and divert the waters so they finally flood my folks' basement.

And talk about floods: These days I'm overwhelmed with all the changes in my life! I'm engaged (literally) in a yearlong process of change—my name, my address, my whole way of thinking about myself. Y'all may call it "planning a wedding," but that's too innocuous a name for what this entails—it certainly doesn't feel like a joining together of any-thing, let alone a celebration. Instead I feel I'm becoming a completely dif-ferent person. I don't know if I'm coming or going with all the appointments with caterers and ministers, the making of guest lists, and playing dress-up, something I didn't even enjoy as a youngster. I'm more likely to bite my fiancé's hand than hold it. Some days I just want to turn back the clock and change into that teen in a ponytail who raced leaf boats with her brother or the young college grad who meditated by the shore—well, maybe not that.

Folks are flitting in and out of my life. Some I need to hold on to; others I should let go. How do I handle my changing relationships with my parents, siblings, and friends and face a new life as a married woman? Just being "affianced" is hard enough on the heart and career! I know I'll spend these next eleven months growing and stretching, and by the year's end I'll have grown leaps and bounds in so many ways, but at the moment, my feet aren't quite big enough for these shoes. But I suppose that will . . . change, God willing and the creek don't rise.

So to those who reassure me that "change is good," I amend, "good and painful." And necessary. Yet, at the end of the day, my heart can rest assured in the unchanging promise found in Habakkuk 3:17-19:

Though the fig tree may not blossom, Nor fruit be on the vines; Though the labor of the olive may fail, And the fields yield no food; Though the flock may be cut off from the fold, And there be no herd in the stalls—Yet I will rejoice in the Lord, I will joy in the God of my salvation. The Lord God is my strength; He will make my feet like deer's feet, And He will make me walk on my high hills.

Maxine closed her laptop and rubbed her eyes with her knuckles. She'd barely met the deadline so her editor could link her blog to her column. Jean was probably having a hissy fit down at the magazine, she'd cut it so close. But she couldn't fret about Jean and her notorious temper.

Interlacing her fingers, she extended her arms way above her head, her eyes on the trees that also stretched their nearly bare limbs heavenward in the evening's half-light. Then she pushed her chair back from her desk, stood, and turned away from the woods and the creek that cut a path through them. She didn't have to see it to know the waters were rising.

February

"For what I am doing, I do not understand.
For what I will to do, that I do not
practice; but what I hate, that I do."

ROMANS 7:15

Chapter Six

"*Watch yourself!*"

Maxine hung on to the first two words JD ever said to her as if her life depended on them. But she never watched herself with him. She let him do that. She was too busy looking for something else she couldn't seem to find.

JD had caught Maxine before she could crack her skull on the concrete, swinging her around so she landed square, breathless and grateful, against his chest. She'd been part of the cavalcade of high school students tumbling out of New Building, and she'd stumbled over the camouflage JanSport backpack balanced on his foot. His amber-colored eyes seemed to laugh at her, even as they warmed her from the flat-ironed roots of her hair to her ebony-tipped toes.

That day after school she spared nary a thought for the

small group of ninth-grade girls waiting to chat it up in the common area. She hopped into the passenger seat of his peeling robin's-egg-blue Chevy, and they drove to Bedlow Park. From then on, that's where they always headed whenever they could steal a moment together. There they talked without Vivienne giving JD the evil eye and Annie casting a wary one in Maxine's direction.

"I don't get why Mother ever married John." After a few weeks together, Maxine had begun picking away at the scar tissue attached to her heart. It hurt, but she could already feel the organ beating more freely, more forcefully, than it had before she'd ever laid eyes on JD. "She didn't need him. She has me."

JD had spread a blanket back where the outstretched arms of the oak trees created a nest of shadows that sheltered them from the sun. And prying eyes. He was plucking at the green strands poking through the woven cotton fibers protecting them from the ground. He threw a handful on her. "So then what, Maxie? The three of us—you, me, and Vivienne— could go for rides in my truck? Maybe you'd have more fun if your mom was sitting here instead of me."

"Stop, JD!" Maxie laughed, brushing off the grass.

"You're the one who needs to stop telling yourself stories. It's simple. Your mom probably missed your dad. She's still pretty young, for somebody's mama anyway, and she needed a man around the house."

"Well, I miss him too."

"Maybe that's why you're here with me."

"But I didn't go looking for you. I just found you." Maxie watched him uproot the grass for a moment. "Or maybe you found me."

JD brushed his hands together before resting them on the thighs of his carpenter jeans. He looked at her and shrugged. "Something like that."

Maxie lay on her side and rested her head in the pillow she created with her bent arms. She watched his slow, deliberate movements. Tired of whining about her own problems, she decided to widen the circle of their conversation. It always seemed to revolve around her. "What about *your* parents?"

"What about them?" He traced a navy thread in the blanket, following it as it intersected a purple star sewn into the fabric. His finger skirted its five-point edge before moving along the navy line once more.

"I want to know about your parents, or did you just sprout from someone's head?"

"Like Athena?" JD laughed. "I've been called good-looking, but handsome enough for Mount Olympus? Nahhh."

"Stop laughing at me." Maxie threw grass at him. "And stop trying to change the subject. You know what I mean."

He grinned as he continued twiddling with the threads on the blanket.

"So?"

"So. Why do you want to know?" At last his eyes met hers.

"Because . . ." *Because I want to know everything about you. Like, where were you born? What were your first words? Why do you like camouflage? Can you hear your heart pounding in your ears the way I can? Do I feel like home to you, too?* But she only managed, "I just do." The words flopped out of her mouth and lay there between them, gasping desperately for air.

"Oh, you 'just do,' huh?"

She could feel his silent laughter but didn't shy from it.

He blinked. "Well, Maxie, since you have such a good reason . . . I lived with my mom and dad for almost seventeen years before he moved out last week. I have a brother who's a year younger and a fourteen-year-old sister."

"You're seventeen!" The words erupted from her brain and spewed through her lips. Maxine hadn't considered his age. She was only a year older than his sister.

"In a couple months. What's up?"

"I just . . ." *I just found you, but soon you'll be leaving me. Just like everybody else.* But again, she didn't say it. Maxie swallowed and played with her ponytail. "I mean, I'm sorry to hear about your folks."

He shrugged.

"You're graduating soon."

He took her hand and linked their fingers. His skin was a full shade browner than hers. "That's a year and a half away. I'm here now. And so are you."

She liked how some of his fingers covered hers while some of hers wrapped around his. Maxie looked up. "Mother used to be there for me. Until she wasn't."

"After your dad died?" JD's voice was so quiet the breeze nearly carried it away before the question reached her ears. "She left you with your grandparents—Mr. and Mrs. Tagle?"

She nodded. "Granddaddy Lerenzo and Mama Ruby, yes."

"And you said she came back about a year later, once she felt she could take care of you and—"

"You mean, once she found somebody to take care of *her*." Maxie extracted her hand from his and flopped onto her back. She tried to figure out the animals formed by the clouds.

JD poked her in the side. "Is that when she became *Mother* and your grandma *Mama*?"

She edged away from him. His insight hurt in places he couldn't see.

"Your mom must be a good-looking lady, if she's anything like you. Did you think she'd never get married again and just be happy chasing you around for the rest of her life?"

"Is that so bad?" Maxie pursed her lips, frustrated. She turned away from the puffy white rabbit and butterfly scudding across the blue above her to study JD instead, a long-legged man-child with peach fuzz dusting his full top lip. Nothing imaginary about him.

"Well, *I* don't think so, but I don't have anything better to do today." JD leaned down and, balancing on his elbows, hovered for a moment over her face. He kissed her when she didn't turn away. "And maybe you wouldn't have skipped band practice again to be here with me right now if she hadn't gotten married." He drew closer.

Maxie rolled to a sitting position. She wrapped her arms around her bent knees. "I bet the band director will call my house. Mr. Freeman and my stepfather are golf buddies." Things were starting to heat up, even back there in the shade. Because they were back there in the shade.

"Do you want me to drive you to practice?"

Maxie felt the weight of his eyes as she lifted her hair, heavy on the back of her neck. She'd blown it dry and then pressed it straight, but it was curling in the humidity. She twisted it into a loose bun, buying time before facing him. *It feels good to be here with him. Like home. Finally.*

"Maxie. Do you want me to drive you back?"

59

"Why do you call me Maxie?" Suddenly this was the only thing she wanted to know.

JD tucked one of her errant strands behind her ear. "Does anybody else call you that?"

"No."

"Well, that's why. Because it's all mine. And so are you."

The tone in his voice forced her to look at him. "Then I'm going to call you Jay." When he nodded, she didn't look away again.

———

"Hello-oo-oo from the mother ship."

The "daughter ship" returned to earth with a thunk. Maxine looked up from her spot on the floor in the family room at her mother's house. The boys tumbled in behind her. "Hey!"

"I'm not sure where you were just now, but I'm glad you're back. I was sayin' don't bother with that. I plan to string some hearts together, add more red lights, and call it a day. Isn't flockin' supposed to preserve that thing?" Vivienne flicked a hand in the direction of the deep-fried Christmas tree sprouting in front of Maxine.

"You should have jettisoned this fire hazard over a month ago, Mother, when the city was still picking up trees at the curb. At this point we're going to have to dump it in the woods somewhere and chop it up." She ruffled Second John's light-brown waves and pulled one of Robert's darker, straighter locks. "How was baseball?"

"We were only getting fitted for our uniforms—" the younger twin started.

"So it wasn't much fun," Second John finished. "Mom, I'm going to practice."

"Okay, but put away all your stuff before you hop on that piano. And what are you about to do, Robert? No video games."

"But, Mom!"

"Butts are for—"

"Obeying," Second John filled in. "Come on, Robbie. I'll help you with your robotics project before I practice." He pulled his obstinate twin toward the stairs.

Maxine patted Robert's shoulder in sympathy and winked at his aider and abettor before turning back to the crispy remains of the Fraser fir.

"Who has time to take down that tree? John is touring with his new book and I've got orders comin' from every hill and dale. You know it's the season of love!" Vivienne set her purse on the settee and joined Maxine. "Besides, it's not a fire hazard. That flockin' is supposed to be a flame retardant, according to the man at the Home Depot." She tugged on a branch and winced when it snapped.

Maxine raised a brow and pointed down to the green needles and white flakes on the wide cherry floor planks. "Maybe that was true in January, but we're headed toward March. What about Celeste? Or the boys? You'd think they'd have time for stuff like this."

"Don't you know by now that homeschoolers are busier than other folks? And that Celeste? 'I've got homework.' 'I have rehearsal.' 'I never get time with my friends!'" Vivienne laughed as she mimicked the thirteen-year-old. "My child is never without an excuse. What are you doin' here anyway?

You don't have anything better to do on Valentine's Day than take down your mama's Christmas tree? I should call Robert and Second John down here. They can work on that robotics project later."

My child. Maxine blinked rapidly at the words she was starting to pay more attention to. She turned to the half-filled box of ornaments by her feet. "No need to bother the boys. Y'all just got home. I have some time before Teddy picks me up for our meeting with Pastor Atwater. Then he's making me dinner." She removed a square of bubble wrap and tucked a ceramic choirgirl into it.

"But that doesn't explain why you're here."

"Well, I got stuck trying to finish my article before tonight, so I thought I'd gather my thoughts over a cup of tea. But then I was out of chai, so I walked over here to raid your tin. And *here* I stand." Maxine used another square to snuggle a crystal angel.

"And here you stand . . . in front of the Christmas tree?"

Maxine reached over to the coffee table on her left. She raised her mug in a mock toast and took a sip. "This is your last bag of chai by the way."

"Find any inspiration in that cup? You seemed pretty lost in thought when I came in." Vivienne retrieved the olive chenille blanket she kept on the arm of the sofa and bunched it on the table before reaching for an ornament. "Ouch!" Vivienne sucked on her thumb and mumbled, "What's stoppin' up your creative flow, besides gettin' stuck by this dead thing?"

As her mother stretched for bulbs hanging near the top of the tree, Maxine walked toward the pocket doors to the hallway and glided them closed. Then she turned and answered simply, "You."

"Me?" Delicate tinkling provided a musical backdrop to Vivienne's exclamation. Red, green, gold, and purple bulbs clinked against each other when she whirled around.

"Yes, you." Maxine slowly drained her cup. "Not what you expected? Or rather, *who* you expected?"

Vivienne swaddled the ornaments in the nest on the table and then sat near the tree. "Is there something specific you want to talk about?"

In no hurry to answer, Maxine eyed Mother as she placed her mug on the coaster. Vivienne used to tell them that the only thing allowed to rest on her Queen Anne chair was their gaze. Now Maxine could see why. Her mother, her lips compressed and eyes narrowed, didn't look comfortable at all perched on the edge of the antique.

"Maxine? I asked you if there was somethin' specific on your mind."

"Not really."

"Well, it sure sounds like it."

"But now that you bring it up—"

"*I* didn't bring anything u—"

"I do want to ask you something." Maxine reached for her tea but remembered she'd finished it. Itching to occupy herself, she popped a few bubbles on the wrapping squares instead. "Did you ever think of leaving me with Mama Ruby and Granddaddy for good?" *Pop! Pop!*

"What are you talking about, girl? And stop messin' with that bubble wrap."

"When I was little, after Daddy died . . . ?" *Pop-pop-pop-pop!*

Vivienne leaned forward, snatched the plastic from Maxine, and threw it to the side. It floated down until it landed atop her daughter's bare feet. "I know *when* you're talking about. I just don't understand why you're bringin' this up twenty years after the fact." She scooted back in the chair and crossed one stockinged leg over the other.

Maybe this wasn't a good idea. Unable to sit any longer, Maxine kicked aside the bubble wrap and stepped over a box of ornaments she'd started packing before her mother returned. She walked to the bay window and focused on the trees hugging the yard.

"Maxine?"

"After Daddy died, you explained why you had to leave me." Maxine's soft response bounced off her shimmery reflection. Her eyes never left Milo sniffing around inside the wrought iron fence. "That you just hurt too much after Daddy's death. You didn't think you were able to raise yourself and me."

"So I asked my parents to watch you a little while."

"For almost two years." Maxine caught and held Vivienne's eyes reflected by the pane. "I didn't think you were coming back." That's when Maxine was forced to find a substitute in Mama Ruby.

"I was comin' back, Maxine. I *came* back, for heaven's sake. This was—"

"A long time ago? It didn't feel like that to me. And it still hurts. I feel like I never got over it. *Never.* I was always looking for you, even when you got back. With First John."

"Your father."

"My *step*father. If you hadn't married him, would you have ever come back for me?"

Vivienne rose and stood beside her daughter. "Maxine Amelia Clark *Owens*, you know that even if you don't know nuthin' else. My love for you and your father healed me. God brought y'all into my life, and that enabled me to recognize love when I found it again with your stepfather. *You* brought me back, not John. He just furnished the transportation."

"But why wasn't your love for me strong enough to keep you here? Or to take me with you in the first place? As bad as it was for me, I didn't leave my baby. I was barely eighteen, practically living on the streets. But I was tied to her. I couldn't have left Celeste, ever. I still can't."

"I never really left you—"

"Yes, you did!"

Vivienne clasped Maxine by both shoulders and turned her away from their dim reflection. "How was what I did any different or less forgivable than what you did when you gave us Celeste to raise?"

"But I didn't leave her."

"Didn't you?"

Maxine reeled back, but Vivienne's words had struck her full on. A direct kick to the gut that wrenched her insides.

Vivienne pinched her nose between her closed eyes. "I didn't mean—"

"Yes, you did."

Vivienne winced. "Max, I don't like to think about that—"

"And you think I do? Seems you've impaled yourself on your own rusty sword." Maxine twisted out of Vivienne's grasp and walked away from the window so she wouldn't have to face her mother or herself. She stalked to the table and knelt by the ornaments nestling in the blanket.

"Maxine, I'm not sayin' you abandoned Celeste. But you did leave her with us, to raise her and care for her because you felt we could do a . . . a . . ."

"Better job?" Maxine's hands stilled on the box, her back to Vivienne.

"An adult job. You were a child."

"Okay, I was a child. 'I thought as a child.' But I was a mother, just like you. And you . . . you were an adult, as you put it, when you left me with Mama Ruby and Granddaddy. Why weren't you capable of taking care of me—or did you just not want to?"

"You can best be sure I wanted to, Maxine. It's just that when Henry died, I didn't know if the sun was yellow or the sky blue. Comin' and goin' was all the same for me. I didn't much care about either one. Mama and Daddy stepped in when they saw I wasn't doin' either of us any good. They loved me enough to do that, just like John and I loved you and Celeste enough to do what was right when you couldn't do right by yourself. I didn't have to *come back* from anywhere. I didn't leave you at a firehouse or on a neighbor's stoop with a note pinned to your blanket. I didn't abandon you, Maxine. And John didn't have to convince me to return to the only daughter I had at the time. I just had to heal. My heart had to start beatin' again."

Maxine looked away from Mother. She fiddled with the bulbs as she recalled what it was like living with Vivienne in those days, weeks, and months after the accident snatched Henry Clark from them. It had stolen her mother just as surely—but not in one swift, decisive blow. His death had been a bleaching agent. Vivienne had slowly faded, wasting away. She nibbled on nuts, grapes, or slices of American cheese, on anything that didn't require cooking or preparation. Maxine survived on the well-meaning hugs and food from visiting family and friends until mercifully, Lerenzo and Ruby packed up their daughter and granddaughter and trucked them over to their farmhouse in Spring Hope.

Maxine's mind churned, her memories as distorted as her mother's image in the Christmas bulb she twirled. A newly widowed Vivienne, floating as a dust mote through her grandparents' house, nothing solid Maxine could cling to. When she had her first cycle, it was Mama Ruby who helped her see the beauty in shedding childhood. Granddaddy wrote her prealgebra problems for her after she fell from the elm in their backyard and broke her wrist. Uncle Roy took her to the movies on Saturday afternoons. Evelyn's Granny B, introduced her to liver pudding and grits while teaching her to know the Bible for herself, showing her that just because folks said Jonah got swallowed by a whale instead of a big fish didn't make it so.

Yet those lessons hadn't hurt as much as the day Vivienne turned her frail profile from Maxine and left her standing on the top step. She hadn't stroked her daughter's hair or kissed her good-bye. She'd just picked up her small suitcase and nudged Maxine out of the way. The child had felt her mama was gone long before her taillights disappeared around the corner.

But standing there with her jaw squared and a fist on one hip, Vivienne seemed no longer content with being a figment of her daughter's imagination. She looked ready to fight for what was rightfully hers—Maxine.

"Now I'm not asking your forgiveness," her mother pronounced. "If you're feelin' some kind of way about that time you spent with your grandparents, you need to work it out with God. To tell you the truth, I don't need you to forgive me for the time you spent with them just like you don't need forgiveness for entrusting Celeste to our care—"

"Mother, I didn't ask for—"

"I know what it's like to live with a lie, and it hurts." Vivienne clenched her side as if she had indeed been pierced. "I did the right thing at that time. It was for good, like what Rahab did for the two spies, I suppose. . . ." Vivienne looked away from Maxine as if she was thinking back thousands of years, picturing herself tucking Celeste under the flax, away from the world's prying eyes. Or perhaps she was envisioning stowing her in a basket on the Nile and setting her afloat under the watchful eyes of her mother-sister. Hiding in plain sight.

Maxine shook her head slowly, then faster.

"What, Max? You stand here accusing me of abandoning you. Of dishonesty. Tellin' me you haven't been able to get over my leaving you for what . . . ? Eighteen months, two years, while I went away to grieve and recover after the death of my husband, so I could come back and be your mama. And you're thirty years old and still dancin' to that same ol' song in your head. How do you think your husband is going to feel two, five, or ten years down the road when he learns I'm Celeste's grandma, not her mama? That her grandma is her *great*-grandma? That his wife asked him to move into the garage apartment so they could keep lookin' over Celeste like a couple of guardian angels?"

Vivienne walked over to the end table beside the sofa and

reached for the box of tissues. "I know I've always considered this family business, but our family is expanding now. It's getting harder to keep this to ourselves."

"You sound like JD."

Vivienne stopped wiping her face and stared at Maxine. "That's the second time you've told me that, and I didn't like it much the first time. You talked to that boy again?"

Maxine bent to pick up the ornaments she'd knocked to the floor in her agitation. "Yes, I talked to that *man* a couple weeks ago. He called. He wants to see Celeste."

Vivienne stalked over to Maxine and plucked a pewter figurine of three wise men from her daughter's hands. The magi huddled together in Vivienne's palm as her fist closed over them. "He called two weeks ago and got you all worked up? That's what sent you over here today, shakin' this old tree?"

Maxine knew the tree her mother was talking about—the past, whose far-reaching, spindly branches had ensnared her. She couldn't just lop off the limbs. She had to cleave it at the root to free herself. "JD hasn't gotten me worked up about anything."

"Just what did he have to say?" Vivienne crossed her arms. Gold, frankincense, and myrrh peeked between her knuckles.

Maxine walked around Mother to the fir. She pretended to search for ornaments, but really she needed a minute to catch her breath.

"Maxine?"

"I told you. He wants to see Celeste. He wants a relationship with his daughter."

"His *daughter*!"

Maxine dug through the dead branches, ignoring the scratches and scrapes on her hands and arms. She unhooked a paper snowflake covered in aluminum foil. She touched the picture of a gap-toothed child glued to the front. When she flipped it over, she read *Celeste, age 6*. Managing a small smile, she turned around and proffered it to Vivienne. "Do you see this? I remember I was home for Christmas, and Celeste ran in with two of these, screaming, 'Here, Mommy! Here, Daddy!' And she ran right past me and gave them to you and First John."

Maxine turned back to the tree. "I determined then to move back home as soon as I could so I wouldn't live on the edges of her life. And as much as it hurts sometimes, I get to see it. I've watched her grow up. He's missed all that."

"JD gave up all that."

Maxine laughed dryly. "That's what I told him." Actually she had told him a lot more during that phone call.

———

"Your *daughter*?" Maxine couldn't stop herself from repeating JD's words.

"Yes. I want to get to know her."

She resisted sticking a finger in each ear to block out the loss and regret that seemed to reverberate from his voice. "What do you want to know? Her favorite color is called punch pink—not hot pink, not light pink. She measured five-two at her last well visit, a mite shorter than I but taller than her best friend—whose name is Jasmine, by the way. Celeste loves to chat to the wee hours. She—"

"I don't want you to tell me about her likes and dislikes and vital statistics. I want to discover them myself."

"'I, I, I.' You're saying what *you* want. Where were you thirteen years ago?" Maxine listened to him shift, heard him take in a deep breath and blow it out.

"The same place you were. Growing up. Going to school. Attending college. Just because you were in the same house with her doesn't mean you didn't let go like I let go. You gave her up just like I did, except I didn't know any better. And then you gave *me* up."

And that's when she'd hung up on him.

"That's all he said?" Vivienne's question brought her back to the here and now.

"That's all I gave him time to say. That was plenty." Maxine moved around the tree, pushing aside branches, checking and rechecking to see if she'd missed any ornaments. White chips and needles floated to the floor.

"And then you come here two weeks later and accuse me of pretty much the same thing. As much as I hate to say it, that boy does have a point."

Maxine dropped the tiny ceramic Nativity scene she was holding. It clunked on the hardwood floor with a crack and rolled away from her. "What did you say?"

"Isn't that what we were talkin' about a minute ago?" Mother pulled another tissue from the box and wiped under her eyes. Tucking the used paper into her pocket, she walked forward a few steps toward the blanket and opened her hand, freeing the wise men. Then she knelt and reached under the table. Vivienne touched the hole in the ceramic figurine where baby Jesus used to lay. "You never told me how you felt about that snowflake."

"How was I supposed to tell you, her *mama*? I'm only a bystander."

"You gave her life, so that means you're not a bystander. You should know I'd understand."

"I don't know anything these days! I'm swimming here, Mother. On one hand, I can empathize with JD. I get it, his sense of . . . of missing out, especially since it wasn't his fault."

"Not his fault!"

"Now living with his mother's suffering probably heightens his sense of loss. She doesn't have the opportunity to get it back, but he does."

"That woman," Vivienne tsked and rolled her eyes. "I know Annie Lester wouldn't care to know Celeste, even if she had the chance. Her memory loss is probably a blessing."

Maxine's mouth fell open.

Her mother huffed and choked down something that seemed to taste bad. "Lord, forgive me for saying that, but who gives a flyin' flip about what the Lesters have lost?"

Maxine's shoulders heaved. "I do, Mother. I care. Isn't Celeste a Lester?"

The grandfather clock in the foyer chimed. Though the sound was muted by the closed pocket doors, Maxine jumped and glanced at her wrist. "Oh, shoot. Teddy will be here in less than an hour, and I'm nowhere near ready to smile in Reverend Atwater's face and pretend all I care about is the beautiful future Teddy and I have." She took in the evidence of her visit. The green blanket creating a pseudo-picnic spread on the table; the nearly bare, brown tree topped by a crooked star; countless needles and white specks decorating the floor; the box of ornaments, its lid askew.

And Vivienne's bleak eyes staring at her from across the room.

"I'm sorry, Mother. Forgive me for blindsiding you. But I . . . I need to go." Maxine patted her pockets. Then she carefully lifted the blanket and set it back down, sending the wise men tumbling out onto the coffee table. She scanned every corner but the one that housed her mother. She could feel Vivienne watching her as she scurried about the family room.

"You're just going to leave?"

"I know I'm leaving a mess, but I'll be back in the morning to finish up." Maxine knelt next to the couch and tossed back first one cushion, then another. She heard the door open between the mudroom and the kitchen, then slam shut seconds later, rattling the pane.

"Girl, it's not the room I care about fixin'. I haven't put a toe in here once this whole week. What *are* you doing? Are you prayin' down there?"

Maxine rose from her knees and finally faced Vivienne. "I can't find my keys."

Jingle, jingle, jingle. "You mean these?" Zander stood by the kitchen island, holding aloft the missing ring. He walked past Celeste, who was opening the refrigerator, and tossed them to Maxine.

They landed—*clang!*—on the floor next to their owner's left foot.

Zander's mouth opened wide enough to catch flies.

"What's up, Max? Why didn't you try to catch 'em? Mom, are you crying?"

Maxine straightened sofa pillows. Vivienne wiped her face and edged around her son, squeezing his shoulder as she passed him into the kitchen.

Celeste peeled a clementine and watched the activity. She seemed to be weighing which road to take before opting for the wider one leading to Vivienne. "Are y'all okay?"

Vivienne pushed closed the trash can and faced her baby girl. "Yes, yes, we're fine, honey. You know Maxine. All this to-do over the weddin'. It's hard on everybody." She moved toward the refrigerator after rubbing Celeste's shoulder in the same way she'd touched her oldest son's. "How was rehearsal? I see you're hungry. What about you, Zan?"

In her periphery Maxine saw Celeste look from Vivienne to her. Maxine made a major production of straightening the family room while she kept one ear on the prowl for her siblings' answers.

"Nope, I stopped on the way home and grabbed a burger. This girl here thinks you can live on SkinnyPop, fruit, and a gallon of water." He raised an arm to block Celeste's blow.

"Are you sure y'all are okay? If this is what a wedding does to you, no thank you." Celeste waved her hands as if warding off a car hurtling toward her.

Maxine had pieced herself together in the few minutes she'd spent fluffing cushions, brushing away needles, and closing the box of ornaments. She hid a grimace as she forced herself to approach the three in the kitchen. Embracing Celeste might split apart the cracks in her armor, spilling her heartful of secrets onto the floor, but it appeared there was no avoiding it. She looped a curl around her earlobe as Celeste reached for her.

"Something's on your mind, but I'll let you keep it to yourself." Celeste grunted as she gripped her big sister. "For now."

"Thanks," Maxine whispered over Celeste's head as she returned the embrace. She couldn't resist stroking the hair at her nape, the silky, dark-brown strands that were the color of JD's.

Jay. Maxine pushed away from Celeste and drew a deep breath. She reached up to ruffle her younger brother's hair because she knew how much he hated it. "Okay, I've gotta go." Maxine exhaled and almost sprinted through the kitchen, angling toward the mudroom. She lifted her coat off a hook and faced the kitchen for one last good-bye.

"V-day plans?" Celeste asked her mother, aiming a thumb in Maxine's direction.

Vivienne pointed at the teenager's trappings nearly blocking the kitchen window.

Celeste ducked her head at her mama's unspoken directive and grabbed her backpack and jacket but stopped short when she reached for the large instrument case. "Um, Zan, can I get some help with my bass? By the way, Sis, I read last month's post. Nice!"

Maxine finished buttoning. "Thanks, knucklehead. Better late than never."

"It made me want to go sit by the creek, float a couple leaves, maybe count some deer, do some bird-watching . . . No, I'm serious! Don't look at me like that!" She laughed. "But can't you slow your roll? You're leaving so quickly, and we just got home."

Maxine looked over Celeste's shoulder. "Zander, First John won't be back until next week, so you'll need to help me lug out the tree. Are you free tomorrow afternoon?"

"After basketball practice." He grabbed Celeste's double bass and slung his backpack over his shoulder. "Mom, okay if I borrow your car? I'm out of gas. Later, Maxine."

"Thanks, Zan. Now I've gotta run myself so I can get ready before Teddy arrives. We'll finish up tomorrow, Mother. Celeste, you and I will catch up then. Bye, y'all!" Maxine stepped closer to the mudroom.

"Okay, okay, but wait. Do you have a minute?" Celeste bounded over as Zander headed up the back stairs.

"For you? Thirty seconds."

Celeste stuck out her tongue and crossed her eyes.

Maxine laughed a bit and relaxed her shoulders. "Of course. What is it?"

Celeste handed her a 3½-by-2-inch rectangle.

Maxine took her hand off the doorknob to reach for it.

"Who's James D. Lester?"

Chapter Seven

"*I'VE BEEN LOOKING FOR AN OPENING, for a way to tell you the truth. . . . You see, James D. Lester is your father, your biological father. And by the way, he might want you to call him Dad now—so keep that in mind when we cozy up at the dinner table to talk about all this. Ignore that woman in the kitchen who's been there for you all your life who, I might add, has lied to you day and night—just like I have, but that's beside the point—and just focus on the facts. I know this is a lot to take in now, but really, I blame you for bringing it up.*"

Maxine swallowed these wild, unspoken thoughts as she soaked in the lettering on the card: *James D. Lester, JD-MBA, Executive Director, Hillsong Community*. When she dragged her eyes from his contact information, she found Celeste's wide-eyed gaze resting on her.

"So do you know Mr. Lester, Maxine? He knows you." Celeste leaned against the doorframe as her fingers tapped out a tune on the cream-colored millwork.

A crater opened where Maxine's mouth used to be. She snapped it closed with a loud click of her teeth before opening it again. "He does?"

"Yes, he said he knew you back in high school. I thought it was funny—not funny ha-ha, but funny weird—because you've never mentioned him. He knows you?"

In what sense? Biblical? Maxine cleared her throat and tried to silence the cowbells, kazoos, and triangles clanging and whirring and tinkling inside her head, all warning her, "Danger! Turn back!" Yet she plowed ahead.

"How did you meet Mr. Lester, Celeste? You had orchestra." Maxine looked around Celeste to Vivienne, who was watching, strangely wordless, over the rim of her glass. "Mother, haven't you explained to her about how risky it is to talk to strangers?"

"You knew him in high school, so he's not a stranger to *you*." Celeste shrugged.

"But he *is* a stranger to you . . . and all you know is what he said to you. Good gracious! This is as bad as 'Hey, little girl, come help me find my puppy' or 'Hello, I have some candy for you. Hop into my black panel van and I'll give you a whole bag of Werther's.' Celeste!"

"Maxine, *really*? I'm not clueless."

"Well, stop acting like you are."

Crash!

Both Maxine and Celeste jumped.

"Shoot!" Vivienne pointed at the closet near the mudroom. "Celeste, grab the broom. No. The vacuum. Glass is everywhere."

Celeste scurried to obey.

Vivienne waved at Maxine. "Go on now. You'd best get ready for your date. We've got this under control. Celeste, be careful. Don't cut yourself. Tell me, did the conductor have any more details about the concert?"

Maxine edged to the door as her mother expertly lured Celeste away from one sticky subject by dangling another one she could adhere to.

"Wait!"

Maxine sighed and rotated in slow motion to face Celeste once more. "Now what?"

"My card." The teen wiggled the fingers on the outstretched hand that wasn't holding the vacuum.

Hillsong Community. JD's business and cell phone numbers played a drum cadence in Maxine's mind as she handed over the rectangle. Then she waggled a good-bye in return and slipped out with a firm thump of the door.

"What's on your mind?"

"What?"

Theodore's knuckles rapped on the ragged nails Maxine had pressed to the arm of her chair. "You haven't said a word in the past seven minutes."

"I just don't like waiting."

He raised a brow. "That didn't stop you from making me wait almost twenty minutes in the car earlier."

"That's because Mother kept me too long, and I needed to shower."

"Okay. But why couldn't I have come inside?"

Maxine's honey-colored cheeks warmed. "Because I was in the *shower*, Teddy! I don't think it's a good idea if you're in my apartment when I'm . . ." She felt uncomfortable saying *naked* in Pastor Atwater's office, and she couldn't come up with another word that didn't sound archaic.

"Indisposed?" Apparently Theodore had traipsed down the same vocabulary trail. He laughed softly and glanced behind him before leaning in closer. "You think I can't control myself?"

"Theodore!" Maxine looked toward the open door and lowered her voice. "It's a small garage apartment. When you're sitting in one room, you can pretty much see everywhere and *everyone* else."

Her fiancé leaned over the arms of their chairs and kissed the tip of her nose. "Miss Virtuous Woman in her horn-rims, pink cardigan, and wool slacks. I love that you're so easily flustered."

Maxine shifted her glasses as Teddy laughed again.

"I see you two are getting along well."

Maxine shielded her eyes with her right hand, as this time, Teddy had the grace to look sheepish before pushing himself to his feet and extending his hand in greeting. "I think we might need to 'bell the pastor.' It'd be nice to hear you coming."

Reverend Atwater shook his head. "That's been tried before. I don't always wear a collar you can attach a bell to, but how about when I enter the room, I'll say something like 'Let the church say amen!'"

"Amen!" Maxine and Teddy chorused.

The pastor shut the door and walked around his desk. "I'm sorry I'm late. My cup runneth over today." He scooted his chair and rested his elbows on the desk. "Okay, enough with the weak church humor. How are you two?"

Maxine turned to Teddy, but he only returned her look, his eyebrows expressing a silent question. She directed her shrug toward the pastor. "Okay, I guess?"

He raised his shoulders exaggeratedly. "Well, don't ask me. Theodore?"

"I think we're both stressed a bit, what with all the wedding prep. Plus our day-to-day commitments. Sometimes it's hard to know whether we're coming or going."

"Do you make time for each other outside of wedding planning?"

Maxine's lips were glued shut. Her mind was also stuck but on a continuous video loop of *JD Lester. Celeste. JD Lester. Celeste.*

Her fiancé tapped her arm. "Any thoughts, Maxine? This isn't the Theodore Charles show."

She forced her lips apart. "Well, we . . ." She sought refuge in the eyes of the man sitting across from them.

Reverend Atwater chuckled. "I think Theodore was looking for some help, but it seems there's nothing but all work and no play for you two. Don't panic. That's normal. It's your big day, one of the biggest of your lives. But it's important you remember that it's easier to *get* married than it is to *stay* married." He leaned back in his chair, looking like he'd just pulled the pin from his hand grenade.

"Well, *that's* encouraging." Maxine shook her head.

Reverend Atwater rested his chin on a fist as he looked up to heaven. "Let's see, how can I put it better?"

Maxine glanced up, also hoping for divine inspiration. *Or maybe I'll just know when to duck.* She noted the answering V formed by Teddy's eyebrows.

"Hmmm. Maybe 'plan the wedding, but work on the marriage'? How's that?"

"Better." Maxine reached across the small distance between her and Teddy, but she didn't touch his hand. Instead, she clasped the arm of his chair. "Our eyes are on the prize, Reverend Atwater. Truly they are. It's just that wedding details have consumed us."

Teddy shifted in his seat. "You mean, consumed *you.* I don't care about quiche tastings, tuxedo fittings, or venue selections. We could convene in my school cafeteria tomorrow, and I'd be happy." He tried to cover her fingers with his.

Maxine's throat felt dry though her words were as smooth as oil. "I don't think that's Reverend Atwater's point, Theodore. And no, you wouldn't be happy sipping from eight-ounce chocolate milk cartons at our wedding reception. At least, your mother wouldn't. The school cafeteria isn't good enough for her only son." *Not that I am either.*

God must have whispered in Reverend Atwater's ear, for he seemed to perk up. "How do you get along with your future in-laws? Any issues?"

"My parents love Teddy. They think he's a sugar cookie, sweet enough to dunk in a cup of milk, chocolate or otherwise."

The pastor's eyes widened. "Oh? And what about Teddy's parents? What type of cookie are you, Maxine?"

She glanced at Teddy before answering. "Maybe we should stretch out on matching chaises. This is starting to feel more like a therapy session than premarital counseling with our future pastor."

Reverend Atwater's eyes twinkled over the steeple his fingers had created. "What—sign your marriage license, pray over you, and call it a wedding day already?"

Maxine shrugged. "I thought we'd talk about our faith, our marriage roles, or our plans for church ministry. And just so you know, I don't want to sing in the choir."

"Duly noted. But I need to get to know the two parts of the whole—especially you, Maxine. I get to look at this one here every week." He smiled at Teddy before turning her way. "Maybe that way I can help you visualize how you fit together. Help you connect your past with the future God has in store for you."

Theodore cleared his throat. "You don't need to reassure us. You're the pastor of this church—*our* pastor. We both believe in the greater purpose behind talking with you. Don't we, Maxine?"

She sighed under the weight of Teddy's expectations. "And what is that 'greater purpose,' Teddy?"

"Well, it's just like Reverend Atwater said. We've been walking our own paths for about thirty years, and now here we are, pledging before God to walk together. Forever. That's a long time. We need to know what we're getting into."

"I don't think that's exactly what *you* said, Pastor. Shouldn't Teddy already know what he's 'getting into'?" Even as Maxine mustered the indignation to pose the question, her insides wiggled and jiggled. But it wasn't because she'd swallowed a fly. The casserole of lies and truth didn't agree with her.

"Maxine. It's true we've only known each other a few months, but I wouldn't have proposed if I wasn't ready."

"But that's exactly my point! Since we're so ready for this, we should be navigating the next fifty years, not dissecting the past thirty." Maxine stood and moved toward the door. She didn't open it, but she stood close enough that she caught a faint whiff of freedom.

Theodore sprang to his feet and landed beside her in two giant steps. He looked from her to the minister and back. "I don't know where all this is coming from. You barely speak to me the whole way here, and now you're talking so much you're not listening."

"Hold up. *I'm* not listening? How many times have I shared my concerns about this premarital counseling? No offense, Pastor—"

"None taken."

"—and you've blown me off with a pat and a smile. Now here we are, on the verge of discussing the eternal implications of what five-year-old Maxine ate for lunch and we're fighting. *Fighting!* Something we never do."

"Never, Maxine?" Reverend Atwater's quiet voice threw water on the fire.

Maxine and Theodore faced him, still smoldering.

"You never argue?"

Maxine shook her head. Theodore seemed to think about it.

"Mrs. Atwater and I do. In fact, that's why I was late getting here. Lilian disagreed with my decision regarding our kitchen remodel. Now she might not want me to talk about it, but we can argue about that later." Reverend Atwater chuckled as he pushed back his chair and propped a hip on the desk's edge.

"Fighting, arguing, disagreeing. They sound worse than they are. At the root, you're each presenting and defending your position. Being vehement about something or some*one* you believe in. You should each be a safe place where the other can demonstrate or express your passion and personality. You seek shelter *in* each other, not *from* each other.

"Maxine, your opinion never differs from Teddy's—well, aside from your views on premarital counseling, that is?"

She fiddled with the buttons on her cardigan and then repositioned her glasses on her nose. "I'm sure it does. Sometimes. But we just think alike. That's what drew us together. According to Mother, it's what attracted her to Daddy, my *real* father. And it's what makes our relationship special, I think."

"So you have the same views on *everything*?"

Probably not about teen pregnancy. Maxine stomped on the thought. "You make that sound wrong. Doesn't the Bible say, 'Submit one to another'?"

"Yes, it does. But it doesn't say, 'Lose yourself in one another.'"

"I don't think Maxine loses herself in me." Again, the lines on Teddy's forehead spelled the letter V. "She does respect my opinion though. And we have a lot in common."

"And you respect hers—although it sounds like she doesn't

have too many that differ from yours." Reverend Atwater returned to his chair.

Teddy sat a second after she'd sunk into her chair.

"Does that include how you feel about your extended families?" He glanced down at a notepad on his desk. "Teddy, I believe Maxine compared you to a sugar cookie."

"More like a snickerdoodle. But yes, her parents seem to like having me around. They think I'm good for her."

"And you, Maxine?"

I'm a lemon square. "Forgive me, but what do my future in-laws have to do with us?"

Reverend Atwater sighed and looked away from them. "Well, okay. Let me show you." He held up a slightly crooked index finger. "When we took the grandkids to Disney World last year, we bought them this intricate 10,000-piece jigsaw puzzle." As he talked, he opened his large center desk drawer and withdrew a thick 8½-by-11 pad. "On each piece are tiny images. We have the exciting job of connecting all these images to form pictures within a bigger picture."

He chose a pen from the caddy on the corner of his desk and sketched a rectangle in the center of the first blank page. "You see, this big rectangle is the bigger picture, the finished puzzle. It's how I see you as a couple." He created wiggly-edged "squares" within the rectangle. Then he roughed in pictures on a few of them that overlapped to other pieces.

"Now I see these smaller pictures as the experiences and people that interconnect and interlock, making you two . . . you. They're your likes and dislikes, your interests and hobbies, your families." He used the pen to show the outline of the rectangle. "You wouldn't be complete without these important parts. But your different parts should fit together, complement each other." He pointed to the squiggles. "You just have to look really closely to see all those tiny pictures." The reverend crossed his hands on his desk. "Now is probably a good time for us to talk about the next step."

Teddy and Maxine stared in silence at his metaphorical masterpiece.

"You need to spend some intentional, quality two-on-two time with other couples. Sharpen some iron, so to speak."

Maxine swallowed. "What couples?"

"Well, Maxine, that's up to you. Do you have married friends or family members you'd voluntarily spend a couple hours with? You would probably feel more comfortable in a natural setting."

"Like seeing a lion on a safari instead of at the zoo?"

"Well said, Theodore." Atwater laughed. "Really, though. I'd like you to choose three or four couples over the next six months and spend twenty-four hours total with each of them."

"Uh—"

"Okay, Maxine, for you, twelve to eighteen. At least. And not for counseling or all at once. Drive over to Thomasville to shop for furniture and eat some barbecue. Visit the natural history museum in Raleigh. Hike or enjoy a long picnic. Just invest some time doing what you enjoy . . . together. Stretch it out between now and the wedding. All I ask is, invest quality time in people who help you interlock your marriage pieces." He tapped his crude drawing of a puzzle as he looked at them. "Who help make you *you*. Frankly, you'll probably get more out of those interactions than sitting here looking at me. How does that sound?"

Teddy squeezed Maxine's hand. "Doable. Max?"

She nodded, grateful they'd at last found common ground. "Do we have to report in? Show you a signed and stamped time sheet at our next session?"

"Let's say we're on the honor system. This isn't for me, after all. It's for you. Come up with some suggestions—or even go on your first date—before we see each other next time. If you want to talk about it when we meet, fine. If not, also fine."

He paused. "Now is there anything you want to share in these last few minutes we have together? Lilian would tell me I've done more than my share of talking." He ripped in two what he'd called their marriage and dropped it in the wastebasket under the desk.

The once-and-future bride gasped.

The minister looked confused. "What? Oh, I'm sorry! Did you want me to save that?"

Chapter Eight

"ARE YOU SURE YOU'RE NOT HUNGRY?"

"And you are?"

Theodore never looked away from the dark road stretching before them. "Well, it is Valentine's Day. Most couples eat dinner together. Especially a young engaged couple with a reservation at Marino's. I know I promised to cook, but since we had that session scheduled, I thought eating out would be easier than whipping something up at home."

But not as romantic, Maxine wanted to say. Since leaving the church, she'd sat like a spoon stuck in a bowl of cold grits. Stiff and unmoving. Aside from announcing she wanted to skip dinner altogether, she'd only mumbled her available dates for their next meeting. She'd rebuffed Teddy's offer to open her car door with a quick shake of her head and had been staring wordlessly out the window at the shadowy outlines of the houses and trees.

"Maxine, I know I've already said it, but it merits saying again. You're not yourself. You haven't been since I picked you up at your apartment. I almost didn't recognize you at church during your outburst, and now you're stewing."

"I wouldn't call it an outburst, and I'm not stewing, Theodore." Maxine picked at one of the edges of clear tape affixed to the crumpled sheet of paper in her lap.

He sighed and squeezed the steering wheel. "Okay, then what would you call it?"

"A difference of opinion—and that's healthy, according to your pastor."

"Oh, so he's *my* pastor now." He reached across the console between the seats. "You know you can talk to me. I want to hear what's going on in your mind, even if we don't agree."

No, you don't want to hear anything of the kind, Teddy. Maxine squeezed his fingers and then she covered their clasp with her free right hand. She tried to shrug off the meeting as well as the memories of the earlier part of her day, but the burden on her shoulders wouldn't let her. One face continued to cling to her, refusing to let go with the casual movement. She forced her lips into a facsimile of a smile. "Maybe it's a mild case of pre-wedding jitters."

"Nooo, I don't think so."

Maxine's heart dropped to her toes.

"I'd call it a major case. Nearly fatal." He grinned weakly. "Happy Valentine's Day?"

"Happy Valentine's Day." She detected the relief in his

eyes, felt the tension in his body ease. "So . . . besides me, who else would you want to invest an entire day in? Or excuse me, at least half a day."

Teddy glanced at her.

"You know, the couples we're supposed to double-date over the next six months."

"O-o-h-h! Well, you know I'm relatively new to town, and I've only recently become half of our couple. Guys don't generally do couple friends on their own."

Maxine laughed. "So there's no one in your art *department*?"

"Funny, but no. It's probably not a good idea to mix business with pleasure anyway. What about that friend of yours—Evelyn, is it?"

She peered at the road. Evelyn and Kevin should be a shoo-in, but . . . *JD.* Maxine tried to dispel his image.

"That's a no for you?"

"No, no . . . I mean, yes . . . no! That's a great idea. I wish we could go out with Uncle Roy and whoever he's dating at the moment, but he's impossible to nail down. How about Mama Ruby and Granddaddy instead? And maybe my parents. It'll give you time to get to know them better, and I'll get to see them in a grown-up light. That's not too much Owens family for you, is it?"

"Maybe." Teddy waited a beat. "Ha! Gotcha. Actually, it sounds perfect. A mix of age ranges and years of marriage. When my mother joins my dad here once their house in New Orleans sells, we can double-date with them. Until then, I can see spending twenty-four hours with those couples." He reached for her hand.

"More like a whole lifetime," she murmured and kissed

his fingertips. She soaked up the peace between them for a moment. "I think I got my appetite back. Let's go to Marino's."

My Daily Grace—Matters of the Hearts . . . and Flowers

I wonder if your day was full of surprises, hearts and flowers, love and romance, and time with loved ones. That's the way Valentine's Day is meant to be, isn't it? Well, that's the way I planned my day: chock-full of hearts and flowers and time with Hubby-to-be. But it seems I forgot to check in with God about my plans, because that's not quite how things turned out.

Most of you know I'm getting married this year, so this is my last Valentine's Day as a single woman. And you know how I'm handling it? I'm not. And it seems I'm not alone when it comes to change. I've learned from your calls, letters, emails, DMs, and tweets that my struggles have reso-nated with many of you enduring your own life's changes—expected and unexpected. Thank you for your prayers, advice, and love. I've been trying to take your advice to heart, even the hard-hitting words to this not-so-wise future bride.

The thing is, God isn't satisfied with just a little remodeling. He wants to gut the whole building, take me down to the bare studs and reveal the cracks in my foundation. He has a way of putting His hand on everything, of shaping and molding me to becoming the person—and wife—I need to be. I'm learning it's not just my name and address that need to change. It's my whole view on life, how I see myself and my world, how I relate to the people around me, who and how I trust.

And trust Him to leave no stone unturned. Today God even put His handprint on the way I celebrated this holiday by teaching me about love—and it ain't all hearts and flowers. It's loving through thick, thin, and everything in between. Loving the warts and the frog that peed on me. He's showing me that loving isn't just planning a wedding—picking a menu, reserving a church, or finding that perfect ring and gown. It's about planning a marriage. Something I thought I knew about. And not just a marriage between Hubby-to-be and me, but between the great I AM and me.

My day turned out to be full of heart-pounding twists and turns, just not the ones I expected. I'm grateful that even when the best-laid plans fail, Jesus never does. First Corinthians 13:8-13 puts it best (now, get ready, because this is a long one):

Love never fails. But whether there are prophecies, they will fail; whether there are tongues, they will cease; whether there is knowledge, it will vanish away. For we know in part and we prophesy in part. But when that which is perfect has come, then that which is in part will be done away. When I was a child, I spoke as a child, I understood as a child, I thought as a child; but when I became a man, I put away childish things. For now we see in a mirror, dimly, but then face to face. Now I know in part, but then I shall know just as I also am known. And now abide faith, hope, love, these three; but the greatest of these is love.

Maxine hit Submit, wishing she felt known by more than the readers she freely bared her heart to. After gently sliding her laptop beneath her night table, she turned off the lamp and tucked herself in bed, pulling up the yellow Egyptian cotton sheets and heavy salmon-colored duvet to her chin. When she scooted down, the glow-in-the-dark clockface drew her eyes—1:52—before they skipped to the vase of chrysanthemums—a dozen real blooms from Teddy that served as a foretaste of the wedding bouquets-in-waiting. They'd finished two movies before she'd sent her groggy fiancé home. Sleepy herself now, Maxine closed her eyes and focused on Karen Carpenter singing about rainy days and Mondays. "It's Valentine's Day that gets me down, Karen," she mumbled and rolled to her other side.

JD always laughed at my love of seventies music.

Maxine's eyes flew open and she flipped over onto her back. "I don't care what you used to laugh about, Jay," she announced to the ceiling. As if to prove it to the furniture, she reached for her phone. Less than a minute ticked off in the time it took her to select a playlist and reclaim her spot between the sheets. She closed her eyes as MercyMe flooded the room.

She opened them and found herself staring at the manne-quins in the window of Kleinfeld. "Ooh! I'll go in. If I can't find the perfect wedding gown in New York, I can't find it anywhere." She pushed open the door and looked up to the tinkling bells above her. "That's strange. That never happened on the TV show."

Maxine strolled through the aisles. She pushed aside layers of tulle . . . satin and silk . . . sheer bodices . . . beads, bling, and sequins . . . and tripped over a three-foot-long chiffon train. She looked down at her feet. Plastic scuba flippers?

"Here, let me." A familiar voice floated from above as a soft hand cupped her elbow and helped her to her feet.

Maxine brushed off her polka-dot, cotton pajamas—why in the world was she wearing pj's and flippers in Kleinfeld?—and looked up. "You're Randy from Say Yes to the Dress! *But it doesn't sound like you."*

Randy smiled. "I'm here to help you. What do you need?"

She stared at him, trying to meld his rich baritone with his well-cut, gelled salt-and-pepper hair and dapper suit.

"Maxine, you're getting married in two weeks. We need to get started."

"Two weeks? But I thought I had ten months! Oh no! Kleinfeld will make me buy from the sample room, and I'm nowhere near a sample size! What am I going to do?"

"I know exactly what to do. Now if you're getting married underwater, you're going to need—"

"Underwater? I'm not getting—"

"Of course you are!" Randy took her hand and led her to a row of colorful gowns. "It's time to take the plunge, girlfriend!" His deep laugh reverberated off the walls of the store. "Here, try this on. It'll show off your beautiful figure."

She plucked at the bold flowers dotting the shimmery lace. "But I can't wear hot pink and yellow. Mother would have a fit. Maybe candlelight, or okay, I could try blush. But hot pink? Yellow? Not on my wedding day!" She handed the gown back to him. "Let's go over there."

But Randy was handing her a shimmery black number with a satiny red hem. "This. This."

"Red. Black . . . Oh, I can't wear white. I can't wear white." She buried her head in her hands. "What was I think-ing? It doesn't matter that I got baptized. I can't wear white this time."

Randy dropped the gown. Organza pooled at his feet, but it didn't trip him up because he seemed to float over to her. "No, no, love. Don't cry. It doesn't matter what you wear when you wade in the water. Hot pink, yellow, polka dots, or stripes. The blood will clean it. Your dress will be white as snow."

"I don't understand. The blood . . . ? Where?" Maxine looked at her hands and feet. She contorted her body, trying to check every inch.

His warm laugh flowed over her, covering her from head to toe. "No, flesh of my flesh. You're not hurt. You're healed. You just see the outside. But it doesn't matter what you wear, because it's the heart that's important."

"My heart?"

"No. Mine. Why don't you wake up? You need to answer the phone."

"Oh! That was the tinkling I heard! The phone, but where is it?" Maxine felt in the tiny pocket on her pajama top and patted her hips. No cell phone. She dropped to her knees, her flippers in the air, and felt along the floor. She peeked under the organza puddle. "The phone. I can hear it, but where is it?"

Ting-a-ling, ting-a-ling. Ting-a-ling, ting-a-ling.

"What . . . ? Wh . . . ?" Half-asleep, Maxine felt along the top of the night table. Something clattered to the floor. Awake at last, she threw the covers aside, dropped to her knees, and lifted the white cotton bed skirt. She stretched under the bed until two fingers snagged the phone. *Buzzz. Buzzz.* She dragged it close enough to hit the green button. "H-hello?"

"Maxine Owens?"

"Yes, yes." Maxine's heart raced. She wriggled her toes in the silky fronds of her rug. No flippers. "Who's calling?"

"Dr. Stacy Jackson at Virtua Memorial. You need to come down as soon as possible."

Suddenly awake, Maxine blinked in the bright morning sunshine squinting through the closed shutters. She retrieved her glasses and slipped them on. She never could seem to hear well without them. "The hospital? Dr. Jackson?" She cleared her throat and pulled off the satin cap keeping her hair back. Curls draped her shoulders.

"Your sister, Celeste Owens, is in the emergency room."

"Celeste? What—?" Maxine glanced at the clock: 9:26. *Okay, it's 9:26 and today is Wed—no, Thursday. Where is Celeste on Thursdays at 9:26?* "But Celeste has her music lesson now. She's practicing her solo. For the concert."

"No, Miss Owens. Celeste collapsed during her lesson, and her instructor called an ambulance. We can't reach your parents—John and Vivienne Owens, correct?"

"I—"

"Maxine. We need you to come down to the hospital. Now. For your sister, Celeste." Dr. Jackson had dropped the careful, gentle tone. In a second, her voice went from patient to brusque, urgent. "It could be her heart."

March

"If your tears had words, what would they say?"

ROSE MERIWEATHER

Chapter Nine

MAXINE LEANED BACK, relishing the sounds of the brass, woodwinds, strings, and percussion playing tag with each other during the warm-up. The trills, tweets, toots, rat-a-tats, bellows, and strums ricocheted off the walls of the nearly empty auditorium, but it was all background music to Maxine. Her eyes were fixed stage left, on the girl wearing the red turtleneck sweater cradling the double bass. Just as they'd been for more than three weeks, since Celeste collapsed during her private lesson.

Today, Maxine hadn't dropped off Celeste at orchestra and headed to Sassafras, the library, or some other nearby spot to wait and write. Instead, she set up shop right under the balcony to enjoy the music and work on her latest post. When the musicians finished their warm-ups and launched into the first piece, however, Maxine's fingers froze after typing *My Daily Grace*. The bright stage lights conjured up images of the thirteen-year-old on a hospital examination table; the sounds of the flutes peeking up from the other instruments reminded her of Celeste's heartbeat on the monitor.

Doctors were still prodding and poking the girl. Yet she took it all in stride—the tests, the attention, the fretting. The unknown. Something Maxine had a hard time doing. She wanted to count every beat, hold a mirror under Celeste's nose while she slept, make the teen quit orchestra and do all her classes from her white four-poster bed.

"Doesn't God have us all in His hand, Maxine?" Mother had reminded her earlier that day.

Maxine watched her shave the carrots before dropping them into the colander in the sink. "Yes, but—"

"Butts are for kneelin' and prayin'." Vivienne turned on the faucet and gently swirled around the vegetables she was preparing for a dinner Manna was catering.

"Not mine. It can work and pray simultaneously. It's called multitasking."

"You think you can take better care of Celeste than He can, the One who knew her before we heard her heartbeat?"

"Before I *felt* her heartbeat, you mean?"

The colander clattered on the bottom of the stainless steel sink. "I didn't know this was over who loved Celeste more or sooner." The water ran unchecked, splashing the carrots and Mother's apron as she stared Maxine down. "Is it?"

Was it? There in Vivienne's kitchen, Maxine had to look away. But sitting in the darkened concert hall, she strained to keep Celeste in her sight as her thoughts and emotions ebbed and flowed with the music. Nearly an hour later, she was no closer to drumming up an answer to the cacophony of questions in her mind.

She kept asking herself, *Why now?* She'd become so territorial over Celeste, when she'd trained herself to think of Celeste as a sister for more than thirteen years. *Now* she wanted to lay claim. *Now* she wanted to establish who had the thickest bloodline. Vivienne was so close to her, she probably imagined she'd felt her heartbeat, that she'd birthed her.

But she didn't. A firmer voice spoke up from her nether regions, and it didn't feel like some third-party, blanched version of Maxine, but her real self, the one who wore hip-hugging jeans and blasted "When Doves Cry" while she washed the car. *I did. And then I left her and took away her father.* Maxine watched the girl flick a twist over her shoulder and bend toward her music stand. *My daughter. How can I make that up to you?*

"Maxine. Is that you?"

"Eee—!" Startled, Maxine smothered her scream with both hands.

The man-of-many-names stood for a second in the shadows at the end of the aisle before scooting sideways down the row toward her. He stopped two feet away and shuffled his weight from one foot to the other. He tucked his hands in his pant pockets and produced a fraction of a smile. "Hi."

Maxine repositioned her glasses on her nose and snapped shut her screen. Her heart felt like it was galloping away from her, but she didn't have the wherewithal to rein it in. "What are you doing here?"

"Probably the same thing you're doing." JD perched on

the edge of a seat. He leaned forward and draped his arms over the row in front of them.

The fingers of the frizzy-haired visiting concert pianist hovered over the keys as the clarinet soloist's mellow tones filled the auditorium. When Maxine faced JD again, she found he, too, only had eyes for the beautiful musician on the double bass. *His* daughter. "How'd you know she was here?"

JD closed his eyes, obviously enjoying the bobbing and weaving of the trombones with the clarinet. "I love 'Rhapsody in Blue.' They're good, for a youth orchestra."

"Gershwin's version is better. And they're good for *any* orchestra. So . . . JD?"

He opened his eyes. "She told me."

"Celeste *told* you what? When?"

"That she played the bass for the Mount Laurel Youth Orchestra. A couple weeks ago, when we met."

"About that."

"About what? The conductor asked me to speak to the musicians about volunteer opportunities with Hillsong, and Celeste and I talked after rehearsal. She's gifted, by the way." His eyes crept back to the stage as the cymbals crashed and the pianist scaled the keyboard.

"You don't have to tell me how good she is. You forget I've heard her play almost every day."

JD's eyes narrowed. "Exactly. You know, Mom plays several instruments. The piano, clarinet, and saxophone, for starters."

"You approached Celeste? She told me she spoke to you before—" She bit off her words, swallowing "before she collapsed." Nothing about Celeste belonged to him, not a hair on her head, her musical gifts, or the irregularity of her heartbeat. Maxine sucked in a deep breath and sat straighter in her chair. "That you spoke to her after the rehearsal. What led you to do that?"

His nostrils flared. "Our genetic connection, obviously. It's not like I walk up to every teenage girl I know. Am I not supposed to ever talk to my daughter? Is that the plan?"

"Plan? I don't have a plan when it comes to you, JD. I never did, not even when I was that starstruck teenager who didn't know better than to abandon the blanket in the woods. I sure didn't plan on you strutting back into Mount Laurel."

"'Strutting'? Did you really say *strutting*?"

When he snickered, it hit her. Dwayne Wayne. Immediately she envisioned JD *strutting* into town in flip-top glasses, a baseball cap, and cargo pants, pretending to be the geeky character from *A Different World*, an old sitcom they once watched together after school. But there was no laugh track there encouraging her to giggle, only the orchestra and a handful of listeners scattered about the auditorium. Maxine inched down in her seat, hoping Celeste couldn't see them.

Sobered, JD bit his full lower lip. "I didn't strut in here, Maxine. I told you weeks ago, I want to get to know Celeste. Even if that means from afar. Since I work around the corner, I pop in for a few minutes to listen, to learn a little about what's important to her. Live on the fringes of her life."

"So you're stalking her."

"Do you hear yourself?"

At JD's throaty outcry the conductor's head turned, his baton raised, just as the bassoonist moistened his reed.

Maxine ducked her head and slid her computer into its neoprene sleeve. She clutched it with her right hand and, with her left, clenched his wrist and leaned in close. She tried to make herself as tiny as possible, praying that Celeste's attention was on her sheet music or on the conductor, not on anyone trickling in and out of the auditorium. "Go. Go," she hissed.

JD didn't speak until they were standing by the tall potted plants in the foyer. "Why are you so angry with me?"

Maxine's curly ponytail tickled the back of her neck as she shook her head. She looked out at Mount Laurel through the windows facing the street to avoid his steady brown gaze. She took a breath and exhaled on a slow count of ten. "My anger is self-directed. You keep getting in the way."

He stroked his beard. This time it was his turn to study the street. He posed there like a model, one hand tucked into the pocket of his flat-front gray slacks, pushing back the lapel of his speckled gray wool blazer. His white shirt hinted at his muscular build and perfectly framed his wide, soft-yellow tie.

All hunk, no geek, Maxine thought.

JD brought his hands together at his chin as if in supplication. "I don't want to stir the pot. That's the last thing I want to do. And I'm not stalking Celeste. I just want to know her, Maxie. She's a part of me. Of you."

"She always has been, Jay. So why now?" Maxine searched his face, hoping for an answer that she'd been unable to supply herself when she was alone, back in the auditorium. "Why are you here now, Jay?" She realized that somehow they'd fallen back into their familiar roles, using the names that signified each other as that safe place they could retreat to when they were navigating through the unknowns of their high school existence.

"I've been praying about this for years. Mustering the courage to reach out. Then this job popped up on LinkedIn and my mom's health started to decline. I knew the Lord had answered my prayer. He made a way for me to come home. To come back and make it right."

She could hear his sincerity. A part of her celebrated his peace, but yet . . . "How can your mother's Alzheimer's be an answered prayer?"

Before he could respond, a door opened, and a custodian pushed a dust mop into the foyer. He glanced at them before he moved from left to right over the parquet floor.

Maxine risked drawing nearer. When she grabbed his wrist and drew him behind the cover of the plants, she was rewarded with a whiff of his cologne. *Cool Water, still?* "There's nothing wrong here for you to fix. Do you think I'm still that lost teen who misses her mommy and daddy?" She felt a stab of memory then of the conversation with Vivienne on Valentine's Day.

"Nothing wrong, Maxie? I gave up my family thirteen years ago. Maybe it was for the best. For her best. But we're all suffering from that choice you tried to make for me. Now even if you don't want anything to do with me, Celeste needs to know her father. You decided for her before, but she's old enough now to choose whether she wants to get to know me."

"She has a father! First John—"

"Is not her father, for one."

"He's the only father she's ever known."

"Exactly." JD seemed to regret the pain his words caused.

"But it's time she knew the truth, Maxie. And you know it. We've been lying to her all these years and one day, when she finds out, she's not going to just hate *me*. You know that, too." His fingers squeezed hers. "Why are you fighting me? Because of Teddy Bear?"

Mortified, Maxine realized her fingers were still wrapped around his wrist. She let go and stepped back. "Don't call him that. His name is Theodore."

"So you've said."

"And it's not just because of him."

"Does he know?"

"It's none of your business."

JD shook his head slowly, his eyes holding hers hostage. "Just like Maxie, always keeping secrets. Baby, when are you going to learn? The truth isn't your enemy."

The double doors behind them flew open, and a potpourri of instrument cases, backpacks, arms and legs, and multi-colored coats erupted through the doors of the auditorium.

Maxine quickly stepped out from behind the planters and scanned the sea of faces for Celeste's. Apparently the teen was taking her usual fifteen extra minutes to extricate herself from her world of music. Relieved, Maxine turned back toward JD, partly visible through the leaves of the ficus. "This—" she drew a circle in the air that enclosed JD, the absentee Celeste, and herself within it—"isn't happening. At least not today. She'll be done any minute, and I should go."

He reached for her as she backed away, but his fingers only grazed her arm. "Can we talk soon, Maxie? I mean, something more than whispering around artificial trees."

Maxine closed her mind's eye to their heartfelt conversations under the very real foliage in Bedlow Park. "Maybe. As long as you keep in mind that Celeste is no more your baby than I am. And I told you, my name is Maxine."

"Did I see you talking to Mr. Lester?"

Maxine dropped her egg roll. Sweet chili sauce and collard greens splattered across her plate. "Excuse me?"

As they were leaving the auditorium, Celeste had thrown an arm to her forehead and pretended to teeter toward the foyer's leatherette chairs. Maxine, intent on safely steering the girl away from any sign of JD, had allowed Celeste to lead her around the block and through the crisp evening air to Sassafras. There, she'd kept the conversation on school, her blog, the wedding, and the piano soloist's missed notes in "Rhapsody in Blue." A lifetime spent circling the wagons. But Maxine plodded where the nimble Vivienne danced, and it wasn't long before Celeste's arrow hit its mark.

"Mr. Lester." Celeste slowly wiped her mouth, seemingly unaware of Maxine's discomfiture. "Earlier, during orchestra. You left the hall together." She slurped another spoonful of French onion soup without taking her eyes off Maxine. "You were talking pretty loud, by the way. You made enough noise to distract Dr. Dennis."

"It's *loudly*, for one thing."

"Whatever." Celeste rolled her eyes.

"And yes, that was JD . . . Mr. Lester." Maxine flicked at the crispy wrapper. *Why can't I ever just eat my egg roll in peace?*

"That's right. *JD*. That's what you called him, so it sounds like you know him pretty well. He's older, isn't he? I got that vibe." Celeste polished off her macaroni and cheese.

"Yes, he's older." Maxine stepped carefully, trying to avoid any hidden, painful traps.

"Oh." Celeste looked beyond Maxine.

Maxine took a bite of her egg roll and chewed slowly, determined not to volunteer more information than was necessary. *Necessary, Maxine? When did the need for truth become debatable or optional?*

"What is it?" Celeste interrupted Maxine's soul-searching.

"Hmm?"

"You don't like him?"

Maxine moved a strand of hair behind her ear. "Don't like who?"

Celeste's mouth dropped open. "Wait. That's it! You do, don't you? Well, at least you *did*. Did you two date or something? Did he carry your lunch pail back and forth to school?" She winked at Maxine.

Maxine's face warmed. "Celeste—"

"I can tell I've stepped on some toes. I know you. You don't *still* have a crush on him, do you? Scandalous!" Celeste sipped her iced tea, her merry brown eyes peeking at her sister above the rim. She sloshed around an ice cube as Maxine shifted in her seat. "I've never seen you like this, struggling for words. Don't you have a smart comeback or . . . ? Wait, what's that word from my Wordly Wise book? *Rejoinder*! Yes! Don't you have a rejoinder?" She chortled over her mouthful.

"Celeste—"

"Don't worry. I won't tell Teddy you're still carrying a

torch for *JD*. He is kinda cute, I must say. While Teddy is more Corbin Bleu, Mr. Lester is like Boris Kodjoe, after a weekend at the beach."

"Celeste—"

"But you have to give me details! Let's have a sleepover so you can—"

"Celeste! This isn't *High School Musical*. We're not a couple of teens giggling over the handsome star of the football team. Did you forget I'm getting married in nine months?"

Celeste twisted her lips and crossed her arms atop the table. "Good gracious, what's wrong with you? You're talking to your maid of honor. We're just having some fun. Well, at least *I* am." She pointed to Maxine's partially eaten meal. "You're not going to finish? You could take it home."

Maxine pushed away her plate and wrinkled her nose. "I've had my fill."

"Then are you going to tell me how you know Mr. Lester?"

Maxine realized that she was working too hard to play it cool, if her armpits were any indication. She sighed and crossed her arms. She leaned back in the chair, away from Celeste. "Well, like I said, we knew each other in high school. When you saw us earlier, we were just catching up."

"Why didn't you mention any of this when I showed you his card?"

"It was . . . kind of awkward. Besides, I was off to my date with Teddy, remember? Premarital counseling, dinner for two, Valentine's Day?"

"But why was Mr. Lester at my rehearsal? Meeting you?"

Maxine answered this question quickly, easily. "Nope. He just happened to see me there."

"What aren't you telling me?"

Maxine squinted at Celeste. "What do you mean?"

"I mean, you're not telling me everything. You've been . . . I don't know . . . off. For weeks."

"Well, this wedding—"

"It's not the wedding. But I can tell you're not going to share what's bothering you, just like you're not sharing the full story about Mr. Lester. So what? You went out. I already knew that, remember? I mean, *hello*." Celeste waved her hand. "I know Mama is all about courtship now, but you're living proof she hasn't always been against dating."

Maxine knew raising her daughter's daughter probably turned her mother against a lot of things. She fought to keep her face impassive.

But it didn't turn God against you.

Maxine sat straighter in her chair and glanced this way and that, past the toddler in the high chair next to them throwing her bottle to the floor and her dad springing to his feet with a "No, Bailey!" . . . the hostess by the door calling out "Letitia, party of four!" before smiling hello at the twentysomethings already holding menus . . . their own server, pencil tip poised on his pad, rolling his eyes over the heads of the couple weighing no-water chai versus skim-milk lattes. No one sat frozen at that familiar, yet disconcerting voice that asserted, louder this time, *God doesn't condemn you.*

Celeste leaned forward and slid her arms into the sleeves of her faded denim jacket. "You're making me cold, sitting over there shaking. Are you okay?"

Maxine summoned the strength to lift the corners of her mouth. "I'm sorry. I'm fine. A bit chilly." Maxine caught the eye of their server. "I'd like a decaf coffee please, with lots of sugar and two pumps of French vanilla creamer. Chai tea, Celeste?" At her sister's nod, she added her request. For a minute after the server squeaked off on sneakered feet, they sat in silence, Maxine rifling through her mental wardrobe stuffed full of memories. She'd long ago smushed them together until they were small enough to stow away. The neighboring toddler's screech jolted her back to the present day, to Celeste, but she emerged with an armload to share.

"Yes, JD and I dated in high school. We met the fall of my freshman year, when he was a junior. When he graduated, he went away to Princeton, so it didn't last."

Celeste rolled her eyes. "Obviously. Was he your first boyfriend?"

You could say that. She blinked away the vision of JD's eyebrows, strong jawline, and eyes as deep as her coffee cup and just as warm. Their replica gazed back at her. "Yes, he was. I l-liked him. A lot."

"More than—?"

"Let's just say we had quite a bit in common."

"Like what?"

You, for one. But before she could answer, the server was setting down their steaming cups. Maxine waved off his offer to box her food and then busied herself shaking sugar packets and sprinkling them into her coffee. She took a test taste and noted that Celeste's wispy curl–framed face had never looked away as her chai tea cooled. "Well, we both liked to read. And he was a good listener."

"What'd y'all talk about?"

"Books. My parents. His parents. Music. *My* parents some

more. JD helped me through . . . an awkward time, made me feel a lot less lonely. High school was hard for me. It wasn't the experience you're having."

"Because I'm homeschooled?"

"Because of a lot of things. We spent a lot of time driving around in his old Chevy that his father had given him. He'd pick me up after band rehearsal—or maybe I'd even skip rehearsal."

"Ooh, Max! Weren't you the rebel!" Celeste scooted her chair closer. "What did Mama say about that?"

Maxine cleared her throat and twirled a strand from her ponytail. "She was too busy being a newlywed and catering to newlyweds to notice much." She swallowed the acrid taste of the memories. "Not that I'd call myself a rebel. I just wasn't always thirty years old. Jesus and I have gotten to know each other a lot better over the years."

"When did y'all break up?"

"During his freshman year of college, after I turned seventeen." Maxine started to take a sip but changed her mind. She considered ordering an iced coffee instead to cool off.

Celeste propped her chin in the palm of her hand and peered at her sister. "But why? Did he cheat on you while he was away?"

Maxine set her cup down with a force that rattled the utensils. "Goodness, Celeste!"

"What?"

"All these questions, that's what. You're not this curious about Teddy."

"That's because we met him before you did."

Celeste had accompanied First John to a dinner at Whitehall Academy last summer when the board had introduced Teddy as its headmaster. "As soon as we got home that night, I told you all about him because I knew you'd like him as much as Daddy did. And I thought he was perfect for you, too." Celeste finally swallowed some tea. "But I don't know anything about your JD. Other than he's cute as all."

Maxine wished she could dip a napkin into the icy tea glass and dab her cheeks. "He's not *my JD*."

"He used to be."

"*I am my beloved's and my beloved is mine.*" The Scripture from the Song of Solomon skittered in and out of her mind. "A very long time ago, Celeste. Just because he's moved back doesn't change the facts. I'm getting married, and Mr. Lester is a grown man with his own plans."

"What are his plans? Is that what you two were talking about during rehearsal?"

You. You are his plan. "Celeste—"

A burst of loud music caught their attention. Celeste turned away from Maxine to dig into the side pocket of her backpack by her feet. She silenced the voice of Adele crooning "Hello" on her iPhone. "Oooh, it's Mama." Adele sang again.

"Aren't you going to answer it?" Maxine worked hard not to express her relief.

Celeste pushed the red *X*. "Nope. I texted her on our way over, and she's probably having a conniption because we stopped to eat. You know how she is about family dinners." She looked at Maxine for a minute, quiet. Then she reached down for her backpack. "Yeah, we should go." She held Maxine's eyes as she slid her chair back. "Thanks for this."

"Of course! I was hungry, too." Maxine slipped on her navy windbreaker and unhooked her purse from the arm of her chair.

"No, I mean *this*. Thanks for letting me in, at least a little." Celeste stood and headed for the front of the café.

Maxine tucked the ticket and thirty dollars under the sugar bowl and followed her sister. "One more thing, Celeste."

"What? Don't tell Mama about our conversation?" The teen glanced over her shoulder.

Maxine laughed. "Okay, make that two more things. That's one. The second is you're wrong about Mr. Lester."

Celeste stopped and half turned toward Maxine, her left eyebrow raised.

Maxine winked. "He's more like Lenny Kravitz—another musician but much taller."

The two bumped fists and left the restaurant.

Chapter Ten

"WHAT?" MAXINE GASPED *and pushed herself up, her fingers sinking into something soft and loamy. She brushed her hands together and down the front of her nightgown to clear away the dirt and leaves that clung to her, but a far-off sound snagged her attention. Maxine stood and craned her neck. A guitar? No, a double bass! She stepped over her bed of earth, straw, and leaves and walked toward the music, ducking under and around low-hanging branches and towering tree trunks. She walked gingerly, yet the sticks, nettles, and pebbles didn't prick her bare feet. The moist ground was plush and spongy between her toes.*

Still, the bow on the strings.

Maxine stopped and squinted in the half-light. Was this morning reveille or evening taps? She took in a chestful of the clear, crisp air and resisted the urge to stretch her arms toward the sky. She felt strangely rested and alert, like she had neither slept for too long or too little. Just right. "Call me Goldilocks," she giggled.

Her low laughter petered out as it struck her that she was the only one listening—save, perhaps, for the invisible musician. Her foot seemed to ask the ground for directions with each hesitant step. But then something familiar glinted at her through the trees and she rushed forward to push aside an outstretched branch. Is that . . . ? Yes, my creek! I'm in my woods! *She half skipped, half ran down toward the silvery-green, slow-moving water, miraculously dodging pines, elms, bushes, and undergrowth.*

"Hello-oo?" Even though she whispered, her voice seemed to bounce off the trees, the rocks, the nearly still water beyond the muddy shore. She walked toward the sound, to the east. The sun crept higher as the humming of the strings grew louder, yet more beautiful—painfully so. Maxine suppressed a shiver and looked behind her. No signs of life. Only her own wet footprints following in a zigzag path behind her. To lose herself, she lifted the silky edge of her nightgown and stepped into the cool water and traversed the creek.

Chill bumps erupted along her arms as the gown clung to her. She slogged across the few remaining feet to the shoreline and scrambled to drier ground. There, she sat and wrapped her arms around her knees, ignoring the mud and grime. She rocked back and forth, in time to the musician's song, as the fully risen sun cooked her from the inside out. Orange, gold, and white light filled the sky as the music finally faded. It was then she picked up other sounds. Birds called to each other, leaves rustled, the creek gurgled over stones.

And someone called, "Maxine."

She turned her head this way and that, trying to find who'd spoken to her, squinting in the wind that suddenly picked up. Wet, loose strands stuck to the sides of her face. Was that the musician standing just over there, obscured by the sun's glare?

"Lie down. Rest. Listen," the voice entreated.

Yet Maxine couldn't rest. She had to find the music. She braced an arm on the ground and rose unsteadily. She turned in a circle, scanning the scene, the woods she'd left behind her on the other side and the thick shadows before her. Maxine looked above her, toward the shadowy treetops, toward the morning light, and she stretched for it . . .

And hit the floor. The area rug softened the fall, but it wasn't plush enough to protect her from the wood beneath. "Ooophf!" she cried, out loud this time. Fully awake, she sprang to her feet, checked her hands for mud, and felt her pajamas for wet splotches. She turned on the lamp and, with a shuddering breath, finally accepted she was in her bedroom.

But not for long.

———

Maxine pushed the button on her key fob to disable the house alarm and let herself into her parents' mudroom. She turned the dead bolt behind her. After stepping out of her fleece-lined slippers and hanging her jacket on the hook she still laid claim to, she tiptoed through the moonlit kitchen toward the freezer.

The evening had inched into night after Maxine had dropped off Celeste. She'd tried to wring out more than the few words she'd typed in the rehearsal hall, but emotionally, she was bone-dry. She snapped shut her laptop and hunted for something—anything—to distract herself. Maxine piddled around her garage apartment, listening to the owls hooting in the woods, moved knickknacks from one shelf to another, and cleaned her refrigerator. Her body ached for rest, but her brain refused to quiet. Finally, hours later, the inky night enveloped her, and she drifted until the dream drove her from bed.

After using the faint, speckled glow from the skylight to find a spoon, she dug directly into the butter pecan ice cream. She vowed silently with her eyes closed, *I'll replace it tomorrow, Mother.* On the other side of the island, she held the stainless steel in her mouth so she could use both hands to lift the heavy stool and set it down noiselessly before hopping onto it.

Teddy. She missed his dimples and the line that formed between his eyes when he listened intently. His humor and his arms were her resting place, but she'd almost cried from relief when he'd told her about his higher education conference. She needed this rest *from* Teddy, however brief, to gear up for Monday's meeting with him and Reverend Atwater. "Ugh," she murmured to herself. *Talk about muck and mire.*

Suddenly the two recessed lights over the stove clicked on, followed by a low woof. Milo pattered over to her and nuzzled her lap.

"Maxine, what are you doing?" First John stood at the foot of the back stairs in a gray Wake Forest University

T-shirt and red- and white-striped pajama bottoms, his hair a spiky silver halo. "Are you eating ice cream at two o'clock in the morning?"

Maxine rubbed the dog's head absently as she greeted her stepfather with a smile as bleary as his blue eyes. "Have some?"

Her stepfather slogged over and sat down on the stool next to her. "Um, no. Are you okay?" He rested his head on a fisted hand. His sleepy eyes pinned her to her spot.

"I am now." Maxine retrieved her spoon and finished what remained on it. She extricated herself from his stare by returning the slightly squishy container to the freezer. "I'm sorry I woke you."

"You woke Milo, and *he* woke me. Viv was worn-out from the wedding Manna catered, so she didn't break a snore."

"I forgot about that!" Maxine leaned against the closed freezer door. "How'd it go? And how was your trip? Where did the travel itinerary take you this time?"

"Dallas, Philadelphia, Chicago, Greensboro, and a dozen little burgs in between. Book signings, commentating, and speaking engagements—good stuff, but I'm tired, and I'm glad it's all over. I'll be home with the family the rest of the year, so now I can focus on writing and Manna's wedding season."

"I can't imagine you'll get to focus on anything besides the NCAA tournament, but at least we can officially celebrate your new syndication agreement. Congratulations, First John." Maxine turned away from him and opened the refrigerator to retrieve the water pitcher.

"Thanks, sweetheart. It just means my newspaper column

ends up in recycling bins in a few more states, that's all." He smiled, however, obviously pleased. "Sometimes I wish I could simply enjoy March Madness like everybody else. As far as today's nuptials . . . they said their 'I dos,' ate some shrimp and grits, and swapped bites of red velvet cake. You know your mother's motto: 'All's well that eats well.'"

He shrugged. "But back to you. Why are you burying your sorrows in a pint of butter pecan this time of night, or should I say morning?"

Maxine set down the water pitcher. "Do you ever need a reason to eat ice cream?"

"You do if it's my Talenti." Dressed in a cream-colored gown and robe sprinkled with pink flowers, Vivienne accepted Milo's lick and nuzzle of greeting near the stair landing. She stroked the dog's head once more before she nudged him aside and entered the kitchen. "Did I miss an invitation to the family reunion?" She rested a hand on her husband's shoulder. "Maxine, why are you standin' here, eatin' my ice cream at two o'clock in the morning?"

Oh, here we go. Maxine returned the pitcher to the refrigerator and faced the giants.

"I was just asking her that same question, hon." First John wrapped an arm around his petite wife's waist and tucked her into his side.

An ugly part of Maxine wanted to wriggle between them, but it would've taken a crowbar. Manna had catered the launch of First John's debut novel. When Mama Ruby had taken sick, she'd sent Vivienne in her place. They'd moved together like interlocking gears since the moment Vivienne discovered John knew that Elena Ruiz wasn't a person, but a

Cuban sandwich—and that he made his with the traditional strawberry jam instead of cranberry sauce. And not only did he appreciate Vivienne's Cuban heritage and food, but he loved dancing, travel, and late-night talks—things she rarely convinced her first husband to do. And she and First John both adored Maxine, or so Mother often said.

A gangly, white, former college basketball player who let his written words speak for him, John Owens was almost everything Vivienne's first husband was not. He was content being the sturdy underpinnings of their family wagon—the axle, hub, and undercarriage—while she sat ready at the reins, with her hands on the brake and the lariat.

As she stared at them, Maxine recalled the night the new Mrs. Owens had returned to resume motherhood, gushing, "I never thought I'd find love again, but not only did I find it, I found myself, my true self."

That's what I want. To be me *and let someone else see it, hear it, love it.*

"What are you lookin' at, Maxine?"

Maxine readjusted her scarf as she focused on her mother's face. "Um . . ."

"No. The truth, girl. Don't tell me something easy on the ears. What?" Vivienne lobbed this last question in John's direction as he squeezed her waist.

Maxine tried to smile. "I think First John is suggesting you lighten up, Mother. Isn't it a little late for full-court press?"

"Well, isn't it a little early for dessert?"

Maxine pictured Celeste saying *rejoinder* and almost laughed out loud. She crossed her arms. "I'll replace it."

"That's not the point, and you know it. Is it JD you're

worried about? Celeste told me about y'all meetin' today during her rehearsal." Vivienne smoothed her husband's spikes.

Maxine snorted. "JD who? Actually, I need your help
with Teddy. Reverend Atwater wants us to spend time with
three other couples, and you and First John top the list."

Vivienne kissed her husband's cheek and disengaged
from his embrace. She walked around the island, opened the
freezer, and withdrew the hotly contested frozen treat. "What
do you have in mind?"

"I'm not sure. He just talked about the impact of family
and friends on our relationship and sent us on our merry
way. We're supposed to spend at least half a day with three
different couples over the next six months. Are you game?"

Vivienne licked a spot of ice cream off her lip. "Sure. We
can go to church and have dinner together on one of Manna's
slow weekends. What do you think, John? I can make steak
and gravy and fry some chicken wings."

He rubbed his eyes and yawned. "Sure, sounds like a plan
to me. I'm sure I can find a game for us to watch."

"Uh-uh, no TV watching. Twelve to twenty-four hours
of interaction, by the pastor's orders. And no need for two
different meats, Mother."

"Girl, you know that's my usual. Even if you don't cook
that way, Theodore can count on his mother-in-law throwin'
down in the kitchen." Vivienne discarded the empty carton.
"Well, now that we've settled that, are you ready to tell me
why you can't sleep? It's not because you're trying to fill up
your social calendar."

Maxine's mouth worked for a second, but no words
squeezed through.

"Maxine, if you want me to leave so you can talk to Viv—"

"You'd better sit right there, John!" Vivienne pointed at him with her spoon. "This is a family matter. If this girl is losin' sleep, it's her own fault and our business."

"So you're saying it's wrong to worry about Celeste. You agree with that, First John?"

"Well—"

"John, stay out of this."

"Wow, Mother. You rescinded that invitation to the club before he had a chance to open the envelope."

"Child, hush, and answer my question."

Maxine glared at Vivienne.

Vivienne's lips pursed. "Have you reached any decisions, Maxine?"

"About?"

"You know what about. The girl dreamin' of butterflies and marigolds upstairs in her room. What are we going to do?"

Maxine's hands flew to her chest as if to protect her sister-child by osmosis. "You can't mean to tell her now, after all those tests on her heart! That's just selfish. Just because I can't sleep . . ." Now, however, Maxine felt she could curl up under a blanket on the hardwood floor and hibernate by the stove for forty years.

"What's selfish is holding this back, Maxine. Maybe it was right before JD came back. But you need to stop pretending this is about respecting his privacy or out of fear for Celeste's health. Livin' in the woods don't make us a tree."

"If I may interrupt."

Both Maxine and Vivienne seemed surprised to find John still perched on the stool in the kitchen. Yet there he'd hunkered down, patient as ever, looking more alert and unruffled than when he'd first stumbled into the room. Maxine imagined his fingers lightly resting on the keys of his ancient Royal typewriter, ready to compose.

First John drew in a breath, eyes on his wife and step-daughter. "Max, you're right. We're all concerned about Celeste's short-term physical health. Viv's got a point, too. We can't forget Celeste's long-term, emotional well-being. But you see . . ." He interlaced his fingers as if he were playing "Here's the church and here's the steeple."

Yet Max failed to see any open doors, even as he continued.

". . . the two views intersect. They don't contradict each other or rule out the other." His eyes beseeched the older woman first and then the younger.

Vivienne seemed to deflate.

Maxine blew up. "Exactly! That's my point *exactly*, First John."

Vivienne moved closer to her daughter and enfolded one of her hands in both her own. "Sweetie, we can't keep lyin' to Celeste. That in itself can do more harm than good. What do you know about JD?"

Maxine slid her hand out of her mother's clasp. "What do you mean, what do I know? I've known him since I was fifteen. You know his parents, Annie and Geoff."

Vivienne waved away her daughter's words like flies hovering over a picnic blanket. "But what do you really *know*? Is Alzheimer's disease genetic? And what about high blood pressure, cancer, stroke, or sickle cell disease—does any of that run in his family? We should know his blood type, family medical history, current medical history. Everything. I imagine you don't."

Maxine's lips were glued shut.

"I thought so. But those are things the doctors need to know. That Celeste should know in an emergency." She cast a bleak look at John. She faced her daughter once more. "We need to help them help Celeste, which means they need to know more than just our side of the medical tree—Celeste has other grandparents, other family. What if the answers are buried somewhere in his DNA? We've had our heads stuck deep in the sand, thinkin' this doesn't involve JD or that all you have to worry about is your relationship with her. We've got bigger fish to fry, my dear. Leave them out any longer, and they'll start stinkin' to high heaven."

John sat there for a moment with his mouth hidden behind his clasped hands. Then he gazed at his wife and step-daughter from across the island. "I think we've been looking at this as a curse, JD's return. But you know what, Maxine? It's a blessing. We need to start thanking God he came back when he did, for Celeste's sake."

First John rose from his chair and walked to Vivienne and took her hand. He drew the three together in a circle, though Maxine's fingers were limp in his. "I'm thinking maybe I should dig out your mama's secret stash of ice cream."

Chapter Eleven

MAXINE PULLED INTO the parking lot of the gray stone church and let the car and her eyes idle for a moment on the Scripture etched in its cornerstone: *"Come unto me, all ye that labour and are heavy laden, and I will give you rest. Take my yoke upon you, and learn of me; for I am meek and lowly in heart: and ye shall find rest unto your souls. For my yoke is easy, and my burden is light." Matthew 11:28-30.*

Built in the mid-1800s, the imposing granite once sheltered runaway slaves in its basement. Now Grace Chapel's highly polished, heavy oak doors opened to men and women of all colors. To get there, congregants walked past deserted buildings and homes, broken windows winking and empty doorways yawning. Dandelions seized the day and the yards.

Cracks in the sidewalk of the once-flourishing neighborhood caught the heels of women headed to Sunday service.

Mount Laurel resembled other notches in the Bible Belt—that Southern swath of the country where houses of worship sprouted like crabgrass on nearly every corner—so on the Sabbath, folks swayed to gospel choirs in an African Methodist Episcopal church down the street and lifted their hands to acoustic guitars strumming contemporary Christian music in a nondenominational megachurch around the block. Hundreds of people still sought spiritual covering from the world's deluge of trouble within Grace's rock-solid walls.

Every first and third Sunday Maxine was one of them as she bumped shoulders with Teddy, mumbling the verses in the hymnal they shared. She stared over her Bible at the back of his father's salt-and-paprika-colored strands, her thoughts skittering away to her dreams from the night before. At the moment, Maxine wanted to skip today's counseling and huddle in her car as Air Supply crooned "The One That You Love." She felt more convicted at each of these sessions with the pastor.

Then Teddy's white Audi Q5 pulled beside Reverend Atwater's silver Volkswagen Passat in the fenced parking lot. There was no turning back. Hastily Maxine removed her glasses and checked her makeup in the rearview mirror. She resettled her frames on her nose, slapped on a smile, and stepped from the car.

"How are you, babe?" Teddy kissed her as they headed toward the church's double doors.

"Más o menos." She waved her hand back and forth, using her grandfather's words for "so-so." "How are you?"

"About the same. It's been a long day, and it's only two o'clock. Are we on for seeing your grandparents this weekend? Remember, we need to report in to the pastor."

"Still trying to get in his good graces?" Maxine teased as they stepped into the vestibule.

Teddy leaned closer and whispered, "I see the seniors are singing this Sunday." He led them toward the church office under the watchful gaze of a choir composed of men and women ranging from fifty-five to eighty years old. They swayed to the beat of their thudding feet as they crooned and moaned their way through a song that was both a testimony and a plea, entreating the couple to "Come on in the room."

Maxine nodded at the choir and then lowered her head, keeping her eyes on the red carpet and Theodore's well-polished shoes.

"I see y'all are still holding hands." Beaming, Reverend Atwater rose from behind his desk.

Teddy waved their clasped fingers in the air as if in victory. "Always, Pastor."

Maxine started when a petite woman in a flowy, knee-length brown dress stepped toward them from the sideboard. Muted flowers in iridescent colors caught the light as she approached.

"By your look of surprise, I can see my husband didn't tell you I'd be here." She frowned at the reverend as she set two glasses of juice down in front of the chairs facing his desk.

Atwater responded with a sheepish smile and drew her into their circle. "Please forgive me for neglecting to mention my wife would be here today, but Lilian's schedule opened up Saturday night, and I jumped on it. I like to have her sit in at least once."

Teddy extended his hand. "It's always good to see you. You know my fiancée, Maxine Owens."

"Maxine, I hope it's okay if I join you." Her smile wrapped itself around the couple.

Maxine noted the *if*, her humble, two-letter request as she doffed her trench coat. After a moment's hesitation she murmured, "Please do. And by the way, I love your dress."

Lilian's eyes peered at her for a second, but then she wiggled her brows and held out her pleated skirt. "You'd better! It cost Willy a love offering or two!"

"Willy?" Teddy glanced at the pastor.

Reverend Atwater's laugh flooded the room. "Believe me, I wasn't born wearing this suit and tie." He motioned a hand toward the two empty, upholstered armchairs—"Please"—as he pulled up an extra seat near his own. Lilian sat down and rested her hand atop his.

"So during our last meeting we talked about the many pieces that make up your relationship—your parents, siblings, friends—and how they fit together to give me, and you most importantly, some perspective on the whole marriage puzzle. It was a good start, I think."

Teddy nodded vigorously. "We've planned a date with Lerenzo and Ruby Tagle, Maxine's grandparents."

Maxine assented, but less enthusiastically, under the unblinking gaze of Mrs. Atwater.

"Sounds good. Today, I thought Lilian and I could show you in a real, practical way how these pieces fit together for us. Maxine, you've grown up in a blended family. Correct?"

Maxine shifted in her chair. "Yes, I guess that's what you'd call it. My biological father died when I was eight, and Mother married First John a few years later. He didn't have any other children though."

"So you're the oldest." Lilian's tone was even.

Maxine swiped at an invisible hair tickling her cheek. "Yes. I have four siblings—three brothers and a sister."

The room was quiet, but it seemed like even the walls knew she had more to say. Teddy turned to face her.

Maxine uncrossed and recrossed her ankles as if she were an English duchess. "I've never told Teddy, but . . . when I was sev—no, eighteen—my parents adopted Celeste."

"What?" Her fiancé loosened his grip on her fingers and then dropped them altogether.

"We don't really talk about it. Or think about it, in fact. Until lately anyway. She's my sister. That's all. It doesn't matter who gave birth to her. Mother has always considered it 'family business.'" Maxine used her now-free hands to make air quotes. "It's no big deal to anybody but us."

"You made it a big deal by not telling me."

"Don't look hurt, Teddy. Another family member couldn't raise her, so my parents decided to. We don't treat her any differently because she's adopted." Maxine risked skating closer to the hole in the ice, her heart contracting painfully in her chest. Each *thump-thump* reminded her of all she hadn't shared.

"Like I said, we just kept it among us. But now you're becoming *us*. And I wanted to make sure it was okay with everybody else first before telling you. They'd already had Zan, and then they later had Second John and Robert. So I feel like I helped raise everybody. They . . . they all seem like my own. We're a very close-knit group. Truly *blended*, to use your word." The lies walked in step with the truth, but the words still tripped her up.

Lilian sat quietly for another moment before she nodded. "I get that. You see, when I was two years old, I, too, was adopted. From China." Then she chuckled at their confused expressions.

Reverend Atwater joined in as he intertwined their fingers. "My wife is known in these parts for her sense of humor." He shook his head. "Lilian grew up in Chicago. She moved to North Carolina in high school."

"I'm glad to see someone else makes bad jokes." Teddy swiped imaginary sweat from his brow as he turned his attention to the other couple.

"You got me." Maxine's shoulders relaxed as the tension between them eased.

"Life's too short for sadness, my dear. God mourns with us, and He laughs with us. Something I've learned over the past sixty years, and especially during my thirty-eight-year marriage to Willy. One of those lessons? Walk in truth and love." Though her smile had faded, the lines around Lilian's brown eyes hinted at her lighthearted spirit as she held up an almond-colored second finger.

"And another lesson? 'Count it all joy' like the book of James says, and then cling to that joy. While I was joking about being adopted from China, I am half-Chinese, half-black. My parents adopted me when I was a toddler, but I could never shake the feeling of being inextricably pulled in two different directions. I'd spent my early years bouncing from one foster home to another, and I'd created pseudo memories of a mother who still wanted me, who was searching for me. I held on for dear life to that sense of abandonment and loss even though I didn't know a thing about my biological parents. Once I was old enough to process that I was different, I resisted the very real love of my family. I resented them for stealing me from my home." Lilian rolled her eyes.

"Unlike your family with Celeste, Maxine, it was something I never stopped thinking about or pointing out, that I was adopted. I was *always* looking for something, *always* afraid that even what I had would be taken away from me, that I was less than because of the blood running through my veins that made my skin lighter and my hair silkier than my parents', my brother's, and my sister's."

Maxine couldn't fathom ever considering the beautiful, poised Lilian as "less than."

Lilian's soft voice never wavered. "I didn't trust my family's very sincere, persistent love. This affected all my relationships and my choices—even before I met Willy and certainly after. And those choices begat more bad choices and more feelings of inadequacy."

Lilian's words seemed tasty morsels to Reverend Atwater, and he didn't miss a single bite. When she stopped talking, she leaned into him and nodded. Only then did he turn from her to address the other members in the room, ravenous diners around the table.

"Lilian acted out—a lot—and put her family through some stuff, let me tell you. When her parents pursued her, showering her with love and forgiveness, she moved out, declared herself independent. Interestingly enough, she never missed a beat in high school. Lilian hid under her report card and convinced herself she wasn't hurting anyone. She even went on to graduate at the top of her class."

Lilian leaned forward. "Valedictorian."

Reverend Atwater winked at his wife over his shoulder. He seemed more and more like "Willy" as he warmed to them. "Yes, but that changed your freshman year at Wheaton College, didn't it?"

"It certainly did. I nearly flunked out!" Lilian sounded like she still didn't believe it.

"But why a Christian school like Wheaton?" Maxine couldn't stem her curiosity.

"Because my parents offered to pay for it. I was rebellious and independent, but I wasn't stupid enough to pass up a free education, especially near Chicago. Once I got there, however, I couldn't continue floating through. It caught up to me. I think that's what God used to wake me up, which is just like Him, isn't it? He allowed my pride to bring me down to a place where I could see Him clearly.

"Wheaton put me on academic probation, and I was forced to come back to North Carolina the fall semester of my sophomore year. And guess what? My parents welcomed me with open arms. They enrolled me in classes at the community college, helped me clean up my act, and most importantly, they took me to church. Again." She looked at her husband.

Reverend Atwater smiled at her as his eyes welled. "But that time she found the Lord, not that He was the one who was lost. He accepted her and she stopped resisting Him."

"Nose piercing and all," Lilian finished. "I finally felt *enough*, just like I was."

Maxine couldn't restrain her eyes from searching out the tiny dot on Lilian's left nostril—which until now, she'd assumed was a mole or a freckle. Lilian caught her stare. She tapped the tiny diamond in her nose and winked at Maxine, who couldn't hold back a smile even as her neck and cheeks warmed. "Where do you come in, Reverend Atwater?"

"Yes, *Willy*," Teddy chimed in.

He laughed a little with the younger man. "Lilian and I met that semester she was home, when I was studying at UNC-G. We both volunteered at a homeless shelter. I saw her curly afro out to here." The pastor held his hands about eighteen inches from his head. "She was beautiful, funny, smart, exciting. I just had to get to know her, and I felt it more and more every time I heard other people talking to her, laughing with her."

The light in Reverend Atwater's eyes warmed Maxine's heart as he continued.

"Then one day after we'd handed out our last blanket, I worked up the nerve to ask her out for a hot dog. I was afraid we wouldn't see each other again because she planned to go back to Wheaton. So while we were sitting there eating in Yum Yum—"

"All beef. With pickle relish, onions, and yellow mustard. The best I've ever had, even better than in Chicago, I might add." Lilian bumped her husband's side.

"So you've said, but nothing beats chili-and-slaw dogs with onions," Reverend Atwater chuckled. "While she ate the *second-best* hot dog in the world, I asked her about the loop in her nose and the tiny diamond cross in the top of her earlobe, and boy, did she lay it on me. There I was, this boy from Mount Airy, North Carolina, whose biggest trial up to that point was convincing his daddy to let him drive his new Thunderbird, hearing how this ball of fire had nearly killed herself. And she loved God and herself enough to trust me, a stranger, with her testimony." He sat silent a second or two.

"I didn't really trust you. I just thought you were cute and good for a meal." Lilian poked Reverend Atwater's shoulder. Then she rested her hand there.

He turned and kissed her fingertips before facing Teddy and Maxine again.

"Now we've never shared any of this before in our premarital sessions. Usually we take this time to share more anecdotal things, debate the nature versus nurture argument and how both sides will affect your future marriage. We field life-application questions from our engaged couples and answer as best we can. Hear about your dates with other couples. Important stuff. But I don't know . . ." He and Lilian exchanged a look.

His wife seemed to complete the pastor's thought. "For some reason, God led us to open up about this today. We both felt it Saturday night, when I told Willy about my canceled luncheon. I don't know why. God's ways are higher, far beyond me. Maybe this was for you. Maybe it's for us. But in all things, it's for God. His glory."

Reverend Atwater brought his hands together in a loud *clap!* and leaned toward them across his desk. "So now's the time to fess up."

Maxine's eyes widened. "What?"

He chuckled and shook his head. "No, no, not to us. To each other. Believe in the love of God and the love He gave you for one another. Consider this your freebie. Seriously, promise that to each other before you say a word."

Maxine cut a glance at Teddy, who was doing the same in her direction.

"Go home. Pray about whatever baggage you're carrying. Then either invite the other to help you carry it, or let it go altogether."

"But first, you need to be honest." Lilian's expression was warm yet sober. "Maxine has already opened the door by sharing about Celeste, right?" Lilian reached over the desk to the younger woman. "Why don't we take it to God and send y'all to Dairy Queen since we're so far from Greensboro?"

Again, Maxine and Teddy's eyes met—and held this time—before their own hands reached for each other across the arms of their chairs.

———

"That was quite the talk!"

Maxine and Teddy stood between their cars in the parking lot. Adrift on a deep lake of thought since uttering "Amen," she didn't respond to Teddy's external processing. He wasn't one to think, *then* speak.

"So, Maxine, what did you think?"

"It was . . . a lot to take in." She pressed Unlock on her key fob as she thought about the stormy weather in their relationship's forecast.

"Hey. Wait." Teddy grabbed her hand and pulled her to

him. The arms encircling her prevented her from erecting a permanent home within herself.

Maxine stiffened at first before she wrapped her arms around his waist and let him press her against her car door.

"Are you okay?" He twirled her curly ponytail and massaged the back of her neck.

"Yes," she answered into his shoulder. "I just need to think."

"What about?" His breath moved the hair on her crown.

"Everything. Don't you?"

Teddy pulled back and searched her face. His eyes looked like a cloudy sky. "Everything like what?"

"Like . . . what the Atwaters said."

"Well, if you're worried, don't be."

Maxine jumped slightly. "Worried about what?"

"What you told us. About Celeste. I won't mention it. And it's okay. I'm not upset . . . anymore. You were right: it was family business. So—"

"So what? You feel like going out to dinner and moving on with our lives?"

"No-o-o. I was going to say, 'So let it go.' I can tell you're taking their story pretty hard. What's wrong, Maxine? I was impacted, too, but you're like this every time we leave his office. Even more so today. Is there some load I can help you carry?"

This is what happens when I *think and speak at the same time.* Over Teddy's shoulder Maxine saw another car pull into the lot. When the driver door opened, a willowy blonde woman stepped out. The stranger laughed as a much shorter red-haired man slammed the passenger door and trotted around the car. They said something Maxine couldn't hear before they kissed and turned toward the church, their clasped hands swinging between them. Free. Unburdened. One.

"Maxine?" Teddy placed a soft fingertip on her chin and gently nudged her face back in his direction. He trapped her eyes. "You have a freebie, remember? Do you have something else you need to tell me?"

She saw how he forced the corners of his lips up, but his eyes still looked troubled. The day remained only partly sunny. Tears welled because she knew she had caused this, this shadow of fear in a face usually so worry free. Maxine caressed his cheek and drew him close. She rested in the security of his embrace and listened to his heartbeat slow before she rose on tiptoe and put her mouth to his ear so she could whisper the words.

"Saturday at six. Let's pretend we're at Yum Yum."

Chapter Twelve

My Daily Grace—From Cover to Cover

I have some confessions to make: I love the sweet cream with pecans folded in at Cold Stone, but a carton of Talenti's butter pecan is a close second. And while I enjoy music from the seventies, thanks to my mother, I always listen to Prince while I clean my bathroom, on long drives, whenever I mop, and while I rake the yard. Also, I don't like talking to people first thing in the morning. So far, that's worked out okay for me as a single woman, but come December, that might be a problem. I'm not sure how Hubby-to-be will take to me walking around at 8 a.m. with a scowl on my face, a silk cap covering my hair, and noise-canceling headphones pressed to my ears.

There are other things I haven't shared with him or anyone else. Take my water bottle. I can't stand when someone else uses it. That's right up there with drying off with my towel, using my toothbrush, and asking for my last bite. Folks say giving these things are all signs of true love, but my last lick of butter pecan ice cream? Never his lips shall meet! For peace in the home, I'll just mark all water bottles, desserts, and linens "His" and "Hers."

Up to now, I've revealed shades of my darker side layer by layer. He knows I hate losing, but not that I stopped speaking to my brother for two days after the Saints lost to the Patriots. We both enjoy playing cards, but I haven't yet told him that I'm a mean spades player. Literally. That I've always wanted to drive to California, but I won't visit Yosemite because I'm scared of grizzlies. And speaking of fear, if it crawls or buzzes, I run.

You might wonder, "So just what does he know?" Perhaps he's asking himself the same question at this very moment. Well, he knows I chose my wedding date because it commemorates the day my parents met each other. That as much as I enjoy my sweets, I crave savory even more, so I'd eat King of Pizza on Main Street over Cold Stone if I had to choose. I consider nothing more important than my faith and my family, and I can already picture where he'll stand in our Christmas photo. And even if he has to use his own toothbrush, towel, and cup, I'll willingly wash them for him because he's my boo.

Mother reassures me that my fiancé will adore and accept all the various parts of me, including the ones marked "selfish," "poor sport," "card sharp," and "scaredy-cat." I'm just grateful that I know we both believe what the Bible says in 1 Peter 4:8: "And above all things have fervent love for one another, for 'love will cover a multitude of sins.'"

But . . . what about all those things that love *un*covers?

Everybody always wants the prettiest, biggest box under the Christmas tree because they expect a puppy or a dollhouse or a television. No one chooses the tiny one with the torn wrapping paper, botched taping job, and the missing bow. Yet the big one might hide a vacuum cleaner, the tiny one diamond earrings. Don't judge a book by its cover, right? Maybe we should stop with the first two words: Don't judge. Period. Something I learned firsthand today.

In terms of books, my fiancé is open wide. I can clearly read what his heart says because he shares it freely. I hope we spend the next several decades pulling back the layers of our relationship and trusting in God, who never changes, who can identify Himself simply as I AM while we reveal our true selves behind what we do, what we believe, and who we know. Whether you have a Hubby- or Wife-to-be, or you're dodging the image in the mirror, trust that God knows. He sees who we are without the bells, whistles, bows, and wrapping. There's no surprise or disappointment and no big reveal.

I wish I could say the same, for my fiancé's sake. Pray for him, y'all.

But the Lord said to Samuel, "Do not look at his appearance or at his physical stature . . . For the Lord does not see as man sees; for man looks at the outward appearance, but the Lord looks at the heart." 1 Samuel 16:7

Maxine reviewed her post for the fifth time and submitted it. She slowly closed her laptop and slipped on her usual doubts and worries as she would a ratty old sweater. Staring past her desk into the dark expanse beyond the window, she vowed, "The day after tomorrow, Teddy. The sun will come out the day after tomorrow."

April

"Salvation—it doesn't change who you are. It changes where you're going."

REVEREND LORAN LIVINGSTON

Chapter Thirteen

"I'm glad you could meet me here. It's so good to see you." The smile Maxine mustered felt like an old pair of jeans: faded, weathered, frayed at the edges.

Evelyn gently cupped the infant's head with her free hand and leaned back in the leather armchair. "It's good to be seen. You know, this is my first outing with Lauren. Thanks for the diapers, by the way. Who knows when I'll get around to writing you a note."

"Girl, please. Just your being here with me is thank you enough. I didn't want to be alone."

"The day after tomorrow" had arrived at its appointed time, but Teddy hadn't. When he'd canceled their date due to a family emergency, Maxine had reached out to Evelyn. From the spot Maxine had claimed by the door of the bookstore, she watched the rain pound the sidewalk, run in rivulets down the street, and swirl around the manhole covers.

"You did me the favor by inviting me. I was able to pick up some nighttime reading."

Maxine peeked at Evelyn's armload. "Ooh, *Guess How Much I Love You . . . Goodnight Moon . . . Owl Babies . . . Good Night Zoo . . . Kia Tanisha Drives Her Car . . . The Snowy Day . . . An American Marriage.* Okay, good choices for Lauren?"

Evelyn laughed. "Mama's gotta read, too."

Buzz. Buzz. She glanced down at her phone and frowned at the familiar number. "It's Teddy."

"While you take that, I'll go check out." Evelyn stood carefully, adjusting the baby in her cotton sling.

Maxine watched them go as she swiped to accept the call. "Teddy?"

"Hey, babe."

"How's your dad? Are you sure you don't need me?" She listened to him blow out a breath.

"I always need you."

Maxine smiled at his familiar answer. It was like the call and response in church.

"But no, you don't need to come to the hospital. Nothing seems broken from his fall, and right now he's getting blood work and X-rays to make sure everything's okay. Frankly, Dad could use this special attention, as expensive as it may be. Since Mother's still in New Orleans, it's mostly been the two of us this year—and you know where *my* attention is these days. It'll be good for him to get this checkup and have some father-son time. For me, too . . ." His voice petered out.

"You're so blessed to have each other, Teddy. Don't take it for granted."

"I don't. But I'm sorry about having to reschedule our talk."

"Oh, that."

"'Oh, that.' It didn't sound like 'Oh, that' the other day."

Maxine watched shoppers enter and exit the store. She gave Evelyn a thumbs-up as the new mother bounced and swayed in the queue. "No worries, Teddy. To me, even a little rain looks like a hurricane." She swallowed. "So what are your plans, exactly?"

"I'll call you tonight once I get the lay of the land, but I've already taken off next week. Maybe Dad and I will drive up to Asheville and visit the art shops there. Do the Biltmore thing. If the doctor gives him the all clear, I might even take him back home to New Orleans, see Mother, see some old friends, reconnect with my Creole roots. Shrimp étouffée goes a long way to heal what ails you."

"Do—?"

"I know what you're going to ask, but I think it's better if it's just him and me. I know you understand, hon. And don't worry about the wedding planning."

If he only knew. But Maxine couldn't—wouldn't—think about that now. "I'm just worried about you. And your father, of course. Since you don't want my company, is there anything I can do from here?"

"How about watering Dad's garden midweek?"

Maxine chuckled. "You know my thumb is brown, Teddy. I shouldn't go anywhere near his plants. Not if you want them to live."

"You're right. I'll ask his neighbor. Hmm . . . I know there was something I thought of while I was sitting here, and I put it in my notes so I wouldn't forget. Oh! For one, you'll need to talk to your grandparents about rescheduling our double date. And for two . . ."

Maxine listened to him think out loud. "Anything."

"Call Pastor Atwater. Let him know what's going on with Dad."

Anything but that, she almost said, but Teddy was off and away before she could find the words to gracefully decline.

Maxine frowned at the gray expanse beyond the window, for it seemed Teddy had taken the sun with him. Turning away from the dreary day, she studied the stacks and considered browsing for new authors but discarded the idea. No telling what book she'd go home with considering her mood.

Suddenly a dark, silky orb blocked her view. It took a second to register that it was actually a swath of Lauren's hair poking out from the sling. The rest of her body was swaddled in that swirl of green fabric across Evelyn's chest. Maxine rose from her seat, grateful for any distraction that delayed her call to Reverend Atwater.

"Is everything okay with Teddy?"

Maxine grimaced. "His dad took a fall, and he's with him at the hospital."

"I'm sorry." Evelyn stroked her baby's head as if to shield the tiny life from any negativity.

"Thanks. He says it's nothing that TLC and Creole food won't cure. So that's the good news. But they're going to take a father-son road trip. That's the bad news, for me anyway. Teddy's relationship with his dad is part of what I love most about him." Maxine shrugged, knowing she didn't have to explain to Evelyn, whose father had also died when she was a teen.

"My goodness. Lauren is too sweet," Maxine whispered, wincing at the unexpected pang.

"She's a treasure. I'd let you hold her, but—"

"Oh, no thanks! Don't get me wrong—I've been around my brothers and sister, and I know you don't wake a sleeping baby. Besides, I'd hate to give her the cooties."

"You're sick?" Evelyn took a step back. Again, her hand shielded the infant.

"No, no," Maxine reassured her friend. "I just mean she seems too new to share. How are you and Kevin adjusting?"

"Well, as you said, you've been around newborns—and you've spent time around parents with newborns. It's not all like this." She pointed toward her chest. Lauren squirmed a bit before settling. "But it's all good." Then she muttered, almost to herself, "Well, at least it's all better."

Evelyn glanced at her wrist and noted the hour, then looked out the window. "The sun is coming out. You have time to walk with me? When Mama heard I was coming to town, she asked me to meet her. I think she just wants to get her hands on Lauren and spirit us back home." The new mother slid a hot-pink crocheted cap over the baby's hair before plopping a waterproof hat on her own short, spiky do.

Anything but that, Maxine thought again, because suddenly she wanted to hide in a corner by herself. Before she knew it, however, she found herself walking out with Evelyn toward Headquarters, the salon owned by Elisabeth Willis, Evelyn's mother. Sure enough, the rain had stopped. She looped her purse over her shoulder and hooked her umbrella over her arm before she fell into step with her old friend, who didn't seem to be in much of a hurry as they sloshed through puddles up Main Street. Maxine was glad for her knee-length rain boots.

Evelyn readjusted the wriggling, whimpering baby. "Are you okay, Maxine? You haven't seemed like the old self I know and love, not for weeks."

Maxine smirked, thinking, *Not since I ran into your brother-in-law in Sassafras.*

"What's that snort all about?" Apparently satisfied she and the baby were safe from the elements, Evelyn reached into her pocket and withdrew a granola bar. She tore off the wrapper and chucked it into the nearest receptacle. "Yes, you. What's going on?"

Maxine moved aside to let a man and his dog pass. "I keep hearing that same old song. 'Maxine, you're not yourself.' Maybe this is really myself. Besides, aren't you the one who hates talking about her own problems?"

"Which my grandma pointed out to me is a problem in itself. Trust her to speak her mind." Evelyn spoke around her mouthful.

Maxine tacitly acknowledged the truth of her statement, for it wasn't until after Evelyn and Kevin had reconciled that she had learned Evelyn had separated from him for a time and the couple had nearly divorced during her pregnancy. "You know, Evelyn, Granny B is the only person who could get me to eat pimiento cheese sandwiches. Mama Ruby's friendship with her probably put ten pounds on me over the years, what with all that recipe swapping."

"You're trying to distract me, and I'm not going to fall for it, so spit it out." The baby started to wail. Without looking down—or missing a step—Evelyn wedged her snack between her teeth, readjusted Lauren, lifted a hidden flap on her shirt, and attached the baby.

Maxine tripped over a crack in the sidewalk.

"Hey, you. My face is up here," Evelyn snickered around a bite as she snapped her fingers. "You're as bad as Kevin."

Maxine nudged Evelyn's shoulder. "It's not you I'm looking at, smarty-pants. You're just really good at that mothering stuff. And she's so precious . . ." Maxine's voice was carried away by the breeze that swirled a strand of hair across her cheek.

The two women covered the next block in silence. Maxine left Evelyn to her snack and breastfeeding while she focused on dodging drips of water from store awnings and counting squares in the sidewalk. And remembering. She finally glanced to her left when a furniture truck rumbled by, and she intercepted Evelyn's look. Her girlfriend's lips were pressed together so tightly they paled around the edges. Maxine hastily feigned interest in an antique chifforobe displayed in a window they were passing.

A car horn broke the seal over Evelyn's mouth, and she took an audible breath. Words tumbled out into the water-logged air between them. "What's up with you and JD?"

Maxine rolled up all her bravado and used it like a megaphone. "There is no 'me and JD'! I'm engaged to Theodore Charles, remember?" *Teddy Bear.* She kicked away the thought as she did a rock under her foot.

"Maxine, it's me. You know that's not what I meant.

And I'm not pointing fingers. I only want you to know you don't have to hide anything from me. We can just skip the salad and the appetizer and get right to the main course." Evelyn plucked the baby from the sling, put her on her right shoulder, and patted her back gently. "Have you told your Theodore?"

Maxine almost said, "Yes," but when she looked at Evelyn, she could see Mama Ruby and Granny B shake their heads and advise, *Tell the truth and shame the devil.* She swallowed her lie and turned away from the windows they passed. "No. At least not yet. Not everything." Maxine belted her short trench coat. Despite the early spring warmth, she restrained a shiver. "I was going to talk to him today and 'let my burdens down,' as Reverend Atwater encouraged me to do. But then his dad fell."

"Well, that's a game changer." Evelyn tucked away Lauren and rubbed the baby's bottom through the sling.

Maxine planted her feet in front of the deli, so drained she couldn't walk another step. The metal *Boar's Head Meats* sign above her head swung to and fro in the breeze. "Who's been flapping their lips about this situation, Evelyn? As if I have to ask."

"No, you don't have to ask. Actually, Kevin and I talked about it, after JD talked to *him* about it. Have mercy, that sounds worse than a game of telephone." Evelyn grasped Maxine's hand and pulled her out of the way of two men hurrying toward the door. She guided Maxine to a bench in a small, grassy curve of the sidewalk. "I promise you we weren't gossiping. It's a husband-and-wife thing. We tend to share everything. Now, anyway." Evelyn shifted the baby to her other side as they sat but kept her eyes on Maxine all the while. "When Jay moved back—"

"I'm trying not to call him that."

"He's my brother-in-law, and I can call him what I want. 'A rose by any other name,' right?"

At that moment, nothing about this smelled sweet to Maxine. The situation reeked, fishier than the Bradford pear trees that bloomed every few yards. "Did he move back to punish me?"

As Evelyn peered into the distance, her eyes seemed to seek an answer that ducked and dodged. "No, he did not. But shame on us, Maxine. Shame on us! That girl has been calling me Auntie Evelyn all her life because you and I are best friends and she doesn't know I'm her real Aunt Evelyn. That my husband is really Uncle Kevin, not Mr. Kevin. And more importantly, of course, that you're her mother. I mean . . . *Maxine*."

Evelyn bounced the baby. "My Granny B toted around a secret almost all her days, and it drained the life out of her, out of the relationships with my aunts and uncles—and with me nearly. And you know what almost happened to Kevin and me."

Evelyn shook her head as if rebuking her husband. Or maybe to clear away a memory. Then she focused on Maxine, who was full of present woes. "That's what living a lie does. It affects generations. I'm not going to let that happen to this baby—or any other baby. Maybe you should be grateful JD came back and all this is coming out. How did you think you'd be able to live with this? I can't believe you've kept it secret all this time."

"Be grateful? You sound like First John! And nothing is 'coming out.' How can I tell her now, at thirteen? It gets harder and harder every day. JD legally gave up his rights to her, so technically he's no longer her father. I'm no longer her mother. We were too ill-equipped to raise a child, and I did what was best for her."

"But now, do you think you did it in the best way?" Evelyn rocked slowly side to side, moving her hand in circles on Lauren's back.

"What about now? You think I should disrupt Celeste's life because JD is all grown-up and regrets his decision and I'm getting married?"

"I don't know if it's regret as much as maturity. You're right. He was young and self-centered. And don't get me started on his mama, bless her heart. Mrs. Lester had her nose too high in the air. She still worries about appearances, even in the state she's in."

Maxine tilted her head back so that the weak sunlight peeking through the clouds wouldn't have to search for her face.

"I know Granny B warned me about sticking my nose in other folks' business, but how do *you* feel, Maxine? I sense your own struggle, and it has nothing to do with JD's return. You said you were meeting with Theodore to talk to him about it. Why, if the matter is said and done?"

"Because we're getting married. Didn't you just say that husbands and wives should share everything?" Maxine crossed her arms and leaned back, uncaring of the water soaking into her coat and pants.

Evelyn squeezed her hand. "So should mothers and daughters."

"Well, Celeste has a mother, and they do share everything. She has a father, too. JD wants to have a relationship with his long-lost daughter, but guess what? She's not lost. She's been here all the time."

Evelyn sat back then and wrapped her arms around Lauren.

Maxine sighed. "Maybe he came back to lay some type of claim on us . . . on *her* . . . but I'm not that person anymore, Evelyn. That girl who cut class. Who sneaked out of her parents' house to party. Who fell in love with a mysterious, cute guy and ran away from home. The person who gave up her daughter. That's not me. But that's who JD expects me to be."

"But you are that person, Maxine. That same woman who's sitting in front of me now, in her gray slacks and striped blouse and glasses, with her hair slicked back, wearing the cute red boots—that's the girl who once loved to skate on Monday nights in her Daisy Dukes and tube tops with her hair flying everywhere. I know, because I was skating beside you.

"You had a baby. Okay. I left my husband. Big whoop. Sure, those are huge, but my temper and your pregnancy don't make us terrible people in God's eyes. They make us who we are, part of the *forgiven*. The people He loves and who He died for. Our pasts make us who Kevin and Teddy—and yes, JD probably—love, too. They expect us to be just who we are. You can slap some paint on a house and make it all open concept inside, but it's still a house. Granny B proved that to me."

"Are you saying a person can't change?"

"Anybody can change. We're supposed to. But the past is another story, Maxine. JD is working on what he *can* change. He left that high-paying law firm in New York to head up a nonprofit in his hometown and help his mother because he's not the same boy who was all about gettin' his. No, he's not perfect. He hasn't thought this through, all the implications of returning here. What it will mean to Celeste. I think he's seeking reconciliation. Forgiveness."

"By causing more pain, more brokenness? This wholeness—it's not mine to give, Evelyn. And it's not ours to take away from Celeste. It's too late." Maxine's tears mixed with the mist from a passing cloud. "And how do you know this anyway?"

"You must have forgotten. Telling Kevin is the same as telling me." Evelyn opened her umbrella and held it over them.

"And is telling you the same as telling Kevin? And telling JD?"

"Well, I can tell you that baring your heart to all your faceless readers isn't the same as talking to the people who know and love you. Do you not trust us with yourself?"

Evelyn smiled and rubbed Maxine's shoulder in the silence. "I'll let you chew on this without my voice yammering away at you. I need to meet Mama anyway. She'd have a fit if she knew I had the baby out in this weather." She rose. "Have you talked to JD?"

Maxine stood slowly. "A little."

"Well, it sounds like you need to talk to him a lot." She embraced Maxine before she jumped back, exclaiming, "Oops, sorry, Lauren!" She made soothing noises over the squirming baby. "Pray about it, and then reach out to JD, Maxine. He'll be able to explain himself better than I can. Love you. We'll talk more later."

Afraid of that very thing, Maxine watched Evelyn look left, right, left, and then dart across the street toward the parking lot beside the glass-and-brick library. Frowning, Maxine opened her umbrella against the sprinkles forming bigger raindrops and gathering speed and splashed back toward her car.

Chapter Fourteen

THE DAYS INCHED BY WITHOUT TEDDY. Every second he was away felt like a nerve-racking stay of execution, a delay of the inevitable guillotine that was sure to drop. Like a teenager sneaking phone calls in the middle of the night, Maxine snuggled against her bed pillows and craned to hear Teddy describe his time in Louisiana with his parents. She thanked God for the news that Franklin was in good physical health, but she couldn't help but fret over the man's impact on her love life.

Her Life & Times editor seemed to think her personal pain directly correlated to her professional gain. At the end of their Saturday morning staff meeting, the editor propped her elbows on her desk and nodded at Maxine. "Keep it coming, all this angst. Your column is generating lots of buzz for the magazine. But stop cutting it so close to the deadline. You're giving me gray hairs." Jean ran her fingertips through the inch-long shock of white hair she kept slicked back from her round face.

But Maxine was only half-listening. She pictured her editor as she'd looked in last night's dream, dressed in a tailored, blush-pink suit, with a large white gardenia tucked behind her left ear—a far cry from the distressed denims and blazer she typically wore to work. Maxine struggled to untangle herself from the tendrils of what seemed a nightmare in the light of day. It clung to her as she feigned interest in the discussion around the conference table.

Maxine was all decked out in her wedding finery as she peeked through the diamond-shaped pane in the door. Each pew was filled to overflowing with well-dressed guests. A votive candle in a crystal holder sprouted from the tub of chrysanthemums blooming at each row, setting the church a-flicker with candlelight. Flower arrangements in the windowsills complemented the greens and golds of the stained glass. Maxine gripped her bouquet and turned to her escort as the last bridesmaid stepped into place at the altar. "I'm ready," she breathed.

At her words, the double doors whispered open and all the congregants turned to behold the bride. Is that Granny B? Look at Granddaddy in his tuxedo! Why won't the twins stand still? *She turned to her left, expecting to see First John in coat and tails, but instead a tall man in a wet suit extended an arm. "Let's go," he managed to offer around his snorkel and mask. Reluctantly Maxine took his neoprene-covered arm.*

As she put a white satin-tipped toe on the carpeted center aisle, she turned to smile at Jean and her gardenia, but the candle at the end of the row blew out. She moved to the next row, and again, a sudden breeze snuffed out the flame, and the ensuing darkness obscured the guests from view. Her escort uttered nary a word as they marched inexorably toward the altar. When Maxine tried to hang back, to discern familiar faces in the shadows, he dragged her forward.

By the time she landed at the front, the inky unknown had swallowed up the entire church. Only the attendants remained, three on one side and three on the other. She turned to hand her bouquet to Celeste, but her maid of honor disappeared in a poof, followed by Evelyn.

"What's happening?" she cried, reaching for Teddy. Her hand grasped nothing but air. She was alone, save for the man in the wet suit who now faced her at the altar, holding a Bible. "Where's everyone? Where did they all go? Teddy!"

Still holding open the Bible with one hand, the mysterious man used his other to reach under his mask and remove his snorkel. He read, "Neither has the Lord chosen this one."

Maxine snapped to attention as everyone gathered files and stood. She scooped up her materials, nodded goodbye to her editor, followed the others from the room, and wove through the cubicles toward the exit. Fed up with the pain and suffering related to the wedding hullabaloo, she dug out her phone and tapped out the ten digits she knew so well.

Maxine smiled when she heard the raspy voice on the other line. "Hey, dear! May I come over?"

Time had abandoned Ruby and Lerenzo's hometown. The only nod to its passage was a Walmart Supercenter that had erupted on an old cornfield, right past the sign that read *Spring Hope City Limits*. Three stoplights broke up Main Street's amble through a place where people ate fried pork chop dinners at the Skillet, shopped for nail polish and wigs at Peggy's, and bought liver pudding and mother of vinegar at the Piggly Wiggly.

Maxine's tires kicked off pebbles as they crunched on one of the side roads, passing large craftsman-style houses families had been handing down for generations. Only a rare soul blindly put a finger on the map and opted to make Spring Hope home. Dirt-covered offshoots wiggled between squat one-story houses, fields, woods, vine-covered abandoned cottages, and knee-high weeds littering yards that had given up the fight to survive.

She had spent nearly two years in her grandparents' historic farmhouse, splitting her time between their kitchen and the front room at Granny B's, two streets over on Carrot Lane. Both Ruby and Beatrice, one related to Maxine by blood, the other by spirit, had plied her with fried fish, fresh corn, sweet tea, stories, prayer, and wisdom. Maxine sighed as she turned onto the gravel drive and pulled behind the house. She was starving.

"Hey there! You just missed Roy. Where you been keepin' yourself?" Mama Ruby—tall, solid, softhearted—enveloped Maxine the minute she slammed her car door.

She rose up on her toes to wrap her arms around her grandma's neck.

After a moment, Ruby pulled back and held Maxine at arm's length. "What's the matter, child?"

"I've just missed you and Granddaddy."

After peering at her a second or two longer, her grandma's chocolaty hand wrapped around Maxine's, and they worked their way toward the wide steps. As they walked, Mama Ruby pointed out the flowers, vegetables, and fruit trees growing out back.

Maxine *tsked-tsked* about the rabbits nibbling on the squash and the stink bugs attacking the tomato vines. She nodded at talk of the fresh corn, blueberry bushes, and the pies and cobblers planned for the summer. By the time they clambered up to the side porch and opened the screen door, she had caught enough bits and pieces about planting to make up for all the meatier chunks of the conversation she had missed. Maxine already felt better, and the smells wafting from the kitchen soothed all her hurt feelings.

"Mmmm. Is that—?"

"Banana pudding." She crooked a finger toward the double ovens. Like Vivienne, Ruby had transformed her kitchen into a chef's paradise, the only updated space in the house.

"Can I help you with anything?"

"Only with eatin' it. And ignore Lerenzo's mess. Since we already had all the ingredients to make his pork roast with you and Theodore, we decided to go on ahead with it." Mama Ruby waved at the oregano, garlic, orange, and lime on the countertop. She moved the bottle of cooking sherry and set out utensils.

"God must have told you I was coming." Maxine found a seat.

Mama Ruby took the pudding from the oven and set it on the counter. It was a concoction of flour, eggs, heavy cream, and vanilla extract that she stirred for nearly thirty minutes before she layered it between cookies and bananas. Then she baked it to brown the meringue. Ruby dug into the topping and delivered a heaping bowlful to the table. "I was keepin' it warm in the oven until I was ready for it. You know I like to eat my dessert first 'cause I might not live long enough to eat it last."

Maxine waited until her grandma had her own serving before biting into a softened vanilla wafer. "This is yummy. I don't know why everybody else likes their pudding cold when they could eat this. And just what I need to warm up."

"Warm up? It's not chilly out there. What's ailin' you?"

Maxine ruminated on her answer.

The back door opened and slapped shut behind a man with gold-kissed skin. His salt-and-pepper shoulder-length waves were pulled back in a leather hair tie, so nothing hid the creases on his cheeks and forehead, gifts from years in the sun.

"Granddaddy!" She dropped her spoon in her half-empty bowl and trotted over to him.

Lerenzo's slight build didn't prevent him from rearing back and lifting his granddaughter's feet off the ground. As a boy, he had toiled in Cuba's sugarcane fields alongside his parents before they spirited him away to the United States. By the time he was twenty-five, he had traveled from Florida to North Carolina and was topping corn in the fields edging Spring Hope. A few decades later, he was planting and harvesting crops on his own farmland, and at seventy-five, he was running Manna Catering and getting paid to cook what his family produced—the sequel to his hardworking success story.

"Ah . . . *preciosa. Cómo estás?*"

"Hmm . . ." Maxine shrugged. *"No importa."*

"It's important if it's somethin' to do with you." Mama Ruby offered her two cents around a mouthful of wafers.

Maxine patted her grandfather's hand as they got comfortable at the table big enough to hold six salsa dancers. "Have some banana pudding with Mama Ruby and me, and we can talk about it."

Lerenzo eyed her before he sighed and accepted a steaming bowl.

Maxine watched him enjoy his first spoonful before she took a deep breath. "JD moved back." They knew all about Celeste's birth, so she made short work of her tale. The end.

Lerenzo pushed away his nearly full bowl. "Will you talk to him?"

Perhaps his soft accent made his question somewhat more palatable. Maxine actually considered the possibility this time instead of rejecting it outright. "What do you think I should do, Granddaddy?"

He glanced at Ruby. Then he ran a gnarled index finger along the rim of his glass dish. "You know, *mi nieta preciosa . . .*"

Maxine smiled a little as his voice faded. She didn't feel like his "precious granddaughter" with the enormity of her burden.

"I was never able to introduce you to your *bisabuelos,* but oh, if you could have traveled to Cuba to meet them! The stories they could've told you about *tu abuelo*. Ah . . ." He and his wife chuckled together. *"Recuerdas cuando me caí en la letrina de mi papá?"*

"*La letrina* . . . outhouse . . . remember when you fell in the outhouse?" Maxine stared at her grandparents, open-mouthed. "What? Why? When?"

"I was four, maybe five. Old enough to remember."

"Like you could forget that smell." Mama Ruby's nose wrinkled. "Girl, when your grandfather told me that story, I liked to fell over myself. I didn't want to kiss him for a week, all those years later!"

"Mmm-mwah!" Lerenzo sat back, pleased with himself after grabbing his wife's face with both hands and planting a wet kiss on her lips. He gave her another smooch before he turned back to his granddaughter and his story. "I was a little rascal in those days."

"You're still a little rascal."

"Hush, woman," he growled. *"Pero es la verdad.* And it was true then, too. My brothers never could keep up with me. That day, when I got away from them, I ran into the outhouse to hide, and I fell into that dirty hole. Whew-wee! They wore me out."

"My great-grandparents? *Mis bisabuelos?*"

"*No. Mis hermanos!* My brothers had to clean me up. And when they did, whew. Believe me, that was the last time I played that dirty trick." He laughed out loud, obviously still relishing the memory, as offensive as it was to the senses. "And you know who reminds me now of me then?"

"Uncle Roy?" Her grandparents' younger child was

Lerenzo's spitting image. Maxine's uncle even wore his hair pulled back into a low ponytail like his father.

Lerenzo's laughter was so full he reared back in his chair to enjoy it. He nodded. "*Sí sí, claro*. Of course, Roy. He looks like me, but *mi nieto* Roberto acts like me. My grandson is always doing something for attention, finding trouble instead. I've talked to him about my own shenanigans, and I think it helps him to know he shares something with his *abuelo*. Comforts him."

"Gives him ideas is more like it." Mama Ruby took their bowls to the sink.

Maxine locked eyes with her grandfather. "I get the feeling this is more than a story about you falling into some poop."

Lerenzo shrugged in his usual exaggerated fashion, raising his palms on either side.

She pushed back her chair. "Let me help you, Mama Ruby."

"Child, I don't need your help. I finally started usin' this dishwasher, and it's done me a heap-a good. What I need you to do is listen to your grandfather. Learn somethin'." Ruby loaded the rinsed bowls.

"How to use an outhouse?" Maxine fiddled with the spices on the counter.

"Don't be sassy. It ain't becomin'."

"Yes, ma'am." Maxine ducked her head.

"He's talkin' about the blessin' of knowin' your family, of talkin' to your grands and great-grands one day, and affectin' their lives. Lerenzo's parents missed out on that. I got to talk to 'em, but I never saw 'em face-to-face. They missed out on holdin' Viv and Roy. As much as you love hearin' these stories about your granddaddy, imagine gettin' 'em firsthand from your great-grandparents. *Tus bisabuelos*." She raised one brow in her husband's direction.

Maxine couldn't help but grin along with Lerenzo at the way her grandma's accent smothered his native language.

"Yes, we have been blessed. To not only hear those stories, but to connect 'em to the man he is today—to how you became my grandbaby. Smart mouth and all." Mama Ruby closed the dishwasher and rested both hands on the counter. "This is Celeste's heritage, too. A rich one, and only half of it."

I'm not much of a prize, and from what Mother says, neither is Annie Lester. Maxine tried not to imagine JD's mother, but she clearly saw the implication of her grandma's words.

Ruby donned oven mitts as she peeled off the gloves with her granddaughter. "I don't know why we're all actin' like this is somethin' new under the sun, 'cause it ain't. In my day, we said a girl was in trouble. The grandparents raised the baby, and she moved on. Nieces and nephews was raised as sisters and brothers. Sisters and brothers was really cousins. Folks knew. Life moved on." She set a thirteen-by-nine-inch dish on a trivet and reached for a long fork.

"That sounds like my day, too, Mama Ruby." Maxine leaned on the counter.

Ruby poked the baked sweet potatoes. "But you're not 'in trouble,' Maxine. You don't have nuthin' to be ashamed of."

"I'm ashamed of living a lie now, but I'm not ashamed of having Celeste. Not now, not really then. That's not why First John and Mother raised her as theirs. I just wanted . . ."

"*Qué?* What did you want?" Lerenzo gripped Maxine's shoulder.

"I wanted her to feel secure. Taken care of. I thought she'd find a real home with them, not with me. Have the love I kept searching for but couldn't hold on to. I wasn't enough, and I wanted more for her. But now . . . it's too late to go back. I can't shake her foundation because I'm struggling. Again. Still."

"What do you mean you weren't enough, *preciosa*? Of course you were. You are."

Precious. Whenever Lerenzo called her precious, Maxine always imagined herself standing by the window on a sunny winter day. She could feel the rays on her face, but the light wasn't strong enough to warm her all the way through to the bone. It was just enough to knock off the chill and make her eyelids flutter.

She kissed her grandfather's hand. "Mother didn't think so, or she never would have campaigned so hard to adopt her."

"Vivienne had her own burdens. Don't carry her load, child." Ruby hung the mitts on a hook by the stovetop. "You're fearfully and wonderfully made—don't forget that."

Maxine soaked up the aroma of the sweet potatoes but turned up a nose to her grandmother's application of Psalm 139, though she respected her enough to acknowledge the one and remain silent on the other. "Are you making a cobbler or a casserole?"

"Child, you best not act like you didn't hear me. Regret is a bitter root to chew on, let me tell you."

"I did hear you, Mama Ruby. I'm taking time to process it all."

Beside Maxine, Lerenzo murmured, "Mmm-hmmm."

The older woman peered at Lerenzo and then at her granddaughter. "I don't see what's to process. You young people today talk about *your* truth and what's real to *you*. Don't you know it's either true and real, an opinion or a lie? Truth don't change. It don't need to be processed, just believed and accepted. I can tell you still after somethin', but you never gon' stop searchin' for more if you don't know you already got it."

Based on past experience, Maxine knew this was no time to argue. She murmured, "Yes, ma'am," and kept it moving.

Ruby sighed as if accepting that this was a battle to fight another day. "While you're being so agreeable, why don't you tell us the real reason you're down here today since you canceled your plans with Theodore. Lerenzo, you want to get that roast out?"

"Woman, just say, 'Lerenzo, take out the meat.' Why must you pretend it's my idea?" When his wife bumped him with her considerable hip as he rounded the island, his laughter curtailed his muttering.

Maxine smiled at their antics. "I came down today because I thought I'd get away from thinking about Celeste and the wedding, but I should've known better. And I canceled our double date since the other half of my double couldn't make it. I'm sad you're going to make it without us."

Lerenzo's eyes skittered to Ruby's. The older woman shrugged.

"What?" Maxine looked from one to the other.

"Well . . ." Her grandmother looked around her as the screen door rattled against the wood frame.

Maxine turned to see long brown fingers pressing against the tiny wire squares.

"JD, you gon' stretch my screen. Get in here!"

Chapter Fifteen

THE FINGERS DISAPPEARED, and the door swung back.

Maxine noticed his teeth first. Yet his smile wasn't for her. JD made that plain when he stepped into the kitchen and embraced Mama Ruby without a glance in Maxine's direction.

"Mama Ruby," he murmured against the older woman's cheek. He reached out and clasped Lerenzo's hand.

Ruby pulled back and rapped his forehead. Then she planted a big kiss where her knuckle had been. "Boy, I hear you been causin' some trouble."

"Mama Ruby." Maxine's low voice tried to stop her grandma in her meddlesome tracks.

"James Dee knows how I'm made."

Lerenzo laughed. "I've always told you this woman is like

a broken refrigerator. She can't hold *nada*. Nothing." He squeezed the younger man's shoulder. "James Dee, it does my heart good to see you."

Everybody in her family had a special name for JD, and her grandparents were no different. Maxine realized she'd have to accept he'd always be family, something Celeste had cemented for them. While Vivienne had never welcomed him to her kitchen table, JD was free to pull up a seat at Ruby's to eat ham hocks and greens, butter beans and neck bones, biscuits and gravy. He helped her uncle pluck weeds in the garden, toted watermelons and pumpkins to their fruit stand, and shelled peas—whatever the older couple needed done. He'd even mowed the lawn when Lerenzo and Roy were down with the flu.

But it wasn't doing Maxine's heart any good to see him standing in their kitchen today. She waved limp fingers in greeting.

JD grimaced, looking like he had an upset stomach, and waved back. "I gather you've been taking my name in vain."

Mama Ruby's smile raised the temperature of the room a notch or two. "Not so, because here you stand. Maxine was supposed to spend the day makin' pork roast and sweet potato cobbler with Lerenzo, but we thought she wasn't gon' make it. Now you're both here."

Maxine slapped her forehead. "So he's the reason for the banana pudding and the sweet potatoes! Shoulda known, since sweet potato cobbler is his favorite. I thought you were expecting Uncle Roy."

Ruby's clipped tone sliced through the air. "*I'm* the reason I cook anything. Nobody's makin' me do nuthin', 'cept the good Lord." She turned to her husband. "I see you still didn't get the roast out, Lerenzo."

He sighed. "And you're the reason I do most things. I see you're not asking this time."

Maxine waved her grandfather back and opened the refrigerator to retrieve the large foil-wrapped lump. She needed to do something more productive than search for words.

"We was gon' teach Maxine how to make Lerenzo's secret pork."

"No, Mama Ruby. You were going to teach Theodore and me how to make it." She peeled back the foil.

"*Así es.*" Lerenzo nodded, setting the covering aside.

"Ah, yes, the mysterious Teddy Bear," JD murmured.

"*No es misterioso. Es su prometido.*" Her grandfather arranged the bottles of spices around the platter of meat.

"That's right. What's mysterious about my fiancé?"

"What is this about a teddy bear?" Mama Ruby sniffed the orange.

JD laughed. "I guess that's some of the trouble you were talking about before I got here. That's my nickname for Maxie's . . . betrothed."

"How can you have a nickname for somebody you never met?" Mama Ruby pointed to a small drawer by the range. "Maxine, get me the measurin' spoons and that small grater."

"Exactly! Jay thinks he knows all about Teddy, and he's never so much as shaken his hand. Mama Ruby, since when did you start using measuring spoons? I didn't even know you owned any."

"I know enough." JD pulled out a seat at the kitchen table.

"You don't know anything—including the recipe for my

cerdo asado. Son, you might as well get up. *Levántate.*" Lerenzo flicked his fingers in the younger man's direction. "The last time you were here, I was beating you in a game of chess, but this time, you and Maxine are doing some cooking."

"That's why you're gettin' those spoons. I don't use 'em because I know my way round the kitchen. You two, on the other hand . . ." Ruby laughed.

"*We're* cooking?" Maxine looked from JD to her grandfather. "Why?"

Lerenzo shrugged. "Well, that was the plan at first."

"Again, the plan was to cook with Theodore, not with Jay."

"Where is Teddy Bear?"

Maxine tried to sear a hole in JD's forehead with her eyes.

He met her glare, looking as cool—and as tart—as the bowl of lemons her grandfather pulled from the refrigerator.

Mama Ruby stepped between the two younger people and plopped a weathered book on the island. She leafed through its pages, landing on one with a large red splatter across the gutter. "Look here, while you're both in my kitchen and got the time, make yourself useful. Take this recipe. If you can read, you can cook. Not like me, mind you, 'cause God intended for me to bless people with my food. But with a little love, it can't help but be good. Your mama proved that.

"Maxine." Ruby dragged her granddaughter's index finger to the first item on the recipe. "See here? It says wash the roast and remove the fat. But I'm tellin' you to leave some for flavor, so don't cut it all off." She stuck a paring knife in JD's left hand. "Now once she's done, score that pork like this." She made slicing motions in the air. "Me and Lerenzo gon' work on pecans until it's time to make the cobbler. You two best behave. Those are the only nuts I plan to crack in my kitchen."

Maxine and JD glanced at each other before nodding in concert at Mama Ruby.

"Good. We'll be sittin' over at the table if y'all have any questions." She stalked to a tall paper bag by the back door. "Lerenzo, honey pot, would you *please* get two bowls and the nutcracker while I get the pecans?" She winked at her granddaughter.

JD touched Maxine's elbow and gestured toward the meat on the counter. "Well, do you think we can do this, make *cerdo asado*?"

"Without killing each other, you mean?" She turned on the faucet and risked a quick look toward the table. Mama Ruby was reaching into a sack full of papershell pecans. Lerenzo already had a small pile beside his own stainless steel bowl. "I don't think we have a choice. Do you need an apron? I'd hate for you to get something on your clothes."

He glanced down, presumably to compare his burgundy cotton hoodie and his wrinkle-free khaki joggers with her pink-and-gray sweat suit. "You're looking mighty cute yourself. If you're okay, I'm okay."

Maxine busied herself with turning on the water and picking up the roast to hide her flush. "Don't say I didn't warn you."

A few minutes later, JD had cut tiny slices across the rinsed and dried pork. "What's next?"

She consulted the cookbook. "How about I work on making a paste out of these spices Granddaddy set out, and you slice the onions and layer them in the pan? It's—"

"Over the refrigerator. I remember." JD opened the upper cabinet doors.

"And don't forget to tuck some slivers in the meat *after* you give that roast some love! Really work it in with your hands," Ruby piped up from the table. The older woman set a trash can between her and Lerenzo, put a nut between her teeth, and commenced to cracking.

"Shh, woman! I thought they were supposed to be doing this *sin ayuda*. No help from you. If they need us, they'll ask." Lerenzo squeezed her shoulder.

Ruby slapped his hand. "I know, I know. But a little *ayuda* goes a long way when it comes time to eat. You'll thank me later."

"How about I thank you now?" He leaned over and kissed her cheek.

Still fresh after sixty years. Maxine smiled to herself.

JD set the heavy cast-iron pan on the counter and separated onion rings before arranging them on the bottom. He set a few slices by her. "Here you go. Or do you want me to tuck those in?"

She shook her head. "I've got it, but you can measure one-third cup orange juice. Then the directions say to squeeze the lime and the lemon into it."

He pointed to the grater. "Don't forget to zest the orange before I squeeze it."

"Oh, that's right! I was supposed to add that to the paste. Grab the sherry, too. Stir in a half cup with that." Maxine laughed when he squirted lemon juice into his eye.

"Oh, you think that's funny?" He aimed the fruit in her direction.

ROBIN W. PEARSON

She raised her arm defensively. "You wouldn't aim at a girl wearing glasses, would you?"

"If I remember your prescription correctly, they're more like safety goggles."

"Ooh, you got jokes now." Maxine focused on grating the orange peel so she wouldn't scrape her knuckles.

"No, I just wish I was wearing them when I sliced these onions. They made me cry like a baby." He swiped at the tip of his nose. "Ugh, now my hands will smell like this for the next two days."

"Not if you scrub them with lemon juice and sugar. Remember how Mama Ruby showed us? I'll help you after you pour that onto the roast."

JD whisked the sherry into the citrus juice mixture, then coated the meat. Then Maxine sprinkled a scoop of sugar and squeezed the remains of a lemon over his hands.

"Scrub them for a couple minutes before you rinse it off. That'll cut the onion odor."

JD sniffed his hand. "Better already."

Crack. Crack. Crack.

Maxine pointed at the nutcracker, forgotten on the table between her grandparents. "When are y'all going to start using one of those?"

Crack. Crack. Crack.

"Or imagine how fast you could go with an electric nut-cracker!"

"And then I couldn't sit outside or at my kitchen table. My teeth go with me wherever I go." Ruby blew shells into the trash can. "Faster isn't always better. You just make a mess in shorter time. Y'all just focus on getting that roast

TIL I WANT NO MORE

into the refrigerator, and leave me to my pecans." *Crack. Crack. Crack.*

"Why the refrigerator and not the oven?" Maxine stowed spices into the pantry.

Lerenzo brushed some shells off the table and into his hands as he rose. "Because it needs to marinate so the flavors can go all through it, *nieta*. We'll baste it the rest of the day and slide it into the oven tonight. Usually we prepare it late in the evening and cook it nice and slow the next morning." He tore off a long sheet of foil and handed it to JD. "Cover it tightly before you slide it in the refrigerator. You didn't know all that went into my *cerdo asado*, huh?"

Maxine smirked. "You've always prided yourself on keeping the recipe a secret."

Ruby chuckled. "Well, now you're ready to learn. And don't you worry. We'll add a touch of this and that once your back is turned. We didn't tell you everything. That roast is like a marriage, which you'll see for yourself one day. A lot goes into it, things you can't anticipate or know about ahead of time—sweet, sour, savory. All that work makes your life together into somethin' go-o-od, let me tell you."

She set their bowls of cracked nuts on the counter. "But jump into things before you're ready to learn? Leave out some ingredients? Don't take off enough fat or leave too much? Cut corners and don't put in the time you should? The flavor won't be as rich."

"Point made. I get it, Mama Ruby. What I won't get is some of this roast we slaved over." Maxine desperately wanted to change the subject.

"Not unless y'all come back tomorrow." Mama Ruby washed and dried her hands.

"Not without her Teddy Bear, I'm sure." JD closed the refrigerator with a thunk.

A molten flow of words threatened to erupt as Maxine rounded on JD. Firm fingers squeezed her shoulder and backed her up a step as they bubbled to the surface.

"Maxine, you ready to make the cobbler? I don't have a recipe for this, but you aren't a stranger to it. Get the flour, sugar, and shortenin'. James Dee, look in that cabinet over there for the cinnamon, allspice, salt, and vanilla extract. We'll make the dough for the double crust and then let it chill while you slice up the sweet potatoes. I'll get the butter."

"I never knew why you don't boil the potatoes. I'd think that was easier." JD moved bottles around in the cabinet.

"Well, you'd think wrong," Maxine chided him. "Boiling them zaps a lot of flavor, so Mama Ruby only uses boiled potatoes when she's making candied yams."

"Child, what's wrong with you?" Mama Ruby propped a hand on her hip.

Lerenzo pushed open the screen door leading to the backyard. "James Dee, *ayúdame por favor*. I need help with something in the shed."

JD set down his armload and followed his host. "I'm just stepping on toes in here anyway. Or getting my own crushed."

The two women watched them go. "Maxine, what's on your mind? And don't tell me, 'Nuthin', Mama Ruby.' You tried to change the subject earlier, but I'm not havin' it."

Maxine twirled the utensils set out beside the sweet potatoes. "I'm fine, really."

"*Fine* is a good word for that man out there with your grandfather. Fine as wine. But I wouldn't use that word to describe your mood right now."

"Mama Ruby!"

"You know it same as I do." She ran her yellowed finger-nail along the skin of a cooled potato and peeled it. "I've never had nuthin' against that child. Hasn't he always done right by me and Lerenzo?"

"But not by me." Maxine used a butter knife to slit her own potato, but at her grandmother's look she amended her response. "Yes, ma'am."

"I appreciate his comin' by here, checkin' on us. We're still family, so I don't see why you're so put out."

"He didn't tell me."

"He's supposed to?"

Maxine focused on discarding the last of the peel.

"Just what I thought. He's my family, too. Ain't that right?"

"I suppose you can put it that way, but—"

"Butts are for sittin' on, not standin' there, tellin' me who I can see and who I can't. And there's no other way to put it."

"I keep forgetting where Mother gets her particular words of wisdom." Maxine went back to work, scooping out flour for the crust. "I'm not trying to dictate JD's comings and goings. I'm only saying it would've been nice to know he'd be here."

"Well, now you know. I didn't even know *you* were comin'. So when you said you and Theodore couldn't be here, we thought to see James Dee now that he's come back home."

"But what if I'd brought Celeste with me?"

"You didn't. So no need to talk about what-ifs. It was like no time had passed, watchin' James Dee season that roast—"

"When I got here, you asked me what was wrong, but you already knew, didn't you?" Maxine cut cold butter into the dry ingredients.

"I just thought him comin' back would stir up things for you. Not just for Celeste. For you. How you feelin'?"

"I'm feeling engaged to Theodore, that's how."

"Chile, stop foolin' with all that." Mama Ruby's hands closed over Maxine's as she was forming the dough into a ball. "Now I know you're engaged, but that don't stop your heart from beatin' a little faster when it comes to James Dee."

"Are you saying you can love two people at the same time?"

"Are you sayin' you still love James Dee?"

Maxine withdrew her hands from the protective cover of her grandma's and opened the long drawer in front of her. She unrolled plastic wrap from the box she'd retrieved to cover the dough ball and walked it to the refrigerator. "I'm saying I need to get going. I promised Celeste I would listen to her practice her solo, and I have an article to write."

"Maxine."

"As much as I'd love to have some cobbler, y'all will have to finish up without me. Maybe I'll swing by tomorrow for some *cerdo asado* and leftover dessert. That is, if Uncle Roy doesn't polish off everything after church." She clasped her grandmother by the shoulders and kissed her papery-soft cheek.

Ruby grabbed one of her hands with both of hers before she could make a getaway. "Maxine Owens. You're as mule-headed as your mama. Sweeter, but just as muleheaded. You ain't stupid though. You know only God controls the twists and turns of the river and the minds and hearts of kings and children. I can't tell you who to love. But I do know fussin' don't change nuthin', and you can't run from it. You only gon' take your heart with you when you go." She kissed her granddaughter's fingers and released them.

Feeling anything but free, Maxine stared at Mama Ruby for a moment before stumbling through the kitchen and out the front door.

Chapter Sixteen

ALL THE CRUMBS LED TO JAMES LESTER, so Monday afternoon, Maxine followed them. Rather than march up to his office and plop down in the middle of his desk, she opted to wait for JD on a shaded bench across the street from Hillsong. Maxine withdrew her laptop from her bag but soon became mesmerized by the sway of the oak tree's leafy branches.

Watching the movement of their shadows on the brick pavers catapulted her thoughts to those long-ago Saturdays when Mama Ruby would drive Maxine into Mount Laurel to shop and pay her telephone and utility bills. Ruby didn't trust debit cards or paying by the mail. She preferred to look folks in the eye when they handled her money. Maxine figured her grandma took such joy in catering because she could witness her clients' satisfaction when they took a bite or returned an empty plate.

From her vantage point across the street, Maxine searched for life in the newly remodeled home of Hillsong, what was once the department store where Mama Ruby shopped for Maxine's school clothes. Pink and white azaleas and variegated hostas sprouted from planters placed every few feet around the white-brick building. Butterflies and bees flitted and buzzed about the vegetation, serving as the outreach center's only visitors, since most people had streamed from the community center and other downtown businesses an hour earlier. Just as she decided to pack up her laptop to head home, out strolled JD. No strutting this time.

He was no unsophisticated nineties sitcom star in his light-blue shirt, burgundy paisley tie, and pin-striped navy slacks. A suit coat draped over the crook in one arm, he walked shoulder to shoulder with a curvy woman with skin the color of amaretto and a smile nearly as sweet. JD's head dipped in her direction as her lips moved, his leather messenger bag bumping against his knee. He mouthed something in return and her lips opened wide, sending laughter skipping across the street.

Suddenly Maxine's last-minute decision to confront JD seemed rash, ill-conceived. She tried to blend into the wooden planks of her seat, feeling sticky and bedraggled from the day's heat that dripped toward evening. She brushed at her limp dress and ran her tongue over the cracked remains of her lipstick. Maxine sucked in a breath and held it as she stowed her laptop in its sleeve and calculated how to get to her car without being seen.

She risked a glance at the couple, who had stopped to converse at the corner. She adjusted a shoulder strap and quick-stepped it to the parking lot. Usually she took care to set her backpack on the passenger seat or even in a bin in the trunk, but today she opened the driver door and threw it across the seat, where it bounced onto the floor. She put a foot inside the car.

"Maxine?"

She gulped down her throaty cry of frustration as she released the wheel and ordered her legs to stand. Trying to surreptitiously smooth her wrinkled hemline, she managed a hoarse "Hey-y-y."

"What are you doing here?" JD set down his bag and shifted his jacket to his shoulder as he moved closer.

Maxine stepped back until her legs bumped against the car. When she couldn't come up with a synonym for "I was looking for a puff of smoke to vanish into," she settled for saying nothing at all.

The vision beside JD extended French-tipped fingers. "Hi, I'm Heather."

Though she wanted to run and hide at the freshness of JD's companion, Maxine reached back out of reflex, for Vivienne's blood ran through her veins. "H-hello. I'm—"

"Maxine, from what I hear."

Silence engulfed them. They shuffled their feet and glanced at each other, at the black-and-white mural of past city leaders on the brick building facing the lot, and back again.

Finally Heather took a step backward. "Well, I guess I'll mosey along to my car. My boys will be waiting for me.

Maxine, it was great to meet you finally. Our own local celebrity! I love your column, by the way. Brings back memories of my own over-the-top wedding." She turned to JD. "See you. Have fun tonight."

JD murmured, "Thanks, Heather. Later."

Maxine watched her crunch away on the gravel lot before she turned toward JD. "Hey! What are you laughing at?"

"Not what. Who. And when did you start adding prepositions to the end of your sentences, Miss Grammar Queen?"

Maxine wanted to punch him in the shoulder that had recently brushed against the mysterious Heather. "You caught me off guard, that's all. I still don't see what's so funny."

"You know what. Jealous much?"

"Jealous?" Maxine's bluster was stronger than the faint waft of air lifting the damp tendrils on her nape.

"Forget it, Maxie. Why are you here? You ran off after our cooking lesson with your grandparents, so I assumed I'd seen the last of you for a while." JD shifted from one foot to the other. He gripped the top of the driver's door with one hand and braced the other against the car.

Maxine felt trapped within the triangle of space. She tucked a strand of hair behind her ear and parted her lips.

JD shook his head. "Uh-uh, nope. Think again."

"What are you talking about?"

"Whatever you thought about *not* telling me, think again. Tell me what's really on your mind, not some reinvention." He looked at the blue face of the large watch on his wrist. "I should be on my way to the Y right now, so out with it."

"The Y?" Maxine grasped at the slim straw he offered and released the breath she didn't know she was holding.

"The reading program. I listen to the beginners. It starts in about twenty minutes, and I'd hoped to change shirts and grab a bite on the way." He glanced at his watch again. "Well, maybe not."

Maxine made a quick decision. "I'll go with you, and we can talk in the car. I mean, if you don't mind." She looked down at her rumpled dress and listened to the weighty pause, so large and heavy it seemed to crowd the air between them. She could barely breathe. "I'm a mess, I know," she whispered.

"You're a vision. As always."

But he didn't linger over his huskily voiced words. Instead, he cleared his throat, retrieved his worn bag, and marched toward his car. As if he expected her to follow.

Which she did, but not until she grabbed her cell and the small purse she'd tucked under the seat.

JD led her to a road-hugging canary-yellow Porsche. After he started the car, he popped the trunk and stowed his things inside.

"Whoa, Jay! In your favorite color, no less!" Maxine tried to whistle but gave up after only managing a breathy *whrrrr*. She caressed the hood.

"I see you still can't whistle," JD laughed. He rounded the car and opened the passenger door.

As she walked toward him, Maxine felt like she had taken a sip from an *Alice in Wonderland* tumbler marked "Drink Me." She felt smaller and smaller until she was but a tiny reflection in his pupil. At last, she looked away, into the yawning darkness of the car's interior. Then with one—final?—glance back at the parking lot, she sank into the butter-soft seat that smelled like JD's cologne.

Maxine closed her eyes after he slammed her door and kept them shut even when he climbed in seconds later. The Porsche reversed and surged forward. Maxine relaxed to the low, steady snarl of the car's engine as JD rounded curves and turns. By the time the car purred to a stop, her eyelids felt weighed down. Blinking slowly, Maxine emerged from her half-dozing, half-wakeful state and smiled when she broke through to the surface.

JD was facing her. "So much for our talk on the way, Sleeping Beauty. I hope you're rested because once we step inside, it is on. No quiet reading time for these kids."

Maxine rotated her shoulders and sat straight in her seat. She looked around her admiringly. "When did you get rid of the truck? I thought it was your baby." Immediately she wished she could retract her words.

JD's face softened. "I didn't, and she still is. Blue is parked at my parents' house because New York isn't the best place for a vintage truck. She's been waiting for me to come back all these years." This time, he himself winced.

I know what you're thinking, Jay. How can I tell you that? Maxine dared to reach across the console, but before her fingers touched his arm, her phone buzzed. She jumped and fumbled with the zipper of her bag.

Teddy Bear. She squashed the forbidden name as she pressed Decline and returned her iPhone to her purse. "Ready?" she asked on a breath.

"Are you?"

"Lead the way!" She stepped from the car. But at the door of the YMCA, the tumult of voices, bodies, and activity swelled over Maxine. She froze.

"See? I tried to warn you. This isn't like any reading program you've ever heard of, is it?" JD spoke over the melee.

Maxine took it all in. Truly, there wasn't much literary going on. Children ran in circles, hurled Cheetos at each other, and raised the roof with their voices. She took a step back as JD's hand pushed her forward. She felt him press close. His breath tickled her ear.

"I started volunteering here to get plugged into the needs of our community. To learn about them firsthand so I can figure out how Hillsong can make a difference in these kids' lives. I don't just want to listen to them read, teach them to sit still, or guard the holding cell until their parents pick them up."

Abruptly JD made a noise like he was spitting out lemon seeds. He pinched a long hair between his fingers. "You've changed your shampoo. Smells nice."

Maxine, her face warm, moved deeper into the "holding cell."

JD scooted around her and bumped fists with a girl with uneven pigtails. She grinned so widely her eyes closed, and he congratulated her on a missing tooth. The sea of children parted as he waded through, high-fiving some, pointing at others, calling each by name.

Maxine trailed him, lost in his wake, marveling at his obvious popularity and sincere care of them. She looked down when she felt a soft hand squeeze hers.

"What's your name? Are you with Mr. Dee?"

Mr. Dee, not Mr. Lester, JD, Jay. Who was this masked man? Maxine smiled over her confusion and bent at the waist to meet the luminous blue eyes of a little boy. "Hi. I'm Miss Owens, and I came with Mr. Dee. What's your name?"

"Ricky. I'm this many." He held up six fingers.

Maxine laughed. "Well, I'm too many to show you with my fingers. Do you like reading with Mr. Dee?"

"Nuh-uh. But he shows me a magic trick after I read five pages. And he'll tell me how to do my own trick when I can read ten. Bye!" Ricky didn't wait to see if she approved of their plan before he dashed off to greet his superhero magician.

Maxine watched Ricky plop down beside JD, who by this time had rolled up his sleeves—*oh, that's right, he wanted to change his shirt*—and found a spot on the floor in a circle of more than a dozen five- and six-year-olds. Each held a book.

JD looked around the room until his eyes settled on her, planted where he'd left her. He shifted to his left and beckoned her over, patting the opening he'd created beside him. At least a dozen pairs of eyes followed his. Sweet, diminutive faces turned in her direction, their compact bodies shifting and squirming as JD waited for her to complete their circle.

Maxine uprooted her feet and took a step in their direction. *Buzz. Buzz.* She stopped and extracted her cell from the bag strapped across her shoulder. Teddy. Again. Maxine looked at the expectant group. *Buzz. Buzz.* She glanced back at her phone, and after a second she pressed Accept.

"Teddy? Hey." Maxine shrugged at JD and backed toward the door. "No, it's okay. I'm not busy. Not anymore."

Chapter Seventeen

"YES, MOTHER, I'M LEAVING NOW. No, I didn't forget the chicken salad."

Actually, Maxine had done just that. She had already taken the left turn out of the neighborhood when she pictured the Cuisinart container perched on the second shelf of Vivienne's refrigerator. Ten minutes later, she was backing out of the driveway and answering her mother's call.

"I should get there in about twenty minutes. I need to stop at the post office first. . . . Don't worry; I won't miss the start of the game." She turned left—once again—out of the neighborhood and onto the road shaded by southern pine, oak, maple, birch, and sweet gum trees and bordered by bright wildflower beds.

Though Maxine considered the national pastime a

national naptime, she craved a distraction—*any* distraction, including suffering through a baseball game in the late-spring sun. She sighed as she sped past a grove of peach trees. She frowned at the inner voice that whispered, *You're failing them.*

"I can't hear you," Maxine responded in a singsong voice. Determined to listen to something other than that voice of condemnation on the seven-mile ride, she opened her console and rifled through the tissues, Chick-fil-A ketchup packets, notepads, and pens. "Gotcha!" She opened the plastic case and inserted the *Diamonds and Pearls* CD. Prince's dulcet tones filled the car, drowning out the medley of thoughts auditioning for a starring role in her brain. By the time she idled at the second traffic light, she'd composed the intro to her latest post.

Love and sacrifice go hand in hand. Take it from me. My brothers had to twist my arm to watch them play baseball. They just wanted me to spend a few hours at a measly game—not give them a kidney or a new car. And they arranged a clear spring day with a nice breeze to boot. So why did it take a kick in the pants and the promise of my mother's chicken salad to take me out to the ball game?

Because I'm selfish, self-centered, and self-seeking, that's why. This submission-dying-to-self thing will take quite some getting used to once I say, "I do." What all will Hubby-to-be ask of me, considering I've already drawn the line with my ice cream and my bath towels? What happens if he asks me to cook spaghetti every week, kill a spider, or change the oil in the car, things I have no interest in doing? Should I give up watching *Home Town* Monday nights because they'll interrupt his football game?

"Now, Maxine, is that how you encourage soon-to-be married couples?" Her eyes flicked to the rearview mirror and back to the road as the mileage sign loomed . . . and as her ears tuned into "Strollin'." She sucked in a breath.

The first time she'd heard this song, she'd kept hitting Repeat, cranking the volume up and the windows down. Laughter and music had trailed out the open windows of Blue as they drove to Myrtle Beach. With her right foot propped on the dashboard and her head on his shoulder, she stayed close enough to nuzzle the spot behind his right ear every time Prince sang the words *strollin'*, *rockin'*, and *rollin'*.

Vivienne had pitched a fit that morning years ago as Maxine slung her beach bag over her shoulder and kissed the air in front of her mother's earlobe. "John, this girl is takin' an inch and runnin' miles and miles away with it!"

"She's a smart girl, honey. Aren't you, Maxine? We don't need to worry. Besides, despite the bad blood between you and Annie, I played high school basketball with Geoff. JD's dad is good people. I know that firsthand."

But what First John hadn't known hurt them all in the long run. Her stepfather hadn't lifted the Coleman's lid in the bed of JD's truck and found the wine coolers packed under the ice-covered soda. No chicken salad to speak of. First John had never suspected that the mysterious "car trouble" preventing Maxine's return had been planned for weeks. He hadn't been told about the other teens sharing the two rooms they'd booked ahead of time so they could party on the beach long into the night. His stepdaughter had walked in the house the next day, a little sunburned and windblown, smug in the knowledge she'd pulled one over on her parents, telling herself it was okay since all they'd done was sleep off their buzz.

Ultimately, the joke was on Maxine herself.

"Just strollin'."

"Oh!" Maxine cried and braked hard as a deer sprang from the brush, leaped across the road, and disappeared into the woods on the other side. Scratching her suddenly itchy underarm, she glanced in the rearview mirror. "Thank God!" she cried, grateful no one was behind her. As she slowly accelerated, Maxine depressed the Power button on the CD player and redirected her thoughts that had raced off and away in a light-blue classic Chevrolet. "Help me, Lord."

Okay, let's talk truth and consequences. And I'm not referring to my parents' old television game show or that city in New Mexico. I mean the realities of life and love. Hubby-to-be just dropped everything to help his family—everything, including me. No worries, dearest readers! It's evidence of his capacity for love, his willingness to lay down his life for his wife should the need ever arise. That give-and-take is worth a Friday evening of baseball, forgoing an episode of *Home Town*, or eating spaghetti. Believe me, that's saying something.

Maxine squinted at the road ahead.

Truth and consequences. The truth is, loving someone has consequences, and sometimes, love hurts. Look at my parents. Every day, I watch them give up their lives to and for each other. I don't think they even consider it giving up. They seem to gain as they lovingly sacrifice. They work together like a refrigerator-freezer combination. And not one of those refrigerator-on-top deals, but a side-by-side model. They're a united front. No good cop, bad cop.

And not only are they willing to kill themselves raising us, but they're willing to kill us, too—or at least threaten to—to make sure we're well in mind, body, and spirit. And my great-grandparents? They sent their son to another country, sight unseen, because they hoped and prayed for something better. Giving up something—someone—for their own good, despite your own wants and needs, your own broken heart . . . what greater love is there?

Maxine blinked back tears. She forced herself to focus on the article.

And what about Jesus? Yes, my friends, it all comes back to Him, as much as I want to make it about me. Like my grandfather, Jesus left His rightful place at home with His Father and came down to earth. Why? For an even greater purpose than my grandparents and great-grandparents envisioned—to submit Himself unto death because He loved us. Ornery, lying, sinful, selfish folks like me who certainly can't be bothered to return the favor.

No, loving submission is not all blood, sweat, and tears. There's joy in taking up the cross, joy in giving, joy in loving, joy in sacrifice. If there weren't any hearts and flowers, I probably wouldn't be here, and neither would any of you, dearest readers. My faith and family have shown me that it feels right to give of myself, to give myself. Period. It's something we do, no matter the consequences. We submit ourselves, one to another, and to our family, one after another. Baseball games, family dinners, family business, schooling, forgiveness, acceptance, love . . . No sacrifice too great. Just like with my hubby-to-be. And I hope, just like with me.

Maxine pulled onto the grassy parking lot at the baseball field and withdrew her journal. When she finished writing, she retrieved her phone from its dashboard mount and quickly found the verses she had in mind. She read aloud Matthew 16:24-25: "'Then Jesus said to His disciples, "If anyone desires to come after Me, let him deny himself, and take up his cross, and follow Me. For whoever desires to save his life will lose it, but whoever loses his life for My sake will find it.""""

Her phone vibrated in her hand. She looked at the screen. "My goodness. Hello?"

"Maxi-ine?"

She noted his slip. "Who else would it be, James Dee?"

"So you're still up in arms about my visit. You left the Y so abruptly, we never got to talk."

"I know." She scribbled down the passage she'd read, put away her leather-bound book, and climbed from the car. She leaned against her closed door and took a deep whiff of fresh pine needles and newly cut grass.

"Ricky says to tell you he can read seven pages."

Maxine couldn't help but smile at the memory of the young reader from the Y. The butterflies settled in her stomach. "Good for him! Did you show him a magic trick?"

"You took care of that, when you disappeared."

"It couldn't be helped. Teddy—"

"I know. Teddy Bear called."

"Yes, my fiancé. I'd already missed Theodore's call the first time, so I had to take that one. Since he was in the area, he swung by and picked me up so we could talk about his problems with his mother."

"You'd already declined his first call, you mean. And Teddy Bear's got more than the problems with his mother to worry about. He just doesn't know it yet."

"Jay—"

"I want to see you." He coughed a little. "To talk in person. About Celeste. We can't keep dancing around this, making it harder for everybody."

"Who's everybody?" Maxine needed something to do besides counting the butterflies that had resumed their flight in her stomach. She walked to the trunk and dug out her collapsible chair, visor, water bottle, and for good measure, a light pullover since North Carolina springs were notoriously mercurial and these baseball games were notoriously drawn out. She dropped each item by her feet.

"You. Me. Our daughter."

"Would you stop calling her that! She's no more yours than mine, JD."

"And she's no less either."

Maxine closed her eyes for a long moment and took a breath that shook her chest. "JD. JD. I just don't know what to do with you."

"Yes, you do. But this isn't about me. It's about—"

"Our daughter." Maxine flinched at a touch on her back and banged her head on the trunk's roof. "Ouch!"

Lilian Atwater leaned around to squint at her. "I didn't mean to startle you. I was just trying to get your attention. Are you okay?"

"Hi." Maxine smoothed down her hair, which had caught on the latch. She looked around, expecting the pastor to pop out of nowhere with a Bible and some holy oil. *The better to save you with, my dear,* she could hear him say. She pressed End on the phone, hoping JD would figure it out, and faced the interloper.

Lilian reached out. "You look like you're about to pass out."

"I'm fine. I'm fine. You surprised me. That's all. What are you doing here?" Though Maxine tried to mask her dismay, she could hear it seep through the edges of her words.

"I had Willy put a trace on your car the last time you were at the church, and this is where it led me."

"What?"

Lilian's lips twitched.

"Oh! Ha-ha. Baseball. You're here to watch the game. Do you have someone playing?" Maxine tied the arms of her jacket around her waist and slapped her cap on her head.

"This is my granddaughter's first season. She plays with the Raptors. I surely wouldn't waste a perfectly good Saturday morning on those hard wooden bleachers for just anybody. And you? Are you a fan, or are you here under duress like me?"

Maxine's heart beat a mile a minute. "Guilty as charged. My brothers play for the Blue Jays." She lowered the trunk. Then she slid her phone and water bottle into the bag holding the chair. Maxine felt like she was gearing up for a long mountain hike rather than a short walk through the parking lot. She wished she could ready her heart as easily.

Lilian reached for the bag Maxine had slung over her shoulder. "Can I help you carry anything? I see you don't plan to sit on those hard bleachers. I wish I'd thought of that."

Maxine waved off the help. "No, no. I'm good. I should let you get to Pastor." She hoped for and feared Atwater's appearance.

"Oh no, no. He's not here. God had mercy on him and arranged a ministerial breakfast this morning. Blessed and highly favored, that man."

Maxine was trying to hotfoot it toward the field, but suddenly she froze. "Actually, would you mind helping me with the cooler? I left the chicken salad in my car."

"No problem. I'm glad to help." Lilian returned to Maxine's Volvo and retrieved the cooler from the backseat. She extended the handle and fell into step beside the younger woman. "Were you talking to Theodore?"

"No. Teddy's probably already here, with my family. Oh, and I'm sorry we had to cancel our last meeting. I meant to call Pastor Atwater back to reschedule, but I just got caught up with all the day-to-day." Maxine flicked away that irritating inner voice that wanted to add, "Day-to-day worrying, avoiding, lying, and procrastination."

"Oh, that's okay. We stretch out our seven sessions over a year's time because, well, life happens. I'll tell Willy. He's probably already talked to Theodore himself. I'm so glad his father is doing better and that they had a good trip." She withdrew a pair of sunglasses from her red cross-body bag. "Mind if I hang with you a minute? It's nice to see a familiar face."

Maxine tried to spot First John and Mother in the crowd. And Celeste. "Are you sure this is okay, talking with you outside of our official counseling sessions? I wouldn't want to make you feel uncomfortable." Maxine adjusted her chair strap.

"You mean, is this unprofessional? Maybe—if we were Philistines or a doctor and her patient." Lilian studied Maxine through her green-tinted shades. "But we're talking about ministry, dear. Jesus walked among the sick, didn't He?" Lilian touched Maxine's shoulder again. "Not that you're sick, but you get the picture. Willy and I believe in making house calls."

Lilian covered her mouth with one hand. "There I go again. You know what I mean. Sometimes I don't know what to do with myself without my husband. I imagine you were scrambling while Teddy was out of town. You also missed your couple's outing with your grandparents, didn't you?"

Maxine squashed the image of cooking with JD and squared her shoulders. She wished she was cloaked by her typical tailored skirt and cardigan rather than her low-slung, gray cargo pants and wrinkled, pink-and-white V-necked tee. She squirmed under the warm brown eyes of Lilian, who looked fashionably comfortable in her lightweight yellow sweater and fitted cropped jeans. Coral-tipped toes peeked out of the holes in her stylish ECCO slides. Feeling like the ugly duckling, inside and out, Maxine focused on picking out the heads of her family among all the people milling about.

But Lilian beat her to it. "Oh, my goodness! Without your glasses, she could almost be your twin!"

Chapter Eighteen

LILIAN LIFTED HER SUNGLASSES. "That must be your sister—Celeste, right?"

Maxine had surely lived a Clark Kent–like existence, hiding behind her tortoiseshell frames and her role of "sister." It had taken Lilian Atwater to point out the obvious. Maxine cleared her throat and waved at her parents. "Yes, that's Celeste. With my family. She's adopted." Maxine hoped her reminder acted as a Danger: Falling Rocks sign, which would have stopped ordinary folks from blundering into an awkward and too-close comparison.

But she'd forgotten Lilian Atwater skipped on the extraordinary side of the street.

"That's incredible that she's adopted, considering the resemblance. How close is the family connection?"

"It's not something we talk about. Celeste is just as much a part of this family as I am."

"But—"

"Dad! Teddy! Uncle Roy!" Maxine plastered on a bright smile as First John walked up with the other two men close behind.

John gaped at her. Then he looked away from the younger woman he didn't seem to recognize to the older woman he'd never met and back again.

"Hey! Did you come over to help me with this stuff?" Maxine slipped the chair from her shoulder and handed it to Teddy. "Thank you, sweetie. And, Uncle Roy, could you grab that cooler?"

Lilian proffered her now-free right hand in his direction. "Hello, I'm Lilian Atwater, Maxine's frie—"

"Teddy's pastor's wife—" Maxine began at the same time. She laughed weakly. "Excuse me. I'm bad at this introduction thing."

"Don't I know it. And I thought this only happened with your old friends." Teddy laughed as he hugged Lilian.

"Especially lately." Celeste peeked out from behind her uncle. "Hi, I'm her sister, Celeste. Maxine, I can't believe the boys dragged you and Teddy out here. They couldn't even get Zander to come. We're leaving by the fourth inning, right, y'all?"

Roy shook his head. "Absolutely not, young lady. I gave up a lunch date with a lovely woman to watch my nephews play, so nobody gets to skip out. Not me. Not your dad and your mama. Not Maxine. Not Theodore."

"Besides, I've packed plenty of goodies to keep us all fat

and happy. And Maxine brought the chicken salad." Vivienne had popped up beside her husband in the flurry of activity.

"But, Mom, I'm bored, not hungry! I have plans tonight."

"Well, you should be hungry. You're losin' too much weight. All that rehearsal is killin' your appetite. And what plans can a thirteen-year-old make that her mama wouldn't already know about?"

"I'm almost fourteen, and you don't know everything." Celeste crossed her arms.

Maxine opened her mouth, but Vivienne stepped between her two daughters and leaned into Celeste. Still, Maxine discerned the warning in her mother's tone.

"Another thing I don't know is who you're talking to."

Celeste unfolded her arms and glared at the field as the players moved to their respective dugouts.

Vivienne stepped away from her younger daughter and back into character of host as she turned her attention to the stranger in their midst. "Hello. I'm Maxine's mother, Vivienne Owens. This is my husband, John, and my brother, Roy. Did I hear you're the wife of Reverend Atwater?"

Lilian seem unfazed by the boisterous group. "Yes, you did. But I'm also Maxine's friend. At least in a *professional capacity*. I think we'll just call this one of our premarital sessions so everybody's comfortable." She threw her head back in a laugh.

Vivienne's red lips shifted in a move that only her inner circle knew was a smile's third or fourth cousin, close enough to be mistaken for the real thing but not immediate family. "Well, professionally or personally, it's nice to meet you. Theodore has told us nothing but good things about his church. We're all on a family date with these two, per your orders."

Teddy beamed and looped his arm through Maxine's. "You can report to Reverend Atwater that we're officially logging in our hours."

For once, Maxine was grateful for her family's typical tornadic arrival. She felt safe floundering about in the headwinds of her mother's take-charge attitude. With one arm in Teddy's, Maxine clasped her free hand in Celeste's and squeezed. At first, the teen seemed to reject Maxine's silent empathy, but then Celeste relaxed her shoulders and squeezed back and made a funny face.

Maxine squinted hard, wrinkled her nose, and flicked out her tongue. Laughing, the two exchanged pokes and hip bumps on their trek. The others fell into step with them, lumbering en masse toward their chairs like elephants on the savanna—graceful, but enough of a force of nature to make others move out of their path or risk getting trampled. It wasn't until they arrived at the jumbled circle their chairs, picnic basket, and bags had created that Mother raised a questioning brow in Maxine's direction.

Maxine responded with a negligible shrug.

Vivienne turned to Lilian. "Care to join us?"

Lilian shook her head and slid her hands in her pockets. "I'd love to, but sadly, no chair. I figured I'd sit in the bleachers with the other hard-core baseball fans."

"The hard-core fans are actually the ones out here." The wide sweep of First John's arm encompassed the grass-covered sea of people setting up seats and food and blankets, preparing for the long haul. "We know better than to think we'd make it through a game on those things." He pointed to the nearly empty bleachers farther down.

"Well, that's good to know. Note to self. Go comfortable, or go home." Lilian beamed at them before peering in Maxine and Celeste's direction.

Maxine turned away from Lilian and her apparent mental note-taking and traded out her glasses for her larger, prescription shades. *The better to hide your face, my dear.* She grimaced. She pressed the button to unfold her chair and hoped her newfound "friend" would mosey on over to the risers.

"I have an extra chair in my car, if you'd like to sit with us." Teddy aimed a thumb toward the parking lot.

"I can go, Theodore. Stay here with your lady love," Roy volunteered.

"It's no trouble. Absence makes the heart grow fonder." Teddy winked at Maxine.

"You're sure?" Lilian seemed to test the temperature of the welcoming waters as her eyes bobbed from one face to another.

Teddy settled the matter. "I'll be right back." He jogged away.

"I'll join you!" Maxine leaped to her feet. As she trotted after him, she heard her mother's voice.

"Lilian, do you want somethin' to tide you over until we bring out the real food?"

Once Maxine reached Teddy's side, she tugged on his fingers, panting, "Why rush? Let's give Mother, First John, and Lilian a chance to get to know each other. Uncle Roy can keep the conversation going, no problem, and they've got food. Worse comes to worst, Lilian can use my empty seat. This *is* supposed to be a date, remember?"

"A double date—with your sister and your uncle tagging along, and now Lilian?" Despite his apparent skepticism, Teddy slowed to a walk.

Maxine squeezed his fingers. "I'll settle for my missing-in-action fiancé."

"Does that mean you're willing to share your last bite of pizza or your water bottle?" Teddy smiled and threw an arm around her shoulders.

She leaned into him. "Don't think I've missed you that much. But close."

He gently pinched her side. "Thanks for understanding about my dad. I've got to take you to New Orleans someday. You'd love it."

"Honeymoon potential?"

"Hmmm. Maybe not that much. But close."

She returned the pinch, then waited as he popped the trunk and retrieved the chair. They locked hands again as they strolled back toward the family's spot.

"In all seriousness, New Orleans is probably not your cup of tea, especially not for our honeymoon."

"Why not?" Maxine let go of his fingers as a group of teenage boys ambled between them.

"The partying, the nightlife. You're not familiar with that type of lifestyle."

You wanna bet? Maxine kept her face blank as she stuffed her hands into her pockets. "You think I'll faint if I smell alcohol? I'm not . . ." She closed her mouth.

Teddy wrapped his hand around her elbow to bring her

closer to him. "Whoa, there. I feel like I offended you some-how."

She fought the urge to yank her arm away. "No, no. It's not like that. But you don't need to shield me like I'm . . ." Again, she reached into the barrel to extract the noun or adjective that reflected who she was. She wanted to wave it high in the air and shout, "This is me! This is who I am!" but she came up empty. All she could think about was what she *wasn't*: innocent.

Out of something to say, she managed a smile. "Thanks for being my Creole knight in shining armor. I guess this woman should learn to be more gracious and recognize chivalry when it presents itself."

"It's not chivalry. Just love." Teddy kissed her forehead.

Maxine closed her eyes. Before, she would've leaned into that kiss, but her heart was an anchor that kept her head in place, unmovable. She couldn't let him see her inner tug-of-war, something that was getting harder and harder to hide. Her feet dragged as he led her back to the group.

It was the bottom of the first. The Raptors had struck out, and Lilian had already hired Manna to cater Grace Chapel's women's retreat. By the middle of the fourth, Vivienne had given Lilian her secret to a perfect potato salad, and by the top of the seventh, First John was referring to the pastor as Willy. Roy had even made tentative plans for a golf foursome with the pastor, his brother-in-law, and Teddy, once he and the pastor had been formally introduced.

"Maxine, can you cook like your mama and grandmama?" Lilian twisted around in her seat toward Maxine, who was seated with Celeste and Teddy behind the main group. She lowered her sunglasses.

"Mmmm . . ." Maxine coughed when she couldn't seem to clear her throat. "Not exactly, but I know my way around the kitchen."

"You'd better, because I hate to cook," Teddy laughed. "I love to eat, but the only things my refrigerator holds are water bottles and French vanilla creamer. And my favorite take-out menus, which I stick to the front."

Celeste pointed at him. "Then you wouldn't have enjoyed your date with Grandma and Granddaddy. I heard they kept Maxine in the kitchen all day."

Teddy looked at Maxine. "I thought we were rescheduling that?"

"We are. We *did*. I stopped by to visit, and they still had all the ingredients out, so . . ." Then Maxine spied Celeste lifting the lid of the cooler. "More water? That's your fourth bottle. The portable bathrooms ain't pretty, let me tell you."

"I'm thirsty. And drinking water is better for you than the deviled eggs you're eating. And that's *your* fourth, you know. Don't you have a wedding dress to squeeze into?"

"Technically, it's her second. Remember you cut the egg in half," Teddy explained.

Maxine glared at her fiancé. "Are you both counting my calories? And hey, you, don't disrespect your elders. My gown will fit just fine." Maxine gently nudged Celeste with the tip of her sneaker and popped the rest of the egg into her mouth.

"Ouch!" Celeste lightly kicked her back, her laughter attesting to the phantom nature of the pain. "Disrespect who? You're not my mother."

Maxine's heart flip-flopped—as it always did when Celeste teased her like that—and she peeked in Lilian's direction.

And was pinned to her seat by the woman's stare.

Maxine swallowed and managed to show her a few teeth.

Roy leaned forward, edging closer to Lilian. "I love watching them go at it."

Lilian's eyes flitted from one to the other.

"Then you'll be happy with us." Celeste snatched off Maxine's hat and ruffled her curls. She giggled as Maxine stretched to reach for it, nearly causing her seat to collapse.

"You'll have to excuse my girls." Vivienne looked askance at them over her shoulder. "Celeste, give your sister her hat. Maxine, act like you're the one gettin' married in a matter of months. Goodness, I can't tell who's the teenager."

"Told you gettin' hitched was no fun," Roy teased his niece.

Vivienne tsked and turned her attention back to the slow-moving game. "Lilian, is that your granddaughter who caught the ball at third?"

"No. She's in the outfield, with the braids." She pointed in that general direction before half turning toward Maxine.

Vivienne squeezed Lilian's knee. "Do you want something else to eat? I think John left one or two chicken wings."

"I'm stuffed. Who brings two types of salad to a baseball game?"

"People who don't want to be here!" First John patted his stomach. "I love my sons, but I tell you, if it wasn't for the food . . ."

Vivienne gathered containers. "Anytime is a great time to

eat good food, Lilian. Don't let anybody tell you different. Maxine, hand me that bag."

Maxine poked Celeste. "Get up, lazybones. We need to pack up. The game is almost over."

Celeste closed her eyes and leaned her head back over the seat. "I'm too tired . . . and I feel sick."

At once, Maxine and Vivienne were at her side. Maxine squatted by Celeste's chair, and her mother tilted up her chin and rested the back of her hand against the girl's forehead. Teddy and Roy hovered nearby, and First John took a knee on Celeste's other side while the women fussed over her. Lilian didn't move.

"Gotcha," Celeste drawled, mischief dancing in her one open eye.

It took a second before they all froze. Then First John squeezed his daughter's toes and returned to his seat. Vivienne tugged on Celeste's hair, a smile squeaking through her pursed lips as she resumed her clean-up duties.

"What in the world, Celeste! Do you think it's funny to make us all worry like that? Well, it's not. It's irresponsible, disrespectful, unkind, and immature."

"Shh. It's okay, Max." Teddy tried to drape an arm around her shoulders.

She shrugged off his embrace. "No, Theodore, it's most certainly *not* okay, and Celeste should know better. Shouldn't you, Celeste?"

"Sorry." Celeste looked down at her toes.

"What? What did you say?" Maxine refused to accept the lame apology for the trick that had her own heart racing. She was just now catching up to it.

Celeste met Maxine's eyes. "I said I'm sorry. I shouldn't have done that, made y'all worry. I didn't realize you'd have heart palpitations." She smiled a little.

Maxine tried to hold on to her outrage, but it was too slippery. Her shoulders relaxed. "I forgive you. But don't ever do that again." She pulled Celeste up from her seat and whispered, "I knew you were stewing over that thing with Mother, but if this was your way of getting back at her, don't do it again. Now get to work." She hugged her quickly but tightly. When she pushed Celeste in the direction of the cooler, she found Lilian eyeing her. Again.

"I don't think I shared about Celeste." Maxine took a deep breath. "She collapsed a couple of months ago during her music lesson, and she's been undergoing some testing. We're all concerned, and just now . . ."

"She scared y'all." Lilian stood there quietly while everyone around them scurried about.

Suddenly Vivienne pointed to the field. "Home run! It's over! Let's go console the boys and get out of here." She, First John, and Teddy cheered and trudged along with the other onlookers toward home plate and the tumbling pile of blue. Roy pulled the recalcitrant Celeste from her seat and fell into step with them. Lilian and Maxine lagged behind.

"Yes, she scared us. She just hasn't been herself. Not eating or sleeping well. Losing weight. Heart racing. And the doctors said we should monitor and note everything. So when I realized Celeste was pretending just now, scared turned to mad fast. She was playing with us, but it's no laughing matter. I know she's young . . ." Maxine searched for the right words, as she had for familiar faces in the crowd hours ago.

Just what does acceptable truth look like?

"You wanted to make sure she was all right. And you wanted her to learn a valuable lesson." Lilian reached out and clasped Maxine's trembling fingers. "Like any loving mother would. Right, Maxine?"

Chapter Nineteen

"Is it okay if I ask you about Celeste?" Lilian proffered Maxine a cup of chai tea, part of the bribe that had coaxed Maxine from the car and was meant to draw her out of the hole she'd crawled into after the twins' baseball game the week before.

Maxine was loath to wade through these waters, though Celeste was the bait on the hook. But she had to face the light of day. If all the messages peppering Maxine's voice mail were any indication, Lilian had overheard her part of the conversation with JD. She relaxed her grip on the fringed pillow and reached for the tea.

"I know you've spent more than a decade trying to hide the truth, and it seems you've been pretty good at it. But I don't care if you wear a snorkel and a Ronald McDonald wig;

that's your daughter. No doubt about it. And I know a man named JD is her father. How did that happen?" Lilian took a deep breath and shifted to a different spot in her seat. "Well, you know what I mean."

Maxine tucked her bare feet beneath her on the Atwaters' overstuffed upholstered sofa. She looked away from Lilian to the window framing the world she wished she could escape to. Her voice was low and deep when she finally spoke.

"JD was like this *island* for me. You know, somewhere I could sail away to. My escape. I was so glad Mother came back when I was eleven, but was it for good? What if something happened to her, like with my dad? I mean, she left me once. And from what I could see, Mother had everything she needed in First John, especially once they had Zander. She didn't need me, not really.

"When I was with JD, I didn't have to think about all of that—Mother, my dad, my fears. I didn't have to listen to my own voice or comfort myself, because I felt at home with him when we met that day. *Immediately.*"

Reverend Atwater's absence gave Maxine wiggle room to let down her burdens, not that she felt safe, exactly. But she had spent the past decade and a half running from her memories, and it was good to slow down long enough to let the past nip at her heels. Those memories swallowed her altogether as she sipped tea in the Atwaters' bungalow.

"Mother got all worked up the moment she met him. She just knew he was trouble, no matter what First John tried to tell her. JD drove me home that afternoon, and when I climbed out of Blue, she had a fit." Maxine waved off an oatmeal lace cookie.

"Blue?"

"His vintage truck, painted the color of the Carolina Tar Heels. Mother couldn't stand the university, the truck, or him."

"Why, do you think?" Lilian set down the plate and settled into her chair with her cup. She peered at Maxine through the wisps of steam.

"A mother knows." *And that's all I'll say about that.* Maxine intuited Lilian's question wasn't referring to Vivienne's fidelity to the old gold and black, the team colors of Wake Forest University, First John's alma mater. She held her peace as she stared at the red lily painted on the side of her host's cup and lifted the lids of different boxes in her brain, discovering and discarding words and memories as she searched for the right ones to explain. "After that day, we were together all the time. And I don't mean . . . It wasn't all . . ."

"Maxine, don't."

"Don't what? Don't try to pretend JD and I spent our time reading poetry in the library? Don't paint a picture of us sitting in Sunday school, working on our memory verses?" Maxine studied the leaves in the bottom of her teacup as if they would shed a clear answer. "No, I'm not going to lie to you, Lilian. I felt like *me* with him, whether we were talking or driving around town or laughing or merely breathing in the same room—and that's what we did, a lot. JD helped me find direction, but most of all, he quieted the noise and gave me room to breathe."

"How so?" Lilian's voice was hushed, as if she were watching a skittish fawn test the air at the edge of the woods.

Soundlessly she slid off her slippers and drew up her feet in the plush chair across from Maxine.

But Maxine smelled danger. She squeezed her lips together to stifle the words and the feelings that bubbled up, threatening to overflow and free themselves. Instead, she drank in the scene around her.

The den was as cozy and eclectic as Lilian's personality. Matching scarlet armchairs flanked the chintz-covered sofa. Emerald, goldenrod, and scarlet throw pillows dotted the furniture. Family photographs in various sizes and exposures dotted the cream-colored walls, along with an oil painting of the Eiffel Tower, a large aerial photograph of Wheaton's campus, and a sepia rendition of Chicago's Magnificent Mile.

Potted plants, real and artificial; a miniature replica of the Cape Hatteras lighthouse; and collections of rocks, shells, and clocks adorned the mahogany end tables and bookshelves. And throughout the room, spots of red peeked out—a bowl of ceramic apples on a bookshelf, a picture of a male cardinal on a leafless branch, a heart-shaped throw pillow, a bowl of dried rose petals. The muted glow of two heavy, cut-glass table lamps and an antique brass floor lamp held at bay the early evening shadows.

"I felt that way about Willy. I still do. I can be my old ugly self with him." Lilian's voice was as low as the lamplight beside her.

Maxine found nothing ugly about the pastor's wife in her slim-fitting chinos, oversize cream silk blouse, and multi-colored head wrap, and she was sure Reverend Atwater would agree with her. *But it's the heart that counts, not the outside,* she heard a voice say.

"What is it?" Lilian swung her legs to the floor. "You look like you've seen a ghost."

"No. But I think I just heard one. I've been talking to myself a lot lately, dreaming crazy things, hearing voices. I just scare myself sometimes. I think it's the stress of the wedding."

"Maybe it's God trying to get your attention." Lilian sounded like she didn't mean *maybe*.

"Well, He certainly has it." The pillows enveloped Maxine as she leaned back.

Lilian said nothing.

"Mother always taught me to be a 'good girl,' to be this 'unwrapped gift' for my future husband." Maxine's eyes lit on Lilian's face for a moment before flitting off to a land far, far away. "JD and I were more than a couple of frisky teenagers, you know. He not only listened, he responded—and boy, I had a lot to say." Maxine laughed at herself, at the young woman who wanted to believe her thoughts and feelings could keep the world spinning in place. Or stop it, if only for a few hours.

"Girl, what are you singing about now? It sure wasn't what I was playing." JD smoothed back her hair with the fingers on his left hand. His right cradled the neck of a guitar.

"My stepfather. He just takes over. Nobody asked his opinion!" Maxine yanked off her dark-blue hair ribbon and stuck it between the pages of her history textbook. Her newly pressed, straight hair draped her shoulders as she flopped back against his chest. It was a wonder JD couldn't feel her heart beating an angry tattoo.

"What happened this time?" He set aside his instrument and drew her closer into him, toward the coolness of the tree covering. The movement of the sun had chased away the shade, and it was now kissing their toes. He lifted her hair from her neck and twirled it.

"I wanted to spend some time with Mama Ruby, away from the gruesome twosome." Her feet were starting to get cooked in the late-summer sun, so she wrapped a leg around his and out of direct light. She felt his laughter.

"I'm surprised the 'gruesome twosome' didn't want a break from you, Miss Susy Sunshine. All up in their groove. Here, let's move this."

The two disentangled themselves for a moment to pack up their lunch remains so they could move the blanket completely under cover of the trees. JD propped his guitar against the tree and they stretched out, her homework and his music forgotten. Maxine tucked her head under his chin and enjoyed the quiet of their spot. She'd missed this, since he'd left for Princeton. She wanted his fall break to go on forever. Her heartbeat slowed as her anger seeped into the fabric of the blanket.

"Nobody asked to be 'all up in their groove,' that's for sure. It would've been so much fun in Spring Hope. Granddaddy was going to teach me how to make his pork roast. He'd already bought the fruit to season it with." She felt his chest rumble under her hand. "What?" She turned to look at him.

"Are you always thinking of your stomach?"

"Hey! That's unfair. It was my excuse to spend time with

them. The pork roast was just icing on the cake. They were going to invite you to dinner, you know." She resettled into her spot.

"I don't get what's so bad about Mr. Owens. You should give him a chance. He loves your mom, and it's obvious he cares about you. He's funny and—"

"How do you know so much about John?"

"He played basketball at the same prep school as my dad. And they still like each other, even though they played for rival ACC teams and our moms don't get along. Really, baby, when *you* talk about him, you don't say anything bad. You just sound jealous."

"Jealous!" Maxine sat up and faced him head-on. "I'm not jealous. I-I'm on the outside, looking in. You should see the two of them, doing all the stuff Mother and I used to do together. And he thinks he's my father, trying to tell me what to do."

JD looped his arms around his bent knees. "He *is* your father."

"No. He's my *step*father. There's a big difference."

"Only if *you* make a difference. I bet he loves you like a daughter. He doesn't have other children besides you and Zander, does he?"

"I'm not his child." Maxine huffed at this unexpected assault. "What if I told you he's moving us to Alabama?" She smirked. "Yes, I thought that would get your attention. Not so big a fan of your Mr. Owens now, are you?"

"He's not mine. What are you talking about, Maxie?"

"He got a writing assignment that would take us to Mobile for who knows how long. I asked him why he couldn't go without us since it's temporary. I offered to watch the house or move back in with Mama Ruby and Granddaddy, but the two lovebirds just had a baby and don't want to break up the family. Who cares what I think, how I feel about leaving school." She looked away from him. "And moving farther from you."

JD's tapered index finger directed her face back in his direction. "I care." He leaned forward and kissed her. "Okay, so maybe your stepdad isn't so great."

She laid her head on his shoulder and wrapped her arms around his waist. She soaked in the smell of Cool Water, the cologne she'd given him as a graduation present.

His breath was warm on her face. "When did you find out about this?"

"Earlier today."

He drew her closer. "Is this the real reason you were so worked up?"

She nodded.

"I knew it was more than cooking with your grandparents. So what are we going to do about it, Maxie? I won't get to see you when I come home."

Maxine's tears ran down his neck. "I know," she squeaked. "What are we going to do, Jay?"

He pulled away slightly but kept her within the circle of his arms. He cupped her face. "You can count on me. I'll find a way to fix this." He kissed her trail of tears, working his way up from her chin. "I promise."

Maxine stopped talking. She studied the vermillion buds on the bromeliad growing by the window.

"So what happened?" By this time, Lilian was leaning forward in her seat, her tea cooling on the end table.

Maxine focused on Lilian. "First John and Mother went to Mobile of course. He wrote an award-winning series of articles on college basketball that sold millions of copies." She sipped from her own lukewarm cup.

"Wait. He's *that* John Owens? Why didn't I know that? I mean, I have your mother's secret potato salad recipe, but I didn't know your stepfather is the bestselling author *Jack Owens*?" Lilian's soft striped socks covered the sound of her footsteps as she padded to the shelves by the bay window. She tapped each book with a closely cut fingernail until finally she withdrew a hardcover and held it aloft. "Aha! Here it is."

"Yep, that's his: *Keeping God in the Game*. You've read it?"

"Twice. Willy even referred to it in a sermon to the youth. I can't believe I didn't recognize him at the game! This book came from that series he wrote while you lived in Mobile?"

Maxine shook her head.

Lilian narrowed her eyes at the book. "No? But this is a compilation of articles—"

"I mean, yes, that's the book. But no, I didn't live in Mobile with them. At least not the whole time."

"Wait. I'm confused." She laid the book on the shelf.

"First John, Mother, and Zan relocated to Mobile for a while. He wrote the articles. And lived happily ever after."

"But what about you?"

"I got married. I got pregnant. I moved to Alabama. Then I ran away from home. End of story." Maxine swung her feet to the floor and reached for the platter on the coffee table. "I think I'm ready for a cookie now."

Chapter Twenty

"WHAT DID YOU SAY?" Lilian whispered, in hot pursuit of her houseguest.

But there in her den, Maxine had sprinted years and miles beyond her reach, back to a scorching hot day in the woods.

———

Whenever JD needed to figure out something, he worked it out through his music. So Maxine let him. After a few bars of "Tears in Heaven," his hands stilled on the strings.

"What if we get married?"

Maxine's puffy, red-rimmed eyes opened wide. "What did you say?"

He rested the guitar on his lap and gazed at the overhang that created their bower.

"Jay, did you say something about marriage?" Maxine hated when he didn't respond—as much as he hated to repeat something needlessly, she knew. "I'm only sixteen."

"I know how old you are." He seemed to be counting the robins that hopped from branch to branch above them. "What does that have to do with anything?"

"I'm only sixteen." She didn't care about his pet peeves. It bore repeating. "I'm too young to get married." She watched him watch the birds. "Or is this about sex?"

They'd been dancing closer and closer to the big s-word for weeks—just uttering the three letters grew the pit in her stomach by another centimeter or two. Yet something or some*one* held them back from consummating a relationship they both believed was forever. And not in that teenage, "I love writing your name over and over in my notebook" type of forever. Even her stepfather admitted to an unexplainable prescience whenever he saw them together or heard her say JD's name. Ever-faithful Vivienne must have gone to her knees the second JD's truck turned in to their driveway, and as much as she resented her mother's fretful interference, the church girl within Maxine was grateful for the intercession.

At this moment, Maxine wondered if JD's suggestion was merely a ruse to finally turn that irrevocable corner in their relationship. But then JD turned away from his nature study, and she looked into the eyes of the little boy who attended Sunday school, the young man who showed such respect for his mother and sister. Who honored and loved her. Maxine gripped the hands poised over his guitar strings. "I'm sorry. I know you don't only want . . . *that*. I just don't understand."

He stopped resisting her, and one hand closed around

hers. "Maxie, yes, I want you, but you're mine already—at least in all the other ways that count. Do you believe that, too?"

She nodded.

"And I'm not coming up with some crazy scheme to keep you with me. It just feels right, like this is what we were meant to do."

"But what about college? And, Jay, I know I already said it twice before, but I'm only sixteen. Mother and John will never let me get married! Won't I have to get their permission?" Maxine crouched on her knees beside him as if pleading with him to come to his senses.

"What *about* college? I'll keep going. And when your mom and stepfather go to Alabama, you can join me in Princeton and study up there or even stay with my parents and finish school here."

"Leave my mother to stay with *yours*?"

"Okay, you have a point." JD set aside his guitar and took her other hand. "But we can make this work. I know you love me, but do you trust me?"

"Of course I trust you."

"We can do this. Your birthday is in a few weeks, and once you're seventeen, you won't need their permission. Then we won't have to feel guilty about feeling the way we do. And yes, acting on it."

He rose to one knee on the blanket and kissed her hand. Then he rained kisses on her cheeks, forehead, and nose, concentrating his attention on her eyes, which were streaming tears. "Maxine, your name means 'noble,' 'bright,' and 'greatest,' and you are all those things to me. Will you marry me?"

Maxine clasped his face with both of her hands and held him there for a few precious seconds as the crickets chirped away in the woods. Then she nodded as a maple leaf drifted down and landed between them. "And in case you didn't hear me, that's a yes," she whispered.

"You married JD?"

Maxine touched her lips and looked around, surprised to find herself on a sofa. But she wasn't out of the woods. She stared across the room at the wide-eyed pastor's wife, planted in her spot by the bookshelf, a hand seemingly holding her heart in her chest.

Lilian slowly crossed to Maxine and plopped beside her on the sofa. She clutched the younger woman's knee. "What in the world did your parents say when they found out?"

"They didn't say anything."

"What? I find that hard to believe."

"I never told them. They still don't know I married JD. I don't know what would disappoint Mother most, getting pregnant outside of marriage or marrying 'that boy' and realizing Annie Lester is family . . ." Maxine's voice faded.

"Or finding out the whole truth now." Lilian's voice was hushed, as if she hadn't meant her thoughts to see the light of day.

Maxine shook her head slowly. Lilian's words sloshed about in her head like water trapped in her ears. One summer she'd accidently slipped into the deep end during a neighbor's pool party. She'd fought her way up for air, her lungs feeling like they'd explode. After bursting through the morass of legs and arms and pool toys, gasping and crying, she'd paddled through the frolicking teenagers to the edge, crawled out, and vowed never to swim again.

She'd kept that promise. And now, as then, Maxine resolved to remain high and dry. No more emotional diving. She brushed away Lilian's hand and headed toward the kitchen. "I've got to go," she managed, sucking in much-needed oxygen.

Lilian trailed her. "But I want to know—"

Maxine whirled on the petite woman on her heels. "*You* want to know! There's so much *I* want to know, but you'll have to take it up with God, Mrs. Atwater. I'm fresh out of answers."

Lilian's eyebrows rose, but she clamped her lips together. Silently she retrieved her visitor's jacket and purse from a chair at the table and handed them over.

When Maxine took her things, she gripped the woman's hands. She opened her mouth and took a deep, trembling breath. At first, nothing. She had to swallow hard to help her words find purchase in her throat, though her voice was as low as her downcast eyes. "Thank you. For tea and . . . everything." Maxine forced herself to meet Lilian's eyes. "And I mean *everything*. I never meant to disrespect you, especially here in your home."

"No disrespect given, by you nor by me." Lilian reached out and embraced Maxine, briefly but tightly. "I'd say, 'No worries,' but that would be disingenuous. You have nothing but worries, and understandably so. I didn't mean to pry, at least not for my sake—though I admit I'm a curious cat by nature. But you need to cast some serious cares upon the Lord, my dear, and use whoever He sends your way to help you bear these burdens."

The weight pressing on Maxine's shoulders eased a bit.

"I'll be frank with you. That free-pass thing Willy and I put on the table last month during your premarital counseling? I have a feeling that won't apply here. But don't let fear stop you from doing the right thing, whatever that is. Teddy is a big boy. He can handle it."

"Handle what? The truth?"

"The truth of your past, definitely. He'll be hurt that you didn't trust him, but healing will follow the pain of your breakup."

"Breakup?" Cool night air rushed past Maxine as she stood in the open storm door. "You don't think he'll forgive me for not telling him about Celeste?"

"Oh, the Teddy I know will accept Celeste. With open arms. He already knows she's adopted, so I guess you can lead him a few more steps down the path that ends with you as her birth mother. But we both know no man worth his salt should marry someone who's holding on to her past with both hands. You're going to have to let go of it if you plan to slide on his wedding band."

Lilian shook her head a little. "Please call me, anytime. And don't worry. For now we'll keep this between friends."

She shut the door, leaving an openmouthed Maxine on the brick steps.

May

*"But Jesus said, 'Somebody touched Me, for
I perceived power going out from Me.' Now
when the woman saw that she was not hidden,
she came trembling; and falling down before
Him, she declared to Him in the presence of
all the people the reason she had touched Him
and how she was healed immediately. And
He said to her, 'Daughter, be of good cheer;
your faith has made you well. Go in peace.'"*

LUKE 8:46-48

Chapter Twenty-One

"You look beautiful."

Maxine resisted the urge to spin. It didn't seem like the place, outside the bathroom door of Bojangles, with the odor of sausage-egg-and-cheese biscuits lingering in the air. Yet she did feel special in the antique white satin dress with its lace overlay she'd driven thirty-seven miles to find. The thrift store had charged an extra five dollars since it was marked "vintage," but no matter. Nothing but the best for her wedding day.

JD took Maxine's hand and kissed it. "You're sure your folks think you're on the college tour?"

Maxine grinned so big it made her eyes squint behind her gold-rimmed glasses. "Yes, we're all set. What they don't know will help us."

Thursday, October 30, a week after her seventeenth birthday. Maxine didn't need permission to marry, and her mother and stepfather thought she was oohing and aahing over Georgetown, Johns Hopkins, and William & Mary with the school's Future Business Leaders of America club, not posing for wedding pictures in front of a poster advertising fried chicken and dirty rice. They wouldn't expect her back for three days.

"What about your parents?" Maxine curled her fingers around his.

"They're too busy avoiding each other to keep up with a son away in college. I'm good as long as I get back to class by Monday." JD opened the passenger door and threw her bag into the back of the borrowed Ford Taurus.

"I wish we could've sneaked back to your house somehow just to get Blue so we could drive to our wedding in style." She smiled at him as she slid in.

Once he sat behind the wheel, he ran his fingers over the squiggly lines on the printout. "According to the map, we're close to the state line. That means we'll soon be Mr. and Mrs. James Lester." He caught her eyes and held them.

Maxine shifted in her seat, not that she was trying to break free. She'd been rolling the words over and over on her tongue all night. Her whole future was so close she could taste it. *Maxine Lester.* She swallowed and breathed, "Your wife."

"Now, don't go signing your married name on your math homework. Remember, we're going to lay low for a few more months."

"I know. I know. And you still think that's going to work?"

"Why wouldn't it?" JD took the exit onto the highway and headed northeast. "You'll finish out your junior year here, and next summer, I'll get an internship and save money. Shoot, I'll even work full-time at Home Depot if I have to. I'll head back to Princeton next fall, and you'll join me after Christmas, once you get accepted early decision. You can finish out your senior year in New Jersey. I've heard about people homeschooling."

"But what if my folks move to Mobile before then?"

"Then you'll come up sooner. They can't make my wife do anything she doesn't want to, including leave her husband."

He made it sound possible, and not only possible but *right*. It was why Maxine found herself dressed in this 1960s sheath on her way to a justice of the peace in Richmond, Virginia. Why she was bailing on John's plans to move them all to Alabama. Why she'd finish up high school in New Jersey. *So why am I shaking?* Maxine tried to focus on the dashed white lines in the road before they disappeared in a blur. But then JD squeezed her hand and drew her eyes back to him. *Oh, that's why.*

Maxine smiled a little less brilliantly, but happiness still warmed her face. "You know we're crazy. This is crazy."

"Why? Why is it crazy? It's not like we're planning to drop out of school, and we're still going to college. We're only getting married a little earlier than most people. Didn't your parents get married at an early age? Mine did."

"Know something else my dad did at an early age? He died. And your parents got divorced." Maxine cracked her window and stared out.

"Maxine." He tickled the back of her hand. "Maxie."

She turned to him.

"I've always been ambitious. When I know what I want, I go after it, and I hold on to it. And I want you. Now stop your worrying. Close your eyes and take a nap. When you wake up, we'll be there. I think we have a long night ahead of us."

Her toes curled as warmth surged into them and crept up her body. She closed her eyes. *Mrs. James Lester.*

Maxine opened her eyes when the music stopped, interrupting her reverie. "Why'd you stop playing? It sounded beautiful—technically. It wasn't coming from your heart though."

"Then what were you smiling about, if something sounded off?" Celeste set her bass on its stand and wiped her hands on her white denim capris.

Maxine watched Celeste shuffle around the music room. She said nothing as the girl plopped on the piano stool and played some notes with her right hand only. C, D, E, F, G, A, B, C. No sharps, no flats.

In the middle of adding a second octave to the first eight notes, the teen rotated to face Maxine. Her fingers left a discordant trail behind her on the baby grand. "I can't do this anymore."

"What? The C scale? You know it backward and forward, like the solo you've been practicing for the past hour." Maxine wanted to lighten the heavy mood swirling about the room like a low-level cloud.

"Not just the solo. My life."

Maxine's heart rate skipped into triple time and the skin on the back of her neck twitched though she fought to keep her face impassive. Swallowing her desire to jump in with both feet, Maxine feigned interest in a torn cuticle. "The solo, I get. But what do you mean, your life?"

"It's too hard. Everything is too hard." Celeste used her toes to set her piano stool in motion.

After a few moments watching first the left side of Celeste's face and then the right . . . left . . . right, Maxine rose from the love seat and caught the girl's shoulder, knocking her off-balance. Maxine knelt on one knee before her as the stool rocked to a standstill. "What's too hard, Celeste? You can tell me." *This is my fault. My own life is spinning out of control, and now so is hers.*

"Can I, Maxine? I don't think so." Celeste caved in on herself.

Maxine gathered her close, and the two sank to the rug. It was then Maxine realized how much weight the teen had lost. She had always been solid, physically and emotionally. But now Maxine could feel Celeste's ribs through her shirt, see her shoulder blades protrude from her thin back in sharp angles. Celeste's arms could hold her double bass and wield her bow but seemed too weak to hold back the sobs as she locked her hands together around her bent knees and shook like the last autumn leaf clinging to a limb.

"Shh. Shh." Afraid words would blow away Celeste altogether, Maxine stroked her braids and rocked her in a circular motion, as if they were still turning on the stool. It wasn't until Celeste shifted that Maxine relaxed her hold. She

peeked at the tear-soaked face and pulled away just enough to stretch for the ever-present box of Kleenex. Mother kept one in each room of their sprawling house. The one on the piano was nearly empty. Maxine shook her head. *Probably since Robert's last tantrum over practicing.*

"Do you want to talk? What can I do to help?"

Celeste shrugged.

"Even if I can't help you feel better, will you help me feel better? If you're this worried about the solo, I can talk to the conductor. Or I can talk to the doctor if it's your heart or you feel weak. Should I call First J—?"

Celeste's head shook *no* vigorously, setting her whole body aquiver.

Maxine sighed and considered for a minute. "Once, when I'd only been living with Mama Ruby two or three months, I came home . . . just *worked up*. She sat there with me on the porch steps and let me cry it out. Then she whispered one of her favorite songs over and over, and we sat some more. Finally I was able to tell her how much I missed Mother."

Maxine cradled Celeste's trembling fingers and hummed what Mama Ruby had sung to her that long-ago day, hoping to reassure the girl that sometimes, it was impossible to find the words to express pain and heartache. After a verse or two, Celeste wiggled her fingers at the right point in the song, and Maxine smiled. It wasn't quite a wave, but she took it as a sign that Celeste understood and was surrendering, accepting help.

Maxine could see herself huddled on those steps in Spring Hope, heartbroken. Wishing Vivienne could attend her school's Mother's Day tea, not her grandmother. She hadn't wanted Ruby to feel rejected, to feel as less than as she felt. After that moment on the porch, Maxine added *Mama* to her grandmother's name. Because that's what she'd become, what Vivienne now was to Celeste.

At that moment, Maxine would've run to either Mama Ruby or her mother and thrown herself in her lap. They'd know what to do in this situation, those constant, loud voices of reason.

"I don't want to press you, but when you say things like 'My life is too hard,' it scares me. A lot. And I just can't ignore it. Should I get Mother?"

"No!" Celeste wrenched away from Maxine. "She'll make a big deal out of this. She's already freaking out about the doctor's visits and this solo, and Elisabeth Willis has been hounding her about her birthday party."

"Okay, okay, I won't get her. But you know Mother's not the 'freak-out' type, Celeste."

"Maybe she doesn't lose it the way you do, but she does in her own way. When she knows something's wrong, she won't stop until she figures out how to fix it, even if that means pulling a magic trick to make us forget there was ever a problem in the first place." Celeste swiped her nose and dropped her used tissue on the rug beside her.

"Eew, Celeste, stop." Maxine scooped the wet tissues into a pile and stuffed them into the now-empty tissue box, anything to mask her shock that Celeste recognized Vivienne's smoke-and-mirrors routine. She walked toward the wastebasket near the pocket doors.

". . . leave me." Celeste's voice seemed to tiptoe across the room.

Maxine glanced at the teen over her shoulder. "I'm sorry, but did you ask me to leave you?"

"No. I said . . ." The girl's chest heaved. "You're always in an all-fired hurry to leave me . . . in Mama's care."

"What?" Maxine blinked slowly, her mouth open. *Girl, stop catching flies,* she imagined Mama Ruby ordering, and she snapped her lips together.

"What does she know that you don't? Or Daddy? Is there something more they can tell me that you can't?"

"Well . . . you should be able to turn to your parents when you need help. They'll love you through the tough times. Isn't that what you want?" This time, it was Maxine's voice that tried to hide.

"How does the song go? 'You can't always get what you want . . .'? You went through a lot yourself as a teenager. How did you handle it?" Celeste plucked at the threads sprouting from the holes in her denim-covered thigh.

By killing your father. Maxine considered the details of the fairy tale she'd woven so long ago, wishing she could mumble *Rumpelstiltskin* and make the whole situation go away, never to be seen again. Maxine let the box tumble from her hand and wished the truth could roll off her tongue as easily. She turned slowly to face Celeste as she weighed her words on a mental scale. "With the help of family."

"Mom and Dad, you mean."

"Well, yes, of course."

"I wish I could."

Maxine strove to get a better read on all that Celeste *hadn't* said, but she couldn't see her face. The girl kept toying with the squished aglets of her shoelaces. Maxine held her breath, knelt before her, and tapped on the hardwood floor beside her sneakers. "Celeste."

Suddenly focused, the teen pressed her fingers against Maxine's lips as she sent her long braids fluttering around her shoulders with a shake of her head. "No worries, I'm okay. I just needed to cry it out, like you did with Grandma. Don't worry. I've worked too hard on this solo to jump off a cliff between now and Saturday night."

Maxine clutched Celeste's fingers. "Celeste! This isn't something to joke about. Maybe it's time we talk."

"Maybe?" Suddenly the girl's voice sounded stronger, more in control. And eerily like her father's. Like JD's. Celeste squeezed Maxine's hand and then stood. The salty outlines on her face were the only evidence of her breakdown. "I said I'm okay. I've always handled it because butts are for gettin' it done, right?"

"But yours doesn't have to go rogue. You're not alone." Maxine pushed herself to her feet and stretched to embrace Celeste.

She moved toward her bass and out of Maxine's reach. "You have Teddy. Mama and Daddy have each other. The twins do their twin thing. Zan is . . . Zan, happy bouncing his basketball. It's always been me. And that's okay, Max. I just had a moment. That's what thirteen-year-olds do, right? Especially soon-to-be fourteen-year-olds." She twiddled with her bow. "I should practice. Two days are going to zip by."

Maxine hesitated. She knew she had dropped a very important, heavy ball. "Do you want me to listen?" She watched Celeste consider it for a moment.

"I think I've got it."

"Well . . . okay. If you're sure. You know where to find me if—when—you need me."

She nodded. "I know you're always looking out for me . . . Sis."

Inwardly, Maxine cringed as she left the room. She leaned against the pocket doors as Celeste resumed her practice. Now it sounded like she was putting her whole heart into it.

Chapter Twenty-Two

MAXINE HOPPED ONTO one of the two stools at the glistening countertop. She balanced her toes on the top rail to keep her feet from swinging back and forth as she gazed around the cavernous kitchen.

"Ready for your blind tasting?" Hands tied a scarf around her eyes.

The soft fabric seemed to hinder her speech as well as her sight. Maxine only nodded as the stainless steel appliances disappeared behind the strip of silk. She swiveled from side to side on the stool while her fingers tapped out "Here Comes the Bride" on the cool marble.

"Here's the first."

Smiling, Maxine gripped the fork and plate and dug in. "Mmm. Sweet. Too sweet."

She set aside the first dish and accepted a second. Maxine wrinkled her nose after only a nibble. "Coffee?" Almost before she could swallow, she felt a whoosh of air and heard the clink of glass. She took a bite—and immediately let it roll out of her mouth onto the plate. "Ugh. Is that fruitcake? For a wedding?"

A large hand gripped her right shoulder before setting down a glass of water.

As Maxine sipped, she turned her head this way and that, awaiting the next serving. It wasn't long in coming. After tasting it, she delicately plucked a minuscule flake from her tongue. Coconut.

The clatter of another dessert plate followed that one. "Mmm. Love carrot cake, but Teddy doesn't like nuts. Where is he anyway? We're supposed to do this stuff together." She patted the empty stool beside her to see if he was there.

Then a swish of air announced another dish. She fiddled around for the fork and slid it into her mouth. A second later, she whipped off her blindfold and tossed it to the counter. "Yes!"

Before her on the counter sat six plates, five partially eaten cakes adorned with varying combinations of fondant, ornate frosting, swirls, flowers, chocolate, and cream cheese. But not the sixth. The last was a plain lemon pound cake. No glaze, icing, or decoration. She recognized Mama Ruby's cake that she usually served with a fried chicken wing, a hunk of cheddar, or both. Maxine's favorite, what she'd known all along.

A voice boomed. "This is the one."

Maxine woke to angry, high-pitched voices.

"Hey!"

"But I want to play this one!"

"I don't care. It's my turn to pick. We played Cranium last time, so this time I pick Qwirkle."

"Ma-*ax*!"

Maxine untangled her legs from her sheets and blanket and walked into her living room to find Robert and Second John shoving each other.

"Uh-uh, guys. Cut it out. What are you two doing here?"

"Mama said you're supposed to watch us. She had to meet Uncle Roy and then buy groceries before the concert." Robert dropped a canvas bag by the door.

"And she has a key, remember?"

Maxine slapped her head, scattering any traces of grogginess. *The concert!*

Robert pointed to her hand. "When did Teddy give you that?"

She looked at her ring finger. *Oops.* "A friend let me borrow it a long time ago. I need to give it back."

"What's her name?" Second John set down his stack of board games.

JD, she answered silently as she gently slid off the ring. She'd fallen asleep after trying it on the night before. "I'll be right back, guys." In her bedroom, Maxine ran her finger around the sapphire's beveled edge. Then she set the white gold band in its small velvet box and slipped it into the zipper pocket in her purse.

When she returned to her brothers, Maxine angled a thumb at the bag by the door. "Whatchya'll got there?"

"Chips and salsa, ham, turkey, Swiss cheese, some bread. Can we eat now?"

"Robbie, you're always hungry. Let's pla-ay!" Second John rolled his eyes.

"Guys, come on. Quit whining and fussing. Mother probably won't be back for several hours, so we'll have plenty of time for *you* to eat." She pulled the curl on Robert's widow's peak. "And for *you* to play." She poked Second John. "But first, I need coffee. Then we'll eat and fight over who plays what first."

Four hours, two board games, some sandwiches, and a bowl of chips and salsa later, Maxine packed up the boys and sent them back across the driveway to help her mother unload groceries from her Volvo. She leaned out the door and called down, "I need to take your key!"

Vivienne smiled over her armload. "You need to give me *yours*! See you at 5:30!"

Maxine shook her head and waved off Vivienne's comment, but once inside, she couldn't dismiss her words. She faced her reflection in the bathroom mirror. *Hmm. Is it time I move out? And leave Celeste? But I'm getting married soon— why now? Because you've never lived on your own. You've gone from your parents, to JD, a group home, back to your parents, and soon to Teddy.*

She turned away from the mirror and flicked on her closet light. "Well, before you pack your things, Maxine, you need to figure out what you're wearing to the concert. Pantsuit? Too stuffy. Gray skirt and cardigan? Blah. Skinny jeans? With a frilly sweater and tall boots? Is that dressy enough? Do I even have a frilly sweater?" She pushed aside a few more hangers before leafing back to the pantsuit. She hooked it across the door.

Bzzz. Bzzz.

Maxine scanned her dresser—*bzzz, bzzz*—and the kitchen counters for her phone. *Bzzz. Bzzz.* She spotted it on her desk, and breathless, she pressed the button. "Hello?"

"I see I still take your breath away."

Her heart tumbled down to her toes. Grateful for the chair, she sank into it. "Jay. JD."

He chuckled low in his throat. "Still don't know what to do with me, huh? That wasn't always the case."

"Oh, I know what to do with you."

"Is that right? And what would that be?"

Maxine pursed her lips. Part of her wished she could chuck him into the deepest ocean, but she suspected he would float rather than sink and make it back to shore.

"Maxie?"

"I see you don't know what to do with me either."

JD's sigh filled the silence humming on the line between them. "No, I don't. And I'm not used to that. I don't like it."

"I don't like it either. How are you? Are you enjoying the new job with Hillsong?" Maxine's shoulders relaxed. His frankness she could always handle.

"I am. Not so much the paperwork and people management, but what's not to love about the kids?"

She pictured her brothers' faces as they fought over board games.

JD continued. "And being with my family. We're getting to know each other again, even as Mom slowly forgets who I am. I'm learning more about Evelyn, and I get to watch my niece grow. It's good. Hard and good. I have to say though, this slower pace of life takes some adjustment. This ain't New York."

Maxine snickered. "Maybe not, but I bet you can't find sweet potato cobbler like Mama Ruby's in the big city."

"You've got that right. Does this mean you're okay with my visiting them?" His low voice tickled her ear.

She touched her cheek, for a second imagining his beard against it. "As my grandparents told me in so many words, your visit is none of my business. You're family. Just making yourself t'home."

"That's the idea. You know how I feel about them."

"Speaking of grandmothers, I was thinking about yours earlier . . . well, at least her ring. I'm sure you'd like to have that back. Keep it in the family."

"You're the one getting married."

Maxine rubbed her brow. "I should give it back to you. I already have one. And I'm sure your mother has missed it."

"Not lately. There's no rush."

"It's not right for me to keep it. Especially now."

"I'm sure Teddy Bear would agree."

"Stop calling him that! You don't even know him."

"Well, he sounds like a teddy bear—he's safe in your arms, but are you safe in his? He must not be man enough to hold *you* up or support *you* since he doesn't know about Celeste. And I bet that means he doesn't know about me either."

Maxine stood so abruptly she almost tipped over her chair. "Like you supported me, you mean, after you found out I was pregnant?"

At first, the sound of her heartbeat whooshing inside her

eardrums was her only answer. That and the loud silence that resonated with their mutual pain and anger and regret. At last, she managed to speak around the rawness of her throat. "I'm sorry. That wasn't fair. Besides, you probably didn't call me to talk about the ring. Or Theodore."

His own voice sounded choked. "No, I didn't. But you tend to give me more than I ask for." He cleared his throat. "We need to talk about Celeste. The last time I called you, we got interrupted."

Maxine shuddered, thinking of what Lilian had overheard.

"But we need to talk in person anyway. This isn't a subject we can handle over the telephone or in a ten-minute car ride. Can we meet for lunch or coffee? I promise to provide tons of cream and sugar."

Maxine walked around her apartment. She stopped at the window and leaned her forehead against the glass. "Mother says I drink it like a child playing grown-up."

"Maybe your coffee helps you keep your sweet disposition."

She snorted. "That's likely. But you're right—we should talk in person. Think we'll behave better?"

"That depends on what you mean by *better*."

"Jay. Stop."

"Stop what?"

"*It*. This . . . this verbal two-step, this . . ." Maxine huffed and focused on the creek peeking through the spray of leaves.

JD sighed again. "I don't know how to talk to you anymore. What to say. I have all these plans before I call you or see you, and then I hear your voice. You either say something that makes me mad or that makes me remember. I find myself *re*acting instead of acting. I'm not used

251

to feeling out of control, and it unsettles me. Makes me uncomfortable."

"You mean, I make you uncomfortable."

"Yes, you make me uncomfortable. This situation. A situation I created."

"That we created." Maxine thought a minute. "Let's start over. Not all the way over, but let's back up a little bit."

"To Sassafras?"

"What?"

"That restaurant I keep going to, hoping to run into you. You won't answer my calls or let me watch Celeste rehearse, and I can't stop by your house. So that left me Sassafras."

"And Mama Ruby's."

He chuckled. "And Mama Ruby's."

"You go to Sassafras looking for me?"

"Let's just say I've probably put on a good five pounds since I moved here. The host? He thinks I'm stalking him. His birthday is next week, by the way."

Her laughter mingled with his.

"Okay. You can stop going to Sassafras. I did. And I didn't ban you from Celeste's rehearsals. Well, I guess I kinda did." She turned away from the woods and saw her pantsuit hanging on her bedroom door. "Why don't you come tonight, to Celeste's concert?"

JD was quiet for a moment. "You mean with you?"

"With us. I'm going with my family. You can meet us there."

"And sit with Mr. and Mrs. Owens? Will there be a sniper waiting on the roof?"

Maxine walked to her bedroom and traced the hem of her

slacks. She picked off lint and flicked it into the air. "No, Jay. I'd hate to deprive you of the opportunity of seeing your . . . seeing Celeste perform her solo. I'm sure we can all behave ourselves for a couple of hours—not that you have to sit with me. With us. I just want you to know you're welcome. And maybe now I won't have to worry about you lying in wait in Spring Hope." She listened to what sounded like his fingers tapping.

"I suppose it's worth the risk of seeing Vivienne. But what about your Teddy B—er, your fiancé?"

"What about Theodore?"

"Will I meet him tonight as well?"

"No, he has a conflict tonight. You'll have to wait for official introductions."

"Does that mean we can meet for coffee after, to talk?"

She froze.

"Maxie?"

This isn't a date, Maxine. He's coming to Celeste's concert, and then he wants to talk about her. There's nothing wrong with talking with him like a grown woman over coffee. Maybe I'll skip the French vanilla creamer.

"Maxie?"

"Okay. Yes. I'll clear it with Mother."

"Clear it with your mother? Aren't you a little engaged for that?"

"I'm not asking her permission, JD. We had dinner plans afterward to celebrate the occasion. I can't simply bail."

"Well, if that's the case, I'll join you. Technically, I'm family, too. Right?"

"Jay."

He chuckled. "I couldn't resist another little cha-cha, Max*ine*. I'll see you tonight. Concert's at . . . ?"

"At 7:30. But we'll be there early to help Celeste and find seats."

"Then I'll see you around 7:00—as long as Mommy says it's okay."

Chapter Twenty-Three

MAXINE CRUNCHED ON AN APPLE SLICE, a far cry from the lemon pound cake of her dreams. "I didn't mean to upset you."

Vivienne slid the cast-iron pot into her oven and adjusted the temperature, then rose with her hands on her hips, glaring at her daughter. "Then what did you mean? Girl, I don't know where you put your head."

Maxine's throat pulsed as she swallowed. "I take it you disagree."

"You darn skippy I disagree! And I bet your Theodore would, too." Vivienne retrieved her apron from the hook by the stove and tied it around her waist.

Celeste's right. Mother does get worked up. Maxine took another bite.

"'I invited JD to attend the concert with us.' That's all you've got to say?" Vivienne looked down. With a furrowed brow, she removed the apron and again, hung it on the hook.

"Actually, no, ma'am. We're going out for coffee afterward. So I can't make it to dinner with you and First John."

"You . . . ! What . . . ? Are you . . . ?"

"Mother, didn't you say JD's return was a good thing?" Maxine hopped down from her perch and walked to the refrigerator.

"Not so you could start datin' that boy again!" She reached for the apron.

Maxine gently took the flower-sprinkled cotton cloth and held it behind her back. "Nobody's talking about a date. He asked me to meet him for coffee to talk about Celeste—and I'm the one who invited him to the concert." She hung up the apron herself and faced Vivienne. "So am I messing up big dinner plans?"

"No. Celeste asked to go out with friends from the orchestra, and we're going to take the boys for pizza nearby. You could join us."

"And watch Second John and Robert fight over the last slice of pepperoni while Zan and First John engage in their Steph Curry versus Lebron debate? No thank you. Then it sounds like we're all set. See you in . . . ?" She drained her glass of water and checked her watch. "An hour fifteen?"

Vivienne caught Maxine by her hand. "Child, listen to me."

"Mother—"

"Listen to me now if you don't ever listen to another thing I say." She set Maxine's glass on the island and clasped her daughter by the shoulders. "Don't mess things up with Theodore just because that boy slid back into town, thinkin' he can pick up where he left off. Yes, you need to iron out this thing with Celeste. Hear him out, but guard your heart. You're a soon-to-be married woman. Act like it."

"Would a 'soon-to-be married woman' ask her mother's permission to go out? Or still be living at home? Hanging out with her little brothers on the weekend? I think it's time we both let me grow up."

"I feel like we're goin' through it all over again."

Maxine gritted her teeth and turned away from the tears welling in Mother's eyes. "Do you really think I've learned nothing in my life, that my commitment to Teddy is that weak?" *But what about your commitment to God, Maxine?*

"No, no. I just worry about the hold that boy has on you."

"I think you should stop calling him 'that boy,' for one. At least use his birth name. James."

"James who?"

Maxine and Vivienne turned toward the back stairs and found Zander standing there, holding his basketball.

"He's an old friend of Max's who just moved back into town. Remember, he's running that community outreach center," Celeste answered from two risers up, just behind him.

"Oh yeah, Hillsong!" Zander stepped into the kitchen, his little sister on his tail. "What's up? Y'all look like Mayweather versus Pacquiao."

Maxine faced Mother in her corner and braced herself for a fight. "We're meeting for coffee, but she doesn't want me to go."

"Can she stop you?" Her brother chuckled at his mother's look. "I know she still lives here, but she's grown. She only answers to Teddy." He dribbled his ball.

"I don't answer to anybody but Jesus, thank you very much. And I don't *still* live here. I live there." Maxine pointed out the back window toward the garage.

"Well, *you* still live here, Zan, so stop bouncin' that ball in my house. And where do you think you're going with that? You should be gettin' ready!"

"Ma, I've got nearly an hour to shoot some hoops. I'm not the one performing tonight."

She pursed her lips. "What about you, Celeste?"

The teen waggled the finger hooked around a hanger. "I need you to iron my blouse."

Maxine lowered her head and walked to the back door.

"Wait, Maxine! You're going out with Mr. Lester? The Lenny Kravitz look-alike?" Celeste raised an eyebrow. "What's up?"

"Nothing's *up*. We're just catching up over coffee. He's coming to the concert."

"He is? You can officially introduce me!"

"Officially introduce who?" Maxine's hand froze on the knob.

"Me! As my sister, you're my in. We want to work at the center this summer."

"Who's we?"

"My friends. Me. *We*."

Maxine turned her back on the perfect O of Vivienne's mouth. "Um. Let's think about that. I don't want you doing too much."

"But tonight's the final concert of the season, and I'll have more time before rehearsals start up again in August."

"We'll see. Today's main objective is getting you to the auditorium on time. Bye for now!"

The last thing she heard before she slammed the back door was, "Boy, if you don't get that ball out my house . . ."

"You have been awfully quiet." First John inclined his head toward his wife.

Indeed, up to then, the twenty-minute drive had been funereal, save for the beeps and taps of the twins' iPods in the rear and the *ca-thunk*, *swish* of the windshield wipers. Maxine's eyes hop-skipped from her stepfather's in the rear-view mirror to the part at the top of her mother's head, all she could see from the middle row of First John's Yukon XL. Beside her, Celeste plucked her imaginary bass with closed eyes, and Zander read *Moby-Dick* in his seat behind his father.

They continued driving through downtown until finally First John turned on his signal and stopped in front of the auditorium. He put an arm across the seat and looked from Maxine to Vivienne. "Is this because we're late? I'm sorry my interview ran long. And I had no idea traffic would be this heavy."

No, First John. I'm the whale on the end of her harpoon this time. But Maxine smiled. "You were only fifteen minutes late."

"So we're all right?" Her stepfather glanced first at Vivienne before catching Maxine's eyes.

Vivienne murmured, "Mmm-hmmm."

"Of course, First John."

"Okay, then . . . Maxine, get Celeste situated. Zan, Second John, and Robert, y'all go in and get us good seats, enough for all of us, plus Roy, Ruby, and Lerenzo—and remember, no horseplay. Your mom and I will park."

"And don't forget Mr. Lester," Vivienne growled.

Maxine decided not to reply. She gathered her light wrap around her, opened her door, and held an umbrella over Celeste as the boys scrambled out after them. As her parents pulled away, Maxine saw her mother's mouth moving and her hands directing an invisible choir.

Backstage was a beehive of activity. A trio of flutists trilled in the corner. Oboists licked their reeds behind trumpet players who were either cleaning their horns or tuning up. Musicians stepped over clarinet cases and saxophones propped up like abandoned bicycles, while other performers reclined against the rear wall or unpacked more instruments.

Maxine and Celeste bumped against mothers and fathers milling through the crowd, listening to their soloists, and dragging younger family members around the curtain and into the concert hall. She waved off her brothers and inspected Celeste.

The teenager turned three hundred sixty degrees. Her black skirt billowed out below her wrinkle-free white blouse. "How do I look?"

"Lovely, of course." Maxine smoothed a strand that had escaped her sister's side bun. *"Très chic."*

A crevice formed in each of Celeste's cheeks as she smiled.

"Thank you. Mama bought me this silver clip. It helps me stand out." She tugged at Maxine's wrap. "It's not raining inside, you know. What are you hiding under there?"

Laughing, she slapped at Celeste's probing hands and gathered the material closer. "Shouldn't you get ready? Check in with the conductor? Warm up or something?"

"You're probably right. It is after six." She craned her neck to see over and around Maxine.

Maxine turned to look before questioning Celeste with an arched brow.

"I'm just looking." Celeste scoured the area again, then smoothed her skirt. "Making sure everybody's here."

"Everybody like who?"

"Everybody like everybody. Anyway, I should unpack my bass." But she scanned the room again before moving toward the string section.

"Okay, I'll go meet Mother and First John. Break a . . . bow or something. You know what I mean."

"Do I though?" Celeste waved a dismissive hand over her shoulder.

Maxine wondered what was going through the girl's mind. As far as Maxine was concerned, it didn't take the sparkly pin to make the willowy, bubbly teen shine in the undulating sea of ebony. She used both hands to part the burgundy velvet curtain and slipped through. She wound her way through the crowd to the foyer and searched among the other concert-goers for her parents.

"Our girl's all situated?"

Maxine approached the deep voice. She nodded at First John and Mother. "She's getting her bass. Want to find our seats? The boys should be holding them down by now. I'll join you in a bit."

"We will, but I'm waiting for . . . There they are!" Vivienne waved. "They don't see me. I'll go get them. Be right back." She stuffed her sweater into her husband's hands.

Maxine moved aside to let a percussionist clicking his drumsticks together push between them. She squared her shoulders. "If you have something to say—"

"Viv has probably said more than enough."

"Yes."

"But just in case she left something out . . ." Her step-father swallowed. "Maxine, I let you down years ago by not saying enough, and I won't make that mistake now."

Maxine opened her mouth to interrupt, but she pressed her lips together.

"I don't care if you're thirty or one hundred and thirty. I will always be your . . . well, you will always be my daughter. When you left us, we were lost. All we could do was pray and hope and believe that God was watching over you. Then you came back to us, with Celeste. And we haven't stopped praying and hoping and believing—for both of you, for all of you.

"And God has answered our prayers. Not just that you would mature into the beautiful, talented young woman that you are. Or that you would develop your own faith in Jesus Christ. But we have been on our knees praying that nothing would ever turn your heart from us or take you away from us again. And here he comes."

"First John, JD didn't break into our house one night, wrap me up in a blanket, and spirit me off somewhere.

I made my own decision." She lowered her voice. "However bad."

"But he was older than you, more mature. He was raised better than that. To just leave you and his baby . . . And now he's come back. You have your whole life ahead of you, Maxine. After all you went through—what *we* went through—now you have a burgeoning career, a husband to look forward to, a family of your own. We've prayed and believed, and now we see the fruit of all those seeds we planted. I hate to see you run headlong into something."

"I'm not rushing into anything! I didn't then, and I'm not now. Did you forget that I was fifteen when I met JD? We didn't get married until I was seventeen!"

First John held up a hand. "What did you say?"

"Who's married?" Celeste popped out from behind First John, holding her bow.

Vivienne strolled up with Ruby and Lerenzo. Vivienne straightened her younger daughter's collar and smoothed her hair. "Child, where's your bass?"

"Large strings and percussions are already set up onstage. Who got married?"

"Hey, sugar." Ruby kissed Celeste's cheek.

"Hey, Grandma. Hey, Granddaddy. Daddy, are you okay? Who's mar—?"

"Vivienne, *hija*, can you call Roy before he parks the car? I think I dropped my glasses in the front seat." Lerenzo patted his blazer pockets.

Celeste waved her arms above her head. "Hello-o-o! An answer please. Maxine, did you run off and get married?"

First John, Vivienne, Ruby, and Lerenzo froze.

And Maxine looked over Celeste's head at Uncle Roy.

He used the arm of a pair of glasses to tap the shoulder of the man at his side.

JD waved, his dimples familiar parentheses enclosing his smile. "Hey."

———

"You picked a fine time to show up."

"I said I'd see you around seven. It was 6:55."

"Shh!"

Maxine glanced at her mother leaning forward in her seat. She mouthed, *"Sorry"* at Vivienne and decided to count the woodwind instruments onstage. *Nineteen, twenty, twenty-one, twenty-two . . .*

"I didn't tell you how beautiful you look."

JD's minty breath widened the breadth of her answering grin. In her periphery, she saw Vivienne throw a heated stare their way. Maxine tugged the hem closer to her knee as she traced one of the bold-orange, blue, and yellow flowers sprouting all over the silky fabric of her dress.

They sat there in the semidarkness of the auditorium while the orchestra launched into the first movement of Vivaldi's *Four Seasons*. Maxine sensed JD's head moving rhythmically and his fingers dancing on the armrests. She soon lost herself in the violins, only coming up for air when JD's shoulder pressed against hers.

"Think your mom will ever like me?"

She shrugged. This time, she sensed rather than felt his exhalation.

He wasn't the only one who was frustrated. She could

tell Vivienne was done—"thoo," as Mama Ruby pronounced when she was too upset to form the *r* in *through*. But JD's arrival had cut off her conversation with First John at the knees. First John had pulled Vivienne close to his side, and they'd all stood there looking for a hole to jump into. Except Celeste. She'd beamed at Mr. Lester after their official introduction, kissed her parents, and bounced off to warm up with the orchestra.

Now Maxine trained her eyes on her favorite bass player, head bent over her instrument, bow at the ready. She tried to tune out JD, her uncle, and her grandparents on her right and First John, Mother, and the boys on her left.

But Vivienne wasn't having it. She was *through*.

Maxine sensed it every time Mother shifted, felt the pain when her eyes flashed their way. Forty-five minutes into the concert, Maxine ached from the effort to appear normal and unaffected.

"Are you okay?"

She nodded almost imperceptibly at JD and studied her program. She tilted the paper toward him and pointed. Celeste's solo!

He squeezed her hand, his anticipation palpable.

On the other side of First John, Vivienne sucked in a breath.

The low notes of the bass swelled through the auditorium, capturing all their attention. Maxine prayed for the strength to hold on until the music ended as she interlaced her fingers with his and squeezed back.

"That was beautiful!"

"Your mama's right, Celeste. Your bass sang." First John's fingers seemed to chase notes in the air.

"You did good, Sis. You did good." Zander clapped soundlessly.

Vivienne's nose lifted toward heaven. "Only Jesus does *good*. Watch your grammar. You know better. And so—" she gripped Robert's shoulder, who was trading elbow pokes with his twin—"do *you*. We're not outside."

"How long have you been playing, Celeste?"

All eyes turned to the man who'd asked the question—JD, drumming on the checkerboard tablecloth.

Celeste's friends had canceled their postconcert plans, and it had become clear to Maxine that skipping off to have coffee with her ex-husband would have the effect of a nuclear air strike. Fearing the caustic residue, she'd invited JD to join the family for pizza instead. Gunfire, she could handle.

"I started the piano at four, the cello when I was six, and I moved to the bass at ten-and-a-half. It took a minute for Mama to get over *that* hit to her pocketbook, especially on top of the piano lessons." Celeste grinned. Still floating from her performance, she didn't seem to notice Vivienne's return smile flicker and go out before it caught.

JD looked at Vivienne for a second. His fingers tapped on the side of the glass jar of Parmesan cheese in the middle of the table. "The cello? Wow. Why not the violin?"

"*Why* the violin?" Vivienne slid her arm on the back of Celeste's ladder-back chair. "Everybody plays the violin. Our daughter isn't everybody."

Zander had been teasing his brothers about their artwork

on their children's menus, but at her words, he cocked an eyebrow in Maxine's direction.

She shrugged.

Vivienne shushed the twins again without taking her eyes off their guest.

"Then why the piano? Everybody and their mama plays that, too, including mine." The gap in JD's teeth winked at them before he doused his grin. "The cello, piano, and bass. Any other instruments in your repertoire?"

"Nope, just the basketball. All of us do, thanks to First John." Celeste pretended to dribble and shoot and laughed when Zan caught the "ball" and returned it.

"Who?" Even sitting at the table, Vivienne propped a hand on her hip as she leaned forward to glare at her daughter.

"Dad knows who I mean." Celeste rolled her eyes.

"I played basketball in school, too, and so did my—" JD began.

"Where are those pizzas? I'm starving!" The metal legs of Maxine's chair screeched on the concrete floor as she scooted her chair closer to the table.

"So am I." First John looked toward the hostess and raised two fingers in the air.

"You played too?" Robert sat on JD's right, at the end of the table where they'd been banished. "I don't like basketball—sorry, *Dad*. We play baseball."

"And the piano," Second John chimed in. "At least Robert does."

JD turned to Robert. "You play the piano too? My mother made me take lessons, but I loved playing the guitar more. And as a matter of fact, Mother played the cello."

"I know good and well what instruments Annie played." Vivienne pushed the words through stiff lips.

"There's Uncle Roy with Mama Ruby and Granddaddy!" Maxine waved her arm wildly as if directing an airplane landing. "Over here!"

JD and First John rose. Zander grabbed Robert's right arm and Second John's left, and the boys stood as Ruby reached the table, with Lerenzo and Roy bringing up the rear.

"Now, y'all know we could've made us some better food than this. Why we eatin' pizza when I could have made short ribs and stewed some greens?" Ruby plopped down heavily into the chair Roy set between Maxine and Celeste. She leaned over and kissed Celeste. "Hey, baby."

"We're here because we're celebrating our granddaughter, and she wanted pizza. *Verdad?*" Lerenzo winked at the teenage girl and pulled up a chair beside JD.

"Yes, that's right, Granddaddy." Her smile seemed to wrap around them both.

"But—" Ruby began.

"Those are for sitting down and eating pizza. Right, Mama Ruby?" JD clasped first Lerenzo's wrinkled hand, then Roy's smoother one. They shook once and then their fingers snapped as their hands slid free. He grinned at Roy as the older man pulled up a chair at the end of the table.

"Boy, you betta . . ." The older woman's eyes crinkled in a grin, belying her threat.

Maxine almost joined in the fun, but Vivienne's frown weighed down the light, playful air at the table. Suddenly it felt like rain. She looked down at her lap.

"I like your dress, Maxine. I never seen it."

"Me neither, Grandma. I thought sure she'd wear one of those pleated skirts she's got a ton of." Celeste reached over and fingered the silky-smooth fabric. "But this is cute. I'd wear this myself."

"As short as it is, you could probably wear it, Celeste. Did you really think that was appropriate for a child's concert, Maxine?" Vivienne looked like she'd dined on a sour pickle.

"What's inappropriate about it?" Maxine forced herself not to fuss with her hem.

JD's eyes caught hold of Maxine's across the table. "I told her earlier how beautiful she looks in those colors."

"And who's the child you're talking about?" Celeste piped up.

Lerenzo reached across the table and patted Celeste's fingertips. *Está bien, nieta.* Vivienne, *hija . . . cálmate.*"

"I am calm, Daddy." Vivienne's smile looked as taut as the strings on Celeste's bass.

Roy leaned in and stage-whispered in Maxine's direction, "As the eye of a hurricane."

Mama Ruby shushed him with a raised eyebrow. Then she sat straight in her chair and looked toward his right. "James Dee, I'm sorry to hear your mama's doing so poorly. Anything I can do?"

JD glanced at Vivienne and Maxine before attending to Mama Ruby. "Yes. It's hard to watch her lose touch, to lose herself, and it's happening so quickly. Thank you for sending the note and the sweet potato cobbler. They meant a lot. Especially the cobbler."

Maxine watched Celeste's head whip from one face to another as Ruby continued.

"I'm happy to help any way we can while she's on this side of heaven. And when the time comes, we'll do you up right for her home goin'."

"Mama Ruby!" Maxine knew JD was used to her grandmother's plain speaking, but she cringed at the shameless plug for Manna's catering business.

JD seemed unfazed. "I know you will, thank you. Kevin told me you really laid it out for the Agnews. I'm sorry Mom didn't ask you when my grandfather died."

Silence fell on the adults at the table like heavy morning dew, but JD's calm statement sparked more questions from Celeste.

"You knew Mr. Lester's grandparents?"

"Well . . . ," Mama Ruby began, looking as if she were planning on digging one to jump into.

"Pizza!" Robert and Second John chorused.

"Finally!" Maxine exhaled.

Celeste's mouth moved as if to say something, but two servers suddenly added plates, utensils, napkins, and five large platters to the table. Soon everyone was distracted by the clamor for food.

"Nobody eats veggies on your pizza?" JD's knife and fork were poised over his plate.

"Nobody else uses utensils to eat pizza either," Maxine pointed out. "And you know I don't like anything on my pizza but pizza stuff."

"And by 'pizza stuff,' she means only pepperoni and extra cheese." Zander wiped his mouth.

Nodding and chewing, JD snickered as he bumped fists with Roy.

"You know how Maxine eats her pizza? Care to share anything else you know?" Celeste giggled.

"Celeste!" Vivienne let her slice fall with a saucy *splat!* that turned the table into a crime scene.

"What? Maxine knows I'm teasing."

"Excuse me." Vivienne dropped her napkin before pushing back her chair and stomping away.

"What's wrong with Mama?"

First John swallowed. "Robert, don't eat—I mean, don't *talk* with your mouth full. Your mama's fine. Probably mad about getting tomato sauce on her new dress."

Maxine noticed that the humor took a wrong turn somewhere before it reached First John's eyes. She set down her crust and looked at JD.

He swiped his mouth and wadded up the napkin. When he stood, his chair rocked and almost fell over. "I should go and let you enjoy your family celebration. If I leave now, I can complete some paperwork before tomorrow."

"But tomorrow's Saturday. And you didn't finish your pizza!"

"Shh, Second John." Maxine slid back her chair.

"The man can find his way out the restaurant, Maxine." Ruby's eyes seemed to order, *Butts are for sitting down.*

First John rose and extended a hand toward JD. "Thanks for coming. I'm sure it means a lot to Celeste . . . and the rest of us . . . that you were here. It's good to see you."

"Thank you, sir. It's always good to be seen on this side of the dirt, as some folks say." JD clasped First John's hand with both of his own.

Maxine knew Mama Ruby was the "folks" JD quoted. She

nodded good-bye as he pushed his chair under the table and walked away. When she glanced at Celeste, she intuited the girl knew it, too. She wondered if Celeste knew how much she looked like her father.

Robert knocked over his cup of Sprite. Zander jogged off to get extra napkins. Celeste broke eye contact with Maxine to help the boys clean up the mess, including the splatters of pizza sauce. Pink swirls in the soda, evidence of the casualties racking up in the family's war.

Maxine scooted closer to her stepfather. "What are y'all doing tomorrow?"

He was quiet for a moment as his fingers plucked sausage from the congealing cheese on his half-eaten slice. "Well, Zan and Celeste have their usual chores. Vivienne is supposed to meet your grandmother around three to lay out catering plans for June, and I'm taking the boys to the Insectarium in the morning and baseball practice at six. Why?" He dabbed his fingertips and slowly folded his napkin. "Zan, get a tray for those wet napkins. Boys, collect all the plates, and cut it out so Roy, Ruby, and Lerenzo can eat in peace."

Maxine leaned toward him on crossed arms. "Um-hmm. I was thinking we could visit Reverend Atwater. Together. You and Mother. With me."

"For marriage counseling?" He rested his chin on his fists.

"I guess the secret is out." Maxine felt like she was dancing on hot coals. "I've kept parts of my life from you and Mother, parts from Teddy, and parts from Celeste. I don't even know my entire self, what I'll look like when they're all stitched together." She studied her intertwined fingers.

"Whole. You'll look and feel whole. And still as beautiful."

"Like Frankenstein?" Her mouth twisted wryly.

"More like his bride." First John shrugged as if he were considering the possibility. He glanced in the boys' direction.

When Maxine followed his look, she noticed how Celeste seemed to float above her brothers' commotion. She kept one eye on the distracted teen while she explained, "When we first met with the pastor, he explained that all the parts of us tell our story, and they affect how Teddy and I will write the next chapter. All of you are part of me. It's like we're all getting married."

First John gripped her forearm, drawing her complete attention his way. "All, including JD? Are we meeting with Reverend Atwater because you're too chicken to tell your mama and me alone?"

Maxine tried to hide her heartburn with a smile. "No. I mean, yes. Partly, I guess. Mother can't flip out in front of a preacher, can she?"

"You know your mama. She'll flip out anywhere she pleases. Are you worried?"

Maxine realized her face was telling on her, despite her best efforts. She grasped his hand. "All is well, First John. So are we going to the chapel tomorrow?"

"As long as you're still going to get married." He squeezed back. Together they watched Vivienne stalk back to the table and plop into a seat next to Roy. "And by the looks of it, it's a good thing we're going to see Reverend Atwater."

———

The darkness in the room nibbled at the circle of light around Maxine's desk where she sat watching the blinking cursor tick away the minutes. She closed her eyes and prayed. Then she typed *My Daily Grace—The Music Maker*.

Music tells a story. I felt that more than ever at my sister's concert. Those melodies and rhythms made my spirit cry, dance, sing, and play along. Oh, if you could have witnessed their fingers dancing over the keys, strings, valves, and slides, heard their hands bang, clap, and pluck . . . ! I could hear and feel such stories. Or maybe I was listening to my own. If I'd had the nerve, I would have run down to the stage, pushed the conductor aside, and directed my own overture.

By now you know I'm more than a bride-to-be. I'm the teenager who doesn't want to grow up. A daughter who still cries on her mother's shoulder. The granddaughter looking for her grandma's lap. A BFF who holds secrets close. A writer passing along her own legends, fairy tales, not-so-tall tales, and tragedies. I suppose my words are the notes I'm playing.

"What does this have to do with getting married?" Good question.

It takes the oboes, the trumpets, the violas—all the woodwinds, the brass, the percussion, and the strings—to form a complete orchestra. To make the music. If a clarinetist splits her reed, she can't play. The piece wouldn't be as full and rich, complete. We need the rumble of the bass drum as well as the trill of the piccolo. They show the thunder and the birds singing. What would "Rhapsody in Blue" be without the piano and the bass? And of course, we need the conductor! He signals each group when to come in, when to crescendo or decrescendo, when to stop altogether.

That's marriage. That's life. Each part tells a story, and altogether, they complete the story. The low notes, the high notes, the sorrows and the joys. The old friends who knew you as a single woman. The new ones who know you as half of a couple. The family who made you, loved you, and even scarred you. Coworkers who get the part-time you. Drivers who honk at you for idling at the light. All these people, all these events—they make up our story. And God directs it all, all the musicians, the entire composition. He knows the beginning, the middle, and the end. He's its Author and Finisher.

Our job is to play it, to share it, to make our stories heard, experienced, and felt. I'm adding another chapter to my life. It's not the chapter I'd outlined necessarily but the one written for me. While I'm grateful for the grace and the gift of the story itself because it's beautiful and painful all at once, I pray for the strength to play this music that makes me cry, laugh, and sing. I'm sure my "audience"—my fiancé, my parents and siblings, my friends, the witnesses and my fellow musicians in this ensemble of life—will be leaning forward in their seats and moving to the beat of the music, alternately applauding or crying.

Is your life a psalm or a Gregorian chant? Maybe it sways to Kirk Franklin or skips to the lilting rhythm of George Gershwin or Scott Joplin. I think mine pulses to the beat of all these, with Gregory Hines as a dance partner and Karen Carpenter crooning on the rainy days. The "Wedding March," Canon in D, or simply "Here Comes the Bride" is always humming in the background.

Yet I know that in the end, I'll give God the highest praise: a standing ovation.

. . . but be filled with the Spirit, speaking to one another in psalms and hymns and spiritual songs, singing and making melody in your heart to the Lord, giving thanks always for all things to God the Father in the name of our Lord Jesus Christ, submitting to one another in the fear of God.
Ephesians 5:18-21

Maxine checked the clock before she closed her laptop with a click. Less than twelve hours to go before her meeting. "For whom the bell tolls . . . ," she murmured to herself.

Chapter Twenty-Four

Maxine pulled into Grace Chapel's now-familiar parking lot. Same cracks, same grass, same Scripture promising sanctuary. Greater weights and worries to bear.

She let her Volvo idle as she waited for her parents to join her, trying to decompress after her weekly meeting with her editor. *More, more, more!* Jean always wanted more. Maxine *was* experiencing more—more pain, more regret, more tears, more fear—but writing about it all wouldn't encourage her readers—or the author. As her stepfather drove through the gate, she wondered how she would encourage her parents after this meeting. Resigned, Maxine waved hello as she turned off the ignition and climbed from her car.

"So what's this all about, Maxine?" Vivienne was never one for mincing words. It seemed in her mind, time was like the gold California miners sifted for—a precious commodity she hoarded. She apparently wasn't up for wasting precious minutes on a reunion in a church parking lot.

"You'll see soon enough, Mother." Maxine looped an arm through Vivienne's and kissed First John on the cheek. "They're waiting on us, so let's head in."

Sure enough, Reverend Atwater flung open his office door before they could knock on it. Lilian, her smile as luminous as her scarlet pencil skirt and matching lip gloss, was perched on a corner of his desk. She hopped to her feet when the group stepped into the room.

"Reverend, I'd like to introduce you to my parents, John and Vivienne Owens. Mother, First John, you already know Lilian Atwater," Maxine managed through stiff lips. She tried to coat her words with oil, but she couldn't pretend they were all friends preparing to dig into a meal of fried chicken and potato salad. She was about to serve up her past, memories and feelings she'd sealed away for decades, and invite those present to feast upon them.

Lilian hugged First John and then Vivienne, even more tightly. When she pulled back, she inclined her head in her husband's direction. "I'm glad you finally get to meet these two. My life—and my waistline—will never be the same after eating that chicken salad."

Vivienne hinted at a smile. "Wait 'til you taste my heavenly cake."

"The kids called it Jesus' favorite cake, but Viv didn't want to be disrespectful," First John explained.

"It gets my vote." Reverend Atwater patted his stomach

and waved toward a small sitting area on the other side of his office. "Let's sit down, Mr. and Mrs. Owens. Maxine."

"Please call us Vivienne and John." Vivienne led the way to an overstuffed love seat.

Maxine trailed behind the group but chose a wooden side chair with a needlepoint cushion. She found comfort in its unyielding frame.

"May I offer you coffee or water? Iced tea? I warn you, it's heavily sweetened." Lilian lifted a crystal pitcher from the server by the pastor's desk.

Vivienne looked at her husband before giving her full attention to Reverend Atwater. "No thank you. I think we'd just like to know what this is all about." The fingertips of her left hand tapped out a rhythm on the arm of her chair while the fingers on the other hand clenched and unclenched in her lap.

First John coughed and clasped his wife's wrist—whether in agreement or as a restraint, Maxine couldn't tell.

Reverend Atwater scooted to the edge of one of the chairs that faced them. "Well, that's why we're here. Your daughter called last night and asked if we all could meet, and I didn't ask any questions." His smile invited Maxine to stay for a spell. "Let's pray, and then you can start whenever you're ready."

At *amen*, Maxine's eyes flitted from one expressive face to another—dread, frustration, patience—before they landed on Lilian's. Expectant.

The pastor's wife touched the twinkling diamond in her nose.

Maxine swallowed. "Well, I hope you cleared the after-noon."

———

It never occurred to Maxine that JD was too old for her or too mature or too driven or too smart or too smooth. He wasn't too *anything*, except maybe too perfect for her, if there was such a thing. God knew he was handsome. And though she'd never thought of the words *charming* or *masculine* as a sheltered fifteen-year-old, she was aware that there was some-thing about the way he carried himself that shouted, "I know where I'm going, and if you knew better, you'd come, too—not that I want you to."

Except for Maxine. Maxie, he wanted.

———

"Manly," Vivienne interjected from the love seat. "Just too manly. I never liked him."

First John patted her hand. "*Shh.* We know all about how you felt. Let the girl talk."

So Maxine did.

———

She would have followed JD to the ends of the world, the man-child who filled a need she'd never voiced or put a fin-ger to. And half-full, or half-empty as she saw herself, that's exactly what she did—she followed him until her world shat-tered into a million pieces. Getting married and pregnant at seventeen had a hand in that.

"Are you ready to tell your mom and dad, Mrs. Lester?" JD took a bite of his sandwich.

"My stepdad. And no, not yet, Mr. Lester." She fiddled with the door lock. Up. Down. Up. Down.

"You're going to break that. You know how old this truck is? She barely got us to Jordan Lake and back." He balled up the wrapping for his Big Mac and polished off the rest of his fries. "Why not?"

"Why not what?" Although she knew "why not," and he knew she knew it. "Because they're not ready to hear it."

"They're not ready to hear, or you're not ready to tell?"

It was obvious he knew the answer to that, too.

"So when?" He twisted and dropped his bag into the truck bed beside their blankets and jackets. A brisk December breeze had driven them from the park, forcing them to "reconfigure" their picnic spot within the confines of Blue's cab. "They're preparing to move. It's only getting harder the longer you wait. Won't they wonder why you aren't packing up your stuff?"

Maxine nibbled on a french fry.

"Maxie?"

"Do you want these?" She wrinkled her nose and dropped the half-eaten fries. Nothing tasted the same these days. The only thing she wanted to eat was cantaloupe and red meat, any kind. Mother couldn't make enough pot roast, beef ribs, meat loaf, or hamburgers. She was glad everybody in her life was too busy to notice her thickening waistline, frequent naps, and change in appetite. "They won't wonder because . . . I'll actually pack up my stuff."

He dropped the fry and stared at her, brown eyes wide enough for her to fall into. "What did you say?"

"I said, I'll—"

"I heard what you said. What do you *mean*?" He threw the carton of uneaten fries into the back. It spilled onto the normally pristine floor of the truck.

"I mean . . . I've decided to go with them to Alabama. We leave in February."

"What?"

Maxine ducked as if to avoid shrapnel when JD sprang from his seat and flung open the door of Blue. She waited a moment before she pulled the handle and stepped out.

"I can't believe this, Maxie! What are you telling me? What about us? You're my *wife*."

But she didn't feel like somebody's wife. She certainly didn't feel like somebody's mama. She felt like a seventeen-year-old girl watching her boyfriend kick the gravel in the parking lot behind McDonald's because he wasn't getting what he wanted. They'd chosen this spot because it faced the woods, and at the moment, Maxine was grateful for the privacy. JD's passion was one of the things she loved about him—until it was vented in her direction.

His chest heaved. "Maxie?"

She stared at him for a second. "Jay, you're heading back to Princeton in a few weeks. You'll be gone all spring semester."

"You knew that when we got married."

"Maybe. But I didn't know I'd get pregnant. At least not while I was in high school."

He froze. "You didn't know . . . *pregnant*?"

As he absorbed her words, Maxine wanted to jump back

into the truck, but she endured his examination as his eyes slowly traveled from her face to her midsection.

His bottom jaw dropped open. "But we only—"

"I see we both skipped Mrs. Bibb's ninth-grade health class. There just has to be an 'only.'" She crossed her arms and leaned on Blue's cooled hood.

JD stared past her. "I don't know what to say."

"That's why I can't go with you to Princeton! We *might* have been able to support ourselves, but a *baby*? I'll go with First John and Mother to Alabama for now. Maybe with their help, I can still finish school."

"So they know?"

JD's voice was so low, Maxine could barely hear him over an 18-wheeler rumbling into the lot. She watched a robin hop about in the grassy edge of the lot, its red chest puffed out. She picked at a light-blue chip on the nose of the truck. *Oh, to be a bird. I could fly away and not answer that question. Lord, do You really care about me as much as You care about this robin?*

"Maxie? What did they say when you told them? I thought we were going to talk to them together."

A sharp edge of paint sliced into her fingertip. She swiped at the blood that seeped under her nail. "We planned to tell them we were *married*, not pregnant."

"Maxie? Will you look at me?" JD's feet crunched on the pebbles as he moved to her side.

But she couldn't face him. He always could tell when she was avoiding the truth. Maxine intended to tell her parents. At some point. It was hard enough telling JD. The truth was the same in the end no matter the way you got to it, she reasoned. And the fact of the matter was, she couldn't go away with JD to Princeton. Not now. Probably not ever.

He stroked her hair.

When she wrenched away from him, she fell to one knee. "Don't touch me! You're the reason we're in this mess! 'Let's get married,' you said. 'We'll go away and live happily ever after.' Does this feel like 'happily ever after' to you?"

"Maxie, let's calm down."

"Just stop, JD. We should've known better than to think this could ever work out. You have a full scholarship to Princeton. Plans to move to New York after graduation. What will you do with a pregnant, teenage wife who doesn't even have a high school diploma?" She rose shakily, ignoring the rip in her khakis and the blood trickling down her shin.

He thrust out his squared jawline. "I would never leave you like this."

"But you have to. If you don't, how will you ever support me, me and a baby—your family? You may not want to go, but you have to."

"*May* not? I won't!"

"You *will*." Though he'd been the force that had driven them to elope, Maxine now wrenched the wheel from him. "You *will*, Jay. We made a mistake. But we can't make another one, a bigger one."

"How can raising our baby together be a bigger mistake?"

"Because I'm barely more than a baby myself. This whole thing has been one big crazy . . . mistake. I . . . I hate you for putting me in this position, talking me into this."

JD's eyes narrowed, but a tear squeezed through and ran

down his cheek, dripped past the throbbing pulse in his neck. "No, Maxie."

"Don't call me that. You've ruined my life, JD. And now . . . now I don't know what I'm going to do. The only thing I do know is I'm not going with you. And one more thing. My name is Maxine. Maxine Amelia Clark *Owens*."

"I can't stand to hear this." Vivienne pushed First John away. "If you say *married* one more time . . . It just burns my buns! Stop it, John. I don't feel like calmin' down. Maxine, how could you not have told me you got married . . . to *him*?" She swatted her husband's hand and, bracing her fists on the sofa, pushed herself to her feet. She stalked to the window and stared out through the venetian blinds.

Maxine silently entreated Reverend Atwater.

He held up a hand in her direction and faced First John. "Please, if I may. I can't imagine how you feel—well, I guess I can *imagine*, but I don't *know*. But neither can you know how Maxine feels now, nor how she felt then. The one way for us to learn, to walk in her shoes, is to listen and listen closely. That's what I once told Maxine . . . and Theodore." He swallowed.

Lilian clasped his shoulder and squeezed. "William."

He looked at her, and she nodded toward Maxine. He took a deep breath and touched his clerical collar that peeked out from his pin-striped suit jacket. He blinked, and he was the same Reverend Atwater who'd greeted them almost an hour ago. "Vivienne. John."

Maxine's mother slowly rotated one hundred eighty degrees toward the group. First John looked up.

"I told Maxine we're all part of her story, her family. And as hard as it is for you to rehash this—and even to hear it for the first time—it has to be even harder for Maxine to share this part of her. To risk your rejection, judgment, her own sense of shame and loss. But God doesn't condemn her for her feelings or her honesty or her past. And neither should you."

He paused as Vivienne shuffled to her spot beside her husband. Then he asked Maxine, "Do you feel like going on? I think we're ready."

"I don't know that I am. Not anymore."

Lilian offered Maxine a box of Kleenex. "Your parents love you. They just hurt when you hurt. *Because* you hurt. It's okay, Maxie."

A tear crept down Maxine's cheek. "Please don't call me that," she whispered. With a dry throat, she resumed.

"Okay. I guess this is good-bye." JD loaded his trunk and closed the hatchback of his mother's Mercedes. He kept his back toward her.

His eyes had widened when she'd strolled up. They hadn't seen each other in nearly two weeks, since their confrontation at McDonald's. For an hour, Maxine watched him stow his things in his parents' Mercedes, but she couldn't let him go without saying something to repair the breach between them. She took a few hesitant steps in his direction. "I'll miss you so much." She winced as JD stiffened like she'd stabbed him between his shoulder blades.

"You said you hated me, Maxine." He didn't turn.

"I could never hate you." When he faced her, she closed the remaining inches between them and wrapped her arms around his waist. She let out the breath she'd been holding as he pulled her closer. "I love you," she choked out.

"Then why are you doing this? What kind of person would I be to leave you? I'd be that self-centered boy your mama already thinks I am." He spoke into her hair.

Each time he said her given name, she felt the rope tying them together unravel. She locked her fingers together in the small of his back, under his cable-knit sweater.

"How can you raise our baby by yourself? I don't care what you say. I'm going to talk to Mr. Owens."

"No!" At his threat, she pushed him away, against his parents' car. "No, JD. That's what I came to tell you." She backed up another step.

"What you came to tell me?"

"About the b-baby. There isn't . . . a baby."

JD's eyebrows furrowed, creating a line on the bridge of his nose. He edged toward her. "What are you saying?"

She inched back. "I lost the baby, so you don't have to worry about that."

"*That?* You mean a baby." He stepped closer until they stood toe-to-toe. Fingers from one hand wrapped around her forearm, keeping her in place, while the fingers on his other moved a flyaway strand of her hair behind her ear. "What happened? Are you okay?"

Maxine tried to disengage herself. "No, I'm not. But I had to tell you. So you wouldn't worry."

"So I wouldn't worry?" JD was breaking all his own rules

by repeating his words. "And you think I won't worry now? How are you feeling?" He scanned her from head to toe as if he wanted to see right through her.

"How do you think I'm feeling?" Seeing the hint of relief in his eyes, Maxine finally broke free with a yank. She started to wrap her arms around herself but thought better of it when the movement tightened her shirt around her midsection. "You're off the hook. Now you know you don't have to say anything to First John, ever. Ever, JD!"

Tears and snot warred for space on her face as they streamed from her eyes and nose. But she didn't care. Maxine just wanted to get away. She had to. "You have to realize this is it for us. Please . . . please . . . go to Princeton and forget about me. Focus on your studies and your music. Another girl. Whatever you have to do. I just don't want . . . this—us. I don't want it anymore. I can't want it."

Behind them a garage door whirred open. Frantic, Maxine rose on her tiptoes, clasped his face between both hands, and kissed him hard—on the lips, his cheeks, his forehead—leaving a moist trail. Then she drank in his eyes as if she'd never see them again and whispered, "Good-bye, James Dee."

And she hopped into her mother's minivan and sped away.

"You lied to him? You told that—" Vivienne gulped down her words before finishing. ". . . JD that you'd miscarried?" She sounded incredulous, like she was working through a difficult puzzle by herself.

Maxine accepted the tissue Lilian pressed between her trembling fingers and offered her a silent thank-you. She dried her face. "It was all I could think to do at that moment to protect him, to protect all of us from making an even bigger mistake. JD was supposed to be my safe place, but all he did was get me kicked out of the church youth choir—which is exactly what would've happened if I'd strolled in there with a belly out to there and no husband to be seen.

"Mother, I didn't know what to do. I just knew what I didn't *want* to do. And that included telling you and First John and listening to you bash JD for the rest of my life, pointing out how wrong he was and how stupid I was and how disappointed you were. It was my decision to let him go so he wouldn't ruin his life, too. He didn't deserve that when he was only trying to help me. So . . . I decided not to say anything until I could figure something out. I threw away every letter JD wrote, ignored all his phone calls, nodded along when you celebrated our breakup."

"You mean your divorce. Something I never would've celebrated had I known." Vivienne didn't try to hide her bitterness.

Maxine held up a hand. "I'm not sure about that. Once I heard you tell Mama Ruby it was about time I 'woke up and left that boy.' But it's okay. You were right. It was time for me to wake up to the truth. As a daughter, I wasn't obedient enough. As a wife, I wasn't mature enough. As a mother, I wasn't good enough."

"Not good enough?" Lilian's and Vivienne's voices formed a duet, their tones expressing varying notes of disbelief.

"Not enough of anything. Regardless of what you

thought, Mother, JD was willing to change his whole life for me, which is exactly what he did! He became my home when it was taken from me—no offense, First John—and he tried to stand up and do what was right when I told him I was pregnant. Then out of respect for what I wanted—for what I *didn't* want—he let me go."

"Maxine, Maxine." First John cradled his head in his hands. "What did you think would happen when he found out you'd had his child? I mean, he *did* find out. What did he say?"

"When I left, I honestly thought I'd never come back. My seventeen-year-old self planned to raise her on my own. Do what Mother couldn't do. It seemed the end of the world as I knew it. But then I did come back. And you forgave me. You accepted us. Not only that—" Maxine took a big breath to fill lungs that seemed deflated—"one day, I was forced to let JD know the truth."

"Forced?"

When they all started at Lilian's interjection, the pastor's wife winced. "I'm sorry. That slipped out. I told you I'm a curious cat. Forgive me. The Lord is still working on me."

Maxine was surprised that she could smile a little at the woman. Actually, she felt a bit lighter. A bit. "I'm the last person to hold it against you, believe me." Sobering, she turned her attention to her family. "And, Mother, even after I told him about the adoption, he agreed. He gave up his own child, all because I convinced him it was the right thing to do, especially after all that time. If I'd been strong enough, I would've stuck it out."

"Or not married him in the first place," Vivienne muttered.

Maxine stared at her. "Or not given up his daughter in the second place."

Mother looked away.

"Anyway. That's what I was thinking then." *And now,* she thought. "I was too weak to tell you before we left for Alabama, and when I couldn't hide my pregnancy any longer, I ran away." Maxine gripped the stiff arms of her chair and leaned back, spent.

Reverend Atwater shifted in his seat. "When we first met and you talked about your family, you never gave any indication."

You lied, a voice accused. *And you're still lying.* "What? I didn't say, 'Hello, I'm Maxine, Teddy's fiancée. And while I'm making introductions, I should tell you about my first husband, JD Lester, and Celeste, my daughter?'"

"Your *daughter*? But isn't that your sister's name?" Atwater sat back.

"Willy, I'll get you some water. How about I just wheel the server over? We could all use some refreshment." Lilian gripped his shoulder and rose.

First John cleared his throat. "Maxine left us for nearly a year. Just up and disappeared one day after we'd moved to Mobile. She left a note that told us not to worry, that she hadn't been kidnapped or killed. We called the police anyway and tried to file a report, but she was over seventeen, so there was nothing they could do—or rather would do. We just prayed, cried, mourned. We stayed in Alabama, hoping she'd return.

"Then one night, we opened our door. And there she was. There *they* were—Maxine and Celeste. I can imagine how Mary and Martha must have felt when they saw Lazarus emerge from the tomb. What was lost found again. Alive." He sniffed and wiped away a tear. He cradled Vivienne's hand and pulled her closer to him on the love seat. "Soon after that, we had a new baby girl, and our oldest daughter had graduated from high school and was attending college. Life was . . . life was . . ."

"Beautiful. Life was beautiful. Everything was as it should be." With her free hand, Vivienne used a handkerchief to dab her cheeks.

Reverend Atwater inhaled slowly. "In one of our earlier sessions, you revealed that Celeste is adopted. She knows?"

Maxine nodded.

"And she knows the circumstances?"

Vivienne volunteered in the pause, "Not everything, no."

"I convinced them that Celeste didn't need to know because I didn't want to undermine her security. She just knew she was adopted and that we'd tell her the rest of the story when she turned sixteen. All she knew was that her birth mother was a family member who loved her enough to do what she thought was best, that she was so young when she had her and that we offered our help because we loved her . . . them. We kept it in the family."

The pastor nodded. "That family business Maxine mentioned."

"Yes. No need to be broadcastin' it to various and sundry. It's our business, and we took care of it."

"But what about the child's birth father?" Atwater pressed.

"What about him?" Vivienne reared up like a threatened swan, prepared to spread her wings and knock senseless a predator with a heavy *thwop* to his head.

As if sensing the threat, Lilian squeezed her husband's knee and ventured gently, "I think what Pastor means, Vivienne, is what did you tell your daughter? Does Celeste know about JD?"

Vivienne scooted back an inch, still eyeing the Atwaters warily. "Oh."

Maxine cleared her throat when they all set their sights on her. "She doesn't know his name, but she knows he gave her up because he loved her. He loved me." She squirmed in their crosshairs.

She soaked in all the faces and emotions in the room, absorbing the benevolent sympathy from the Atwaters and the overwhelming regret flowing from her parents. "But we've been living in the past. Every day. Pretending I was still a kid, living at home. For years, I got to be the obedient teen, not the rebellious one. Have a mother and a father, be the best babysitter for my little brothers and *sister*. The virginal bride-to-be to an upstanding man my parents picked out for me. Until now. JD's back, and we're reliving the nightmare of my teen years."

"Maxine, no," Lilian whispered.

"Yes. Yes! Except today I'm not just devastating my parents, I'm also taking my fiancé and my daughter down with me. And let's not forget JD."

Reverend Atwater retrieved his Bible from the table between them and opened it. "Let's see what the Word says about this. Here . . ." He flipped through his well-worn pages. "According to Psalm 103, God forgets all our iniquities, heals all our diseases, and redeems our life from destruction. In His great, everlasting mercy, He has removed our transgressions as far as the east is from the west." He moved the ribbon to the page and closed his Bible. "If God forgives and remembers our sins no more, then why do you cling to them, Maxine? Celeste is a gift."

She hung her head. "Because I continue living a lie, Pastor. As long as Teddy doesn't know I have an ex-husband, I lie. As long as he and Celeste think I'm her sister, I lie. As long as she thinks JD is—" Maxine's voice broke. "My sins are this close." Only a hair's breadth separated her thumb and index fingers.

Lilian handed Maxine a glass of ice water. "Then 'go, and sin no more,' as Jesus told the woman caught in adultery. No one here condemns you—not God. Not Pastor or me. Not your parents." She glanced at Vivienne and John before turning back to Maxine. "So if you need to sit Celeste down, talk to Teddy, or confront JD, do it, whatever the case. Go. And sin. No more. Then, when guilt's not hunting you down, you can see what you're chasing and figure out just what you want."

June

"*Behavior follows belief. You will act consistently with what you believe about yourself. That's why you've got to know your identity in Christ. What you've done is not who you are. Failure is an event. It's not who you are.*"

UNKNOWN

.

Chapter Twenty-Five

"Maxine, I know what your granddaddy said about me. But he's the broken refrigerator." Ruby straightened the white damask tablecloth.

"*Mi rubí preciosa*, that customer left with a smile on his face. *No te preocupes.*" Lerenzo waved away his wife's concerns like a nagging fly.

Ruby put a fist on an ample hip. "'*No te preocupes*'? Don't worry? Even though you told a stranger what I put in my baked beans!"

"And he'll be back to order even more. No matter how much bacon fat he adds to his beans, they won't taste like yours. *Sí o sí, nietecita?*" Lerenzo winked at Maxine, who was helping him even out the table linen on the other side of the round table.

"*Claro que sí.* You're right, Granddaddy." Maxine yawned. Mama Ruby's phone call had yanked her from bed just before the sun crept from its resting place that Saturday morning.

"I still can't understand how that child got it into her head to leave me with this luncheon. She knew what was happenin' today! Flittin' off to the mountains like she don't have a care in the world." Ruby yanked on the linen.

Maxine held her peace, knowing the "child" her grandma referred to was Vivienne and her last-minute getaway with First John to their mountain house. Since Jean had canceled the staff meeting, Maxine had hoped to hide under the covers until she picked Teddy up for their date with Evelyn, Kevin, and baby Lauren. But here she was, filling in at a Manna catering job in Raleigh. No rest for the soul weary.

Run, run, run, as fast as you can . . . Been there, done that. Maxine buried her regrets in a mental grave. Then she tossed in her thoughts about the meeting with the Atwaters and piled imaginary dirt on top for good measure. She surveyed the five tables they still needed to prepare.

"Thanks for steppin' in, Maxine. Can't keep good help. Folks always complainin' about not having money, but they won't do somethin' to change their situations. If only they knew workin' hard fills an empty pocketbook and an empty spirit." Ruby smoothed out the wrinkles in a tablecloth and moved on to another. "Hand me that over there."

"Does it, Mama Ruby? I'm not so sure." Maxine retrieved the box.

"It helped your mama." Another tablecloth billowed out like a cloud as Ruby nodded at the ceramic salt- and pepper shakers nestled in plastic. "Put a set on each table."

"Because she met First John?"

"Because she was doing something besides feelin' sorry for herself." Ruby pointed to the back of the room. "Now go do what I told you, girl."

Maxine frowned—internally—and obeyed.

Her grandmother disappeared behind the kitchen's swinging doors.

Lerenzo stroked Maxine's arm. "*Tu abuela* has a good point, even if it stings when she pokes you with it. Fretting never solved a problem. Know what does? *Oración y fe.*"

Prayer and faith. His gentle pressure balanced out Mama Ruby's firm push. "I know, Granddaddy. Sometimes worrying feels easier." Maxine moved to the next table.

He nodded as he reached into the box and retrieved a few shaker sets. "It may seem that way."

"Because it *is* that way." Ruby seemed to materialize from thin air, smelling like baked chicken and the grape jelly–chili sauce mixture for her meatballs. She pushed a cartload of dishes. "Trusting God is an act of the will. It isn't easy to fight your nature. Worryin' and fussin' over a matter come easy to you. That don't mean you do *nuthin'*, but that *somethin'* may mean standin' still. Believers spend much of their time waitin' and watchin'."

"Sounds like fun," Maxine said under her breath.

"It's more fun than cleanin' up the mess from your mistakes when you rush ahead of God. Anyway, I don't have time for pulling weeds. Child, come over here and push this cart. Lerenzo, start with the utensils. Oh, goodness, the flowers!"

Ruby called out to two women who breezed into the room bearing containers of violet, white, and indigo asters and anemones set in greenery. "Y'all can start placing those centerpieces on the finished tables in the back and work up this way. We'll be outta your hair in a minute."

Maxine hustled over to grasp the cart's handle as her grandmother centered plates in front of chairs. Lerenzo followed behind, arranging forks, knives, and spoons.

Ruby flicked a hand around the hall. "Now you and Lerenzo finish up. I'm goin' back to the kitchen to check the food. Hungry folks will be here any minute. See if the florists need any help, but keep them outta my kitchen. We got to get crackin'." She cast a look over her shoulder. "And that means you, Maxine."

Her grandfather leaned toward her. "It probably means me, too."

Maxine and Lerenzo repositioned tables and chairs and rearranged centerpieces after the florists had left while Ruby basted, stirred, sliced, and pointed out their mistakes. Right after Maxine set out the last chafing dish and slipped a serving spoon into the ambrosia, the host of the luncheon braced open the double doors and ushered in the first group of septuagenarians. Gradually the room filled with chatter, chuckling, and the clanking of utensils on glass dishes.

For more than an hour, Maxine followed her grandmother's directions, refilling iced tea and replacing dropped forks and napkins. She lost count after the thirty-fifth "bless your heart" and rolled her eyes the third time she returned a saucer holding dentures. When at last the event's hostess climbed the two steps of the dais and spoke into the microphone, Maxine sloughed off to the industrial-size kitchen and threw herself across the stainless steel countertop.

"My hat is off to you and Granddaddy. These folks wore me out. The slippers—is that how you do it?" Maxine pointed to Mama Ruby's polka-dot, terry cloth slides, her normal work attire whether she was cooking at home or in a four-star restaurant. "If one more lady in a flowered dress and hat shakes her cup of ice at me and calls me honey, I'm going to explode. And if I had to listen to another story that starts off with 'When I was your age . . .' or 'Back in . . .'"

Ruby stopped wiping the counter and propped a hand on her hip. "If you had to listen to another story, what? Now tell me somethin', child."

Maxine clamped her lips together.

"Mmm-hmmm. That's what I thought. Those folks in there been through some things, and you'd best pick up a basket and gather up some wisdom. You could use it right now. Consider it a blessin' to serve them and listen to their stories. Some of those people marched with Dr. King. They carried the newspaper yesterday—*when they were your age*—so you could write your articles today. They bore the stripes so you could vote, marry whoever you wanted to, and sit up in here moanin' and groanin' about the sorry state of your life. Sure, they may not be able to text on that phone and play games on the computer like Robert and Second John, but there's plenty more important things those folks know and did—and can still do, let me tell you."

Ruby tsked. "Now go see to the dishes and stow these boxes in the van while I slice this red velvet cake. And make it quick. You'd best believe that speaker won't be too long. They're all ready for a nap after that heavy lunch."

"Yes, ma'am," Maxine murmured and pushed herself upright.

Lerenzo's eyes twinkled at the chastened Maxine as he clicked open a plastic container storing a sheet cake. He set it on the counter and reached for the next.

Maxine tried to make herself as small and as useful as possible as Ruby continued to grumble, throwing daggers her granddaughter's way as she sliced the cake. Contritely, Maxine rinsed and dried the dishes, then packed red velvet squares into small white boxes each lunch guest would take home as a favor. Her grandmother was cutting the second cake when she froze, the tip of her stainless steel knife just breaking through the frosting.

"What is it, Mama Ruby?" Maxine set down a dish.

"Who's that?" The older woman shuffled to the paneled door and peeked through its diamond-shaped window. Apparently unsatisfied with the view, she pushed open the door slightly.

Maxine heard a resonant, well-modulated voice say, ". . . inviting me. As you heard, I'm Hugh Anthony McMillan, but please, call me what my wife calls me. Hugh Anthony McMillan."

Mama Ruby watched for a minute, then slowly let the door swing shut. "He didn't sound like no Hugh Anthony." Ruby's voice was hushed as she stood eye level with the glass pane.

"Entonces quién?" Lerenzo unloaded the last of their cookware from the dishwasher.

"Then who, I can't say. He just puts me in the mind of . . . Nah, ain't no way." Mama Ruby seemed to be shaking herself free of a thought and returned to her cake distribution.

Maxine assumed her grandmother's spot at the door and checked out the speaker, a man who appeared to be around the age of most of the people in the room. But he exuded a warmth and vitality that rivaled the June sun streaming through the windows around them while looking as cool and fresh as the spring breeze. Maxine propped her foot in the opening in order to hear him.

". . . so I said, consider my hat my calling card." Hugh Anthony twirled his fedora in the pause as he delivered what must have been the punch line. Laughter swelled and rolled through the room like a wave, and he flashed a hundred-watt smile that rivaled the gleam of the gold buttons on his smart tan blazer and green vest. He ran his free hand over wavy gray hair that was brushed back from his high cheek-bones and curled just above the collar of his crisp white shirt. The amber topography of his face—a map of lines, wrinkles, and crevices—was the backdrop for light-brown eyes that seemed to weigh and measure each face before moving on to the next.

Maxine whispered over her shoulder, "I bet he was quite the man about town back in his day. He wouldn't have had to shake his glass to get some attention from the ladies. I could cut myself on the crease in those slacks."

"Child, come from that door. You've got work to do."

"Right." Maxine returned to her post beside Mama Ruby.

"I've got the cake, *nieta*. Why don't you take the crates and load them in the van."

"Right, Granddaddy." She wiped her hands and stacked a tray atop the others on the cart, then pushed the cart through the back door into the alleyway behind the building. She resolved to crawl into the cradle with Lauren when she got to Evelyn's. If she got there.

"Ma'am?" an aged voice called from behind her.

Maxine closed her eyes and clenched the handle as she prayed for strength. She slowly pivoted, half-expecting to see someone shaking an empty glass.

"Teddy?"

"Baby." The "elderly" gentleman she'd soon pledge her life to smiled and held out his arms wide enough to embrace her, the cart, and any other baggage she toted. Teddy pressed her close and buried his face in her hair. "Mmm. This is what I needed. You smell so good. You *feel* so good. Miss me much?"

Maxine barely got to nod before his lips touched hers. For a few seconds, she was fully present, relishing the feel of his hands on her back, his mouth on hers, and his heartbeat against her chest. But then inch by inch she withdrew from him. At first her thoughts flew to another time, another place, to another unexpected reunion. She braced her arms against his chest. Her pulse slowed to a faint crawl while his heartbeat continued to race in his chest. Maxine couldn't breathe.

Teddy pulled away and held her at arm's length, his physical retreat mirroring her emotional one. "What is it, Maxine? You're not happy to see me?"

"Of course. It's been a long day." A long life. She tried to smile as she removed her glasses to clean them with the edge of her shirt. "You caught me off guard. What happened to your day out with your mother? I thought I was picking you up on the way to Evelyn's, not meeting you here in Raleigh."

Teddy captured her fingers. "Mom wanted to do some

shopping and try out a new place in the area for brunch. When I checked your location, I saw we weren't that far from you, so I asked her to bring me here. I thought maybe you needed me."

She caressed his face. "I always need you. But I hate to steal you away from her when she's only here for the weekend."

He brought her fingers to his mouth and kissed them. "Dropping me off now just gives her more time with Dad. Come say hello to the first Mrs. Charles, Future Mrs. Charles, before she leaves."

"I should really get back to my grandparents. They'll think I ran away."

"You'll only be a minute. Just a quick hug." Teddy grabbed her fingers and tugged her toward the corner of the redbrick building.

Maxine swallowed. "Okay. I wish I'd had time to freshen up. I'm a mess."

He gave her a quick once-over. He licked a finger and swiped at her cheek. "You'll do. She knows you've been helping your grandmother."

You were supposed to say, "You're a vision. As always." Maxine shrugged away the memory and smoothed her hair back. She whipped off the white jacket with the Manna logo on its pocket as they approached his mother's sedan. Maxine waved at the diminutive woman who stepped from the car. "Mrs. Charles, hi! Good to see you."

"Hello, dear. It's good to see you, too. It's been too long." A cloud of Estée Lauder enveloped Maxine as Corinne Charles kissed each cheek. When she pulled back, she nodded at the younger woman's feet. "Working hard, I see?"

Maxine grimaced at her sturdy black loafers. "I had to wear my clodhoppers today. Manna needed a fill-in while my folks are in the mountains."

She smiled. "Ooh, a getaway! Celebrating something?"

Maxine returned the smile and put a wink with it. "Yes, getting away from their troublemaking daughter."

Teddy laughed, and after a quizzical look at them both, his mother joined in.

Maxine noticed some people slowly making their way from the building. "I should get back. The luncheon must be over, and Mama Ruby and Granddaddy will need my help packing up." She embraced her future mother-in-law. "It was good to see you again. You look beautiful. As always."

"And you, too, *chérie*. Did you enjoy those pralines I brought you from New Orleans?" Corinne squished the name into one reimagined word, *Nahlins*.

"Yes, and so did my hips! You must not want me to fit into my wedding dress."

The woman's eyebrows knit together. "Oh, did you have your next fitting? I'd hoped to accompany you on my next trip to North Carolina."

Teddy's face mirrored his mother's disappointment. "Yes, I thought she was accompanying you?"

"No, no, don't worry. You haven't missed it. Of course we're still going together—you, Mother, and me. Next month, right?" Maxine looked over the woman's shoulder. "I really should go. They sent me out here to load the van, and I went missing. Mama Ruby was already irritated with me. Long story," she added quickly with a wave of her hand. "I'll call you about a time for the fitting."

"Okay, darling. Teddy, I'll see you later." Mrs. Charles climbed into her car and slowly pulled away.

Maxine looped her arm through Teddy's as they headed toward the kitchen entrance. "It's really sweet of you to surprise me like this."

He winked. "It is, isn't it? Plus, we never had our date with your grandparents, so I hoped to squeeze some time in, have a two-for-one day before we see Reverend Atwater again."

Maxine shook her head as they reached the cart, still piled high beside the Tagles' van. "Always Mr. Practical. And here I thought you just wanted me." She squeezed his fingers before letting them go. She reached for a box. "Since this is all official, you can help us pack up the rest of the stuff in the kitchen."

But he reached for her. "Maxine, you seem different."

"Is that you, Theodore? Yes, it *is* you!" Ruby set her load atop the pile on the cart. "Maxine, you didn't tell me Theodore was comin'!" She enveloped him in a hug and glared at her granddaughter over his shoulder.

"I didn't know, Mama Ruby." She steadied the precarious tower.

"Really, she didn't know, Mrs. Tagle." Theodore kissed the wrinkles on Ruby's cheek. "I thought it'd be fun to surprise her."

"Then how did you know where to find her? Lerenzo, put that stuff down before you hurt your back."

"I'll take that, Mr. Tagle." Theodore took Lerenzo's armful and slid it into the van.

"*Gracias, hijo.*"

"I used my iPhone. Maxine has shared her location with me, so Mom dropped me here."

"Shared her location? So you did tell him, Maxine."

Maxine laughed out loud for the first time that day. "No, Mama Ruby. That's not—never mind. I apologize for holding you up. Teddy surprised me, and we took a few minutes to say good-bye to his mother." She hauled shut the door.

"Why don't you take Maxine and go? Lerenzo and I can handle the rest. We're about finished anyhow."

"Oh, we are?" Lerenzo chuckled when Ruby shot him a look. "*Sí, sí*, we can finish up."

"No, Granddaddy, we won't end our date early, right, Teddy? Besides, many hands make light work."

Teddy took her hand. "Especially these beautiful hands. Mr. and Mrs. Tagle, lead the way."

Ruby seemed unconvinced, so Maxine tugged Teddy toward the building. Her grandparents' footsteps crunched the gravel beside them.

"I'm sorry we missed seein' your mama, Theodore. How is she? I've been praying for her, that the house will sell soon and she can move up." Ruby clasped the younger man's arm.

"I can tell, thank you. They're considering an offer that came in this morning. You must have been praying for my school's graduation, too."

"Why is that?" Ruby's brow furrowed.

Maxine answered for him. "The commencement speaker canceled last week, and he's been searching for a replacement. Did something happen, Teddy, or should we get Hugh Anthony McMillan?"

"Hush your mouth!" Mama Ruby chuckled. "Let Theodore talk."

Teddy shook his head. "I don't know who that Hugh guy is, but I have a good idea who our speaker will be." Teddy held open the back door.

"Really? That's great, sweetie!" Maxine squeezed his arm as she entered the kitchen.

Inside, Ruby and Lerenzo wiped the countertops and swept. Maxine and Teddy folded the remaining tablecloths and napkins and collected stray utensils in the banquet hall.

"I'll check behind Granddaddy and Mama Ruby and make sure none of the servers mixed up our equipment. Then we can go, Teddy." Maxine stuffed the last of the linen into baskets.

"Just in time!"

"For what?" She didn't break her stride toward the swinging door.

He picked up the baskets and fell into step beside her. "What do you want first—the good news or the bad news?"

Maxine stopped walking and gave him the eye.

"The school secretary just texted me. It's official. We have a commencement speaker."

"I take it that's the good news."

He smiled a little. "Yes, but it means I need to work on the program this afternoon."

"Okay, I can deal with that kind of bad news. We can stop by the school on the way to Evelyn's. It'll give me time to change out of these work clothes into something cute. Look at you, Teddy, a three-for-one day! You get to work and put two dates under your belt." She winked at him and pushed open the door.

Teddy cleared his throat.

"Uh-oh." Maxine's inquiring eye pinned him to the spot. "Don't give me that look."

"What—the 'you're canceling our date with Evelyn and Kevin' look?"

"Not canceling, per se. Reconfiguring. I'll ride with you to their house and explain what's going on. Then I'll take your car back to the school because I'll need to spend the better part of the day ironing out the details about graduation. I'll pick you up, maybe in time to meet you for dessert even?"

"Teddy!"

"Maxine, I'm sorry. You know this isn't what I wanted, but we don't have long before the big day. My first as headmaster, you know."

"Uh-huh." Maxine started opening lower cabinets while Ruby checked the uppers, using the time to work through her thoughts. Lerenzo snapped closed the dishwasher and gave a thumbs-up. Maxine moved toward the master switches, barely glancing at Teddy, who had remained by the back door. After they filed past her, she turned off the lights.

Teddy made a back-and-forth motion in the air between the two of them as they trooped behind Lerenzo and Ruby to the parking lot. "Are we good?"

Maxine wanted to ask, "How can you really know me without learning about all the puzzle pieces—my friends and my family—that make up my life? These dates aren't about checking off Reverend Atwater's list." Instead, she nodded and fed him a line he'd find more palatable. "I'm really disappointed, but I understand the position you're in."

Teddy took her hand. "I know, and I appreciate you, babe. I just don't know what else I can do. We'll have plenty of opportunities to get together with Evelyn and Kevin, but I have only one chance to get this right. I have a feeling this speaker is going to make this graduation, at least from what I know so far."

As they walked to the car, Maxine half listened as he described his school board's search.

". . . better than our original choice, actually. Local student makes good, returns home to give back. He wasn't one of the academy's students, but he'll still connect with the graduates."

A frisson of fear crept up Maxine's spine as she finally fully attended to Teddy. She stopped by the back door of the van. "You said it's a local student returning home?"

"Yep. I think he graduated a few years ahead of you, or maybe while you were in Alabama. His name is James Lester, and he was an attorney in New York. Ever heard of him?" Teddy set the hampers inside the van and closed the door as Ruby and Lerenzo climbed in. He waved good-bye to the Tagles as they drove onto the main road.

Chapter Twenty-Six

THEODORE SHIFTED in the passenger seat and faced Maxine. "You've barely said anything for more than thirty minutes. Are you still upset?"

"Go. And sin. No more."

She brushed away the command like it was a worrisome hair tickling her cheek. "Yes. No." She fiddled with the air conditioner.

He filled the extra heartbeat Maxine took to consider her answer. "Which is it?"

"Both." When she touched the radio dial, she felt his fingers wrap around hers.

"Both?"

Maxine's eyes skipped to his and back to the white lines dividing the highway. "No, I'm not still upset. But you asked me if I know JD—Mr. Lester—and I didn't answer. Yes, I know him. He's Evelyn's brother-in-law."

Theodore's fingers loosened their hold on hers. "Her brother-in-law? What are the chances?"

"Apparently, pretty good," Maxine muttered. She adjusted the volume and MercyMe reminded her that she was redeemed and more than enough. She pushed another preprogrammed station and Kirk Franklin was saying goodbye to fear because grace had replaced it. She depressed the radio dial and redirected the air vents. Silence wrapped itself around them for a moment.

"So. Do you know this JD person well?"

An artificial breeze lifted Maxine's bangs, cooling her brow. "We went to high school together, and yes, to your earlier question. He was a couple years ahead of me."

"Is there another 'no' coming with that?"

Maxine's eyes skipped to his and back to the road. "No. I mean, yes, kinda. We dated."

Theodore's head rocked back a bit, like he'd taken a soft punch to his chin. "Kinda yes, or you kinda dated? You've never mentioned him before."

Maxine kept her eyes on a slow-moving minivan she passed. She waved to one of the children making funny faces in its back window. For a few minutes she listened to the hum of the engine. The staccato of the turning signal broke the quiet as she flowed right off the interstate onto a grooved road that created its own duet with the tires.

"Maxine, how long did you go out?"

"Long enough," she murmured. Subconsciously she pressed the accelerator, and the speedometer crept past the posted forty-five miles an hour limit . . . to fifty . . . to fifty-five. A textile mill was a blur on their left as she sped over the bridge denoting Mount Laurel's city limits. Soon they were passing fallow fields filled with junky, rusting cars and farmland dotted with cattle.

Theodore braced a hand on the car's roof. "Hey, you nearly hit that dog back there. Why are you in such a hurry?"

"I'm not in a hurry, but didn't you say you needed to get to the school to nail down your graduation speaker?" Maxine relaxed her foot on the gas pedal.

"It sounds like he's more *your* graduation speaker."

Maxine braked suddenly, making their seat belts lock and their heads rock forward. As she resumed a legal speed, she glanced at him.

His eyes narrowed, the humor fighting a losing battle with doubt in his face. "What? Is that what he was? A boyfriend?"

Maxine tucked some hair behind her ear and considered how much truth to share, if this was the time. She fought the urge to accelerate again. "Maybe. Yes."

"Maybe or yes?"

She couldn't run from that Voice in her mind, that spoke to her heart. "Yes. He was my boyfriend. We met when I was a freshman and he was a junior in high school. We dated until he went away to college. To Princeton." Maxine's eyes flicked to her engagement ring sparkling in the afternoon sunlight.

"Hmm," he murmured, his mouth an upside-down U and his eyebrows the mirror opposite.

I wonder what made the bigger impression—dating me or

going to Princeton? She focused on her turn, trusting her ears to piece together his true emotions.

"That sounds serious."

"You could say that. Didn't you date in high school?"

"Sure, but nothing like that. I was having too much fun on the soccer field. Of course, if I'd met you then, maybe you would've changed that."

And after meeting her, a lot of things changed for JD. Maxine cleared her throat. She hadn't intended to open up this mental yearbook. She pushed down the signaling arm. After a U-Haul rumbled by, she slowly turned left on the lane leading to the Lesters' neighborhood.

She saw only the back of Teddy's head in her peripheral vision. She sensed that he wasn't staring at the stately brick homes rising behind the wrought iron fence, however. Maxine expected Teddy to pepper her with more questions as he worked through their conversation, but uncharacteristically, he said nothing. By the time she negotiated the twists and curves to Evelyn's cul-de-sac, she was so unsettled she'd begun to lose feeling in her fingers gripping the wheel.

"Are we good?" Maxine used Teddy's own words to chip at the ice between them. She angled his way as he reached for his door handle.

But Teddy's tone was cold. "Are we?"

Taptaptap!

"Hey, Auntie Maxine! Are you getting out sometime today?" Evelyn stood in the driveway, waving one of Lauren's tiny fists. A Yorkshire terrier tugged at the leash attached to Evelyn's wrist.

Maxine held up a finger. She faced Teddy's direction again, but he was slamming shut his door. "Well, all righty then," she mumbled to his empty seat and climbed out.

Maxine watched Evelyn settle the baby into her stroller with a snap of the harness, adjust the domed cover, and push Lauren onto the sun-drenched deck. She wondered at all the accoutrements of today's infant care, extras the church ministry couldn't provide when she'd lived in a home with other young mothers. But then she hadn't needed a night-vision camera to see Celeste in their ten-by-ten bedroom or a luxury Old English–style pram so her baby could nap in the sunshine. Maxine had nestled Celeste in the crook of her arm most of the time, and the two hadn't ventured much farther than the local library, where Maxine kept up with her studies.

Evelyn smiled and exhaled. "Okay, all fed and changed. Now you can tell me what you said to Teddy. I feel like I'm watching *All My Children* in Mama Ruby's den, waiting to find out what Erica Kane was up to. Spit it out—and quick, before my man gets back with dinner."

"I think I mumbled something about JD being your brother-in-law and knowing him in high school." Maxine pinched the bridge of her nose.

Evelyn slowly pushed the stroller back and forth. "You remind me of your mama, doing that. Did Teddy accept your answer? If you looked anything like the way you do now, I'd guess a big, fat, and hairy no."

"You know Teddy—well, actually, you don't. He's not like me. He's trustworthy and trusting, and he loves unconditionally. True blue."

"Or he's simply clueless, self-involved, or a serial killer. And you didn't answer my question." Evelyn peeked at the sleeping baby and parked the stroller. She retrieved a watering can and started sprinkling the lilies of the valley planted in large clay pots in the corners of the deck.

"Evelyn."

Her friend pushed aside a tender white blossom and soaked the soil. "I'm sorry, Max, but the man's not a saint. I don't know him, but he didn't look very 'true blue' in the two minutes he spent talking to Kevin and me. More like green around the gills. Something was up."

"You have quite a way with plants, Evelyn."

"But I do know you." Evelyn rolled like a train over her friend's attempt to derail the lecture. "It's obvious you're a mess. If you're this unhinged now, what were you like when Teddy first dropped the bomb about his commencement speaker?"

"I'm not unhinged."

"Come on. You're not the only writer here. When I say 'unhinged,' that's exactly what I mean. I can't believe he didn't notice you falling to pieces right there in front of him." Evelyn stepped down to the backyard, picked up the hose, and turned on the spigot with a squeak.

Maxine crossed her arms on the wood railing and watched Evelyn tend the flower beds. She growled under her breath, "I'm not falling apart, and I'm not unhinged." *But she's got a point. What does it mean if he didn't notice?*

"Only unhinged people talk to themselves," Evelyn laughed.

"This isn't funny!" But the corners of Maxine's mouth twitched.

"You're right. It's not. So when are you going to talk to your future husband about your former husband?"

Maxine glared at her.

Evelyn returned her unblinking stare as she flicked the nozzle in Maxine's direction.

Maxine jumped out of the spray and nearly fell over the stroller. Cocoa, resting in its shade, yipped when Maxine nearly stepped on her paw. "Hey! You know black women don't play like that. You've been hanging around your sister-in-law too long!"

Evelyn laughed. "Girl, she's been around us long enough to know the rules. She'd never mess with my hair—just like I didn't mess with yours. I'm just trying to wash away the dirt."

Maxine brushed off the beads of water on her gray shorts and cantaloupe-colored top. "Dirt? What dirt?"

"In your ears, from sticking your head in the sand." Evelyn squished through the wet grass and turned off the spigot.

"You sound like Granny B."

"Good. A wise woman, my grandma." Evelyn coiled the hose and put it away. "Come down here with me. We can hear the baby if she wakes up."

Maxine descended the steps.

"What about Celeste, Maxine? JD and your Theodore are big boys, and they'll be able to handle this better than your—"

"Sister. My sister. That's what you were about to say, right?"

Evelyn faced Maxine, hands on her hips. The baseball cap on her closely cropped curls slightly shielded her eyes.

Maxine still could see the truth in them, so instead, she studied a lemon-colored butterfly as it danced among the tiny buds breaking through. "She's . . . Celeste. Thirteen going on thirty-three. We're still not sure what's going on with her physically."

"Is that why you're waiting to talk to her about JD?"

"It's just not the right moment. You think it's time, and my parents think it's time, but I'm not sure. Am I putting it off because I'm afraid? Partly. But mostly I wonder what she'll think of the person who was wild enough to marry in high school, who didn't have the sense to raise her own daughter and wasn't courageous enough to admit the truth."

"Max—"

"And I also simply want to make the right decision, do what's best for her, what I've always tried to do since she was born." She flicked away a tear before she continued, running roughshod over Evelyn's refutations.

"You know, when I was little, I trusted Daddy to fix all my boo-boos and make everything better. After he died, I tried to rely on Mother, but that was like trying to walk on a broken foot. So I turned to Mama Ruby and Granddaddy. Nearly two years later, Mother gets it all together and comes back with First John, and they step into my grandparents' shoes and expect me to naturally follow in their footsteps. But I couldn't. I just . . . couldn't. Then here comes JD, and he takes charge. I thought that was what I wanted, but the next thing I know, I'm married and pregnant, still looking for answers."

"Aren't we all looking for an answer of some kind?"

"Maybe. But we don't all run away to find them. That's what I did, Evelyn. I couldn't hear my own thoughts and figure out for myself what I needed to do. When I could do that, I came back."

Evelyn walked toward her friend. "But are you sure it was *your* voice that spoke to you in Georgia, after you got saved and made the decision to return home? From what I'm hearing now, listening to your voice isn't helping much." She stroked Maxine's shoulder, still damp from her gentle dousing. Slumped from the not-so-gentle peer pressure of a loving kind. "Can I get you some iced tea?"

"No thanks. I just want to ice this subject. I'm tired of talking about it. I'm tired of thinking about it. I'm tired of worrying about it."

"Then don't talk, think, or worry about it." Evelyn lifted a canvas tote stuffed with tools off a hook on the deck. She intertwined their fingers and pulled Maxine farther into the yard. "Come out to the garden with me. Let's not spoil this time together, rehashing. I'm so glad you took the time to drive out here because we haven't seen each other enough."

Maxine bumped her friend's shoulder with her own. "And it'll be a few years before I come back again if you keep abusing me." But she smiled. "How're Dominick and Peter?"

Evelyn had left her teaching position to write a children's book about a character named Peter and his dog, Dominick. "Dominick got lost, which forced Peter to learn his home address. I was so excited when I signed that three-book publishing contract, but I'm exhausted. I can barely stand upright. And of course Kevin still gets . . . ideas . . . if we get in bed at the same time. Girl, I'm tired!"

Maxine shook her head, reliving those early days with a new baby. Those months without a husband and with a new baby.

"But I wouldn't change a thing. Kevin and I are in a much better place than we were a year ago, and now I can call myself a published author! Most importantly, we have Lauren. She's worth all the long days and nights when I don't look, feel, or smell very cute."

By this time, they'd reached the right side of the yard by the back fence. Evelyn glanced back at the deck before dropping to her knees in the dirt. She pulled up what looked to Maxine like perfectly good green plants and tossed them aside. Maxine watched her dig, snip, and discard for a moment, then murmured, "I'm glad you and Kevin are doing better."

"Don't get me wrong. This peace between us has been a long time comin'. I didn't think I'd ever trust him again. But strangely, all that heartache and betrayal strengthened our commitment to each other. It's not unconditional—I'm not as perfect as your Mr. Theodore—but it's real, God-given love." She stopped plucking vegetation to glance at Maxine. "But I still can't hear the name Samantha Jane without making a fist."

"Who's Samantha Jane? Wow—you did make a fist."

Evelyn stabbed at the dirt. "What did we say about 'not rehashing'? Well, that applies to me as well."

Maxine watched her girlfriend for a moment, wondering

whether to press. A cry from the deck decided for her. "Want me to get Lauren?"

"Would you? Tell her Mommy will bring dinner in a sec." Evelyn's voice sounded like she was trying to talk around a mouth full of cotton swabs. She swiped at her face, leaving a swath of black dirt across her cheekbone.

Maxine hurried to the deck. There, she scooped up Lauren, whose wails sounded like something between a sheep's baaing and a hiccup. She rubbed the tiny back in a circular motion as the infant flailed. "Shh . . . there, there. Auntie loves you," she crooned.

The longer she held Lauren, the more that statement proved true. She tucked her under her chin and tried to recall how she'd quieted Celeste. It felt like she was unlocking a treasure chest buried for decades under deep ocean waters. She closed her eyes and dove deep into her creaky storehouse of memories and emotions until she retrieved a song about a dark-brown river and golden sand. Maxine hummed the melody when the lyrics ebbed and murmured "with trees on either hand" when they flowed again. She inhaled that precious, one-of-a-kind baby's breath that transported her to another time and place that consisted of a ten-by-ten room holding a twin bed, a dresser, a chair, and a crib that smelled like Johnson & Johnson's lavender-scented soap.

"Maxine?"

But she wasn't in the group home. She wasn't singing Celeste to sleep. When she turned around and opened her eyes, she wasn't looking into her own newborn's face.

"I'm back . . . bearing gifts." Kevin raised the brown paper bags emblazoned with the red MingFu logo and cocked his head to his right—not that there was a need to, for it was obvious what, and who, he'd brought home.

JD smiled weakly and scooped up Cocoa, who was jumping at his leg. "Hey, Maxie. Guess who's coming to dinner."

Chapter Twenty-Seven

"Please, Celeste, prettypleaseprettypleaseprettyplease . . ." She mouthed the words over the baby as she settled her into the white Jenny Lind crib she'd pushed against her own twin bed. She put in the CD she'd permanently "borrowed" from the library and slipped under the covers, careful not to make the thin mattress squeak on its hard springs.

Seventeen-year-old Maxine lived in a twilight state. Celeste wasn't one of those "good babies" the others had birthed, the children they crowed about as they moved back and forth in their gliders after supper. Every night she headed up to the second floor, leaving the other girls smacking their gum and their jaws in the den, hoping against hope something would change. She tucked Celeste into her crib, swaddled just like the nurse had shown her and smelling like that calming soap she'd paid $4.99 for at Rite Aid.

But it didn't do any good. It never did. Just like all the other nights, Maxine scooped up Celeste, squeezed her into the space between herself and the wall, and sang "Where Go the Boats" until she was hoarse. She groaned, "Maybe you don't want to listen to stolen lullabies. Or is this recompense for my own mother's sleepless nights?" Maxine's heart ached for Vivienne, whose misery was palpable across the miles.

Ten minutes later Maxine found herself in her usual position, hovering on the edge of wakefulness, on her left side in her twin bed, with one arm tucked under her head and the other tented over a wailing Celeste. Maxine wondered if letting go of a little thing like sleep would provide Celeste what she'd spent her life seeking—belonging, acceptance. She leaned closer to smell the baby's breath and thought about the girl she once was. And about JD.

Until Miss Vicky threw open Maxine's door. "Child, I hear y'all carryin' on all the way down the hall. What are you doin' up at two o'clock in the mornin'?"

To Maxine, bone-tired and nearly blind because her glasses were on the floor beside her bed, Miss Vicky appeared as an angel in her white housecoat with its wide, winglike arms, her feet in fuzzy light-blue slippers as if she balanced on a cloud, her large, pink sponge rollers her halo. The young mother burst into tears and thrust Celeste at her savior. "I can't do this! I give up. I give up. Just take her. I'm no good at this."

"My goodness! Quiet now, before you get the whole house goin'." Miss Vicky shut the door and *shoosh-shooshed* over to the bed, bringing with her a waft of Noxzema. She took the baby and settled her firmly in the crook of her arm. Her pale fingers smoothed the fine, silky hair plastered to Celeste's teary cheek.

"See, I'm a terrible mother! I can't even put my own baby to sleep," she sobbed.

"If you don't hush up . . . First of all, you don't 'put a baby to sleep.' That's what they do to dogs at animal shelters. Celeste is no more abandoned than you are."

Maxine's shoulders heaved with the force of her sniffles.

"Secondly, if *you* cain't calm down, *she* cain't calm down. Celeste is just overtired, is all. You both need to stop hanging out, jaw jackin' with the girls after dinner and get upstairs so this baby can settle down for the night. Nine o'clock is just too late for a four-month-old. And it's gettin' on too late for a girl raisin' both herself and her baby while goin' to school."

Watching Miss Vicky sway side to side had the same calming effect on Maxine as it had on the baby. The young mother's tears slowed.

"And the third thing really should've been first. Have you prayed over this baby? Or do you just sit there rockin' and cryin' along with her?"

Mama Ruby talked to God enough to cover everybody else, so Maxine's knees never touched the floor. Her grandmother toted her prayer closet around with her and stepped into it at will. She entreated God for any situation—when to plant her tomatoes, where to bury her brother, how to handle the Jehovah's Witness handing her a tract or the injured bird that smacked into her front window. Maxine figured if Mama Ruby's prayers could reach God's ears, surely they'd cover her in Valdosta, Georgia.

"Just as I thought," tsked Miss Vicky. "This baby here needs more than some breast milk and a lullaby for nourishment. She needs God's Word mornin', noon, and night. I know I'm not supposed to be evangelizin', but how will you young girls ever become proper mothers without walkin' with Jesus?"

Maxine hesitated, then shrugged.

Miss Vicky kept swaying as she patted Celeste's diapered bottom. "Do you know how much the Lord loves you? He sees you here talkin' and cryin' with this baby—what I suspect you do every night. He wouldn't have you despairin', as if your sufferin' paid a debt you owed Him."

Maxine dried her face with her sleeve, her eyes never leaving her angel.

"Maybe you know Jesus, maybe you don't, but you should spend as much time with Him as you do with this baby. When you find rest for your soul in Him, you'll find rest for your body over there." Miss Vicky pointed to the bed. "Now, this Sunday we're goin' to church—you, me, and this precious child. As for tonight, I'm takin' her."

"No! Please don't take her!" Maxine nearly fell off the bed and onto the crib.

"Hush, child. I'm just watchin' her tonight so you can get some sleep. By the looks of it, you ain't been gettin' much. Come get her in the mornin' bright and early, before my shift ends. I'll have you a Bible to read by then. Nobody's gonna take your baby, so don't worry."

"Are you sure?" Maxine managed, her throat dry.

Miss Vicky laughed. "Child, do you know how many other girls have begged me for help so they could sleep? Why do you think they're so happy to see me when I get here at seven?"

"But I thought—"

"I know what you thought because I know what they told you. It's not only my pecan pie they love. Just listen to this voice that's been up, down, and around the block a time or two, and get some sleep. The sun will be shinin' in your eyes soon enough." Miss Vicky took a blanket and the baby bag. "And move this crib back to the wall before you get your head tangled between those rails."

"Maxine? I'll take the baby. Maxine?"

Maxine stopped swaying and patting and set Lauren into her mama's waiting arms.

Evelyn plopped down in the porch swing and draped a blanket across her shoulder and over the baby. "Hey, honey, once you set down the food, find the lighter for the citronella candles and open the umbrella over the table. I thought we'd eat outside. Maxine, could you grab the paper products from the kitchen counter? And put Cocoa inside too. JD, mind going to the garden to gather my tools? I left them to get the baby. Good to see you, by the way."

By the time they each returned from their respective tasks, Maxine had nearly recovered from the painful shock of seeing not one, but two Lester men. She joined Evelyn on the double porch swing and watched the brothers set up dinner. She whispered, "Did you know he was coming?"

"You think I'd blindside you like that, after our conversation in the yard?" Evelyn moved Lauren to her right side.

"No, but you also know I wouldn't have stayed if you'd

warned me. And *I* know how much you want all this out in the open."

"Well, it *should* be out in the open."

"Hey, what are you two talking about over there?" Kevin lit one of the citronella lanterns.

JD locked eyes with Maxine as he leaned against the deck railing and murmured, "I can imagine."

"You're going to have to because it's about time for dinner. Lauren's not the only one who's hungry. Excuse me." Evelyn propped the baby on her shoulder and patted her back as she rose, leaving Maxine with JD.

Maxine's eyes ranged from his mustache to the small gold loop in his earlobe, but finally settled for the curls on his hairline. "Hey."

"Hey. Where's Theodore F. Charles?"

She met his deep-brown eyes. "I think I liked it better when you called him Teddy Bear. At least you didn't smirk when you said it."

JD threw his head back and laughed.

After a beat, Maxine joined in. "You're a mess, Jay."

"We're a mess." When he sat beside her, he set the swing in motion.

"Jay, I . . ." She tried to find somewhere else to look, anywhere but in his direction. It was hard to ignore the long fingers tapping the cushion near her shoulder. "I'm sorry."

"You don't—"

"No. I do need to say this. I'm sorry I lied to you. I kept you from your daughter."

"You were seventeen." JD's hand found a resting place on the skin of her neck.

She tried not to relax into its warmth. "I *was*, but I can't keep blaming seventeen-year-old Maxine for thirty-year-old Maxine's choices. Fear has shaped a lot of my decisions and hurt a lot of people. It took courage for you to come back to Mount Laurel."

"I didn't just come back for you. For Celeste, I mean. My mother needs me." JD shifted in the swing.

Maxine's neck felt cool when his hand fell away. "I know you're right about telling Celeste the truth. We'd agreed to tell her when she was sixteen, but I think it's time now."

He covered her shaking hands with his. "How about the adult Maxine and JD work together to forgive our teenage selves?"

"As long as that's all the adult Maxine and JD do together."

"You two, bring that over here. My wife has worked up an appetite." Kevin waved them over to the glass table.

"Want me to hold her?" Maxine nodded toward Lauren.

Evelyn laid the sleeping infant in the stroller. "Nope, we're good for now, but don't get comfortable with those chopsticks. She fell asleep almost immediately, so she's likely to wake up the minute I start eating."

"Her uncle is here to help, too. Here you go, Maxie." JD pulled out a chair.

The next-to-last thing Maxine wanted was to get closer to him. The last thing was to call attention to that. She sat down and allowed him to scoot her closer to the table. "Thank you."

"Want a spring roll, Evie?" Kevin scooped honey shrimp, fried rice, and egg foo young onto a plate and set it before his wife. "Max, tell me about the writing. Evie reads me your posts. You're almost as good a writer as my Evelyn."

Maxine snickered. "Thank you? Things are great. Slow. Wonderful. Terrible. You know I've always been a rebel." She could feel JD's eyes on her though she aimed her words at Kevin and Evelyn.

"I loved writing when I could do it according to my own schedule. I hate deadlines, commitments, dancing to the tunes other people play, having their opinions and thoughts override mine. Sometimes all I hear is my editor's voice, not my own. It saps my creativity." She spooned sweet-and-sour chicken and lo mein onto her plate.

"Pressure makes diamonds, right?" Kevin dipped crispy wontons in the duck sauce.

"Or mud," JD and Maxine chorused.

Evelyn cleared her throat in the awkward silence that felt as heavy as the waterlogged evening air. "I do know what you mean, Max, but life takes you outside your comfort zone sometimes. It's a good thing, even if it hurts. Getting organized and establishing a routine will start to feel good after a while. Maybe it's not your editor's—Jean's?—voice you're hearing after all."

Maxine fumbled with her chopsticks. "Maybe that applies to my life, but my writing? That's a different story. Evelyn, you worked for the man before you quit teaching, but I've always done my own thing on my own time. I've freelanced and blogged since grad school up to now, writing and editing what I wanted, *when* I wanted. Inspiration doesn't strike just because something is due at 5 p.m."

At that moment, Maxine felt a gentle touch slide the chopsticks from between her fingers.

JD extended a plastic fork. "Why don't you stop pretending you know what you're doing?"

For a minute, the only sound at the table was *crunch, crunch* as Kevin ate his wontons before Maxine shot a fortune cookie at JD and protested, "Hey!"

"Hay is for horses," JD began.

"And cows eat it, too." Evelyn finished their old line from high school.

"Just not with chopsticks," JD snorted, nearly choking on his rice.

"That's what you get." Maxine feigned a jab at his hand with the tines of her fork.

Evelyn sipped her sweet tea. "How's Annie, Kev? Is this a good day for her?"

Kevin glanced at JD before answering. "I don't know if I'd say 'good,' but Mom has had worse."

Maxine's touch on JD's hand was that of a butterfly landing on the porch rail, delicate, fleeting, attention grabbing. "I'm sorry about your mother. She's still so young."

"That's the very definition of early onset Alzheimer's. Her symptoms just appeared out of the blue, and she wasn't even sixty. It nearly killed her to take early retirement, but she worried about compromising her research when she started forgetting the simplest details. Today, she thought I was Dad."

"Ouch," Evelyn murmured. She turned to her husband. "I can't imagine that, since your parents' divorce was so acrimonious."

Maxine opened, then closed her mouth.

JD must have noticed. He smiled a little, though his eyes

didn't. "Don't worry. I didn't know what to say either. I just went with it—until she aimed a pencil at my head!"

Kevin chuckled and pointed at a scar on his left arm. "That's nothing, bruh. I feel you. Your return takes a huge load off of us. It's been hard, especially with Lauren's arrival and a new company to keep off the ground."

"I'm sorry it took me so long to get it together."

They ate in silence for a few minutes.

Evelyn scooped up the last of her rice. "Welp—I think we all deserve to lose ourselves in a game of spades after dinner, if the little one cooperates. What do you think? We never get to play because we don't know another couple who knows how. And I think we all could use some fun."

Kevin smiled. "Wow, Evie, spades. That brings back memories. I'm game, no pun intended. How about you, man?"

"I haven't played in like . . . forever. Since the tournaments held by the BSU, I think. My roommate nearly choked me when I reneged."

Maxine had marked some habits, activities, people, and styles as "BCC"—and playing spades was one of them. But the wistfulness of his tone pummeled the wall she'd erected between the past and the present. "Maybe, if Evelyn and I are partners. It sounds like you can't keep your books straight, and I don't plan on getting set tonight."

"Oh, I can keep my books straight, so we'll be okay as a team. You shouldn't come between a married couple anyway."

What about an engaged couple? Do Teddy and I count? When did you get marked "ACC"? As she closed the containers and stacked their empty plates, Maxine hoped her face didn't betray her thoughts about all the changes in her "after Christ and Celeste" life.

"Let's make sure we all play the same way. Big joker, little joker, deuce of spades, the ace . . ." He counted off the rules on his fingers.

"And no kitty," Kevin interjected.

Maxine dropped her handful. "Did you say 'no kitty'? Uh-uh! Those two cards can change a whole hand."

Evelyn laughed. "Look what you did, Kevin. Your crazy talk woke Lauren. Y'all put this stuff away and find the cards while I take care of her. Let's move this party to the den because this humidity is wreaking havoc on my do. We're not all natural like Maxine. Hon, give me a hand." She and Kevin left the table and walked over to the stroller.

Maxine watched Evelyn snuggle Lauren's cheek, gulping down a sigh as the baby sucked on her mama's chin. She gasped when long brown fingers clasped hers.

JD's shoulder pressed against her own for a second, although his eyes held on and didn't let go. "Are you all right?"

She brushed away a strand before squeezing his hand in return, silently acknowledging the bitter and the sweet tastes of this meal with baby Lauren. But that was the only answer she was prepared to give, that brief touch.

Fireflies had come out to entertain them while they ate. One landed on the table and crawled around, its tail blinking like a tiny hazard light. As JD trailed its movement with his index finger, Maxine noted that he still chewed his nails. They both ignored Kevin as he cleared away the remains of their meal and only looked up after he'd swiped away their six-legged visitor with the crumbs and water rings.

Maxine looked for a way to redirect the conversation. "Why the complete job shift from profit to nonprofit?"

JD shrugged. "Since my hair isn't long enough to fiddle with, let's say I wanted a fresh start."

Maxine saw she hadn't fooled him. She also recognized the truth buried six feet under his simple statement. A fresh start. Getting baptized and changing her wardrobe had served that purpose for her. But she was starting to realize she couldn't shed her true self like dead skin, as her mother had hinted at months ago—even saved, sanctified, and dressed in wool from head to toe. She could run as fast as she could, but like a turtle, she wouldn't get far. Maxine and Maxie were inextricably connected. She wouldn't survive as herself if the two were separated.

"But I'm the same JD you know and love. You know that, right, Maxie?"

This time, Maxine did poke him. Gently, and with the tip of her finger, so as to leave an impression but not a mark. She purposely bumped his chair with her hip as she left the table. "Butts are for winning spades, Jay, so don't let me down."

Chapter Twenty-Eight

Her bloody hands yanked up another reed and another and another. Her arms full, she sloshed through the marsh to higher ground and dumped her burden on the mat. Maxine sneezed when a feathery tip tickled her nose. She glanced over her left shoulder toward the distant rumble of voices, but they continued without pause. She dragged the pile of sticks closer to where the reeds were tallest and thickest. Sunrays pelted her. Sweat dripped off her nose and mixed with the blood on her hands, turning the yellow reeds pink. No matter. The water would wash it clean.

Her fingers deftly wove the stems together, adding layer after layer. She slathered on pitch before beginning another row. She pushed the reeds together and slapped on more of the thick mud that soothed the cuts on her hands as it waterproofed the small basket. Maxine carefully used a blade to thin the globs, for the vessel had to be light enough to float and move along with the current, even with its load. Especially because of its load. Dear Lord, please don't let it sink. Show me what to do to keep her safe.

Leaves crackled and branches snapped behind her. Maxine craned to listen. The faraway voices had faded to a barely discernible hum, but she was certain she'd heard her name and now footsteps. Panting, she tucked the jar of pitch under her chin and snatched up two armloads of reeds. When she realized she couldn't tote the basket, too, she dropped the sticks. She pinched two corners of the mat and tried to lift everything at once, but she couldn't maneuver her load around the squirming bundle tied at her middle. Maxine whimpered and glanced in the direction of the approaching footfalls. They were nearly upon her.

She hugged the baby to her and threaded her way through the thick water reeds. "Shh, shh." She crouched, praying for deliverance from whoever or whatever was coming.

"Maxine! Maxine!" a voice hissed.

When she peeked through her cover, she nearly wept with relief. She ignored the sharp stems scratching her face and arms as she burst into the clearing. "Mama!"

"Yes, it's me, your mama." Vivienne covered her forehead and cheeks with kisses. She clasped her daughter's face with both hands. "It's okay. Listen to me. You have my word nothing will happen to her, so don't fret. But we have to get going."

Maxine nodded, her eyes welling. As she cradled the crying infant, she reached behind her neck and untied the wrap. Vivienne shook the debris from the mat and fitted the cushion into the bottom of the basket. Still singing words of comfort, Maxine settled the wailing baby inside and tucked the wrap around her. She stepped back as her mama fastened the lid.

The two women's eyes held for a second before Vivienne nodded. She clasped her daughter's shoulder, squeezed it, and whispered, "Remember, the Lord is on your side, so don't be afraid. What can somebody else do to you?"

Then she picked up the wiggling basket with one arm, and using the other to push aside the resisting plants, she squished through the mud and waded into the dark-brown water.

Maxine felt like she was still splooshing through her dream as her eyelids fluttered open. Limbs heavy and her mind muddy, she squinted at her palms in the dim light. After her search revealed no scratches or blood, she relaxed on the pillow. *Where am I?*

Then a baby wailed and a dog barked.

Evelyn's! I slept over. The four had stayed up late playing spades and eating chocolate chip cookies. To give her fiancé—and herself—a bit of wiggle room to recover from their discussion, Maxine had texted Teddy, telling him not to worry about rushing through his graduation planning. Kevin had promised to drive her home if she stayed the night in their guest room. Maxine blinked, stretched, and sat up as her eyes adjusted and the fog cleared from her brain.

When Maxine fiddled around on the night table for her frames, a blurry something thunked to the floor. She slid on her glasses, and the dresser, chest, and television came into focus. She retrieved her phone from under the bed and set it beside the Bible, which was still open to Psalm 118 from the night before. Maxine checked the time: 8:30. Time to go home, by the looks of the text messages on her home screen.

Her bare feet crossed the cool hardwood floor to the attached bath. There, she slipped out of Evelyn's borrowed pajamas and cleaned up, grateful for the extra toothbrush and new underwear her friend had left for her. Maxine stared at herself in the mirror as she twisted her curls into a bun at the base of her neck. "Oh, well, girl, I think that's the best you can do. You're starting to look unhinged," she chuckled to herself as she collected her shoes and left the bedroom.

The scent of bacon and the sound of voices wafted up the stairs. She recognized Kevin's mellow tones and the baritone of . . . JD? Maxine ignored another ding of her phone as she paused to gather herself on the turn of the back stairs leading to the kitchen.

Clink, clink. ". . . cup on the counter."

"Thanks, *Jay.*" Kevin snickered. "You don't mind if I call you that, do you?"

"Not funny, Bro. You convinced me to unload on you. Don't use it against me."

Maxine crossed her arms and leaned against the railing as she listened to the men moving about the kitchen.

"I'm sorry; you're right. I'm just trying to get you to smile. Are you going to tell her what—?"

"Maxine, why are you hiding here?" Evelyn hissed in her ear.

She nearly tumbled down the remaining steps before she caught herself, but not her phone or her sneakers. They clattered down the wood planks and landed at the base of the stairs.

Two sets of heavy footsteps clopped toward them, accompanied by the *tickety-tap* of Cocoa's nails on the hardwood.

JD reached them first. "Morning. Is this a private club, or may we join?"

Maxine raised her chin. "I could ask you the same."

"How about you take the baby and hold that thought, JD? I'm beat, and I need a shower." Evelyn gently handed over her armful.

He settled the baby on his shoulder and turned back toward the kitchen. Kevin shrugged at the women. He retrieved Maxine's phone and stuck it in one of her shoes, then followed his brother.

Evelyn shook her head as she stalked upstairs. "Shame on you, Maxine." She patted her leg, and the dog trotted upstairs after her.

Head hanging low, Maxine scooped up her shoes and walked into the kitchen. She accepted the steaming cup of coffee JD thrust at her before he sat down at the island. "Thank you," she murmured to his back.

Kevin flipped bacon at the gas range. "So, Maxine, how'd you sleep?"

"With my eyes closed." She smoothed back her hair and pretended she was totally comfortable standing in a kitchen drinking coffee with her ex-husband while he held someone else's baby. Maxine glanced down at yesterday's well-worn shirt and shorts and compared her outfit with JD's wrinkle-free striped polo and khaki shorts. "How about you?"

"With my eyes wide-open, and I'm not joking. Lauren wasn't very cooperative last night. Evelyn's going to shower and get a nap, and then we'll do church at home. Of course,

I'm wiped, too, since my brother and I talked until the wee hours. Didn't we, Jay?" Kevin turned off the flame and perched on a stool beside JD. He tore off the plastic around a glossy magazine.

"Mm-hm," JD mumbled. He rubbed Lauren's bare feet.

Maxine slapped her forehead. *Sunday. Church! I'm glad Mother and First John are out of town.*

"Need a ride home?" Kevin sipped from his cup.

"I'll have some bacon first—there is enough for me, right?—and finish my coffee. Then, yes, I could use a ride. Thanks!"

"Because Jay offered while you were upstairs. Though he might have changed his mind since then." His eyes never left the magazine.

Maxine dropped the English muffin she'd split. She brushed it off and popped it into the toaster.

"I'm still willing to suffer through the drive with Maxine," JD responded dryly, twiddling with the gold loop in his ear. "I know how much you could use a Sabbath rest, Kevin, to cuddle with your girls. But if you call me Jay one more time . . ."

"By the way, nice column this month." Kevin spun the magazine around on the counter. He pointed to Maxine's tiny image over her column and gave her a thumbs-up.

Maxine opened the refrigerator door and buried her head between the shelves holding the milk, coffee creamer, eggs, and butter.

"Have you read it, JD? Assuming not, this is what our writer friend over there had to say. She calls it 'Move-In Ready.'"

Mouth agape, cheeks cool, Maxine emerged holding the tub of Country Crock. "You're really going to read it out loud?"

"Why not? Isn't it the same as passing it to him once I'm done?" Kevin shrugged in the answering silence to his question and resumed.

"So what's 'home' to you?

At the moment, my home may not look like much to an observer, casual or otherwise. It's certainly not one of those tiny houses currently in fashion, though if you squint, you might deem it 'cozy.' It's big enough to hold everything that's near and dear to me: my mother's old bedroom set, a sofa I got in grad school, the walnut desk I refinished myself, and my laptop, my faithful frenemy. I can't host a family reunion here, but I have the space to cook a mean pot of ramen and enjoy my morning coffee. I lovingly refer to it as my 'room with a view.'

And what a view!

From here, I keep a watchful eye on my home away from home—my family. Sure, they can be a little too close for comfort, and I get the sense sometimes that Mother feels the same way about me. But when I'm in need of that comfort—and butter pecan ice cream, a private string concert, a rousing game of Qwirkle, or a plate of anything other than noodles—they're a mere heartbeat away.

Isn't that what home is anyway? It sounds cliché, but it's where the heart lives, breathes, cooks, bathes, fights . . . and expands. For the past few months, that's exactly what I've been working on—expanding my home, planning for the day when Hubby-to-be quite literally (and figuratively) officially moves in. I've been preparing to accommodate another towel, a few suits, some red beans and rice, and a turtle of all things. They'll have to move over for a standard poodle, a baby grand piano, and midnight bowls of Frosted Flakes.

343

I'd thought my 'renovated space' meant moving in his mother and her quilting squares and his dad's antique cars, his sister who only calls when we eat dinner, my brothers and their jokes about body functions, my sister's giggling girlfriends, my parents' cast-iron pots and pans, and my grand-parents' stories . . . all under one blood-pumping roof.

Yet God had more heartrending work in mind for His fixer-upper, more than a mere change of address. He's knocking down walls of miscommuni-cation and shoring up binding ties. He's deep cleaning and power washing, making everything new. And He won't complete His makeover within an hour-long episode. It'll take a lifetime, which means it won't be finished in time for the wedding. But that's okay, even if this process hasn't gone the way I expected. It's all according to His plans.

Yes, my home is where the heart is. But most important, my heart is where Jesus is. He's reassured me there's always room for one more: Him.

Are you undergoing renovations of your own? I'd love to be a part of your family's journey, so drop me a line and tell me about it. Here's a Word of encouragement from Ruth 1:16 in case you need it:

Entreat me not to leave you, Or to turn back from following after you; For wherever you go, I will go; And wherever you lodge, I will lodge; Your people shall be my people, And your God, my God."

By that time, JD had been reading silently over Kevin's shoulder as he gently rocked the baby. Without looking up, he asked, "So, Maxie, are you bringing your Teddy Bear home to the garage apartment?"

"That was the plan," she answered around a mouthful of bacon and muffin.

"When are you going to tell him your 'home' includes an ex-husband and a daughter?"

Kevin ruffled the pages. "Come on, man. Now's not the time. I'd hoped to break the ice between you two, not go into a deep freeze up in here."

"It's going to take more than a touchy-feely magazine column to do that." JD stalked over to the coffee maker.

Ding-dong!

Kevin looked from JD to Maxine.

"I've got the baby." JD nodded at Lauren, snoring softly in his arms.

Maxine shrugged. "I don't live here. You'd better get the door before the dog wakes Evelyn."

Kevin left the kitchen.

Maxine tapped in the password on her phone and opened the app for her texts.

Ding-dong!

"Oh no." Maxine's phone clattered on the cherry tabletop as she sprang from the table. She sprinted for the foyer. "Kevin, wait!"

Her fiancé stood on the threshold, framed by the sunlight, his face obscured by Kevin, who had thrown open the door. As Teddy stepped forward with arms outstretched, Maxine saw his warm smile widen . . . and freeze as JD strolled up beside her, still holding the sleeping baby. Teddy's arms fell limp to his sides.

Chapter Twenty-Nine

"TEDDY, I JUST GOT YOUR MESSAGE." Maxine, breathless, kissed his cheek. "I'm ready. Let me grab my purse and phone from the kitchen, and we can go." She patted his forearm and turned to dash back to the kitchen.

But he clasped her fingers as they brushed his. "Still struggling with introductions, Maxine?"

"Oh, right. Well, you remember Kevin, Evelyn's husband, from yesterday. Evelyn's upstairs catching up on sleep after a bad night with the baby. Otherwise, she'd be here with us. And this . . . this is Kevin's brother, Jay, uh, JD . . . I mean, James D. Lester. He came over this morning. For breakfast. Well, it wasn't really breakfast, more like bacon and coffee." *I sound unhinged even to my own ears.*

"Jay, JD, James Lester. . . . Wow, you must have spent

three years in kindergarten trying to keep all that straight."
Teddy stepped forward, hand outstretched. "I'm Theodore,
Maxine's fiancé. Didn't think I'd meet you in person before
the commencement."

JD reached out with his left hand and gave Teddy an
awkward-looking, abrupt shake while still cupping the baby's
back with his right. "Theodore. Teddy. Headmaster. Fiancé.
It's nice to put a face to your many names as well."

Kevin shut the door. "Well, you can call me Mr. Tibbs. . . .
You know, the movie with Sidney Poitier . . . *In the Heat of
the Night*?" He winced as his joke seemed to miss its mark
and landed somewhere beyond the other, silent people in the
foyer. "Now that we've cleared all that up, would you like
to come in, Teddy? We were having—how did Maxine put
it?—'like coffee and bacon.'"

Maxine no longer cared about the bacon. "I don't think
we have time."

"Sure." Teddy draped his arm around her shoulders. "It's
probably a good idea to learn more about the man speaking
at our graduation. You already seem to have a way with the
ladies in the audience." He nodded at Lauren, nestled into
JD's neck.

JD's eyes narrowed.

His look reminded Maxine of the day he happened upon
her poring over tenth-grade geometry proofs with Carl
Schwartz. He sized up the other boy right away, his smirk
announcing that he recognized Carl was more interested
in the female figure sitting across from him than the geo-
metric ones. He left Carl and Maxine there with their heads
together, swapping No. 2 pencils and college-ruled notebook

paper. Before sauntering away, he even pointed out a mathematical error in Carl's proof and mouthed, *"QED"* over the boy's head. *Quod erat demonstrandum.*

When she glanced at Teddy, she saw a similar look, one that measured the length, width, and breadth of JD, that took stock of his intentions and his chance of success. She imagined two male lions on the savannah, circling each other, calculating when, how, and where to strike.

Maxine leaned into Teddy and tightened her grip on his hand. "Okay, let's get to know each other. We can sit in the keeping room." As she led the group to the back of the house, she listened to their footsteps fall into step behind her.

"I'll make more coffee before I check on Evelyn," Kevin offered.

They sat quietly around the coffee table in the keeping room just off the kitchen—she and Teddy on the love seat in front of the window, JD and Lauren across from them in a leather armchair—while their host ground fresh beans and filled the filter. Then Kevin lifted the baby from JD's arms and exited the room. *Take me with you!* Maxine nearly cried.

"So, James—is that what you'd prefer?—Maxine tells me you and she dated in high school." Teddy's fingers played with the stray hairs on the back of Maxine's neck.

She watched JD watch Teddy's hand.

"Actually, those who knew me when tend to call me Jay, with a James Dee thrown in for good measure. Colleagues call me James or JD. But it's par for the course, a Southern thing. I've called some of my own cousins by their nicknames for so long, I don't even remember their real names—Big

Boy, Schoolgirl, Sistah. So, yes, James is fine." He paused. "You're not from around here, are you?"

"I'm from farther South. I grew up in New Orleans, but I graduated from Boston College. You know, *pahk* the *cah* near the *hahbah* and all that. What about you?" Teddy's trailing hand settled along her neckline.

"I followed my brother to Princeton. He transferred back to school in North Carolina, but I stayed and eventually went to work in New York. But home never leaves you."

Maxine's eyes flicked to the magazine and back to JD.

JD crossed his leg and rested his hand on a knee. "How'd you end up in our sleepy burg, Theodore?"

"Apparently, the same way you did, by what I've read in your curriculum vitae: work, pure and simple. And I'm grateful, because I would never have met Maxine." He turned to her as his fingers busied themselves once again, tracing her jawline near her ear.

Yet the flatness of his eyes belied his show of affection. He seemed to have traveled to some faraway place with accommodations only for one. Maxine almost reached for his hand to interlace her fingers with his, to center him in the moment with her, but suddenly she heard, *It's time.* She blinked, and Teddy turned away.

JD's fingertips played a slow drumbeat against his shin. "So when did you two get engaged?"

Now, Maxine. Now's the time. She inhaled deeply.

"December. Didn't she tell you?"

"No, she can be pretty closemouthed about her personal life."

Maxine felt like she was poised on the back stairs, listening to the two men talk about her. She stood and walked deeper into the kitchen, feeling the heat of their eyes on her back. Her eyes landed on her column.

Tell them what home means to you.

She wanted to cover her ears to shut out the voice, but it reverberated from somewhere deep inside, exuding from her body in waves.

Who is home to you, Maxine?

Suddenly Teddy was beside her, turning her to face him. His eyes now burned with questions.

"In the car yesterday, you asked me about JD . . ." Maxine's voice faded as JD twisted around in his chair, catching her words as they fell from her mouth. Unable to focus on him for long without running out of breath, Maxine averted her eyes to the Japanese maple framed by the window. It glowed red in the late-spring sun. The movement of its delicate leaves mirrored the slight tremor of her body.

"I told you we dated pretty seriously."

"You didn't say 'pretty seriously.'"

"Well, it was. I mean, we did. In fact . . . in fact, we more than dated."

"What's 'more than dated'?" Again, Teddy turned her face toward his.

"For goodness' sake, man, give her room to speak!" JD's voice exploded from his seat though he never stood.

Upstairs, the baby cried.

Maxine moved away from Teddy and gripped the counter, her eyes squeezed shut. *Please, Lord. Help me get this out somehow.* Her exhaled breath seemed to make her eyelids flutter as she opened them.

"Do you mean you had . . . a sexual relationship?" Teddy backed away.

Maxine fought the urge to check herself for visible, oozing sores, to shout, *"Unclean! Unclean!"* and distance herself from her fiancé. Her brain searched for the right answer while her mouth spouted, "Yes."

"No. No, it wasn't a *sexual relationship*. Don't you dare stand there and try to shame her, to shame *us*. Neither one of us is about to pin an *A* to our shirts and hang our heads. We were married. She was my wife. I was her husband."

"What did you say?" Teddy erupted.

Again they heard Lauren's cry from the second floor. This time, Cocoa's faint *ruff-ruff, ruff-ruff* followed up.

Maxine reached out, but her fiancé stepped out of reach. Her fingers floated there in the air for a second before they were gripped by another.

JD shook his head, but he didn't let go of Maxine. If anything, he held on more tightly. His *no* seemed to be about Teddy—*no* to saying more, *no* to explaining her past away, *no* to making excuses, *no* to feelings of disgrace. *No* to her engagement.

Two pairs of feet thundered down the back stairs.

"What's going on down here? Every time we get this close to settling Lauren, we hear shouting." Evelyn stood by the range in a rumpled T-shirt and sweatpants. Her hair stood up. Behind his wife, Kevin, eyelids drooping, silently rocked Lauren, whose tiny arms pummeled his chest as she screeched.

Teddy spotted Maxine and JD's clasped hands. His mouth worked but didn't muster a sound.

Kevin edged by Evelyn and laid a hand on JD's shoulder. "Bruh, why don't we let Theodore and Maxine have a moment? We can stream the worship service down in the media room while we work on getting the little one back to sleep."

Though JD started to shake his head, Maxine withdrew her hand from his and stepped closer to her fiancé. "Thank you, Kev. We could use that moment. Teddy, do you want to sit on the deck?" She waited for his answer, ignoring the others as they shuffled from the room. It wasn't until she heard the basement's pocket door slide closed that she pointed to the back door. "Teddy?"

He looked at her a moment before heading toward the double front doors.

Chapter Thirty

By the time Maxine caught up with Teddy on the side-walk, she'd broken into a light sweat. The sunrays were hot fingers pressing on the skin between her shoulder blades through her thin shirt. She hoped Teddy would cross over to a shadier side of the street, but he seemed oblivious to the late-spring heat that was quickly turning the corner to summer. When she glanced at his grim profile, guilt suffused her.

"It's starting to feel like New Orleans out here. I'd suggest walking under those dogwoods, but I know you'll be afraid of the bees or bugs."

"I-I'll be okay. I don't think I'd even notice a bee sting today." Feeling worse after his thoughtful suggestion, she took a step off the sidewalk.

"Whoa!" He threw an arm out as a sedan blew by them,

going too fast on the neighborhood road. Then he took her hand. Once they'd safely crossed, he let go. "So let's hear it, Maxine."

She kept her eyes on her feet as they moved slowly, but she took no notice of the delicate mounds of white and yellow blossoms dying on the sidewalk. Though she yearned to feel the security of her hand in his, she didn't dare stretch for his fingers dangling at his side.

"Maxine?" Teddy stopped walking.

She sighed and turned to face him, squinting into the sun that framed his face. "Can I start by telling you how sorry I am?"

"I'd rather you told me how much you love me, but I suppose I'll take that." He shifted to his left, deeper in the shade of an overhanging branch, forcing her to follow.

Maxine's face flushed, despite the cooler temperature in the shadows.

"Come on. Tell me what's going on. You and this JD person were married? When did that happen?"

"When I was seventeen. And—" she swallowed—"and I got pregnant."

"You mean, you got pregnant, so you eloped." He shook his head as if judging the sad ending to her story.

"No, that's not what happened."

"Then what happened?"

"That's what I'm trying to tell you." She took a deep breath.

"Don't try. Just tell me."

"Yes, we eloped when I was seventeen, and he was a freshman at Princeton. I got pregnant right away, before we could tell our families about our marriage. Instead of following him to New Jersey the way I'd planned, I told him I'd miscarried, and then I ran away and had the baby." Her chest heaved with the effort to catch up with her words.

"Where's the baby now?"

"Here, in Mount Laurel." Maxine cleared her throat. "Celeste, Celeste is . . . *was* . . . my baby."

Teddy's eyes flattened; then they fluttered like butterflies before they closed altogether. "Of course," he whispered under his breath. "Of course she is. That makes sense." His eyes opened to such narrow slits his lashes nearly covered his pupils. "The family business."

"Yes, I suppose you can say that."

"Why did you run away only to come back and give her up? Was that the plan so people wouldn't know?"

"No! At least not like that. I didn't have a plan at all. Only to get away. But while I was gone, the Lord helped me see—"

"The Lord. The Lord helped you see what exactly? I love when people use God to explain away their bad choices." Teddy pivoted and took a step toward Kevin and Evelyn's house.

Maxine clutched his arm. "Wait, Teddy. Let me explain. Can we sit and talk?" She pointed to a bench in the neighborhood park. As they made their way over, she thought back to the day Vivienne first planted the seeds that later bloomed into their present circumstances.

Maxine sat on the edge of her seat. "I'd been back in Alabama almost a month. I remember . . . I remember sitting at the table, feeding Celeste green peas, and she was twisting every which way. She's always hated peas." Maxine swallowed.

"Max—"

"Mother said something like 'I know you think I'm crazy, but forgoin' your education to work forty hours a week churnin' milkshakes and fryin' nuggets at McDonald's makes even less sense. How are you supposed to make a life for you and that baby selling chicken nuggets?'" Maxine shook her head a little at her imitation of Vivienne. "And then she moved me out of the way and somehow got more peas into Celeste than Celeste smeared on her apron.

"For a while, this powerful . . . *inertia* . . . just dragged me along. I'm serious, Teddy. I didn't have the energy to change the status quo. I focused on being a good girl and getting us both used to our new life. Then one day, Mother drops these brochures on the coffee table, and they're filled with pictures of people cavorting on the quad, a chapel spire stretching into the sky, libraries stocked with books and computers . . ." Maxine's hands spread wide as she recalled those pictures.

"And she tells me, 'Evelyn's really enjoying college, and you could, too, Maxine. It would be my honor to relive your baby days. Celeste and Zan play together so well already, just like brother and sister. You can hang with your friends, instead of sitting on my sofa in your sleepin' cap on a Friday night. Let us help you.'" This time, Maxine was too busy being *in* the moment to impersonate it.

"So they helped you." Teddy seemed to join her in it, for he scooted forward.

"So they helped me. I quit my job and enrolled in a couple of classes at the community college. First John bought me a car with his book advance and moved Celeste's car seat to his SUV. They started asking *me* to babysit instead of the other way around. And yes, I filled out one of those applications. But then I forgot about it."

"I bet Miss Viv didn't."

Maxine shook her head. "You know Mother. One night, I got home from my writing club, determined to spend one-on-one time with Celeste and read *Guess How Much I Love You* with her bunny puppet. But when I peeked through the crack in the door, I saw Zander building a tower with his DUPLOs and Celeste propped up by pillows beside him. First John and Mother laughed with them when the tower toppled over and—"

When Teddy slipped his hand into hers and squeezed it, she leaned into him and let her tears soak into his shoulder. "They were this perfect picture of a happy family. I tried to sneak away, but Mother spied me at the door and crooked her finger. 'We've been waitin' for you. Guess what came today!'" Maxine waved her hand as if holding that long-ago letter.

"So First John scoops up Celeste, and she's bouncing on his arm to some music only she can hear and patting his cheeks. He's swinging Zan like a pendulum from his other hand, and Mother's thrusting this letter at me as she dances from one foot to the other and clapping her hands. I can feel my stepfather watching me, *questioning me*, with those intense blue eyes of his the whole time I'm reading it."

She looked at Teddy. "Kinda like the way you're looking at me now."

"What did it say?" By now, Teddy's voice was as quiet as Maxine's.

"'Congratulations! We're excited to offer you a full,

four-year scholarship . . .' Mother shouts, 'Praise the Lord!' and starts doing the cha-cha with Zan. First John keeps watching, watching, watching. And Celeste just throws her head back and crows, 'Yay!'"

Maxine sat up as elementary-age boys ran onto the playground. The tallest beat the other two to the swings and hopped on. "All I could think about when I saw her tiny teeth was that Mother and First John saw them come in while I was at work and at school, and they'd be the ones to put the money under her pillow. Shoot, as far as everyone was concerned, the Lord seemed to answer Mother's prayers with a loud and clear *'Go,'* and why not? It felt like I was already gone.

"So I packed up and went, to college first and then to grad school for another eighteen months. After that, I worked in Atlanta before I shimmied back home, this time with two degrees and a few paychecks in my suitcase instead of a pack of disposable diapers and hand-me-down baby clothes. By the time I returned, they were all settled into their life in Mount Laurel again, and I'd made my parents' temporary guardianship of Celeste permanent. But that was understandable, right, Teddy?"

For a moment, they both seemed to listen to the *squeak-squeak* of the swings. Maxine watched their legs pumping, sending the boys higher and higher toward the sky.

"Why haven't you ever told me any of this before? Did you think I wouldn't support you or love you? That I wouldn't understand?"

Instead of meeting his eyes, Maxine scanned the facades of the houses built around the park. She wondered where the playful boys lived. If they had sisters and brothers, mothers and fathers. *Squeak-squeak, squeak-squeak, squeak-squeak.*

Teddy released her hand and leaned forward, blocking her view of the children. "Is that why you live over your parents' garage, to keep an eye on your sis . . . daugh . . . Celeste?"

"Celeste doesn't need me to keep an eye on her. She's got two perfectly good parents to do that. I just can't bring myself to leave her. For my own sake." Maxine squinted at Teddy, the sun bright behind him. "Are you willing to move in there with me when we get married?"

When—the ginormous elephant squeezing between them, sucking up most of the available air through its four-letter trunk, and leaving little for Maxine. She held her breath as she awaited his answer.

"I don't think there's room for the three of us."

Teddy shifted, and suddenly Maxine could see his face. "Celeste wouldn't live with us."

"But Mr. James D. Lester would." He aimed a finger behind him, in the direction from which they'd come. "You still haven't told me how he fits into all this. How can you forgive him and welcome him back into your life?"

"Forgive him?" Maxine swiped at her face.

"I mean, it was great that you had your parents' support, but you could've used Celeste's father. Your *husband.*" Teddy squared his jaw and averted his gaze toward the boys, who leaped from the swings and ran to the slide.

"I didn't need to forgive JD anything." Maxine's voice was as low as her spirits.

"What?" Teddy raised his voice over the youngsters, who were now pushing each other at the bottom of the ladder.

"I didn't—"

"I heard that. I just don't understand." He scooted toward her on the bench.

But Maxine inched away until her back was pressed against the wood. She watched the smallest boy reach the middle rung and kick out at one of his tormentors. "As I said, before I ran away, I told JD I'd miscarried. So you can't blame him. He didn't know about Celeste until we'd moved back to Mount Laurel, after we ran into his mother at the library. The minute she saw Celeste and me together, she knew. So I had to tell him."

"How did she feel about meeting her granddaughter?"

Maxine snorted. "Annie Lester? She didn't feel anything but horror. She was worried about JD giving up his life in New York and coming home to a ready-made family—oh, the shame. Mrs. Lester never liked me. Something to do with her and Mother. Anyway, she helped convince JD to sign away his rights since so much time had passed. She even paid for the divorce, assistance I needed since my folks didn't know I was married. With all that taken care of, my folks made the adoption final."

"And Celeste didn't mind all this?"

The neighborhood children seemed to have worked out their differences. One after the other they climbed the ladder and slid down, climbed and slid. Maxine's eyes never left them. "What's there to mind? She already knew she was adopted, and as part of our agreement, First John and Mother said we could wait until Celeste was sixteen to tell her about me. I said I wanted to make sure she was ready, but really, I wanted to make sure *I* was ready."

"And her father? What about him?"

"Well, I couldn't have her searching for her father, finding out how I'd kept the news from JD. So basically . . . I killed him. I told her he died. Just like my own biological father had years ago. That way she wouldn't search for him. She had First John."

"Maxine." Teddy groaned. He braced himself on the arm of the bench and stood.

Maxine looked up at him from her seat. "I just couldn't let her think she wasn't wanted. That nearly destroyed me when Mother left me with my grandparents, feeling like I wasn't enough to keep her home. That she didn't love me enough to stay. I couldn't have Celeste trying to earn someone's attention and love for the rest of her life. It was enough her own mother had given her up. At the time, I thought, 'She'll never want for love, not if I can help it.' But now, I realize, that wasn't up to me."

Teddy stared at her as if she was a rare specimen at the zoo. Behind him, the boys gave up on the slide and raced for the jungle gym in the middle of the park. After a minute, Teddy stalked through the grass back to the sidewalk.

At first, Maxine followed him, but then she stopped after a few steps. She took a deep breath and planted her feet among the dead petals in her square of concrete and watched him tuck his head into his chest and stuff his hands in his pockets as he left her.

Chapter Thirty-One

"Oof!" Maxine twisted her ankle as she trudged up the gravel drive. She squatted to massage it and eyed the remaining one hundred feet of gravel leading to the house. She straightened when she heard a garage door open. She rotated her foot and sighed, "I guess I'll limp the last half."

First John stepped around the side of the house, pulling the recycling bin. He met her as she tramped haltingly toward him.

"Hey! You're back early," she observed. She glanced over her shoulder. The leaves of the oak, sweet gum, and maple trees nearly obscured the road. The receding purr of a car floated on the breeze.

First John stood the bin upright and walked over to her as

he pointed toward the garage. "Where are you coming from? I didn't see your Volvo."

Maxine returned his kiss and hug of greeting. "I spent the night at Evelyn's. Did you have a good trip?"

He shrugged. "We didn't go for fun." First John looked down at her sandaled feet. "Did you walk there?"

"No, Teddy dropped me there yesterday and borrowed my car."

"So you decided to come back, huh?" Zander called from the front porch. The glass-paneled storm door slowly whispered closed behind him. He bounded down the four steps to the walkway and sauntered over.

Maxine punched him in the shoulder. "Yes, Zan, I *finally* decided to come back. Don't tell me you missed me. And with all those muscles you're showing off in that sleeveless tee, you're too buff to need my protection."

He laughed and pounded his chest with a fist. "Nope. I know how to handle things just fine without you. I'm nearly seventeen. 'Bout time you started acting your age anyway. When I'm thirty, you won't catch me living at home."

Maxine tried not to think about what she was handling at Zan's age. "I don't live at—"

"Then what do you call—?"

"*Kids.*" First John ran his hands through his closely cropped hair. "Knock it off. Maxine, I know my oldest son is more than capable of handling his brothers and younger sister for twenty-four hours, but we would've appreciated a heads-up. When we left Friday night, we thought you'd be around, at least during the overnight hours."

Zander smirked at Maxine.

She rolled her eyes at her younger brother before giving him the cold shoulder. "Zander didn't tell you, First John? I was here Friday, but I asked Mama Ruby and Granddaddy to stay in my apartment last night. I thought they'd take them to church this morning."

"You know we don't like to go to Old-Fashioned Baptist. All they do is sing hymns. It's boring. The kids and I worshiped at home." Zander crossed his arms.

Maxine readjusted the strap of her canvas bag. "I bet you did. Anyway, Mother warned you about using that name for Mama Ruby's church. You very well know worship isn't about strobe lights and rock music. You should be able to sit still without a PowerPoint presentation."

"Who told you that? The person driving that yellow Porsche? I guess it was a come-as-you-are Sunday where *you* attended today." Zander gave Maxine a once-over.

First John held up two hands and effectively put the brakes on the argument. "Yellow Porsche? Since when did Theodore start driving a Porsche?"

"Since never. I caught a ride home." Maxine brushed back a flyaway wisp of hair and cast a sideways glance at her stepfather. "You know, just like the good ol' days with your wild orchid."

"Huh?" Her brother's teasing grin died on his face.

"Zander, take this to the curb." First John pointed toward the recycling bin.

"But—"

His father's mouth tightened and he inhaled loudly through his nose.

Zan shut up and tilted the large blue bin on its wheeled

side and started down the drive. He called over his shoulder. "Mama was looking for you, Max."

I bet she is. Maxine stared up at the second story.

"That's not true, you know."

She turned to First John. "What? She isn't looking for me?"

"No. What you said a minute ago, about 'the good ol' days.' Nobody's reliving those. And what's this about a 'wild orchid'?"

Maxine pictured JD speeding off not fifteen minutes before. By some folks' estimation, not much had changed since she was sixteen years old. Just the getaway car.

"Maxine? Did you hear me? And what's up with that smile?"

Hearing the crunch of Zander's sneakers as he ascended the hill toward them, she crooked a thumb in the direction of the main house. "Mother's in there unpacking? I'm going to shower, change, and throw my Manna uniform into the washing machine before I come over."

"Doing laundry herself. Preparing for the week. But whoa there, Maxine."

She'd taken a step toward the house, but she stopped to look at First John and then Zander, who stood beside the older man.

The teen's eyes skipped between his father and his sister before he marched to the porch, muttering under his breath.

Once the glass storm door swung open and shut, First John cleared his throat. He thrust his hands into the pockets of his khaki shorts and kicked at the rocks with his Dockers.

Maxine fixed her eyes on the green alligator stitched over his heart.

"Your mom and I did a lot of talking about this situation while we were gone." *Rattle, rattle.* His feet continued their steady movement over the driveway, sending gravel cascading down the hill. "Too much has gone said and unsaid by too many people for too long. It's time we had a family meeting, at least that's what I told Vivienne."

Maxine squinted at him and shifted her weight from her injured ankle. "What does that mean exactly, a 'family meeting'?"

His feet stilled. "Don't you think we have a lot to discuss, Maxine? As a whole family? I thought we were close-knit, but based on all that's been happening, these ties seem to be made of spider silk."

She grimaced. "Because they're virtually invisible and they capture the unsuspecting?" Her eyes widened at First John's laughter. "What's so funny?"

"You've always had a way with words. Guess you get that from your dad." He draped an arm around her shoulders and tucked her into his side. "And I mean me."

After a moment's hesitation, Maxine wrapped her arm around his waist and fell into step with him as they tramped toward the garage.

"As far as my poor web analogy goes . . . not only does it catch those unsuspecting bugs, spiders use it to wrap up their young. To protect them. It's strong as steel, Maxine. So is the bond between us. But yes, things have gotten sticky."

They'd reached the corner of the house, the point where Maxine could continue up the stairs leading to her apartment and he could open the side door that connected to the mudroom. He squeezed her and pulled away.

"But as strong as that web is, a spider still has to repair it and rebuild it when it gets tangled. And we need to fix this, Maxine. We have to if we're going to go on."

"I know you're right." Maxine looked off into the woods that flanked the sides and back of the house and took a deep breath. "But if I recall correctly, you led with 'at least that's what I told Vivienne.' I gather she doesn't agree."

First John's head leaned toward first one shoulder, then the other.

"So neither a yes nor a no. What does that mean?" Maxine could only imagine.

First John pounded his right fist into the palm of his left hand like a gavel. "It means I'm calling our family meeting to order. Let's coordinate everybody's schedules and get through graduation."

Maxine winced, thinking of Teddy's excitement over his speaker. Some hometown hero JD turned out to be.

"I'll reach out to Ruby and Lerenzo, and you . . ."

"I'll be there."

First John clasped her fingers. "*You* call JD. I'm sure his yellow Porsche has Bluetooth."

Maxine tapped lightly on the back door before stepping inside. The large glass pane rattled when she shut it. When she turned into the mudroom, she ran smack into Uncle Roy.

"Whoa there, little mama!" He grabbed his niece by the shoulders and steadied her.

She gripped his forearms. "Uncle Roy! I didn't know you were here."

"Party planning, corn shucking, and fussing. A typical Sunday afternoon at your mama's house," he laughed, snuggling her close as they walked into the kitchen.

"Fussing because you think you know everything," Vivienne growled by the cooktop.

"And because you don't."

"Just tell me if you found those cartons in the storeroom." Vivienne propped a fist on her hip and glared at her baby brother.

"Nope. Like I told you the first and second time, they're not in there. Did you check over the stove?" He left Maxine by the window and approached his sister. He reached for the cabinet door.

Vivienne swatted Roy as she brushed by him. "You think I don't know my own kitchen?" Vivienne kissed her daughter's cheek as she huffed from the room.

"Business as usual, I see," Maxine murmured, grateful. She'd wondered about her mother's demeanor after her earlier conversation with First John, so she'd deliberately taken her time doing laundry and straightening her small apartment before coming over. Maxine surveyed the kitchen as she walked to the refrigerator. One overflowing bushel of corn still in its husks, one bushel partially shucked, and a basket of yellow corn on the cob sat by the table amid a sea of corn silk. A ceramic bowl of kernels and a knife were in the middle of the table.

"What's going on? That's normally an outside project." Maxine plucked some red grapes from a stalk on a refrigerator shelf.

"Funny you should say that. Viv sent Celeste and the boys upstairs to put on some shoes so they can take this mess out to the porch. They thought they'd 'help' by getting started before she got home. You can imagine how that went over when your mama walked in." Roy arched an eyebrow.

Maxine mouthed, *"Ouch."*

"See! I told you." Vivienne marched into the kitchen, bearing an armload of heavy-duty, quart-size storage containers. She set them down on the island and faced her brother. "You know what I'm going to do, don't you?"

He sighed deeply, held out his hands, and then grabbed his backside.

"Still there?" Vivienne laughed and squeezed his shoulder as she moved to stir the kernels frying away in the large cast-iron pan on the stove. "Nearly made me burn my corn, messin' with you."

Maxine chuckled at the long-running joke between the siblings. Her mother had always said, "Roy never could find his behind with both hands."

"Where've you been?" Vivienne adjusted the stove dial and flipped and stirred the corn, revealing a golden-brown crust.

Maxine's stomach gurgled. "Washing clothes."

"I meant before that. Where were you?"

"At Evelyn's. I stayed the night." Maxine went for more grapes.

"Or did *we* stay the night?"

Uncle Roy froze before the pile of silk he'd amassed, his hands wrapped around the broom handle. "Vivienne."

"Roy."

"Mama!"

Maxine, Vivienne, and Roy all looked toward the ceiling, in the direction of Celeste's call.

Thirty seconds later, footsteps creaked down the back stairs and the teen stepped through the door. "Oh, hey, y'all! Didn't mean to interrupt. I couldn't find my other sneaker at first. Mama, we're going to set up in the driveway, if that's okay. When did you get back, Max? Will you be here for dinner?"

"A few hours ago." Maxine glanced at Vivienne. "I'll stay if I'm welcome."

"Child, hush. You can help Roy and me plan this party while we finish up dinner." Vivienne set a Dutch oven on a trivet. She lifted the lid, revealing a pot roast, and poked at it with a fork. Murmuring, "Not tender enough," she replaced the lid and returned it to the oven as what sounded like elephants tumbled down the stairs.

"So, Max, if you're going to be around, can we talk later? After dinner?" Celeste braced a hand on the molding when Zan, Robert, and Second John bumped her as they rounded the corner into the kitchen.

"If y'all don't slow up and be quiet . . ." Vivienne glared at her sons. "Your dad is lyin' down."

"Sorry, Mom." Zan reached for a basket.

"Sorry didn't do it, and it didn't do it to me. Make sure you grab the full one, and, Robert, finish sweeping up. Your uncle didn't make the mess, so he shouldn't clean it."

"*I'm* sorry, Celeste," Zan amended, singing the words. He hoisted a different basket and headed for the door, followed by Second John with the half-full bushel.

Maxine laughed and stepped back as Robert swept over her sandaled feet. "You're going to take away all my luck, and I need all I can get these days." She flicked him on the head when he swiped her toes again before collecting all the trash in a dustpan. "Sure, Celeste. I'll be here for dinner. Something in particular on your mind?"

But Celeste spun and trailed her brothers out the door.

"Have any idea what that's about, Mother?" Maxine retrieved a sharp knife and a bowl. She looked from Vivienne to her uncle, who by now was seated at the table slicing off the cob.

"Your guess is as good as mine. The girl has been in her own world lately. Son, that's the best it's gonna get. You'll have to vacuum after dinner. Take something to collect the corn, and go on outside." Vivienne pulled out a chair across from her brother and sat.

Once the back door had rattled shut, Maxine found a place across from Roy. "Okay, what party?"

"That's what I want to know from you, Maxine," Vivienne grumbled.

"Viv—"

She jabbed a finger on the planner in front of her brother. "Roy, stop trying to shush me. I'm talkin' to Maxine. You just keep brainstorming about Lis's birthday party. Look back in the book from last year, and work from there. You know Evelyn canceled her mama's last summer with all the goings-on with Granny B, so we need to make up for that somehow. Think big. Lis likes to show off, and she's been workin' my nerves, wantin' to see what we've come up with."

Then Vivienne seared Maxine with her eyes. "Now tell me what happened at Evelyn's and with whom." After she spared a glance at Roy, she added, "Please."

Maxine surprised herself by smiling. She set to work with the corncob. "I got what I wanted."

"Well, that makes one of us."

The group turned toward the voice coming from the archway between the kitchen and family room and found a tousle-headed First John shaking his iPhone. "I just talked to Theodore. He tapped three seniors to—how did he say it?— 'take back our graduation.' They'll each give five- to seven-minute speeches."

Maxine's eyes widened. "Does this mean—?"

"That JD won't serve as the commencement speaker?" First John nodded. "Exactly. Theodore wanted to make sure all the board members knew, starting with me."

"You mean, starting with Maxine." Vivienne's voice was as dry as the discarded corncobs in the cardboard box by her feet. "*Mmm-hmmm.* I guess we know how that party went last night."

Maxine squeezed a quarter-size circle of hair product into her palm and massaged it from her scalp down to the tips of her wet curls. She scrunched together strands as she stared at her reflection. Her eyes strayed to the clock on the shelf beside the mirror: 8:47. She dried her hands on the towel around her neck and braced them on the countertop. In thirteen minutes, Teddy would be knocking on her door. "Make that twelve," she amended as the second hand circled the hour.

The rest of the evening had crawled the minute she received Teddy's text during dinner—Okay to come over at 9 tonight? No way could she have held it together over a game of Scrabble, while fielding questions from a wily Vivienne or chatting with Celeste. Another glance at the shelf informed her she had ten minutes to spare, less than that based on Teddy's love affair with punctuality.

Thump, thump, thump.

"Okay, a lot less," she groaned. Maxine gathered together the hot-pink folds of her robe and padded from her bedroom on slippered feet. She unlocked the front door and opened it to her fiancé.

Teddy ran his hands over his head, apparently attempting to smooth the brown spikes, usually kempt and wavy. His red-rimmed eyes met hers only briefly as he brushed past her.

Maxine swallowed the urge to offer him some hair cream and resisted rubbing his back as he moved deeper into the apartment. She shut the door and dead-bolted it, preventing unexpected drop-ins from using their key. She studied the back of Teddy's plaid short-sleeved shirt for a moment. He seemed captivated by the stars twinkling in the darkening skies over the treetops beyond the large window. Then she cleared her throat. "Can I get you something while you wait for me to change?"

He crossed his arms across his chest and hunched his shoulders, but he didn't turn. "I remember not so long ago, you wouldn't let me in when you weren't fully dressed. Why now?"

"Because you see me as I am." But Maxine clutched her robe more tightly, feeling exposed, laid bare in the quiet. "There's coffee," she murmured, then *shooshed-shooshed* to the back, determining to take her whole ten minutes.

And not a minute earlier, Maxine emerged in a pair of wrinkled purple gym shorts and a pink T-shirt with a bedazzled *PRINCESS* emblazoned across her chest, a Christmas gift from Celeste. She'd brushed her hair into a tight ponytail that dangled down her back to prevent her fiddling. When she stepped into the main room of the apartment, she found Teddy right where she'd left him, staring through the window overlooking the backyard. Night had completely swallowed the sky. She padded to a spot beside him, seeking solace in the creek she had to imagine was there.

"I keep wondering . . . would you have ever told me, if this whole graduation debacle hadn't happened?"

Maxine flinched.

Teddy's eyes narrowed. "That's what I thought."

"That's not fair, Teddy. Yes, I was going to tell you. It was just a matter of when and how."

"When? How? I'd think you'd have more to say to help me understand this. Especially since you've heard about my plan to cancel JD's commencement address. You don't have anything to say to convince me otherwise?"

"Convince you? So you expect me to plead my case or his? Frankly, I can't think of anything else to say. I don't rightly care what you do about graduation. Not at this moment. That's the last thing on my mind." She rubbed her brow. "Maybe we should stick a pin in this until our meeting with Reverend Atwater next week."

"Excuse me, but did you say 'stick a pin in this'? You've been lying to me for months. For months. Sitting beside me in my pastor's office, planning our wedding like you're some blushing bride. Meanwhile . . ."

"What, Teddy? I suppose you think I'm a bride who lost her right to blush."

"You said it. I didn't." He rattled loose change in his pockets and studied his shifting feet.

"I guess it was 'if' not 'when,'" she muttered, retreating again to the woods beyond the window. She leaned her forehead against the pane.

"What?"

"Nothing. It only means something to me. But do you know what also means something? That all you can talk about is what you're going through. How you've been hurt and lied to and misled for months. That your pastor has been the victim of my . . . subterfuge, to put it lightly. Well, my daughter, Celeste—you know, the one you struggled to name earlier today?—she has a lot more to deal with than you. I'm ashamed to say I've been lying to her since she was barely walking, and what I have to tell her may break her heart. Not just her *pride*."

Teddy didn't flinch, which irked her enough to embolden her.

"And I'll let you in on another secret. Your pastor knows everything. I told the Atwaters last month. So that should save you some embarrassment. You only need to save face with your parents. You can include them in the big reveal First John's got planned, a family meeting."

"Maxine, I have a feeling I'll be odd man out at a family meeting, so I won't be there. I was hoping coming here would change things. And it's not my reputation I'm trying to protect. It's my heart. Too little too late though." He seemed to drag himself to the door.

"Teddy, is it? Is it too late? Am I not worth the effort?"

He braced a hand on the frame and stretched for the knob.

"What effort? I don't have to make an effort to love you, Maxine. It's as easy as breathing. Loving you is something I want to do. I need to do." He spun and wedged his back on the door, his legs locked to keep him from sliding to the floor.

Maxine thought it would be hard to look into his eyes, but her eyes met and held them. She stepped closer, and when he reached out, she reached back.

"What's hard right now is trusting you." He clasped her hand between both of his and brought them under his chin, forcing her even closer. "Trusting you want nothing more than to marry me. You're looking for something, Maxine. You need or want something more or something *else*. I'm not asking to be all you want in life, only that you want me. Me. Us."

Maxine reached up with her free hand and completed the sphere their fingers made. "Did I ever say I didn't want you?"

"Did you ever say you did?" Teddy extricated his fingers and straightened to his full five feet eleven inches.

Maxine twirled a strand of damp hair that had worked out of her hair tie and edged backward until her heels bumped against her sofa. "Sounds like you're calling me a liar, Theodore F. Charles." Usually her tone was teasing when she used his full given name. Some day she hoped to laugh at the irony, but tonight, her lightly spoken words carried the weight of accusation.

Teddy never broke his gaze as he met her in the middle of the room. He smoothed her hair and kissed her gently on the cheek. "If the glass slipper fits."

July

"The Lord is my shepherd;
I shall not want.
He makes me to lie down in green pastures;
He leads me beside the still waters.
He restores my soul . . ."

PSALM 23:1-3

Chapter Thirty-Two

MAXINE SPREAD THE LAST of their blankets in between the roots of a large oak tree and plopped down. She craned her head around the tall woman with the perfect posture who'd dared to set up shop in front of her. *Don't folks know by now this is* our *spot? She either forgot herself, or she's new to town.*

The seats designated for the musicians were empty, save for their instruments. Celeste's double bass rested on a stand near the edge of the dais. Crossing her legs at the ankle, Maxine counted the five empty chairs around the tall stranger in front of her. She stopped herself from praying the stranger would get a sudden cramp in her back. "But, dear Lord, please get her to remove that wide-brimmed hat," she muttered.

"Hi, honey. Watch your mama's purse, and don't let the

wind take these flags. Be right back." First John dropped his things on one of the blankets. He strode through the grass, dodging women in flowing summer dresses and sandals, men in T-shirts and polo shirts, and children in shorts and sundresses yanking on the hands of their chatting parents.

Maxine searched for Vivienne. She had helped Celeste set up her bass but had since disappeared in the crowd milling about the field. There!

"Over here!" Maxine called and threw a hand up, but her fingers stopped midflight as she recognized the light-brown curls of the man beside her mother.

The wind must have carried her voice to Vivienne, for she turned toward her daughter. Teddy followed suit.

Maxine knew she was easy to spot in her sparkly red-, white-, and blue-striped T-shirt and red shorts, so she didn't duck for cover. Committed, she waved and smiled.

Teddy nodded at her. He leaned into Vivienne and murmured a couple words, then quick-stepped in the opposite direction, nearly tripping over a woman pulling a Chihuahua in a Radio Flyer wagon.

Vivienne turned back to Maxine and shrugged, palms up, as Teddy's navy-blue shirt bobbed and wove through the crowd until it disappeared behind the grandstand decked out with bunting.

Maxine shrugged herself and tried to focus on the holiday fun. Her whole family attended the July Fourth picnic and concert at Bedlow Park every year, but this was the first time Celeste would play. She wondered if the night's fireworks would hold a candle to her explosion with Teddy.

"Still haven't talked to Theodore?"

Maxine's eyes angled upward toward her stepfather's deep voice. When he bent his long frame and gently planted a kiss on her forehead, she closed her eyes and leaned into it. She opened them and noted the way the fading sunlight glinted off the silver weaving through First John's short blond hair. "Nope. Not a word since the two we exchanged last week during our meeting with Reverend Atwater. But it's okay. We said enough to last us awhile that Sunday he came by the apartment. I've had about thirteen years to process this. He can take a few weeks." She flicked away a stray thread from the American flag emblazoned on her stepfather's otherwise-pristine white T-shirt. "Or however long it takes."

"So you've fully processed this, have you?" First John lowered himself to the ground and clasped his hands around his bent knees.

Picking up on his skepticism, Maxine nodded once, firmly, as the breeze lifted her curls. She crossed her bare legs at the ankles. "Yes. I'm all ready for our family meeting. I just need to pick out an outfit." She offered a smile.

He didn't return it. "Does that mean you've contacted JD?"

"Not yet, but I will. That's not a problem. Really, my biggest question is skirt versus no skirt," Maxine chuckled.

First John clasped her shoulder. "In that case, I don't need to warn you that he's behind you."

"What?" she sputtered, her laughter dying so abruptly she choked on it.

"Just trying to see if you're as cool a cucumber as you pretend to be. Seems to me like you're not quite ready to be sliced and tossed into a salad."

"That's not funny." But she laughed.

First John sighed and pushed himself to his feet. "I see your grandparents and the boys." He looked over her head, waved his arm, and then pointed to the ground around them. "You stay here, Maxine. Looks like they need reinforcements."

Maxine knew Mama Ruby and Granddaddy always brought lawn chairs, so she rose to redesign the space she'd saved. When she stretched her arms wide to move the blanket, the wind whipped it, and it knocked askew the hat on the head in front of her. "I'm sorry!" she exclaimed, though she hoped her mistake would prompt the woman to remove the offending accessory altogether.

The stranger didn't move, so Maxine reached for her shoulder. "Excuse me."

Tap, tap, tap. "Hey, Niece!"

Maxine turned at the touch to find Uncle Roy. She took a big whiff. "Ooh, you smell like baked beans!"

"Ha-ha. Eau de molasses?" He set down a food carrier and released the handle of a large cooler. "Your grandmother is trying out a new scent, too—fried chicken with honey."

"What happened to your date? I'm not used to seeing you without a honey of your own." Maxine nudged him with her elbow.

"Not today. Not for a *while*, actually. I'm trying out the single man thing and giving my heart and wallet a rest." He crouched down on one knee and unzipped the bag he'd toted over.

Maxine laughed. "What does the Bible say? 'Who can find a virtuous woman? For her worth is far above rubies.'"

Her uncle snorted. "Well, I'm not in the market for *any*

woman, virtuous or otherwise. And speaking of rubies, there's your grandma."

Still chuckling, Maxine dove into her grandmother's hug first and then her grandfather's. "You do smell . . . I mean . . . *look* good! Let's set you up there. Uncle Roy, you can stay here with Mother." She pointed to the blanket where she'd been sitting. "And I'll move over with the boys. Celeste will join us for the fireworks. What'd you bring us, Mama Ruby?"

"What I always do, plus some million dollar pies for dessert. Did your mama make the potato salad?"

"Yes, ma'am. It's in the cooler. Where are Zan, Robert, and Second John?" Maxine scanned the crowd for her brothers' heads.

"They went with your dad to grab Viv. She was running her mouth, as usual." Roy unfolded a chair.

My dad. Maxine slowly set up the second chair.

"But they'd best hurry back. The musicians are arriving." Ruby nodded toward the stage.

"*Hola, nieta!*" Lerenzo waved at Celeste as she took her place behind her bass.

"The orchestra usually takes some time to warm up, and then they play while we eat. We're okay, Mama Ruby," Maxine reminded. "Look at her." She smiled but didn't wave at her sister, trying to keep her pride low-key. *I should've focused more on my music when I was in high school,* she thought. *But then if I had, maybe Celeste wouldn't be here.*

Mama Ruby squeezed her hand. "God is our great Redeemer."

She returned the squeeze. "You always know what I need to hear, even if it's not what I *want* to hear."

Roy shuffled around the group, unpacking paper goods and food storage containers. "Good, I see John. Viv's with him. And she's holding somebody's ears hostage. Who's that she's talkin' to—Lis Agnew?"

Maxine stood on tiptoe so she could see around the throng milling about, slowly making their way to their seats as the instruments launched into a scale. "You mean Lis Willis. And there's Evelyn! I thought she was afraid the noise would scare Lauren. Oh, my goodness," she gasped.

"What is it, child?" Sounding alarmed, Mama Ruby braced her hands on the arms of her seat and went to push herself to her feet, but Granddaddy and Maxine gently pressed her back down.

Roy moved closer to his niece. "Everybody calm down. It's gonna be all right. It's just Kevin and—"

"Geoff!" yelled the woman in front of them, clapping her hands. "I did it, honey. I did just what you told me. I sat here, and I didn't move!"

"Geoff" strolled up with the rest of his entourage and gently took her hand. He smiled and wrapped an arm around her shoulders. "Good job, Mother! I'm JD. James David. Dad isn't here. Thanks for saving our seats.

"I'm sorry it took me so long to get back, but look who I brought—Kevin, Evelyn, and the baby. And this is Evelyn's mom, Lis." Then JD guided the wide-eyed woman to face the people behind her. "Mother, you remember—I mean, let me introduce you to Ruby and Lerenzo Tagle, Roy, and John and Vivienne and their sons. And their daughter Maxine. Y'all know my mother."

Just then, the wind whisked away Annie Lester's large

straw hat and sent it sailing across the park—along with whatever Maxine could think to say.

"I can't believe I'm sitting with that woman," Vivienne hissed.

At least she's taken your mind off "that boy." Maxine tried not to smirk. Her head nearly touched her mother's as they crouched together by the cooler. "It's okay, Mother. Whatever it is between you and Annie, you need to let it go. She certainly won't remember it now."

Maxine had positioned herself on the large blanket with the boys. First John and Vivienne had squeezed onto it with them. Roy had turned his and his parents' seats toward the group on the ground so they formed an enclave amid the other concert-goers, namely the Lester party chatting away by them. Yet her mother's anxiety was as contagious as a yawn, and when Vivienne glanced over her shoulder, Maxine's eyes followed. She forced herself to turn back to her family, inhale, and take the rest of the evening one forkful of potato salad at a time.

"Are you going to eat that?" Robert's fork was poised over her strawberries and blueberries.

"Nope. They're all yours. I just put them in the bowl to make it look festive. I'm saving my sugar fix for Mama Ruby's pie." Maxine scooped the fruit into her brother's pool of whipped cream. Her head moved to the melody of "America the Beautiful."

"Mom, okay if I sit with Jackson? I'm done. Y'all need me to take your plates?" Zan stood. He and Evelyn's younger brother had become friends after spending years tagging along behind their older sisters.

"You should stay back here with us. Don't bother those folks."

"Vivienne, by 'those folks,' do you mean your good friend Lis and her family?" First John took a bite of his chicken wing.

Roy wiped his mouth and whispered, "And, Zan, if you're going over there, I'm going, too. That Lis is lookin' mighty fine today."

Maxine shook her head. "Uncle Roy, didn't you just tell me you were done with dating?"

"I didn't say anything about dating, little girl. I need to talk to her about her birthday party. Nail down some of these plans." He winked at her, then grabbed his nephews' empty plates and took them to the large trash receptacles near the parking lot.

Maxine noticed Lis watching her uncle. She cupped a hand over her mouth and elbowed Vivienne. "I don't know, Mother. Looks like Mrs. Willis might not be averse to discussing her 'birthday party.'" She snorted.

Mama Ruby cackled. "Wouldn't that be somethin'? Didn't I tell you God would bring him the right woman someday?"

"Shh, Mama!" Vivienne looked stricken. "They'll hear us!"

"They just gon' hear *you*." But Ruby silenced her laughter as her chest continued to heave with it.

First John tried to plug his grin with a chicken leg.

Maxine lowered her voice so her brothers wouldn't kiss and tell. "How sweet that would be for Uncle Roy."

Her uncle knelt on the ground near Lis, and Zan peered around Jackson to beckon his younger brothers. After their silent request and Vivienne's stony nod, they ran over. Maxine wondered what JD was telling Kevin as the orchestra launched into "You're a Grand Old Flag."

"Y'all are just determined to give me a heart attack, aren't you? You won't be keepin' this from Celeste much longer, with all this fraternization," Vivienne huffed.

"We're not supposed to, remember?" Maxine waved her flag in the air with the rest of the audience. "Isn't that what you said months ago? No more 'family business.'"

"That child has a point, Vivienne. They're part of our 'family business,' and Celeste has a right to know all her people. Isn't that right, Lerenzo?"

Granddaddy nodded. *"Así es."*

"You don't count, Daddy. You always agree with Mama," Vivienne growled, her eyes trained on the back of Annie Lester's head.

"Isn't he supposed to, honey?" First John stroked his wife's hair.

Vivienne cut her eyes at her husband. "Then why aren't you agreeing with me?"

"But I am. We talked about this, and we were all on the same page about the importance of telling the whole truth, not serving up bits and pieces that can't fully satisfy. I'm glad that Maxine finally agreed to get this all out in the open."

"There's nuthin' to be ashamed of. Not one thang," Mama Ruby pronounced. "Mistake's been made and paid for."

"Mother, just what do you have against that woman? It can't be solely because she's JD's mama. You've never liked her." Maxine scooped out a wedge of million dollar pie. She knew it came with a million calories as well, with its mixture of sweetened condensed milk, whipped topping, crushed pineapple, and pecans served on a graham cracker crust. She closed her eyes as she savored the costly bite.

"You shouldn't like her either, the way she treated you and Celeste. She thought you weren't worth her precious son's time of day."

Vivienne's bitter tone soured the sweetness of Maxine's dessert. She dropped her fork. "But you've never liked her. Even before I met JD, you couldn't stand her. And whatever you two had between you affected how she felt about me—and you about him, I suspect. Now it's too late to change things with Mrs. Lester, but we can make a difference between Jay and Celeste."

"But she has a father, Maxine!" Vivienne's quiet voice had a steel beam running through it. "What about *their* relationship?"

"JD doesn't threaten me. The lies do."

Maxine wanted to hug First John. She settled for squeezing his arm as she turned to her mother. "So . . . ?"

Vivienne's eyes tangoed with Ruby's.

Maxine looked from one woman to the other. "What?"

"It's time to sing." Lerenzo cradled his wife's elbow and helped her to her feet. He snapped a finger in his daughter's direction and motioned for her and First John to rise. Then he placed his hand over his heart.

Starting just before dusk every year, the orchestra performed a repertoire that included patriotic favorites, breaks for readings, and choral accompaniments. The national anthem marked the end of the concert when the first star twinkled in the night sky. Then the fireworks commenced, instead of applause, and at that point, the musicians joined their families in the audience. As she awaited Celeste's arrival,

Maxine concentrated on the large flag waving over the orchestra, asking herself, *Is this what a "perilous fight" feels like?*

She jumped when she felt a weight settle around her shoulders.

"*Estás bien?*"

"*Sí, abuelo.*" She nodded as the crowd belted, "'. . . and the home of the brave.'"

Boom! Whoosh! Zing!

"Aaaah!" Annie Lester screeched, covering her hands with her ears.

Gathering his mother close to his side didn't seem to help much. JD murmured in her ear, but Annie pushed him away.

Maxine started toward mother and son, but then she took a half step back. "I feel like I should do something. I hope she's okay."

After patting her granddaughter's arm, Ruby pointed out, "Just hopin' won't do no good. Prayer's the most we can do right now."

"Hey! Did y'all enjoy the concert? Could you hear me?" Celeste bounded up, out of breath. She threw her arms around First John's waist.

"Yes, darlin'. You did beautifully."

Sizzzzle . . . pop-pop-pop-pop-pop!

Annie started beating at JD's arms. Her protestations grew louder and more violent, drawing stares and murmurs from the people scattered about the park. Zan peeled away from the Lesters and returned to his family. Eyes wide, Robert and Second John trailed their older brother, followed by their friend Jackson.

Whirreee . . . pow! Each explosion lit up the darkening sky, sparking Annie Lester's agitation.

"Y'all, shouldn't we do something besides standing here, ogling like this is part of the show? Mama Ruby, I think we need to put some hands and feet to our prayers." Maxine moved forward, but a restraining hand stopped her.

It was Vivienne. "Let them handle her, Maxine."

"I'm through with running away from trouble, Mother."

"But you don't need to run to it either. They have enough family involved."

Wheeee!

Though the fireworks seemed to be entertaining most of the crowd, Maxine only had eyes for the Lesters. Helplessly, she watched Kevin give Evelyn the baby, who passed Lauren to her mother. Cradling her granddaughter to her chest with one arm, Lis and her son stood back with Uncle Roy. Evelyn, JD, and Kevin encircled Annie.

Pop . . . pop . . . fsssss! The sky seemed to sizzle and catch fire.

"I remember her! And is that Mr. Lester and Auntie Evelyn?" Apparently the heavenly commotion didn't hold a candle to the one on the ground as far as Celeste was concerned.

"Shh, shh. What I tell you about pointin'?" Vivienne put a finger to Celeste's lips. "Yes, that's Annie Lester, Evelyn's mother-in-law."

Maxine sighed. "Which makes her JD's mother, too, right, Mother? Celeste, remember, we talked about her condition. I think all this activity and these loud noises are too much for her. I should help them pack up so they can get out of here before those cannons go off."

"Poor woman," Mama Ruby murmured. She entwined her fingers with Lerenzo's and they both closed their eyes.

"Celeste, you stay here with me. Don't involve yourself. Maxine!"

But Maxine ignored her mother. As she walked away, she heard First John hiss, "Viv, what's wrong with you? Boys, come with me."

Lis bounced and patted Lauren while Roy and Jackson stowed food and gathered blankets. They all looked relieved to see them walk over. First John whispered instructions to the twins and he and Zan folded the chairs.

Annie Lester continued to fight.

The fireworks whistled and sizzled around them as they worked. It seemed to Maxine that Evelyn had a way with her mother-in-law. Annie started to calm as she clutched the younger woman's hand like a life raft.

As Maxine bent to retrieve the cooler, Celeste approached her.

"Need help?" the girl asked.

"Mother's going to have a fit you're here." Maxine could feel the heat radiating from Vivienne.

"Mama will be fine. What can I do?"

"You! It's you again!" growled a voice. Annie Lester was dragging Evelyn toward Celeste and Maxine.

"I'm not going to let you have him! Not this time. You took Henry away, but I won't let you take Geoff. You can't have him!" Annie Lester grabbed Maxine's arm despite Evelyn's efforts to restrain her. When JD tried to wrap his mother in a bear hug, she slapped him.

Celeste gasped.

Suddenly Vivienne was there, edging her daughters aside, out of harm's way. "Annie, see here."

Pow! Pow! Pow! Pow! Whizzzzzz!

When Annie faced Vivienne, her eyes narrowed and she cocked her head. She moved her mouth soundlessly as she stared at each Owens woman. So intent, she didn't seem to notice JD, holding his cheek.

"Annie Lester, nobody here wants your Geoff. Didn't want him then, and don't want him now. And *my* Henry's long gone, so let's calm down now." Vivienne's voice was low but loud enough to be heard as she raised her hands, palms up. "Just get ahold of yourself, and let them help you get situated. It's going to be all right. Hush, now."

Annie Lester squinted at Maxine and Celeste. She held up her right index finger and moved it side to side. "Taking Henry wasn't enough for you. I see that now. You just had to have my Geoff, no-account man that he is."

JD stroked his mother's back. "Mother, let's go. Dad—Geoff—isn't here. I'm JD, okay? Not your ex-husband. I'm James David, your son. Everything will be better as soon as we get you back home." He looked back at his brother, Kevin, as if for confirmation.

Tears snaked down Annie's face. "No, it won't! It will *not* be okay. It's too late, Geoff. You know how I hate Vivienne, and you went and had a child with her." Her mouth curled in disgust as she glanced at Maxine. Then she pointed at Celeste as she turned stricken eyes on JD. "Look at her. Try to deny it, Geoff. Anybody can see that child is yours!"

Boom! Boom! Boom! Boom! Boom!

First John exhaled a shaky breath. "I guess we didn't get out before the cannon fire."

———————

This must be how it feels to ride in a hearse, Maxine thought. The spirit of heaviness in the car seemed to have pressed Second John and Robert into silence. Refraining from their usual backseat tussling, they shrugged at Maxine when she glanced back. Beside them, Celeste stared out the window, her fist propping up her chin. In front of Celeste sat Zander. He'd braced his head against his window and closed his eyes the minute they'd loaded up. First John and Vivienne focused on the road ahead. Only their clasped hands resting on the armrest between them betrayed their inner turmoil, for her stepfather was a strict "ten-and-two, both hands on the steering wheel" guy.

Vivienne had hushed any and all talk after Annie Lester's accusation and hustled everybody into operation recovery. Evelyn trusted Kevin to see to the baby, her own mother, and her baby brother because an inconsolable Annie resisted all other comfort but hers. When Roy offered an abandoned Lis and Jackson a ride, a shell-shocked JD offered to escort the Tagles. Before they dragged themselves to their SUV, First John, Vivienne, and the rest of the Owenses helped everyone pack, fold, and stow their belongings. Maxine figured she'd save her personal breakdown for later.

"I'm tired," Maxine announced to anyone who would listen on the seemingly interminable ride home.

First John met his stepdaughter's eyes in the rearview mirror. "Then why don't you take a quick nap? We're almost there."

Maxine knew her exhaustion was emotional, not merely physical, but she didn't have the strength to explain. She leaned against the headrest and closed her eyes.

The boom-boom-boom *from downstairs forced her eyes open. She realized someone was pounding on the front door, even though it was the middle of the night. Maxine stumbled out of bed and down the stairs just as the door crashed open and a large shadowy figure squeezed under the frame. It had to bend nearly in half to make it inside. She froze—but only for a minute. Then she hightailed it through the family room, around the kitchen island, and out the back door, which mercifully, gaped open.*

Hearing the footsteps thunder after her, she looked this way and that for a hideaway. Spying a U-Haul parked in her driveway, she scrambled under it. And just in the nick of time. Heavy breathing sounded from everywhere—in front of the trailer, behind it, under it! Then . . . was that the moon? With a whoosh, something—someone—had lifted the end of the U-Haul and exposed her crouching there. Maxine rolled to her feet and sprinted into the woods.

In her mad dash, she nearly careened into the contorted limbs of a humongous oak tree. She held up an arm to cover her face and protect her eyes. An outstretched root sent her tumbling to the ground. But she had to keep moving. She bear-crawled to a hollowed-out log. "Here. I can hide in here."

Maxine tried to stem her harsh panting by focusing on an owl's distant screech. Seconds later, all she heard were footsteps crashing through the undergrowth and her own "Aiiaa!" when an eye peeked through a knothole. As she backed out, splinters and thorns stabbed her hands and knees. Once her feet found purchase, she scrambled upright and took off.

But she was tired. So tired. Each time she found a place to hide, the giant discovered her. He remained just a heart-stopping step away. If she could only make it to the creek . . . but even though she could see it glimmering ahead, she couldn't reach it. It seemed a mirage. "He-e-l-p," she panted. "H-h-e-l-p . . ."

Just when she felt she couldn't run any longer, that she had to give up, a familiar outline stepped from behind a pine tree. He held out a hand. "Maxine, Maxine, here. Run this way."

Her heart obeyed the voice even though her mind warned her of danger. "But wh-what about the giant?" Sure enough, the ground shook with his hot pursuit. Limbs and needles rained down as he snapped off treetops.

"Don't worry. It is well, Maxine. Shh." When she reached him, he pulled her close and tucked her behind him.

"It's well? How can it be? Don't you hear that?" She pointed around him, her chest heaving. "Every . . . time . . . I try . . . to hide, the . . . giant . . . finds me."

He said nothing as he reached down and plucked a smooth stone from the five at his feet. Each had a letter etched into it. As the figure burst through the trees, he nodded at her and reassured, "Don't worry. I'm a man after God's own heart," and he took aim.

"Truth!" Maxine exclaimed, rearing up. The belt scratched her neck.

"Girl, what's wrong with you?" Vivienne eyeballed her daughter from the front passenger seat.

Maxine panted, still picturing the letters on the stones. Then she took in the shocked faces of her family sitting around her as a line from an old Jurassic Park movie struck her. "Well . . . we're back in the car again."

"Yes, we're still in the car. You liked to scare us to death!"

"As tired as I am, it wouldn't take much," First John sighed. "I say we unpack what's necessary and get inside. It's been a long day." The overhead light flicked on as First John climbed from the truck.

"Indeed," Vivienne murmured.

"I have a feeling the next few days will feel even longer because I think First John's right. It's time for a family meeting." Maxine reached into the backseat and squeezed Celeste's knee. "Starting with you. Want to sleep over?"

"Not tonight. I'm pretty tired." The girl shifted her knee, pushed the middle seat forward, and stepped into the garage.

"Since she won't, we will." Second John clambered out the truck after his twin. Zander used the cooler he was toting to nudge his brothers toward the steps leading into the house.

First John patted Maxine's shoulder and followed the rest of his family as they shuffled toward the back door. He paused on the top step, one finger on the garage door opener, and looked over his shoulder at Maxine. "Give her some time. We're all worn-out."

Maxine nodded and headed up to her apartment. The garage door whirred closed behind her.

At home, she collapsed on the sofa in the dark, her mind clogged with the day's events, faces, and voices. Before she could free her thoughts and drag herself to bed, she heard a light *tap-tap-tap* at her door. Hopeful, she walked to the door and flung it open.

Indeed, Celeste stood there on Maxine's stoop. And she did have a bag looped over her shoulder, a frayed, army-green duffel Maxine hadn't seen since Celeste was so small, she could've tucked the girl inside it. Before Maxine could speak, Celeste slowly extracted a worn, yet familiar thin blanket speckled with green and yellow flowers and held it out.

Maxine reached for the cotton cloth and clutched it to her chest, much as her mother had held her daughter and granddaughter thirteen years ago. But instead of coming in and staying put, as Maxine and baby Celeste had, the teen turned on her heel and quickly descended the wooden steps.

Celeste's feet didn't stop moving until they'd carried her back home.

Chapter Thirty-Three

"*Anybody can see that child is yours!*"

Maxine couldn't stop thinking about Annie Lester and her vituperative words. Confused or not, she'd spoken truth, however harshly. Maxine jabbed a pin into her topknot, trying to recoup some of the damage from last night's humidity. Not that it mattered. Celeste certainly wouldn't give a whit about her hair, and neither would anyone else. "But who told you to go to bed without your silk cap?" she asked her reflection.

Out of sorts, Maxine opened her bathroom door and walked into the main living space. In the middle of the sofa was the blanket. Maxine had curled up with it, crying on the sofa most of the night. Emotionally wrung out, Maxine padded to the window. She pulled back the curtains to let in the sunlight and caught sight of a small figure in gray down by the water. She squared her shoulders. "Time to face the music."

Suddenly energized, Maxine threw on clothes. She only stopped to respond to a buzz from her phone before taking the steps to the driveway two at a time. She had to force herself not to run down the path to the creek, to slowly take in the moments leading up to this meeting with Celeste. To savor the time before their relationship changed forever, before trust was irrevocably broken, before doubt and blame replaced confidence and love. So she focused on the crunch of the nettles and acorns under her feet and the spiky needles and wavy leaves that brushed her. By the time she reached the water, her heartbeat had sufficiently slowed and she could speak.

"Celeste."

The girl was crouched by the water's edge, dragging a stick in the mud. Straightening, she turned and brushed her hands on the back of her denim shorts. She met Maxine's gaze unflinchingly.

Maxine's breath hitched. For a second, she considered running back to her apartment, drawing the curtains, and hiding under the nethermost part of the bed with the blanket. She took a deep whiff of air through her nose.

"Obviously I know what you're going to say, Maxine. That's what I was trying to tell you last night. It's okay."

And Celeste did look okay, despite the huge tear running from the corner of one eye. She brushed it away as if it were a pesky gnat she couldn't be bothered with. Maxine parted her lips to speak again.

But the teen's dirt-streaked, outstretched hand stayed her. "I know you love me. Otherwise, why would you have stayed here all this time, living in Mama and Daddy's garage apartment, working at some dinky, small-town magazine? You could have traveled the world, writing columns for big-time newspapers like Daddy. Had a bestseller on the shelves in your own big house, been married. Had kids of your own."

Of my own? Maxine gaped at the woman-child in her shorts that showed entirely too much leg, limbs that were too skinny for their own good. *If she were* my *daughter . . .*

She blinked.

"But you didn't," Celeste said. "You stayed here. With me. You gave up all that to be here with me. You've sat through every concert, corrected every double negative, shooed away the boys, braided my hair. You sat beside me in church, convinced Mama to let me go to the spring formal even though I'm not in high school yet, and showed me how much fun grandparents can be. So I know you love me.

"You've given me the best of both worlds—a sister who loves me like a mama. *Like* a mama. You're not, though. You're not, Maxine. Because a mother would have told me a long time ago. And you know what? She did. Mama did."

Maxine's tears seemed to dry on her face from the rush of heat to her cheeks. "Is that how you had the duffel bag and the blanket?"

"Yes, Mama told me."

Maxine tried to calm down. She'd agonized over telling her sister—her daughter—the truth, and she already knew. What right did Vivienne have to tell her?

Every right, a voice whispered. Maxine struggled between

embracing or rejecting her anger. She knelt and untied her sneakers. "Let's walk."

After a moment, Celeste unstrapped her sandals. She fell into step beside Maxine in the shallows, their hands brushing each other's as they waded into the creek.

"Teddy's proposal triggered something. For so long, I hid my hurt and ugliness behind my faith. Did and said what I thought I should. I told people what I thought they needed to hear. But then I got engaged, and the dreams started. And it got harder and harder to hide the truth. From you and from myself."

"What dreams?"

"I thought they were about the wedding, but God was showing me something. I'm still working on figuring them out. But I struggled with marrying someone who didn't know everything about me—the most important part about me. You. Only I was afraid. Petrified."

Maxine moved deeper into the water. "I guess Mother got tired of waiting on me to get it together. When did she tell you? After your concert?"

"Not exactly."

Maxine turned around and found Celeste had stooped to pick up a stone. She watched her turn it over in her hand. She splashed back to her. "'Exactly' when?"

Celeste dug out another from the mud. She seemed to compare their smoothness as she rubbed them. "When I was eight years old."

Maxine burrowed her feet deep into the creek bed to keep from running back to the house to shake Vivienne and implore, *"Why? Why?"* She squinted hard at the water, following the current's gentle twists and turns away from them, and wished she could burn the image into her brain.

"I was making a family tree for co-op. And we had a guest historian teaching that semester. You could tell she thought she was somethin' else. This expert had planned a project she said would be something easy for third graders, a way we could practice our interview skills and learn about the past. Homeschoolers make a two-in-one lesson out of *everything*." Celeste threw one of the rocks.

"It turns out it wasn't so easy for me. I'd always known I was adopted, but when I stared at the blank branches of that big tree, *I* felt empty. Sure, I could've picked up the Sharpie and written John and Vivienne and then Ruby and Lerenzo on that poster paper, but those names felt like lies. Maybe if I'd used pencil, but permanent marker . . . ? Nope. Couldn't do it."

Maxine couldn't watch her sister relive that day, so she focused on the trees and the brush bordering the other side of the water. Part of her wished she could make a leaf boat and race after it until both she and the vessel were swept into the ocean. Anywhere but there.

"So I tore up my paper. I had a fit right there in class. And you know Vivienne Owens's children do not cut up in public, especially not when there are only ten black children total at co-op. We have to—"

"'Set an example,'" Maxine mumbled the words with Celeste, for she'd heard them time and again. Snatched back from her imaginary waterfall, she knelt in the creek and fished out a leaf.

Celeste crouched beside her. "So the teacher took me into

the hall and she got someone to run for Mama. When Mama got there, you should've seen her face when she saw us."

Maxine felt her own hair frizz from the steam that must have blown from Vivienne's ears, though she knew it was the moisture from the creek. "Mother hates to draw that kind of attention."

"Especially when it comes to Annie Lester."

Maxine had been searching for a small stick to make a mast for her boat. Her hands froze as she stared at the girl. "What did you say?"

"Mrs. Lester was the guest historian that day. She told Mama about the project we were working on and how I'd behaved in class. How I'd torn up that paper. And you thought *I'd* flipped out! When Mama heard from Mrs. Lester's own lips the assignment she'd given, I thought she was going to slap her right then and there. But that was neither the time nor the place, as she told me later. Mama just took my hand and we went home. She asked Uncle Roy to pick up Zander and the twins, and she took me out for ice cream."

Celeste rose. Water dripped from her legs and her shorts were damp. "Mama started by explaining that Mrs. Lester was punishing me for something she thought Mama did. It seems Annie was dating your biological father."

"That's why she accused Mother of taking Henry!"

Celeste nodded absently. She didn't seem invested in this part of the story, her history. "Then he met Mama, and as they say, 'That's all she wrote.' Mama and Henry fell in love and got married. Annie married Mr. Lester on the rebound, and they fought like cats and dogs until they eventually divorced. Sounds like Mrs. Lester took your dad's death as hard as Mama did."

My dad. Your grandfather. I took it hard too. Maxine blinked away tears and focused on the moment, for Celeste had more to say.

"Mama went on to tell me how I was born, that you were my mother and that my father had left us. You were in high school when it had happened, and you'd run away. When you came back home, you brought me with you, and Mama and Daddy wanted to raise both of us. So that's what they did. That's how much you loved me and they loved us."

"But it's not that simple, Celeste!" Dropping the materials for her boat, Maxine sloshed to the shore. She felt Celeste follow. "Please forgive me for telling you your father died. He didn't. And he didn't just leave you. We tried to do the right thing by getting married first. We did love each other, but there was a lot more we needed to understand to make it work." Maxine looked around before retrieving something from the ground.

She held up an acorn. "See this? Inside is everything you need to grow an oak tree. Maybe even a mighty one like that one up there." She pointed up the hill. "But if I set it aside instead of planting it and giving it time to grow, it won't mature and strengthen. This—" she pinched the seed between her index finger and thumb—"was me. Immature in my faith, how I saw myself and life. I sought my value in who I loved and who I thought loved me back. But I didn't realize God had given me everything I needed, all I could have ever wanted. And not in my parents or in my husband, but inside. In Him."

Maxine stuffed the acorn into the front pocket of her shorts. "What we felt for each other was real, even if I had a lot of other emotions tied up in it. But we acted too fast. We didn't give it time to mature. When I found out I was pregnant, I freaked out. Yet at the same time, I grew up a little. I realized that acting out and getting married hadn't solved anything. Then I made everything worse by lying to him and telling him I'd had a miscarriage. I didn't want anything else to do with him."

"Why would you do that?"

Maxine reached for her hair but stopped herself. She tucked her hands in her front pockets and rolled the acorn between her fingers. "I don't know exactly. Maybe because I wanted somebody to love me for me, to be there for me. But once I got pregnant, I had to grow up fast to be there for somebody else. In some misguided effort to make up for my mistakes—of which there were plenty—I sent him away so he could finish school and get over me. If only I'd stayed and trusted my family, but I ran away."

Maxine started walking again toward the water. Her legs had miles of walking in them though her heart felt like it would give out.

"You keep saying 'him,' but we're talking about Mr. Lester, aren't we?" Celeste's voice was quiet at her shoulder.

Maxine was too spent to be shocked. "Yes, of course you know that, too."

"Don't worry; Mama didn't tell me that part. She hated him."

"Don't say *hate*, Celeste."

"But it's true. Or close enough. I just put two and two

together. The way she acted with Annie Lester all those years ago. How you flipped your wig when he came back to town. I knew my biological father wasn't dead or missing, despite what you'd said. While I didn't know why he'd given me up, I knew it was him."

"And that's why you didn't seem surprised last night after the concert."

"Right. I was just tired of it all, Maxine. Watching you run from the truth is exhausting." Celeste sighed. "Should we head back? Mama's going to wonder what's keeping us. And I'm really tired. I need food."

With a wry twist of her lips, Maxine reached in her back pocket and pulled out a packet of peanuts and a Nature Valley bar. "Mother texted me before I left and told me to bring these. Which do you want first?" She waited for Celeste to choose one. "Why didn't you tell me you knew? To see me twist in the wind, get back at me somehow?"

The teen finished off the peanuts and stuffed the empty package in her back pocket. Her cheeks full, she managed, "You know better than that. When Mama told me, she explained that someday, when you were ready, when it was time for you to tell me, you would. 'In God's own time, not ours' was how she put it. That day, it was time for me to know. Today, it was time for you to tell me."

Maxine stared at the thirteen-year-old in wonder, expecting to see Vivienne pop out of the girl's skin.

"You can't be mad at Mama, Max. She was looking out for me. Thanks to her, I felt like I belonged, really belonged. If I can forgive you for *not* telling me, can't you forgive her for telling me?" Celeste looped her arm through Maxine's.

411

Maxine tucked her elbow into her side to hold the girl close. "You seem too cool with all this, Celeste. What about your father?"

"Dad? Mama didn't tell him I knew. She wanted to keep it between us girls. But when he did find out, he had a cow! That's why they went to the mountains, to talk about it. That trip wasn't all about you. You know he usually lets Mama have her way, but he rolled over her to call the family meeting."

Celeste's mouth rounded in an O and her eyebrows nearly merged with her hairline when she looked at Maxine's face. "Wait. You meant Mr. Lester, not Daddy. Don't get it twisted. I'm not cool with all this, how you kept it from me. I've just had time to work through some of it. Ask my doctors." She withdrew from Maxine and stopped.

Maxine filed away the information about First John and shut up so she could study Celeste's face. The girl looked a little green. "Are you okay? Is there something going on with your heart you haven't told me?"

Eyes closed, Celeste took short breaths as if each word weighed a ton. "Yes, but not in the way you think." When she opened her eyes, fresh tears wet the salty tracks on her cheeks. "I'm grateful you gave me life, Max, and I'm even happier you finally told me the whole truth. We can stop all this dancing around it, put an end to the secrets."

Maxine stared at the teen. While she'd felt Celeste's heartbeat, it was Vivienne who'd guarded it ever since.

"But it really hurt, Maxine. It still does. I know you love me, but having to be strong enough for you and me both got old. Don't forget I'm the teenager, not you! And then, when you got engaged, I knew you'd be leaving and having your own children. You'd leave me for . . . for *them*. I started wondering if I was good enough, and I couldn't eat or sleep. I couldn't play. Part of me wanted to force you to pay me more attention. To do something that made you admit it, to explain. And according to everybody else who seems to know everything, going through puberty makes it worse. Then of course, meeting Mr. Lester made everything go *whoo!*" She spread all her fingers like her head had exploded.

Maxine's hand flew to her chest as she accepted responsibility for the trauma she'd caused. "Please forgive me, Celeste! I tried to protect you, to keep you from feeling 'less than' without a father. But I'm the one who made you feel that way. Why you're dealing with anorexia."

"Cut it out, Max. It's not all about you. And no, it's not anorexia. It's not really about the food. I started out seeing a medical doctor when I collapsed, but now I talk to a counselor. You're right about the word you used—*trigger*. My counselor likened it to post-traumatic stress, and something sets it off. Maybe it was Teddy's proposal for you."

Maxine nodded. "For both of us."

"The counselor really helped. And so did Mama. If she hadn't been praying with me all this time . . . and feeding me. I know I'm too skinny, and she's doing her best to fatten me up. Which is why I need to get home. These peanuts ain't cuttin' it."

"Okay, let's head back," Maxine acceded. They slowly trudged along the soft ground. "Why didn't you tell me about the counselor?"

"Because you didn't need to know. Mama did. I guess I stopped eating to get attention, and Mama gave me everything

I needed. And then some." Celeste's voice was matter-of-fact. Not angry or accusatory. Just a simple statement that had complex truths weaving through it. She picked up a large, fallen branch and plucked off its dead leaves.

For a few minutes, Maxine focused on the swish and squish of their feet as they trekked toward the shoes they'd piled in the grass. A chittering squirrel made her look up, through the twists of limbs and foliage. She turned her face up to the sun, glimmering off the water. Maxine could feel warmth traveling all the way through her.

"Celeste, could I bribe you?" Maxine held out the granola bar.

"Depends on what you want."

"I'd really love to race leaf boats. We'll just have to wade across the creek to gather the widest leaves. If you're up for it."

Celeste sighed and glanced back over her shoulder at the direction from which they'd come. Propping a hand over her eyes, she peered into the sun toward the house. Then she plucked the bar from Maxine's hand.

Maxine smiled. "I'll take that as a yes."

Chapter Thirty-Four

MAXINE SHOULD HAVE BEEN writing notes for her latest article, praying, studying her to-do list, anything but trying to find a new outfit for her bitmoji. She scrolled through the options. Skirts, workout clothes, fan gear, holiday wear. Finally she settled on shorts and a T-shirt.

"Hey, there! Sorry we're late."

She set down her phone and looked up. "Reverend and Mrs. Atwater . . . hey! You're right on time. I'm afraid it's Teddy who's late." She stood and embraced them both. When Maxine pulled away, she got a look at Lilian's outfit. Then she threw her head back and laughed.

As usual, Lilian was nattily dressed, this time in an A-line, coral summer dress with cap sleeves and a hemline that swayed gently just above her knees when she moved. The same dress Maxine wore. The older woman pointed and chuckled. "Tiffany's Boutique?"

Maxine spun. "I hope I look half as good in mine as you do in yours." She glanced down at her feet, clad in white low-top Chuck Taylors, courtesy of Celeste. "Next time, I'll wear a pair of cute sandals like those." She nodded toward Lilian's feet.

Reverend Atwater held out his arms. "What about me? Nothing for the man in the polo shirt and khaki pants?"

The women's eyes met. Lilian's rolled first. The shaking of her head made the diamond in her nose flash in the sunlight. "Maybe we should just sit down and wait for Theodore."

"If he's coming," Maxine murmured after she hugged the minister and sat down, not counting on *when* this time. A scan of her watch told her he was eight minutes late.

"I'll wait for him outside." Reverend Atwater headed for the front of the restaurant.

Maxine focused on the menu. It had been a long time since she'd been to Dairy Queen.

When Teddy had called her to set up this date with the Atwaters, Maxine was taken aback. Technically, this would be their seventh and final premarital counseling session, not that either of them saw it that way. She couldn't even see it as a "date." At first, his choice of meeting place had flummoxed her. Maxine only had time to murmur, "Yes," and jot down the time and location in her calendar before he'd ended the call.

Lilian's fingertips danced along the tabletop to some invisible band. "So how've you been?"

Relieved to stop feigning interest in the plastic menu in her hands, Maxine dropped it on the table. "Okay. Busy. How about you?"

The woman arched an eyebrow. "Just okay and busy?"

"How about 'better'?" Maxine felt a light touch on the back of her neck, and she looked up. *Better, much better.* That was how she'd describe Teddy as well. She scooted back her chair.

Theodore took her hand with one of his and stared at her for a moment. Then he extended a long white box.

Maxine slowly unfolded her hand from his, but she took his offering, set it on the table, and lifted the lid. When she peeled away the green tissue, her breath hitched. One blaze of orange nestled in the midst of cranberry, purple, and green. Holding back a sob, she dropped the cardboard with a clonk on the floor and stepped toward him.

Teddy drew her close.

Maxine ignored the smell of chili, the crinkle of paper-wrapped sandwiches, the whir of the blender from the kitchen, and the Atwaters, who must have been looking on. She closed her eyes and held Teddy, something she hadn't been able to do for weeks. Something she'd wanted to do but feared she'd never do again. Her heart full, she pressed him closer and let the tears trickle down his neck.

They both released each other in small increments. First, she braced her hands on his shoulders. Then he cupped her face. They leaned their foreheads together, and he kissed her near her ear as he stepped away. His fingers trailed down her arms, then squeezed her hands before letting go altogether. Cool air rushed between them when they parted.

"Friends?" Teddy's lips hinted at a smile, and he extended his hand.

Maxine reached in her pocket and set a ring-shaped box in his palm. "Always."

My Daily Grace—At the Table

When my grandma bakes a peach cobbler, she makes sure her topping crunches when she breaks through it with a spoon. That sound shows it can support a scoop of ice cream without getting mushy. Thing is, she can tell that it'll make that sound just by peeking at it through the oven door. She doesn't have to test it or use a timer. Grandma knows when it's ready by its color.

She developed that insight over time, from experience. It's not that she was born wearing an apron. Once upon a time she probably forgot to stir her butter beans from the bottom and she kneaded her biscuits too long. It's hard to believe she'd ever serve a mushy crust, but I know it's possible. As far as I'm concerned, she's the best thing in the kitchen since sliced bread—and I'm talking about her corn bread that tastes like pound cake— but Grandma isn't perfect, in the kitchen or otherwise.

All those healed scars on her forearms and on the backs of her hands attest to what she does—that she can really burn in the kitchen. In the best way possible, mind you. They also reveal her mistakes, that she's constantly misjudging how far she should reach into the oven or how close she is to a baking dish. Yet they don't reveal who she is—a loving wife, precious mother and grandmother, a faithful friend, an only daughter. Nouns that don't say enough.

People, places, and things . . . chapters in my story, all. The tan lines around my ring finger? That sparkly diamond that rested there before I returned it in its original box? My daughter, my past, my broken heart? Some people might think these stand out like Grandma's scar tissue, proof of my mistakes and poor judgment. I know I used to.

But they're my testimony. They remind me of lessons learned, of how I can love and live better. The scars don't reveal faults and weakness. They prove I'm a warrior princess. A true princess doesn't hide her tiara in her jewelry box when she appears in public. She doesn't hide behind the throne when she doesn't feel good enough. As a daughter of the King, I need to own the proof of my heritage. Show off my "crown jewels," the evidence that I'm one of His and that I have as much right to stand before the throne as the next heir.

No, I'm not perfect. But I'm "fearfully and wonderfully made," as Psalm 139:14 attests. I'm not trouble free. Yet God has tried me. He knows my anxieties and my cares. I'm not less than because He is more than enough, and I take after my Father. All my shortcomings, troubles, and scars are as much part of my story as my blessings and successes. They all reveal the faith in the Man who sacrificed all for me, the Spirit breathing new life within me, and the Father who has always loved me.

God made me who I am, and in case I ever feel empty, I can look to Psalm 107:9: "For He satisfies the longing soul, And fills the hungry soul with goodness."

Maxine gave a war whoop and stowed away her laptop. That was her last column about the-wedding-that-wasn't. Taking a deep breath, she counted the cars in her grandparents' yard. It looked like a nearly full house. She relaxed her grip on the wheel and reached for the box of chrysanthemums. She didn't want the flowers to die.

As Maxine tramped across the yard, she stopped to admire the wide fields around the house. Empty cornstalks waved in the sun just beyond the patch of blueberry and blackberry bushes. Eventually local hog farmers would help cut the stalks to use on their own property while leaving some behind to fertilize the Tagles' soil. She wondered when she'd be called upon to pick the cantaloupe and butter beans planted in the back. Surely they were ready for harvest.

"Finally! I was startin' to wonder if somebody had swooped you up and toted you off."

Maxine laughed and walked to the porch, where Mama Ruby had planted herself, a hand braced on each hip. "Mama Ruby, nobody would want me. At the very least, they'd bring me back the minute they realized what they'd gotten ahold of."

Ruby held her granddaughter at arm's length and peered into Maxine's eyes for a long moment before pulling her in. They rocked together from one foot to the other.

Maxine inhaled the kitchen smells embedded in her grandmother's hair. "Mmm . . . I see I finally get to have some pork roast."

Ruby pulled back but didn't let go. "I figure it's about time. Whatchyou think? What's in the box?"

"Flowers, to honor the occasion." She let herself be led from the porch and into the wide foyer. She cocked her head. "Who's here? There's a lot of clanking going on."

"Everybody. We got tired of waitin' on you, so we got things started. It's startin' to warm up back there." Her grandmother looked at her, knowingly.

"I imagine the temperature is pretty hot right about now. Sorry I missed the fireworks."

"Well, you didn't miss them all, from what I recall."

Maxine and Ruby turned toward the voice that was as dry as the bare cornstalks flanking the house. Vivienne had a hand balanced on the frame of the doorway opening to the kitchen.

She beckoned. "Come on here, girl. You're needed."

"I'm going to see what's happenin' with my blueberries." Ruby took the box and gently pushed Maxine in the middle of her back to set her granddaughter's feet in motion.

She heard the screen door slap closed behind her as she moved toward her mother. She stopped a few inches from her. Vivienne pulled her the rest of the way. But Maxine didn't need anyone to make her wrap her arms around her mother's waist. She wanted to.

"Did you have a good meeting with the Atwaters?" Vivienne spoke into her daughter's neck.

Maxine inhaled a whiff of Estée Lauder's Beautiful. As usual, the scent transported her back twenty-five years to the day she broke that perfume bottle in Vivienne's bathroom. Since then, she'd always equated the scent with a spanking. That was Mother, a heady mixture of love and discipline. Maxine pulled away so she could see her face.

"What?" Vivienne's forehead wrinkled.

"Nothing."

"Uh-oh."

"No 'uh-oh.' It was good to see Teddy, to talk things out with the Atwaters present. We finally had the premarital session we should have had months ago—just without the 'marital' part happening. I guess you would call it bitter-sweet." Maxine paused and squeezed her mother's free hand. "Kinda like my conversation with you last night."

Vivienne squeezed back. "Emphasis on the sweet, I hope."

Maxine released her. She crossed her arms and leaned a shoulder against the wall. "I remember a long time ago you told me mothers and daughters couldn't be friends. Do you remember that day?"

"Yes. You were fourteen, and you wanted to wear my fiery-red lipstick and have me drop you and Evelyn off at the mall." Mirroring her daughter's stance, Vivienne crossed her arms.

"I remember you looked at me like I was crazy. Kinda like you are now, just thinking about it," Maxine laughed. "But I thought if you loved me, you would do it, give me what I wanted. Be my friend. And you told me then you were even better than a friend because you didn't give me what I wanted. You gave me what I needed. It stung because I wanted more."

"Like what?" Vivienne uncrossed her arms.

Maxine looked over her mother's shoulder into the kitchen and past the murmuring, hustle and bustle, and clinking of utensils and pans, background music for her thoughts. "To feel worthy. I thought I found it in that baptismal pool. But that only motivated me to change my outside and hope the inside would follow."

"Just like raising your baby didn't make up for me leaving mine. I know I already told you, but I'm so sorry. We're all in the same needy boat, love." Vivienne swiped under her eyes.

"Sometimes sinking, sometimes floating. But God saves, He redeems, and He fulfills. Celeste came out of all this with the best of both worlds, a sister who loved her like a mother." Maxine smiled at Vivienne. "And I have a mother who's becoming a friend."

"But you better not ever call me by my first name."

Maxine knew she'd never dare. Thinking of her as "mama" was good enough.

The front door creaked open. "Y'all still jibber-jabberin' away in here?"

Vivienne bumped her hip against Maxine's and told Ruby, "Perfect timing. Just wrapped up our girlfriend chat."

Ruby harrumphed as she walked through the foyer toward the women. "Well, I need to put some water on these flowers and see to my kitchen help. Sounds like too much fun and not enough work's going on in there. Y'all gon' let me by?"

Maxine noticed her grandmother's hands. "I don't see any blueberries."

"That's because you're not outside," Ruby laughed. She flicked her empty hand forward as if shooing flies. "Now excuse me, ladies."

They stepped through the doorway. Ruby set the box on the counter and dug out a tall glass vase from under the kitchen sink. Vivienne kept walking through the kitchen, headed for the back door.

"I'm going to find your grandfather and Celeste. I suspect he's lettin' her drive the tractor again. James David, don't shell all the beans. Snap a few and mix 'em in like I showed you."

"Yes, ma'am."

There sat JD—"everybody"—grinning at the table with his hands in a bowl of butter beans. Maxine tried to slow her heartbeat with her hand. "You scared the dickens out of me! How did I miss that yellow Porsche?"

"I drove Blue. She's parked in back."

Robert bounded from the table and sprinted to Maxine. "Finally you're here! They don't play the right way." He aimed an index finger at Zan and Second John, who sat in front of a Blokus game board.

His twin shook his head. "Robert likes to play with you because you give him extra chances, and Zan and I don't. You should think twice and move once. Face the consequences."

Maxine snuggled her baby brother. "Second chances are a thing, right, Bro?"

Zan cast his eyes toward the ceiling with a beleaguered sigh as he put away the last of the colored tiles. "Grandma, can I help you with those flowers?"

Maxine cupped Robert's shoulder. "Here's another willing worker."

The back screen creaked open. Vivienne held it wide, and her husband walked in, burdened with a wooden crate of peaches. "Somebody can help me with these. They need to be washed and sliced for the pies," her stepfather ordered, out of breath.

Maxine rushed over. "Sure thing, Dad." She reached for the crate, but when he didn't move, she looked up. "Mama Ruby would tell you to 'stop catching flies.' Why are you standing there with your mouth wide-open?"

"You just called me Dad."

Maxine ignored the suspicious gleam in his eyes. "That's what you are, aren't you?" She kissed his cheek and hoisted the crate to the counter.

"Excuse me; I don't mean to interrupt your conversation with *Dad*, but I'll help you scrub and slice those peaches." Vivienne turned on the faucet. "So we're retiring *First John*?"

Maxine glanced at her stepfather and back at her mother. "It's about time, don't you think?"

"It's *been* time, that's what I think."

"Come on now, Viv. All in God's time. It doesn't matter what she calls me. The relationship is still the same. Where's Roy? We can't have a family meeting without the rest of the family."

"He's at Lis's, but he'll be here directly. They went out for breakfast. I think they discovered they have more to talk about than her birthday." Ruby wiped her hands on her apron and approached the three at the sink. "As soon as your granddaddy and Celeste get in here, we can pray and get started. Can I get y'all somethin' to tide you over 'til then?"

Maxine tucked her hands in her front pockets and looked around the room. She shrugged, content. "No, I can't think of anything. Oh, that's right . . ." She withdrew a tiny object and let it roll around in the palm of her hand.

JD's eyebrows furrowed as he peered at the acorn.

Maxine laughed at his unspoken question and closed her fingers around the seed. "Maybe Celeste and I will explain it to you later."

Return to Spring Hope, North Carolina, in

"Robin W. Pearson delivers a fresh new voice for Southern fiction, treating readers to an inspiring journey through the complex matters of the heart."

JULIE CANTRELL, *New York Times* and *USA Today* bestselling author

a long time comin'

a novel

Robin W. Pearson

turn the page for a preview

"Pearson's excellent debut explores forgiveness and the burden of secrets."

PUBLISHERS WEEKLY, starred review

Chapter One

That night when my man eased through the door, his clothes felt and smelled like the summer rain tapping on the roof. There sure aint nothing like a North Carolina rain. He bout scared the breath out of me, but then he grinned and whispered my name in that way he had. I started missing him on the spot cause I figured he'd be gone by the time the first rays of sunlight tickled the floorboards. I slipped to the kitchen anyway and made him a plate since I never could say no to them eyes. To this day when I fry up pork chops, I can still see him gnawing on that bone.

Know what else I see? Me pushing him out that same door not even two hours later. Only the Lord coulda made me do it. And that man made such a fuss! My heart practically thudded to a stop when I heard the children stir. A part of me ached to pull him inside and wrap my arms round him, but my bones said, Bee, there aint no coming back from this. He probly heard my heart pounding in my chest as he stood there with the rain dripping off his brim and his mouth a straight line. His eyes weren't laughing then. And they weren't asking me for nothing either. He just tipped his hat to me—and he sure never looked back. I know. Cause I waited.

But deep inside I could tell he wouldn't come creeping back in a month or so to melt away my anger with them smiles and empty promises and sliding out the door before sunrise. I just wish I coulda told my fool self—Bee, get away from that window and either stop wishing for your husband to come back or stop fearing it. You can't have both.

Beatrice tucked her pencil into the gutter of her worn leather journal and dragged her eyes from the page. She readjusted the thin watch on her left wrist. 10:42. Holding her book to her chest, she hefted herself from the chair. Her bones creaked as they made themselves comfortable in her new upright position by the window of her Spring Hope, North Carolina, home. She strained her neck, aiming to see where the once-graveled road, now paved, turned the corner. Her fingers fiddled with the long gray braid curled across her right shoulder as she imagined his knee-length black coat and matching black felt fedora worn so low it almost covered one eye.

Then, sighing, Beatrice removed the pencil and closed the book altogether. She pulled the strip of rubber from her wrist and snapped it around her diary to secure the pencil. She'd been spending too much time these days looking backwards, getting lost meandering through those long-ago days. "Keep yo' hand to the plow, Bee."

Peeking around the curtain one last time, Beatrice cast a disparaging eye on the Wilson boys in their daddy's car. "Mm-mm, flying down the road like they ain't had no sense." As the noise from their engine faded, she stepped away from the window, retrieved the box from the bed, and laid the journal atop the papers inside. She'd just stow it all in her closet for now. *Too much trouble gettin' out that key to the steamer trunk.*

She shut her closet door and glanced around her bedroom. Sunrays streamed through the parted curtains and struck the mirror. The reflected glare revealed not one speck of dust. It had taken her the better part of a week of stops and starts to scrub her room and the rest of the house with orange-scented Murphy oil soap, and the wood floors seemed to smile at her, they were so shiny. Two fluffed pillows adorned her otherwise-plain light-blue bedcover, the hem of which hung exactly one-half inch from the floor. Nothing needed fixing, straightening, dusting, sweeping, or spraying.

In the front room, Beatrice found something to straighten: the black-and-white photograph of her mam and pap, one of the two framed pictures on the eggshell-colored wall. The back bedroom sat empty, undisturbed. She walked the few steps to the kitchen, but there even the stainless steel sink proved true to its name. Everything was cut, canned, wiped, washed, or stored away. Sighing again, she retrieved the empty clothes basket on the washing machine and tramped from the kitchen out to the clothesline.

The heat slapped her. Beatrice reached toward the first wooden pin and unclipped the underwear. She worked her way down the line, folding the stiff laundry and dropping it into the basket at her feet. She grimaced—*Too heavy a hand with that bleach*—and edged the now-overflowing basket to her right. Panting as much from exertion as from the oppressive heat, Beatrice bent and hoisted the basket to her waist and plodded to the kitchen.

The kitchen clock read 11:17. Beatrice fetched the garden hose from the shed and brought it to the front yard to water the roses her granddaughter had planted by the mailbox for Mother's Day. After she finished dousing the wilting plants and any other hint of vegetation in the yard, she walked to the hose bib. With a squeak of the spigot and a stiff turn of the wrist, she extinguished the stream and detached the hose. She coiled it loosely around her elbow and trooped toward the porch to enter the house by the front door, too tired to go around to the shed. After she dragged her slight frame up the steps, she noticed her water-splattered legs and mud-covered brogans. Shoulders slumped, she eased down the steps—even more slowly this time—to go around back. Worn-out once she reached the door, Beatrice plopped down on the stoop to catch her breath. She couldn't even make it up the one step.

"I told Ev'lyn them flowers was mo' trouble than they's worth." The hose uncoiled on the ground around her ankles.

Some time later, Beatrice pushed herself to her feet with great effort and left the hose in a loose pile, forgotten. She unlaced and removed her shoes before entering the kitchen. Inside, her hot, wet skin greedily sucked in the cool air from the window unit. Refreshed a bit, Beatrice glanced at the clock over the sink: 11:55. *It ain't too early to eat some lunch. I've worked me up quite a hunger.*

The refrigerator yielded just enough pimiento cheese for a nice-size sandwich, and she plucked a Granny Smith apple from the bin in the pantry. Sitting at the table facing down her food, she prepared her stomach to eat.

Lord, You know what I need 'cause You the one who gave it to me and blessed it. Thank You. Amen. She took her time chewing, talking her way through her meal, frequently sipping the water, all the while ordering her stomach to stay in line. And just like many of the people in Beatrice's life, it obeyed.

When it was nearly half past noon, Beatrice slid her bookmark on James 1 and closed her Bible. She ignored the scrape of the chair's feet as she pushed away from the table. She scrubbed her lunch dishes, dried them, put them away, and retreated to her bedroom. There she resisted the urge to flip back the curtain to see whatever busied itself on the other side. Instead, she cast an eye at the clock. Its hands told her, *"Time for a nap."*

Nearly two hours later, refreshed and back on the porch, Beatrice leaned on the cushions and replaited her hair. She wound it, tucked it, and pinned the one long, silver braid into a bun at the nape of her neck. By now, the sun had crept toward the rear of the house, mercifully sparing the front porch. She basked in the nothingness stretching out beyond the yard and the street running in front of it. Then, "My Lord!" she entreated, gripping her side. She hunched over as pain speared her insides, inched around her spine and over her hip, and took hold somewhere in the area around her chest. It stole her breath. She sat still as stone, gripping her dress, eyes squeezed shut.

Seconds . . . a minute . . . forever passed until at last, the fist of pain loosened its hold, finger by finger, and finally let go altogether. The breeze that merely dislodged the heavy air raised chill bumps on her clammy skin. Doctors had warned her, but the suddenness of this spell caught Beatrice off guard. She had half a mind to cancel her afternoon plans, but before the other half caught up, a car crunched into the drive.

Piece by piece Beatrice put herself together, and then she stepped into her house far enough to retrieve her keys and turn the lock. She'd already pushed the heavy baskets laden with clean laundry onto the porch. Wordlessly Beatrice lifted her head a notch as she passed the hand that tried to help and stiffly took the three concrete steps to the ground.

"How you doin' today, Granny B?"

"Same as always." Beatrice looked neither to the right nor the left as she marched to the ancient burgundy metallic Monte Carlo, much as the second hand had ticked away the time. "You can put them two baskets in back." She threw the words over her shoulder as she climbed in. Beatrice drew from her pride rather than from her depleted stores of energy to slam closed her door behind her.

The other door opened and the seat was let down before

the driver scooted the laundry baskets across the back. Then he slammed shut his own door and the engine chugged to life. Reverend Farrow turned to his passenger. "Granny B, are you ready?"

Beatrice nodded briskly. "If I ain't now, I ain't never gon' be."

A Note from the Author

ACCORDING TO DOROTHY in *The Wizard of Oz*, "There's no place like home." There's also no place like Mount Laurel in North Carolina. I do hope the Owens family and the other characters who live there have found a warm and comfy place in your heart!

Acknowledgments

"THANK YOU" MIGHT SOUND BANAL. It's what I say after some-one passes me the salt. Now, if that same person smushes a funnel web spider on the way to the dinner table, I'll use those very same words—only this time with feeling. So to the One who is Salt and Light and in whom I live, move, and have my being . . . thank You. You are the Author of my life's story and the One who waits for me at its end.

God alone knew how much I'd need these folks who sit around my kitchen table every day, consuming anything they can cover in ketchup or hot sauce or eat with a side of bacon. I used to think I couldn't write because of my peeps, but He showed me I *wouldn't* write without Eddie, Nicholas, Kate, Benjamin, Faith, Hillary Grace, Hallie, August, and yes, even my four-legged baby, Oscar. And without the history and experiences of Daddy, Mama, Dad, Mother, and *their* parents, I wouldn't have a story to share with my readers or new chap-ters to live and breathe with Hubby and my little people. They make me laugh until I have to wipe the tears off my glasses.

But not all my peeps fit around my table. Just like Jesus

Christ said in Matthew 12:50, my family also includes "whoever does the will of My Father in heaven"—people like Tammy Grant with Sunflower Creatives who don't mind my "I love it, but just one more thing"; the Hannah Circle, my prayer partners of twenty-plus years; my church; precious friends; fellow authors who've endorsed, advised, and exhorted me; and all the readers and reviewers who see themselves in my fiction.

And I can't forget the people I get to work with, who continually show me Jesus in them. My agent, Cynthia Ruchti with Books & Such Literary, smooths the worry lines from my forehead with her fitly spoken words, "apples of gold in settings of silver" (Proverbs 25:11). She reminds me of the *why* of my work when I focus on the *what* and *how*. Karen Watson and Jan Stob gave me a comfy seat at the Tyndale House table, and their warmth and attention make their home my home. My editor, Caleb Sjogren, makes sure my stories aren't filled with mere words found in the dictionary; they're based on truth that comes from the Bible. Eva Winters designs amazing covers that drive each story straight to the heart, while Elizabeth Jackson, Andrea Garcia, Mariah León, and the rest of my family at Tyndale keep my plate full of all manner of good things.

So to all who bring flavor to my life, and who keep me in stitches and joyfully bug free, thank you. My faith and you, my family, are my bread and butter, sustaining me, inspiring me, and feeding me. I couldn't want for more. Blessings!

About the Author

Robin W. Pearson's writing sprouts from her Southern roots. While sitting in her grandmothers' kitchens, she learned what happens if you sweep someone's feet, how to make corn bread taste like pound cake, and the all-purpose uses of Vaseline. She also learned about the power of God and how His grace led her grandmothers to care for their large families after their husbands were long gone, a grace that has endured through the generations. Robin's family's faith and superstitions, life lessons, and life's longings inspired her to write about God's love for us and how this love affects our relationships with others. In her debut novel, *A Long Time Comin'*, Robin weaves a family drama rich in Southern flavor that a starred review from *Publishers Weekly* called "enjoyable and uncomfortable, but also funny and persistent in the way that only family can be."

While her family history gave her the stories to tell, her professional experiences gave her the skills to tell them effectively. Armed with her degree from Wake Forest University, she has corrected grammar up and down the East Coast in her career as an editor and writer that started with Houghton Mifflin Company more than twenty-five years ago. Since then she has freelanced with magazines, parenting journals, textbooks, and homeschooling resources.

At the heart of it all abides her love of God and the family He's given her. It's her focus as a wife and homeschooling mother of seven. It's what she writes about on her blog, *Mommy, Concentrated*, where she shares her adventures in faith, family, and freelancing. And it's the source and subject of her fiction—in her novels, in the new characters currently living and breathing on her computer screen, and in the stories waiting to be told about her belief in Jesus Christ and the experiences at her own kitchen sink.

Follow Robin at robinwpearson.com.

Discussion Questions

1. Mama Ruby says, "Forgiveness don't always soften the consequences." What consequences is Maxine facing at the beginning of the story? What about JD? Celeste? Vivienne? Which characters extend or receive forgiveness, and what happens as a result?

2. At the end of her first premarital counseling session, Maxine says, "I wonder what else God sees when He sees me." Why does Maxine wrestle with her identity? What do you learn about her struggles through her dreams and monthly columns? How does your view of her change as the pages of her story unfold? How well do you know yourself? What do you think God sees when He sees you?

3. Maxine's past inserts itself into her life when her childhood friend calls her Maxie, a nickname Maxine had left behind her. JD needles Maxine when he refers to her fiancé as Teddy Bear. And Maxine has special reasons for calling Vivienne Mother and her grandmother Mama Ruby. What do these names and nickname preferences say about how these characters

see themselves and others? Why did some biblical characters (Abraham, Sarah, Paul) get new names?

4. After Maxine and Teddy begin arguing during one of their premarital counseling sessions, Pastor Atwater reminds them, "You should each be a safe place where the other can demonstrate or express your passion and personality. You seek shelter *in* each other, not *from* each other." Do you have a spouse or close friend who is your safe place? Are you a safe place for someone else? Why is this so important in relationships?

5. JD warns Maxine, "The truth isn't your enemy." Evelyn believes that living a lie "affects generations." Mama Ruby tells her, "You young people today talk about *your* truth and what's real to *you*. Don't you know it's either true and real, an opinion or a lie? Truth don't change. It don't need to be processed, just believed and accepted." Why does it sometimes feel safer to hide the truth? What are some benefits of having the truth come to light, even if it's painful or unpleasant? In a world filled with relativism, do you still believe in this absolute? How might a lens you have—the way you were raised or something you experienced—affect your views?

6. Mama Ruby likens her special pork roast recipe to a marriage: "A lot goes into it, things you can't anticipate or know about ahead of time—sweet, sour, savory," all of which works together to make a good marriage.

What are some of the "sweet, sour, savory" things that have gone into your marriage or family? Do you agree that they work together for good?

7. Maxine feels she's "not enough" in many ways, and she isn't sure of what her "whole self" will look like when all the pieces of her life are stitched together and the truth is revealed. What would you say to her if you were Vivienne or Lilian or Reverend Atwater? Have you ever felt "not enough"? Who or what are some of the more memorable parts of your life story, past or present? Are there chapters you wish you could rewrite? What are some new chapters you're looking forward to?

8. Maxine thought she was making a fresh start when she was baptized in that church in Valdosta, Georgia. But "even saved [and] sanctified" hasn't stopped Maxine from responding to challenging situations by shutting down or running away. Mama Ruby reminds her: "Trusting God is an act of the will. It isn't easy to fight your nature. Worryin' and fussin' over a matter come easy to you. That don't mean you do *nuthin'*, but that *somethin'* may mean standin' still. Believers spend much of their time waitin' and watchin'." What's your go-to response when you're looking for answers to questions life throws at you? Read Luke 9:23. How often must we deny our true nature? What does Maxine need to do to truly start over? What does waiting and watching look like to you?

9. When Teddy bails on a date with Maxine, she wonders, "How can you really know me without learning about all the puzzle pieces—my friends and my family—that make up my life?" What advice would you give to Maxine and Teddy as they go through premarital counseling? Do you have someone in your life who knows all your puzzle pieces? Or are parts of the puzzle hidden from certain people?

10. Both Vivienne and Maxine make difficult choices for their daughters' sakes. How does what Vivienne did with Maxine affect Maxine's decisions for Celeste? Was it right for Vivienne to reveal the truth to Celeste without Maxine's knowledge or approval? What regrets does each woman have? What life-changing decisions have left you with regrets? Have you ever faced a situation where you felt utterly inadequate to the task ahead? What happened?

11. When Maxine was fourteen years old, Vivienne told her mothers and daughters can't be friends. Do you agree with that? Is there a point at which parents and children can become friends or will parents always be "better than a friend" because they give what their child needs rather than what he or she wants?

12. Maxine views her scars not as battle wounds but as testimony about the God who loves her. What scars or marks have been left on you? How do you view them? Can you see how they provide evidence of God's love for you?

TYNDALE HOUSE PUBLISHERS
IS CRAZY4FICTION!

Fiction that entertains and inspires

Get to know us! Become a member of the Crazy4Fiction community. Whether you read our blog, like us on Facebook, follow us on Twitter, or receive our e-newsletter, you're sure to get the latest news on the best in Christian fiction. You might even win something along the way!

JOIN IN THE FUN TODAY.

 crazy4fiction.com

 Crazy4Fiction

 @Crazy4Fiction